PRAISE FOR **THE EPIDEMIC**

★ "Young's latest book perfectly illustrates how good intentions
can lead to horrible results."—*VOYA*, starred review

"Series fans will be delighted."—*Booklist*

PRAISE FOR **THE REMEDY**

"A visceral exploration of the eternal and misguided search for pain-free
happiness in an almost-now Brave New World."—*Kirkus Reviews*

"The intriguing premise, swift pace, plentiful chapter hooks,
and shocking ending (which demands a sequel) will have
readers staying up late to finish it."—*Booklist*

PRAISE FOR **THE TREATMENT**

★ "With romance, mystery, adventure, and the complications
and suspense of a thriller, it will be difficult to find a reader who
will not enjoy the series."—*VOYA*, starred review

"This jarring thriller looks at the cost of societal complacency
while lauding heroism and remembrance."—*Kirkus Reviews*

PRAISE FOR **THE PROGRAM**

★ "Readers will devour this fast-paced story that combines an intriguing
premise, a sexy romance, and a shifting landscape of truth. With big
questions still unanswered and promising twists, this first volume in a
new series will leave readers primed for more."—*Booklist*, starred review

★ "With this powerful psychological drama, Young contributes
a unique, attention-worthy standout from the crowd of young
adult dystopias."—*BCCB*, starred review

ALSO BY SUZANNE YOUNG

The Program Series
Book 1: *The Program*
Book 2: *The Treatment*
Book 3: *The Remedy*
Book 5: *The Adjustment*
Still to come . . . Book 6: *The Complication*

Hotel for the Lost

All in Pieces

Just Like Fate
(with Cat Patrick)

A PROGRAM NOVEL

Book 4

THE EPIDEMIC

SUZANNE YOUNG

SIMON PULSE

New York   London   Toronto   Sydney   New Delhi

SIMON PULSE

An imprint of Simon & Schuster Children's Publishing Division

1230 Avenue of the Americas, New York, NY 10020

First Simon Pulse paperback edition April 2017

Text copyright © 2016 by Suzanne Young

Cover photographs of models copyright © 2017 by Michael Frost

Cover photographs of backgrounds copyright © 2017 by Thinkstock

Also available in a Simon Pulse hardcover edition.

For information about special discounts for bulk purchases, please contact Simon & Schuster Special Sales at 1-866-506-1949 or business@simonandschuster.com.

The Simon & Schuster Speakers Bureau can bring authors to your live event. For more information or to book an event contact the Simon & Schuster Speakers Bureau at 1-866-248-3049 or visit our website at www.simonspeakers.com.

Cover designed by Russell Gordon

Interior designed by Mike Rosamilia

The text of this book was set in Adobe Garamond Pro.

Manufactured in the United States of America

2 4 6 8 10 9 7 5 3 1

The Library of Congress has cataloged the hardcover edition as follows:

Names: Young, Suzanne, author.

Title: The Epidemic / by Suzanne Young.

Description: First Simon Pulse hardcover edition. | New York : Simon Pulse, 2016. |

Sequel to: The Remedy. | Companion book to: The Program and The Treatment. |

Summary: "After discovering that everything she's ever known, including her own identity, has been a lie, Quinlan McKee is determined to find out the truth about her past. But in her search for answers, she discovers a cover-up more chilling than she can imagine. An epidemic is coming, and there's no way to stop it"—Provided by publisher.

Identifiers: LCCN 2015043249 | ISBN 9781481444705 (hc) |

ISBN 9781481444682 (pbk) | ISBN 9781481444699 (eBook)

Subjects: | CYAC: Identity—Fiction. | Death—Fiction. | Suicide—Fiction. | Grief—Fiction. | Epidemics—Fiction. | Science fiction. | BISAC: JUVENILE FICTION / Social Issues / Death & Dying. | JUVENILE FICTION / Social Issues / Emotions & Feelings.

Classification: LCC PZ7.Y887 Ep 2016 | DDC [Fic]—dc23

LC record available at https://lccn.loc.gov/2015043249

To Brandi
This is for our grandmothers
Josephine Parzych and Mary Cavallaro

ENTER THE WORLD

THE PROGRAM

The Program—a memory-wiping therapy—was created to combat the outbreak of a suicide cluster. Sloane and James will do everything they can to survive both the epidemic and its cure.

THE TREATMENT

On the run from The Program, Sloane and James must figure out a way to take down the system that ruined their lives before it can expand.

BOOK ONE

BOOK THREE

BOOK TWO

THE REMEDY

Before The Program, there was the grief department. Quinn and Deacon spent their lives as closers, offering grieving families a chance to say good-bye—until Quinn discovers her life is not at all what it seems.

OF *THE PROGRAM*

THE ADJUSTMENT

Tatum and Wes undergo the Adjustment—a new procedure to replace memories that The Program erased. But what happens when the past you thought you had was a lie?

THE COMPLICATION

After learning the truth about her past, Tatum must find a way to stop the Adjustment before it sets off a new epidemic.

BOOK FIVE

BOOK FOUR

BOOK SIX

THE EPIDEMIC

Quinn will enlist the help of other closers to save a girl she hardly knows, setting off the series of events that lead to the suicide epidemic.

PART I

EVERYTHING IN
ITS WRONG PLACE

CHAPTER ONE

MY ENTIRE LIFE IS A LIE. I'M NOTHING MORE THAN A carefully crafted story about a dead girl—a recently discovered truth that's left me questioning my existence. I was brought in to close out her life, but somehow I forgot mine along the way. I don't remember my real name or my real family; I truly thought *I* was Quinlan McKee.

But now I'm nobody.

The tires roll over a bump in the road, rattling the windows of the bus, and I sway in my padded seat. The world moves past me in silhouettes against the darkening night. My fingertips tingle and my lips are numb. Cold sweat beads on my skin. I think I'm in shock.

Deacon sits next to me, the music from his earbuds playing loudly enough for me to hear a faint hum. We're on an evening bus to Roseburg, Oregon—a poorly planned trip to find my identity. But now I know we're heading toward an uncertain future. I thought Deacon and I had finally figured each other out, found a way to be together despite all the lies surrounding me. But the last twenty minutes have cured me of such naïve thinking.

I look sideways at Deacon and study his features, seeking out his misdirection. Instead I find the soft brown color of his eyes, which can read my soul, the perfect curve of his lips, and the sharp angles of his jaw—a face that's so familiar I would know it in the dark. He gives nothing away as he subtly bobs his head to the music, staring straight ahead. Betrayal suddenly hardens in my veins, and I have to turn away from him. All of my relationships have been a lie too.

I face the window, my suspicion going unnoticed. My heart would surely be shattered by this if it hadn't already been damaged several times today, maybe broken beyond repair. Because after finding out I wasn't who I thought I was, I trusted Deacon—the only person left to trust. But twenty minutes ago a text popped up on his phone:

HAVE YOU FOUND HER YET?

There are only a handful of people who would have sent that text, none of whom I'd want knowing my location. Every time I try to find a rational explanation for the message, I remind myself that Deacon *did* find me. He tracked me down at the bus station because he knew exactly what I would do. He knows me better than anyone. And that makes me an easy mark for a closer. Trust and love are our greatest weapons for manipulation.

Deacon and I have both been closers, reading people and their emotions for a living. For years I willingly took on the roles of deceased girls in order to help their families through grief. I was a remedy for broken hearts, a tool for loved ones to use to get closure. But I had no idea that I was a closer for my own life. Quinlan McKee died when she was six. I was brought in by Dr. Arthur Pritchard to play her role. My father . . .

I close my eyes, cursing my sentimentality. *Stop thinking of him like that,* I demand. Tom McKee isn't my father.

But despite my attempts to compartmentalize the pain, my breath hitches from the loss. He *was* my father, wasn't he? I can't deny that. Tom McKee raised me, even if he lied to me the entire time. When I was a little girl, he'd brush my hair and cook my meals. We'd watch movies together and, of course, train to be better within the department. Ultimately, what he needed was for me to help him get over the grief of losing his daughter. He kept me to avoid his own pain. In turn he caused mine. But he was still my dad.

Deacon's fingers brush over my hand on the bus seat, startling me. I lift my eyes to his, struck down by how my heart swells when he meets my gaze. How my insides burn at the possibility that he's deceived me more than anybody. And yet I still can't find that betrayal in his expression.

"You okay?" Deacon asks, taking out one of his earbuds. I wait a beat and then press my lips into a sad smile—half acting, half pained. Determined to find the crack in his veneer.

"Yeah," I say. "Just thinking about my dad."

He winces sympathetically and slides his fingers between mine, squeezing them for comfort. "Don't do that," he says. "Don't give him that. He doesn't deserve your loyalty."

He's right, which is ironic considering the mysterious text Deacon received. I look down at our hands, so perfectly matched. *He's mine,* I think, my chest aching. *Hasn't he always been mine?*

But how many times has Deacon lied to me? How long has he been manipulating me?

Who sent that text?

"Remember the last time we tried to run away?" he asks, leaning his temple against the seat as he gazes lovingly at me. It's almost enough to distract me completely.

"'Tried' being the operative word," I say. "We failed."

"Hey." He sniffs a laugh. "We made it as far as your driveway before your dad pulled up and you chickened out. It's the farthest we ever got." His eyes soften. "Until now. And we're all in this time, right?" he asks.

"All in," I repeat, looking down at our hands again. Deacon's thumb strokes my wrist, pausing slightly on my pulse point. For a moment I'm lost in his touch, but then I realize he could be monitoring my heartrate—acting as a lie detector.

I haven't been careful enough. I haven't been protecting myself, even though my father told me that the grief department would be after me. He said they wouldn't let me go because they plan to *transition* me within the department. He didn't know exactly what they were transitioning me into. Maybe someone at the grief department is behind that text.

"What's wrong?" Deacon asks, narrowing his eyes slightly. "I mean, beyond the obvious part where your dad is a raging asshole."

"It's all just a little much, you know?" I say as naturally as possible. I casually take my hand from Deacon's and run it through my short hair, bringing it to rest on my lap instead. Deacon follows the movement but doesn't mention it. "I don't know what we'll find when we get to Roseburg," I add.

Dr. Arthur Pritchard is in Roseburg, along with his daughter, Virginia. Although I agreed to check on Virginia's well-being after the suicide of my last assignment, Arthur's the one I'm after. My father said that Arthur might be able to get the grief department off my back, but more than that, Arthur knows my real identity; he might be the only person who does.

Until then I have to avoid getting picked up by the grief department—I don't know what they're capable of. Clearly, they're not just a treatment program; they're involved in cover-ups and lies. My father is afraid of them. Marie, my advisor, skipped town before they could find her. I don't even know what I'm up against, and that makes them scarier than anything.

And I'm stuck on a bus with the person I love, the person who is possibly working against me. Am I being paranoid? Am I not paranoid enough? If the situation were different, I could act like all is well with Deacon and wait for reinforcements—another counselor to take my place because I'm compromised. But, of course, there's no one coming to help me. I'm all alone. I've always been alone. And so I have to run until I'm certain where Deacon's loyalties lie.

Deacon slips his earbud back in his right ear, exhaling heavily like he's exhausted. "The first thing we should do when we get to Roseburg," he says, "is grab dinner. We're both a little high-strung right now." He turns up the corner of his mouth when he looks over at me.

"Agreed," I say, playing along. A passing sign outside the window announcing the Eugene bus station catches my attention, and I think I've figured a way off this bus. "One change," I say to Deacon, holding up my finger like this is important. "We should eat in Eugene. I can't make it to Roseburg—I'm starving."

Deacon furrows his brow and leans forward to look out the window, checking our location. "You sure?" he asks, turning to me. "We don't have much time at this stop."

"I'm hungry." I smile winningly, as if trying to convince him.

Deacon darts his eyes quickly toward the back of the bus, and I feel my stomach sink. He's searching for someone. He has backup. Then again, maybe I'm jumping to all the wrong conclusions. Only problem is that I don't have the time to figure out which it is.

"Okay, sure," Deacon says, lifting his shoulder in a shrug. "Yeah, we can grab something quick. Anything for you."

He says it like he means it, and it's the cruelest thing he

could have done. I press my lips into a smile and turn away. My heart aches like I've been punched in the chest, each breath cracking my ribs, pressing on my soul.

He doesn't love you, I tell myself. *That's why he's never said it. That's why he never will.*

Whether or not the statement is true, I repeat it until I start to build a wall between us. I continue to push until my feelings are locked away behind the bricks. Like this is just another assignment. I imagine that Deacon is a client and that our time is up. I need to slip away as if I've never been here—take no mementos, no baggage. I'll leave it all here on this bus. I'll leave him.

The brakes hiss, and gravity pulls us forward in our seats as we come to a stop in front of a small but crowded building. The overhead lights on the bus flick on, and the people around us immediately start to angle for a position in line—as if the bus would leave without letting them off first.

"We've got to be back on here in fifteen minutes," Deacon says. He grabs his bag from under the seat and sets it between us. He zips it closed without ever checking his phone. He doesn't know he got a message. But more importantly, he doesn't know that I've already seen it.

I pull my backpack straps onto my shoulders, and as we wait for a break in aisle traffic, I subtly glance toward the back of the bus. A woman four rows behind us sticks out—an anomaly in the crowd. I don't recognize her, but the rigidity of her posture and her stoic expression remind me of a doctor. And when her dark eyes flash momentarily to mine before darting away, I know immediately that she's from the grief department. I know that she's here for me.

I spin around, a lump forming in my throat. I could cry right now if I let myself, break down completely. I could cling to Deacon and beg for his help—*would he help me?* I could return to my father's house and go on with the lie, live as Quinlan McKee and work for the grief department. It would be easier, in a way. Because right now I'm so scared that I don't know if I can get off this bus. I don't know if I can do this alone.

But when there is no other choice . . . you find a way. By the time Deacon steps out into the aisle, making room for me to walk ahead of him, I'm ready to nod politely and put one foot in front of the other.

"Excuse me," a woman's voice says. I freeze, afraid to turn around. The tone is husky and deep, and I imagine it's the woman I noticed a moment ago. "Excuse me, sir," she says, and I hear another passenger tell her to go ahead. She's getting off the bus too.

I inch closer to the businessman in front of me, wishing I could squeeze by him and just run. Instead I'm trapped in the line with everyone else, all of us pressed together and waiting. My fear continues to ratchet up as I hear the woman getting closer. Deacon's hand moves to rest on my hip, guiding me forward.

Panic is running rampant as I try to piece my situation into something that makes sense, but there are too many broken edges. I don't have enough time to make a clean getaway. I don't know if there is enough time to disappear.

"Excuse me, son," the woman's voice says, and she's so close that I swear she's talking to Deacon. Her tone has warmed, but Deacon's hand is still firmly placed on my hip.

"Sorry," he tells her. "We're all packed in here pretty tight." I don't turn back to them, but I read people's reactions for a living: I hear the annoyance in Deacon's voice, and I can only hope he doesn't know her. Hope that he's not trying to hand me over to the very people we're running from. I can't believe he ever would.

Stop, I think, forcing myself cold. I can't let my love for him blind me. I have to get somewhere safe. The stakes are too high to take a chance. Even on Deacon.

I stare ahead until I notice a frail older woman two rows up. She huffs out in pain, trying to lift her bag with one hand while balancing herself with her cane. I narrow my eyes, and when it's clear no one else plans to help her, I elbow my way past the businessman in her direction.

"Sorry," I murmur. "I have to help her."

The man nods as the crowd ahead of the old woman thins—he doesn't want to hold up the line. I stop next to the woman and look down.

"Do you want me to grab that for you?" I ask.

She looks me over and then smiles kindly, the wrinkles around her bright blue eyes deepening. "Why, thank you, honey." She steadies herself on her cane, leaving her small suitcase behind for me to grab.

She starts down the aisle, and I turn to find Deacon watching me, a soft smile on his lips—as if my kindness impresses him. I nod toward the window to say I'll meet him outside. He looks oblivious to my true intentions, and I give myself one last chance to back out. To ask for his help. But then I catch a glimpse of the woman just behind him. There's a flicker of panic in her expression. I have no choice but to run.

I let the part of me that loves Deacon desperately drain away; I feel it flow down my arms and legs, out my fingers and toes. And I turn, cold and empty—ready to take on whatever identity I want—and start down the aisle behind the old woman. I thought this was the beginning of something new. Getting answers to my past, starting a life with Deacon. But now I know I'll have to find the truth on my own. I am the only person I can trust. There is no time for sentimentality.

Disappearing should be easy for me, but with Deacon, someone deft at recreating himself and blending in, it won't be that simple. I mentally tick off the items I have at my disposal. I still have my father's credit cards, which I can probably use at least once more before they're reported stolen. Also in my backpack is a change of clothes, the DVD that Marie left me, and some cash. Nothing that can actually help me disguise myself, though. I look out the window at the bus station.

I'm in Eugene, I think. *And once upon a time I played a dead girl here.*

Melanie Saunders was fourteen when she died in a car accident. She lived in a charming area of older homes, and her parents were understandably devastated. She was an only child, and I remember hoping they'd have another when I left. They were good people.

My memory of the area hasn't completely faded, and I'm sure if I go downtown, I can find a place to hide. Regroup and flee in the morning. Deacon will assume I'm leaving immediately—why would I stay? I hope the grief department draws the same conclusion.

Now I just have to slip away.

I walk down the steep bus stairs and set the small suitcase in front of the old woman. She starts to say thank you, but I slide past her and walk swiftly toward the building. I'm nearly to the door when I hear Deacon call my name. I flinch, but I reach for the handle anyway. I have only seconds, and as I step over the threshold into the building, I know I've just changed everything.

Now it's time to be smart. I'll have to be smarter than the entire grief department. But first I have to be smarter than Deacon.

I walk calmly toward the restrooms. I don't look back—never look back when trying to disappear. I scan the crowd as I slip in and out of people's way, making it a point to shift into their space so that they have to step aside. I take over their walking path. It helps me become invisible, like the sleight of hand a magician might use when hiding a rubber ball under a shell.

I step in front of a mom with a wiggling toddler on her hip, murmuring a quiet apology, and after a few feet I walk in front of a man in a business suit who's talking on his cell phone. My movements are smooth and rapid. I see an older woman heading toward the restroom, and I stand at her side, blocking the view of me from the back entrance.

Once inside the bathroom, I pause. A thick floral scent hangs in the air, and the constant sound of flushing toilets and hand dryers is exactly the kind of white noise that keeps people distracted. I go to stand near the baby changing station and slip off my backpack. I'll have to leave it. I take off my sweater and pull out my favorite hoodie. I grab a fresh plastic bag from the changing station and throw in my Rolling Stones T-shirt, the DVD from my file, and a few pairs of underwear and some basic toiletries. Once done, I drop my backpack and sweater into the trash. No one notices me.

I glance at my reflection, and emotions try to fight their way out, but I lock them away. Not now. Not here. I take the hair tie from my pocket and scrape my hair into a barely enough ponytail, disguising the pale blond color. I look sideways at the woman washing her hands two sinks down. She has a baseball cap snapped onto the handle of her suitcase. Near the door someone has left her denim jacket on the counter as she uses the restroom.

I hate the thought of stealing. Sure, when I was a closer, I would take . . . a souvenir from my assignment's house: a shirt, a necklace. But that was different—she was dead. Now it feels like stealing. But it's my way out of here.

In a swift motion I start toward the door. As I pass the woman at the sink, I reach down and unclip the back of her baseball hat and slip it under my hoodie without missing a step. I keep walking and casually pick up the jacket as if it were mine all along. Again—no one notices me.

The moment I exit the bathroom, I put the hat on my head and push my arms into the sleeves of the jacket. I pop the collar for more coverage. My steps are fast, but not fast enough to arouse notice. Another corridor is coming up, and I continue to take over other people's walking paths. Just before I turn, I glance up to the mirror perched in the corner of the ceiling. I look toward the food court, and sure enough I find Deacon standing facing my direction, brow furrowed as he looks around, his hands folded behind his head as he searches. He knows that something is wrong. He feels it. The woman from the bus is nowhere in sight. And I realize that I could have been wrong about her; she could have nothing to do with the grief department. But there's no time to think.

I quickly dart around the corner and head for the exit. I'm careful not to look panicked, just hurried. I can't check back to see if Deacon's following me, so I stick to the wall. The sliding doors of the exit come into view. It's started to rain, and I say a quiet thank-you. It'll be harder to find me this way.

I walk purposefully toward the sliding glass doors of the exit. The minute I'm outside, I pull my hood over the baseball cap, acceptable fashion while in the rain, and walk down the curb until I see a cab. I put out my hand, careful to keep my face turned from the doors in case Deacon walks out here. A cab stops, and I'm nearly out of breath as I get inside. I lock the door, and the cabdriver lifts his dark eyes to mine in the rearview mirror.

"Corner of Fifth and Pearl, please," I say, and sit back, sinking down slightly. The man shifts into gear, but keeps his foot on the brake and turns to look at me. "You know that's just a few blocks from here, right?" he asks.

"Yeah," I say, although I had forgotten. "But it's raining and I'm in a hurry." Each second the driver delays, the closer Deacon gets to finding me.

The man shrugs. "It's your money." He eases off the brake and pulls into the street.

Once we're moving, I check the mirror on the passenger side for Deacon's reflection. I watch until the bus station fades from view, and when it's gone completely, I hurt more than ever.

I'm all alone.

CHAPTER TWO

WHEN I WAS A LITTLE GIRL, A DOCTOR BROUGHT ME to a man who'd just lost his child. This man, my eventual father, was suffering from the death of his wife and daughter. I should have been a temporary relief from grief, but Dr. Arthur Pritchard had different plans for me. He let my father keep me and raise me as his dead daughter. I was brainwashed to believe it—although I don't know how.

For years after, the grief department employed me, teaching me ways to adjust my personality to suit their clients. With the exception of my last assignment, the one that changed things, I was always able to adapt. But I fell in love with a family and lost myself. I was almost gone completely.

As I sit in the backseat of the taxi, I push up my sleeve and stare down at the gold bracelet around my wrist. I trace my finger along the delicate band, determined to keep my mind clear this time. Isaac Perez, the boyfriend of my last assignment, gave me this bracelet. During my time with him, we crossed a few lines, made it all too real. It nearly destroyed me. But in the end Isaac found closure, and he gave this to me as a gift. And right now it adds to my strength. It resets me in my purpose.

Despite my fear of the grief department, I have to find Arthur Pritchard and demand he tell me who I really am. I won't leave until he does. And while he's at it, he can tell me what the grief department wants with me—what they're *really* doing there. My father warned me that Arthur doesn't have much clout there anymore, saying a board of directors has taken over. But Arthur created the department; I have to believe he knows how to stop them too. I just want a life that's my own. I want the truth.

The cabdriver pulls to the corner of Pearl and Fifth and bumps the curb, startling me from my thoughts. My head is a mess. In the last forty-eight hours I've lost my identity, my family, my friends. Even Deacon. It's hard to keep on a mask of calm when I lean forward and ask the driver how much.

The guy swings his arm over the seat as he turns back to look at me. "Five fifty, sweetheart," he says, prickling my nerves. I fish out a ten from my pocket and tell him to keep the change.

I lower my hood and climb out of the cab, glad when it drives away; the smell of pine air freshener is still in my nose. The rain is barely a drizzle now, and I glance around, trying to reacquaint myself with the surroundings of the area. Things

SUZANNE YOUNG

have changed since the last time I was here, updates to the two-story market next to the light-rail tracks.

The building has a brick façade and lush flower baskets hinting at its charm. There's a restaurant with a covered patio out front, twinkling white lights on its posts, and the smell of grilled food thick in the air. Now that I'm out of immediate danger, even the horror and anxiety of the day isn't enough to cover the fact that I haven't eaten since this morning.

I walk over to scan the restaurant menu at the front desk, but the dinners are overpriced, so I head into the indoor market and glance at the stores. There's a candy shop, and I slip inside and buy a handful of chocolates and a lollipop for a dollar twenty-five. My nose twitches, and I notice a barrel of roasted almonds. My eyes start to itch with allergies, and I thank the woman behind the counter before fleeing for another area of the market.

I stop by the food court and buy a rice bowl with avocado. I gulp it down, and when I'm done eating, I wander over to a bench near the center fountain. I sit and pull my legs up to wrap my arms around them, resting my chin on my knees. I eat the chocolates I bought earlier, saving the lollipop.

Deacon should be here, I think miserably as I crumple a candy wrapper in my hand. *He should be here with me.*

But he's not here. I made sure of that.

I squeeze my eyes shut at the sudden hole in my chest. I didn't even give Deacon a chance to explain. And now I've left him . . . again. *What if I was wrong?*

My breath catches on the start of a cry, but I force it down. I bury it. When it's only a pinprick of agony, I open my eyes and steady my gaze on a flower pot across from the fountain.

What if I was right? Deacon himself would tell me to play it safe first. So I will. Even if it feels like I've ripped out my heart and left it on a bus to Roseburg.

I glance around at the shops, feeling suddenly aware of how vulnerable I am in public. Several of the stores start to lower their gates, and I take it as my cue to head back outside.

It's not dark yet, but the rain has let up. The hazy evening reminds me of the times I'd sit on Deacon's back porch, watching the sky clear. We would feel small; our problems as closers felt small. And the universe offers me that same small measure of comfort now.

I begin to walk, feeling contented by the slow pace of the town. Eugene houses the University of Oregon, but it's still quiet here. Peaceful. I wouldn't mind staying for a while, even though I know I can't.

It's when I cross into another neighborhood, still not having found a place to stay, that I remember a detail from when I was on assignment here. The Saunders family used to own a bike shop nearby. It's past business hours by now, so I don't have to worry about running into them—traumatizing them. But . . . they used to hide a key. Maybe it's still there.

I continue down the road, and when I finally arrive at the store, the sky has dimmed considerably. The lights inside

SUZANNE YOUNG

the bike shop are all off with the exception of a safety light behind the counter. I check that the street is empty, and then I round the brick building toward the back door.

There's a rock in the garden trim that used to mark a hidden key, and I pick it up and dig into the mulch below. But the key is no longer there. I spend a few more minutes searching obvious areas but eventually resign myself to the fact that the family doesn't leave the key to their business hidden in the back parking lot anymore.

It's been years since I've been here, and it's entirely possible that the Saunders family no longer owns the business. But from what I remember, they were dedicated. The shop had been started by Mr. Saunders's father, passed down through the family. I don't think they'd walk away from that.

Frustrated, I set my dirty hands on my hips and look up at the overhead streetlamps illuminating the empty back lot. I only wanted a few hours of sleep; my head is foggy. My heart is broken. I'm completely overwhelmed, and I can't hold back the wave of sadness that rushes over me. I've lost everything.

I slide down the locked door until I'm sitting on the ground, knees bent. I lower my head into my hands, about ready to fall apart completely. I'm worn down, but not like when I broke with reality the other day. This exhaustion is something different. Like a struggle to figure out how all my problems fit together, only I'm missing a piece.

I've felt this way before. It was about six months ago, a

night I'd nearly forgotten about. I was at Aaron's apartment, sitting on the couch with Deacon. We'd been broken up for nearly two months, and we were just starting to figure out what it meant to be forever friends with no other benefits.

"Come on, Quinn," Deacon said from the other end of the couch while flashing that devastating smile. "Turn your frown upside down before I come over there and cheer you up."

"I love that you think moving closer would make me happier," I told him.

"Sassy," he murmured, making me laugh.

Aaron was playing a video game while Myra was at the store buying alcohol with a fake ID she'd gotten from Deacon. Aaron and I were between assignments, and Deacon was enjoying his retirement from the grief department.

I felt emotionally bankrupt. My last assignment had been painful. I was still wearing the socks of the dead girl I'd been impersonating; I didn't know why I'd taken them. They were a gift from her grandma, and I suppose it was because I'd never had a grandmother. Or maybe I just wanted those socks. Either way, I took them. I wore them.

But it didn't explain the lost feeling still festering in my chest, as if something in me was missing. As if I'd changed.

"Quinlan," Deacon said like he'd called me once already. It startled me and I looked over at him. His brown eyes narrowed with concern. "Are you okay?" he asked, all joking aside.

I ran my hand through my long blond hair, thinking over the question. "I'm not sure," I said. Aaron stopped pressing the buttons on his game controller and turned to watch me. Deacon's posture straightened.

"I'm . . ." I paused, and the best word I could think of was "lonely." "I think I'm lonely, but it's like I miss . . . myself." And damn, once I said it, the force of the words hit me in the chest. The sense of loss was so heavy. It wasn't grief; it was as if something had been taken from me, and it hurt. The feeling was disconcerting to say the least.

Deacon appeared immediately at my side and gathered me in a hug, probably thinking it was all about him. And even though it wasn't, I rested against his chest and closed my eyes to listen to his heartbeat. I loved him so much, and for a moment I entertained the thought of letting his affection feed me—cure my loneliness. But I knew better. And so I pulled away, seeing his expression flicker with hurt before he could cover it up, and I looked at Aaron, who seemed ready to pounce if his worry got any deeper.

The front door opened, and Myra came in, holding a heavy-looking brown bag. She kicked the door shut with her foot. "Who wants a drink?" she called in her harsh voice.

And I was the first one up. "Me," I said, and followed her into the kitchen, setting aside my loneliness and its forgotten reason.

The squeak of bicycle brakes and a scatter of gravel startles me from where I'm sitting against the shop door. My eyes fly open, and I find a stranger straddling the seat of his bike a few yards away. Although the light is dim, I see that he's a little younger than me, with shoulder-length dark hair and a flannel shirt. He looks nonthreatening, but I'm careful nonetheless.

"Uh, can I help you?" the guy asks.

"No," I respond quickly, and climb to my feet. I'm disheveled, and I use my fingers to poke my hair back under my hat. I lower my eyes, ready to disappear. "I was just leaving." I've started to walk away when the guy laughs, loud and hearty. I glance back over my shoulder at him.

He rubs his palm over his chin. "Wasn't trying to scare you off," he says, smiling. "I'm August. And you are?"

"Does it matter?" I ask.

"Guess not," he allows. "I can just call you Girl Lurking in the Shadows Looking to Break into My Uncle's Shop." He pauses. "But it's a mouthful."

"Your uncle?" I ask. I look him over again, to see if there's any resemblance to Melanie's family. Nothing immediately sticks out, but it was nearly four years ago.

"Unless," August says, looking around dramatically, "you have a bike stashed that needs a new chain or something?"

I know I should leave, get out of here before he realizes who I am. Once a family has had a closer in their lives, they don't forget it. But . . . I'm not a closer anymore. That should count for something. Feeling brave, I step toward him and take off my hat. The light from the streetlamp falls across my face. August gives a reflexive smile, but I watch it slowly fade.

"Wait," he says, furrowing his brow as he thinks. "I know you." He climbs off his bike and lays it on its side, approaching as he studies me. I feel it coming, and sure enough, I see his Adam's apple bob as the realization falls over him. "You're . . ." He takes a step back like I might hurt him. "You're her," August says, his expression calm but his voice pitched higher. "You're the closer for Melanie."

I only went out in public with the family once or twice. But he could have seen me. Could have seen pictures from a reenacted moment. And when you see a person acting as someone you know is dead, you don't tend to forget their face. Only the clients can do that, and that's because they're sick with grief.

"I was a closer," I admit, waiting for him to tear out of here or, worse, tell me I'm a monster. "But I don't do that anymore," I add, hoping it makes a difference.

August stares at me and then nods slowly. "That's good, I guess," he responds. "Because closers are creepy as fuck."

My mouth flinches with a smile, even though I don't think he's joking. But it reminds me of something Deacon would say if he hadn't been a closer himself. Even August's brown eyes are the same shade as Deacon's. Or maybe I just really want this guy to be Deacon right now.

"So what are you doing here, then?" August asks. "If my uncle sees you, he'll—"

"I wasn't sure where else to go. I thought maybe . . ." I shake my head, feeling stupid. "I don't know what I thought. I'm leaving town tomorrow anyway. I'll probably just go to a motel."

August seems to think this over, and then he scrunches up his nose like he has a horrible idea. "I'm heading back to my house," he says tentatively. "If you don't have a place to go . . . you can come with. My roommate's cool. I'm sure Eva will have a million questions for you. Closers fascinate her."

"Roommate?" I ask. "You don't live at home?"

"Nope," he responds. "Not anymore. I've been on my own for over a year."

It would be dumb to go with him, but his tiny show of damage makes me trust him—as if we have it in common. But I hesitate. People are hostile toward closers: We make them confront mortality. We prove they're replaceable, even if only for a short time. The bruise on my cheek from when I was punched by my last assignment's best friend has barely faded. I touch the spot, worried I could be walking into something worse.

"Look," August says. "Eva's my roommate. We have a shitty house near campus that never warms up and has a constant stream of stray dogs that we rehome. I promise we're not stranglers. I can call her first if you want. Make sure it's cool."

Fact is, I do want to go. Not just because it's a hiding place either. I want to hang out with regular people, not people who spend their lives as others. I miss my time with Aaron, Deacon, and Myra, but there's something to be said for being normal. I had that for a little while on my last assignment, and I'm craving it now. I'm craving a chance to be myself—not as a closer, but as a girl starting over. A girl without a name of her own.

I want to figure out who I am. I want to get to know me.

And I'll never figure that out surrounded by a bunch of fakers.

"Would your roommate have to know who I am?" I ask August. "Do you have to tell her?"

He waits a painfully long moment and then shrugs. "Yeah," he says. "I wouldn't bring a closer into our house without telling her."

Although he says them kindly, his words sting. Not even a week ago, when I was Catalina, Isaac brought me to meet his friend Jason. When Jason found out who I was, what I was, he wasn't kind. He acted as if I were an infection. A disease. A *monster*. At least August knows who I am already. I won't have to worry about being discovered.

"Okay," I say, nodding. "Thank you." I wait while he takes out his phone, turns away from me, and talks in a low voice to the person on the other end. He laughs.

"I swear," he says. He glances back over his shoulder at me. "No, she looks cool. All right. See you in a few." August puts his phone away and smiles. "Eva is totally stoked. You ready?"

I say a silent prayer that I'm not about to get murdered, and then nod my head. "Let's go."

CHAPTER THREE

I WALK BESIDE AUGUST AS HE RIDES HIS BIKE IN the street. He stands on his pedals, swerving back and forth along the pavement to keep his balance. He tells me about his uncle and how after I'd given them closure, the family started doing better. That they even had another child. I'm glad—glad the family is okay. It sets me at ease, proving it wasn't all a waste. I gave them peace. Now if only I could find a bit of my own.

"What about you?" August asks, glancing over at me. "What have you done since? Have you been busy *being* other people?"

"Yeah," I say, looking at the sidewalk beneath my boots as I walk. "A lot of them, I guess. I've lost count. The last one . . ." I stop myself. Now is not the time to overshare. "The last one finished my contract," I lie, looking over. "I'm a regular person again." *Or for the first time.*

"Eh." August shrugs. "Being regular isn't all that great." He watches me a long moment and smiles broadly. "Man, Eva is going to love this. She looked into becoming a closer, you know."

"What happened?" I ask. "Did she apply?"

"Nah. The statistics scared her. Some of you can't hack it, end up hospitalized . . . or at least that's what the local paper reported."

I widen my eyes. "The paper wrote about us?"

"An op-ed," August says. "It was tucked in the back of the paper, but Eva found it. The paper never followed up. I used to joke that the grief department probably whacked the journalist and covered it up. Either way," he continues, "Eva will be excited to meet you. You're way better than the stray dog I brought in last week."

I laugh. "Well, I do have all of my shots."

"That's good. Although I'm not sure Eva does."

We continue on, and after a strenuous trip uphill, August pauses in front of a two-story, ramshackle house lit up under the streetlamp. The paint on the shutters is peeling, and the porch pitches dramatically to the left. Despite its condition, it's kind of cute. There's a flower planter outside the second-story window with petals that glow orange in the low light.

"Having second thoughts?" August asks.

"No," I tell him honestly, "I think it's nice. It looks lived in."

He smiles. "Now, that is such a closer thing to say. Come on." He hops off his bike and bumps it up the stairs before stashing it in the corner of the porch. I'm nervous, but excited for something different. I want to be a part of society. I'm sick of being an outcast.

The door is unlocked, and August leads me inside to a small, split-level foyer. We start up the staircase; it's dark even when August flips on the light. I follow him toward the door at the top. He knocks once to announce our arrival and walks in.

I step in just behind him, immediately comforted by the colorful tapestries tacked to the wall and the mishmash of thrift-store furniture. In a way it reminds me of Marie's apartment. The cluttered residence of my advisor was a touchstone for my real life—or at least what I thought was my real life. Despite the lies she told me, I long for her now: her trusted advice, her confidence. But she's a liar, and I quickly squash the nostalgia I've dredged up.

August reaches behind me to close the door, and thankfully, he doesn't lock it. He pulls off his flannel—he's wearing a white T-shirt underneath—and tosses it on top of a cluttered table.

I look around the meager apartment, no stray animals in sight. In the next room I find a girl on the couch, legs crisscrossed in front of her. She leans forward to stare at me. Her already-big eyes widen impossibly large; her fake lashes are painted to points like she's an anime character. Her brown hair is shaved in a buzz cut, but she wears a headband with a pretty pink bow.

"Eva," August says, dropping into what looks like a curb-rescue recliner. "This is the closer."

I flinch internally, wishing to be introduced as something else. *Someone* else. But I don't know who I am yet.

August purses his lips and turns to look at me. "Actually," he says, shaking his head as if just realizing, "what *is* your name?"

"Brooke," I answer, calling up the first name that doesn't immediately relate back to a case. I turn to Eva. "It's nice to meet you," I say before August can ask about my last name. "And I'm not a closer anymore," I clarify.

Eva stares at me for a long moment, and just when I think she's going to ask me to leave, she laughs loudly, filling up the whole room. "This is so fucking awesome!" she calls out, startling me. She pats the couch cushion beside her. "Sit here. I want to know *everything*."

I take a seat on the patterned sofa next to Eva and set my bag of items on the floor next to my feet. Eva leans forward to grab a glass of soda from the dusty trunk they use for a coffee table. I feel suddenly warm in my layers of clothes. I take off my jacket and fold it in my lap.

"I've never actually met one of you before," she says, and takes a hurried slurp from her drink. "You're pretty," she adds, "even though I can tell you're trying to look plain." She smiles and takes another sip before setting down her drink. "You didn't cover your freckles." Eva runs her finger in a line over her cheeks and nose to mimic where mine are. "But I like them. I wouldn't cover them up anyway." She turns her body toward me, and her knees nearly touch the side of my thigh.

"Thank you," I say. "To be honest, I never really wear makeup outside of my assignments." I smile. "Too much work."

"Oh, I love makeup. Beauty makeup is totally my thing. But enough about me." She bites down on her lip nervously. "I have so many questions. . . . Do you mind?"

"Ask away," I tell her, truly not minding. She makes me feel interesting, not hated. Not feared. That's typically the default setting, so this is a nice change.

"I've always wondered if closers go to regular school," she starts. "I mean, I'm sure you'd miss a lot of classes and all that."

"Some do," I say. "But I haven't gone to school in a long while."

"Cool," August says from the chair, as if a lack of education is the ultimate goal.

I laugh. "Not really," I say. "I take online classes, but I kind of hate them. It's isolating. There's no life there. It's all just words on a screen."

"There's life at school," Eva says, "but I'm not sure it counts if all the heartbeats belong to judgmental douche bags." She grins. "But I get what you're saying about technology. In fact, our computer systems got shut down last month. Someone hacked into the online journals they make us keep and started leaking pages. Same thing happened in Roseburg. A sophomore girl there got really upset." Eva takes another sip of her drink. "I think she killed herself."

"Yep," August says, leaning forward in the chair. "It was on the news a few weeks ago. There were two of them. Another boy killed himself in between classes."

I feel the blood drain from my face, the realization settling in. It's happening there, too, just like with Catalina and Mitchel, who was Aaron's assignment. A suicide cluster. My heart starts to beat faster.

"Do you know which school it was in Roseburg?" I ask, betting that it's the same school Virginia Pritchard attends.

"Marshall, I think," Eva says. "Why?"

"Just curious," I tell her. "I hadn't heard about it."

"Really?" August says, sounding surprised. "It's been all over the news here. Even on CNN. Pretty sure that's all anyone talks about anymore." He stands up, rolling out his shoulders as he stretches. "It's depressing," he adds, and then looks over at Eva. "Hey, is there any pizza left?"

"Yeah," she tells him, waving him toward the kitchen. When she turns back to me, she smiles. Unaffected by the thought of suicides. Untouched by it. I'm envious of how clear her emotional palate is—how free of loss it seems.

August escapes into the kitchen, and Eva studies me admiringly. She leans in, her elbows on her thighs. "Have you ever wanted to stay in a role?" she asks. "Like, stay as one of the dead people?" The question catches me off guard, opening a wound in my heart.

"Once," I tell her, surprisingly honest. "The family was very sweet to me. Accepting. I cared about them, and they wanted me to stay—even after we'd completed the closure. But I realized eventually that I didn't want to live a life that wasn't mine. It wouldn't be fair to any of us."

"I don't think I would mind it," she says wistfully. "Taking someone else's place would be nice. My life is shit. My family sucks—I left the moment I turned eighteen. Maybe a different life would be a good thing."

There's the loud clap of a cupboard door as August gets out a plate for his pizza. I take another look around the room. It's painfully average in the most perfect way—an ease that can't be replicated by any closer.

"You're lucky," I tell her. "This is yours. Your life is yours."

"At least you're not replaceable," she tells me. "Not many people can do what you do."

I lower my eyes. "Yeah, well. I gave up a lot to be a closer."

This seems to pique her interest. "I bet it was hard. I can tell you're different, though—different from us."

My stomach twists, and I look up to meet her gaze. *Us*— she means regular people.

"Not in a bad way," she clarifies. "I can see that you're kind. And I think you take death more seriously than most people— death of complete strangers. But there's also . . ." She pauses, narrowing her eyes as if trying to figure something out. "I'm not sure what it is," she says, "but you seem . . . fluid. Like, you're here . . . but not really."

I understand what she means. I'm unfinished. Closers are always acting as someone else. It changes who we are and who we can be—even if I did know my real self. It's amazing that Eva can see that.

"You probably would have been a great closer," I say, making her smile.

"Now that I think about it," Eva says, "maybe I just wanted to play with makeup."

I laugh. "Well, it just so happens I'm fantastic with makeup. At least, I'm fantastic with the kind that can turn you into someone else."

Her eyes light up. "Can you turn me into someone else?"

I shift in my seat.

"Just for fun," she says. "No one dead or anything. I want to look completely different. Come on," she adds. "It'll be awesome."

I hesitate. Although Myra and I have done this same thing a million times—she loved how different I could make her look—I've never done a makeover on a stranger.

The memory makes me suddenly miss my friends with a deep ache, and the only way I know how to deal with loss is to replace it. So I smile and nod my head.

"Do you have makeup?" I ask. "I don't have any with me."

"Girl," Eva says, jumping up, "I work part-time at Sephora. Come on." She reaches out her hand to me, a movement that probably means nothing to her, but to me, a person who is rarely touched by a noncloser, it shocks me. I slip my hand into hers and follow her toward the bathroom, pretending that she and I have been best friends for years.

Eva sits on the edge of the tub, her eyes turned up to the ceiling as I paint another layer of mascara on her lower lashes. I've contoured her cheeks to thin them out, overlined her lips to plump them up. I've made her large eyes smaller and her nose more defined.

"I hope this isn't too personal," she says, staring up as I finish her lashes, "but what's your family like?"

"I don't have one," I say quietly, and push the mascara brush back into its tube and seal it shut. "I'm a ward of the state. Most underage closers are."

"Oh." Eva lowers her eyes to look at me. "Sorry," she says.

"It's okay," I lie. "The grief department takes good care of us."

"That's nice, I guess. I always wondered what kind of parent would let their kid be a closer. You must see some messed-up shit."

I grab a blush brush and run it over her cheek, sharpening the contour. "I have," I tell her. "But the clients were always good people. And we were monitored, so we were never in any danger." What I don't say is that the truly 'messed-up shit' came from my own life, not my assignments.

I straighten and look over her face, proud of my work. "All done," I say, and step aside.

Eva flashes me a smile and then goes to the mirror, her hands on either side of the porcelain sink. Her mouth hangs open as she examines her reflection. She falls silent, and I worry that she hates the change, or worse, that she realizes what I can do. Realizes that if I really wanted to, I could buzz my hair and become her in the matter of an afternoon.

I start to put away the makeup, and when I turn around, Eva smiles at me. "You're crazy talented," she says. Her expression grows more thoughtful. "And I appreciate what you do," she adds.

"You look great," I say.

"No. Not this." She motions to her face. "I appreciate what you do for families. I don't have any brothers and sisters, but if I did, and if one of them . . . died, I would want your help. I would want you to save my parents from that."

"I used to think the same way," I tell her. "But now I wonder if we shouldn't just feel the hurt. Maybe not hurting is hurting us."

She nods like she's considering my words. "I like being pain-free," she says after a moment. "I suspect a lot of people do. Now . . ." She motions for me to follow her out of the bathroom. In the hall she glances over her shoulder at me.

"August said you needed a place to stay," she says. "Want a beer?"

I feel embarrassed that I've already imposed so much. I'm a random stranger August found and brought home. I don't belong here. I'm about to say so when Eva holds up her hand as if anticipating my excuse.

"You don't have to be so polite, Brooke. We have an extra room. Our roommate just graduated from U of O, and it probably still smells like his feet there. But there are clean sheets in the closet, and it's better than a park bench. We *want* you to stay."

I thank her, overwhelmed with gratitude. But I'm afraid I'm letting my guard down just because she's being nice to me.

Don't I deserve this bit of kindness, though? I can go back to being a heartless closer tomorrow. "Thanks," I tell Eva again, smiling brightly. "Now about that beer . . ."

CHAPTER FOUR

EVA AND I ARE ON THE COUCH WHILE AUGUST, complaining that he's still hungry, grabs me a beer from the kitchen before going back in to make mac 'n' cheese. For a while Eva and I don't talk about anything too serious—mostly about TV shows and music. But halfway through my drink, my inhibitions are lowered, and my mind keeps turning back to the things I miss, to the life I miss—the one that wasn't even my own.

"Is it hard to make friends?" Eva asks. "I mean, I think you're lovely"—she grins—"but I'm guessing other girls might be threatened by you. You know, because you can *be* them."

"I have a few friends," I say, although I make "few" sound like it means more than literally three people. I didn't have any friends growing up. Not a damn one. I had my father, and then

I had Deacon, and then Aaron and Myra. Now that I think about it, it's a wonder I'm not more screwed up.

Eva closes her eyes, exhaling heavily. I turn back to the television, which is playing an hour-long commercial for moisturizer. There's a buzz under my skin, and I find myself smiling when August comes back into the room, holding a blue bowl. He sits in the chair across from me and uses an oversize spoon to scoop a heap of macaroni into his mouth. When he finishes, he tilts his head inquisitively.

"Are you dating anyone?" he asks. The minute the words are out of his mouth, his cheeks start to redden. "Sorry," he says quickly. "I didn't mean it to sound . . ." He laughs. "Honestly just curious. I mean, would you have to date another closer? Do other people understand what you do?"

My insides scream as he opens a wound that I've tried to close, and the pleasant tingle on my skin turns to needle pricks. I don't want to think about Deacon. I can't let myself feel this.

"Being a closer definitely doesn't go over well at parties," I tell August, trying to keep my tone upbeat, but ultimately I fail. Sadness creeps in along with thoughts of Deacon. "I've only had one relationship," I add. "And he did happen to be a closer. It's not easy, you know." I lean back on the couch cushion, the weight of my head suddenly heavy after I take the final sip of my drink. "Even though another closer understands the difficulties of what we do, the fact is, he's a liar," I say. "We're all liars. Our entire life is a system of pretending. And when you're trained to be a skilled liar, it starts to come naturally."

August furrows his brow, and I realize I've said too much. Given away too much of my truth. I lift my head. "Sorry," I say, flashing a smile. "I think I've had too much." I wiggle the empty bottle and then lean forward to set it on the trunk with a clink. When I look to the side, I see that Eva has fallen asleep on the couch. August watches me, his uncertainty easy to read.

"Do you want another?" he asks, motioning toward the beer. "It's still early."

"No, I'm going to go to bed," I say. August sits up straighter, like he doesn't want me to go. "I've had a long day," I add politely. "Thanks again for bringing me back here. Hope I worked out better than the dog."

"We rehomed him," August says, his tone flat. "I really hope you find your forever home soon, Brooke."

"I hope so too," I tell him.

He smiles then, friendly, like he's known me for years. "You could always leave the country, you know," he says. "Go to Europe and start over. Fake mustache and all that."

My heart skips a beat. Deacon and I used to talk about going to Europe to escape my father—that *exact* joke, in fact. But coming from August, the idea is absurd. I stand quickly, uncomfortable with the mood in the room. I grab my jacket and bag and murmur my good night. I start down the hall to where Eva showed me the extra room. The minute I close the door, I lock it—just in case. After all, they are strangers.

I grab the clean sheets out of the closet and smooth them onto the bare mattress. When I lie down, a coil pokes my back, but if I shift to the side, I don't even notice. I lie there, light filtering in the window from the streetlamps, and stare at the closet door. I only had one drink, but I feel fuzzy. And it could be from the alcohol or just the general fucked-up-ness of my life, but my emotions have come to the surface, like I can't hold them back. I'm submerged in a loneliness that is deep and dark and absolutely crushing.

"My name is Quinlan McKee," I whisper, trying to pull myself out of it. But I can't even finish my mantra, the one that used to keep me grounded after an assignment. I'm not Quinlan McKee. I'm no one.

I turn to the side and see a phone on the side table, a landline, and my fingers itch to pick it up. Tears gather in my eyes: Who can I call? Deacon is working against me, because no matter who sent that text, it was outside us. We should have been everything to each other—it was the only way to ensure our safety. He betrayed that. I would hate him for it if I could. I want to.

I squeeze my eyes shut, feeling the tears slip down my cheeks. It hurts too much to imagine my life without him. It hurts too much to believe that none of it was real. But if I'm going to survive this, I need to forget him for now. Forget what he's done.

My father, I think suddenly. I ran to him the last time Deacon hurt me—the time he broke up with me and left me shattered. Yes, my dad's a liar too. But he's the only family I have. The only family I know.

And hasn't he loved me? Would my real father, whoever he is, treat me as well? The idea that I have another father strikes me as odd. I've never considered it. I've daydreamed about a mother, but my Tom McKee has always been a constant; I can't imagine it any other way. I'm going to change that by discovering the truth.

I put my palm flat on my chest, as if I can relieve the ache there somehow. Right now I need something. *Someone.* If I can just talk to my father . . .Tom. I'm not sure what to call him anymore. I saw him only a few hours ago; I don't know what more there is to say. But I'm like a little kid running home to tell her dad that she scraped her knee, only to find that it hurts worse once he acknowledges the wound.

But maybe I just need him to acknowledge that I'm hurt.

Calling my dad right now is surely a sign of weakness, but I decide that I'm allowed to be weak once in a while. My entire life I've been manipulated into playing the permanent role of a dead girl, so yeah, it's understandable that I need to hear my father's voice again so I feel like a real person. My feelings for him don't disappear just because I want them to. Despite all his lies, part of me trusts him. Believes he doesn't want me hurt. Right now . . . he's all I've got.

I reach for the phone, pulling myself to sit up despite the wave of dizziness that accompanies it. *What is wrong with me?* I blink several times to get my bearings, and then I pick up the phone and stare at the numbers. It takes a second for them to come completely into focus.

It occurs to me that my father won't be home. From what I

know of him, which admittedly isn't nearly as much as I thought, he will try to act as if everything is normal. I've memorized my father's behaviors, a side effect of being a closer: observation. He's a creature of habit, and when he's stressed out, he likes Mexican food from a little joint near the college. When I'm not around to call it in, he heads there himself straight from work.

I can't call his cell phone—the number is too easily monitored. Luckily, I know the number to the restaurant by heart.

I dial, and when the line rings, I dart a careful glance at the closed door of the bedroom, worried that August or Eva will come in and ask me what I'm doing. I'm just using their phone, of course, but with each ring my paranoia grows. Again my emotions are exaggerated.

"Barrio's on University," a man answers in a thick accent, making me snap to attention. I feel a rush of warmth at the familiarity of his voice, a small reminder of home.

"Hi, Rubio," I say, able to picture him with the phone resting between his ear and shoulder, his finger tapping the keys of the register as he multitasks. "It's Quinn. I'm wondering if my . . . dad is there."

Rubio laughs. "No, not yet. Is he fetching his own order tonight?"

My heart sinks. "I guess not," I say, disappointed. I'd taken for granted that I knew his routines. Which was stupid. I never knew him at all. "Thanks any—"

"Oh, hold on, Q," he interrupts. "He just came in. See you soon, all right?"

"Yeah, all—" But I hear the phone shifting as he hands it over the counter. The anticipation sticks in my throat.

"For me?" I hear my father's voice say to Rubio. There's another rustle and then, "This is Thomas McKee," he says.

It's been only a few hours, but it feels like weeks since I've spoken to him. I'm flooded with anger and hurt, mixed with the heaviest sense of loss I've ever known. My voice hitches when I murmur, "Hi, Dad"—the only name I know to call him.

I hear him shift the phone to his other ear, a hush in his tone. "What's wrong?" he asks immediately. "Are you okay?"

That's the stupidest question he could have asked. Of course I'm not okay—and so much of that is his fault. But . . . I miss him. I miss having a family. I miss the lie of it all. I begin to cry, fighting the tears as fast as they fall.

"Quinn, where's Deacon?" he asks. "Can you put him on the phone?"

Despite their strained relationship, my father always thought Deacon was an excellent closer. He trusts him to protect me. I did too. All the people in my life who were supposed to love me have betrayed me instead. The horror of the thought helps me pull myself back together.

"I left him," I say, swiping my palm over my cheeks to clear the tears. "I left him at the bus station. That's why I'm calling *you*," I add with bitterness. "I don't have anyone else."

"What happened?" he asks, alarmed. "You two are inseparable. Believe me, I've tried. I understand you've had your problems," he concedes. "But Deacon will watch out for you. Now isn't the time to—"

"Deacon's hiding something, Dad," I say, my lips pulling taut. "I can't trust him. He got a text from someone looking for me. And then there was a woman who I think was following me on the bus. I couldn't tell if Deacon was in on it. I . . . I don't know where he stands. So I had to slip away—I had to disappear."

"You think Deacon's involved with someone at the grief department?" he asks. "I . . . I'm not sure I believe that."

"I don't know who texted him, but he shouldn't be talking to anyone about me. He's put me in danger. Why would he do that?" My father doesn't answer right away, and I assume he's shocked by this revelation. I don't blame him. "I don't know what to do, Dad," I say. "I have to get to Arthur Pritchard, though. Find out who I really am. I have to—"

"Honey," my dad says, making me flinch at the softness of the word. "I don't think that's a good idea anymore. Arthur isn't the kind of man you can make deals with. You have to let that go. Get far away from all of this."

"I'm sure that's what you'd want," I say, growing angry. "You kept my life from me. You deceived me and pretended—"

"I never pretended to love you," he says, cutting me off before I say it. "And you know that, or you wouldn't be calling me now. I'm your father. I'm the only father you know," he corrects. "And I will do everything I can to keep you safe."

"Then I need to know who I am," I say simply. I'm desperate, but part of that desperation is building on a wave of emotion in my chest, a clarity I can't seem to find in my head.

"I understand," my father says. "But please, Quinlan. We have to be careful. Arthur isn't even your biggest problem. Like I told you earlier, there are people at the grief department who will be very concerned by your absence. Since the board took over, there's been a shift in their goals. And I'm uncomfortable with some of their tactics. I don't want you under their control."

The fuzziness in my head continues, and I lie back on the bed, stare up at the swirling fan. "What kind of goals?" I ask. "What more can they take from me?"

My father pauses. "Are you all right?" he asks. "You have . . . you have a slight slur in your words."

"I had a beer," I admit, feeling my cheeks grow warm as if waiting for my father to scold me.

"Who did you have a drink with?"

"I met some people after getting off the bus. They're letting me crash at their house. I swear I only had one drink, Dad. I guess my tolerance just sucks. And I'm really emotional right now."

"Quinlan," my father says, his voice growing very serious. "I don't think you're drunk. You need to get out of that house right now."

My heart rate spikes, and I sit up, my head feeling two feet behind me as I rise. "What are you talking about?" I ask.

"I think you've been drugged."

I laugh. "No," I say. "I've been with them the entire time. How would they—" But slowly, through the haziness, I realize there was a moment when I didn't have my drink. It had already been opened when August handed it to me. But there's no way . . . There's no way, right?

I went to the workplace of a former client. That's where August found me. The grief department would have access to that information. But . . . how would they know where to look? My mind can't follow the logic, but I know suddenly that I was reckless in going there. I should have thought it through.

"Just indulge me on this," my father says. "I may sound paranoid, and I probably am. But I know what the department is capable of. And—" He stops abruptly.

The bustling sound of the taco shop has gone silent in the background. Something's wrong, and a sudden sense of panic makes me jump to my feet.

My father clears his throat. "Listen, Quinn," he says, sounding suddenly lighter, "everything's going to be okay." But under his tone I hear a falseness that people get only when they know they have an audience. A pitch to his voice. "I'll speak to the department, get this all cleared up. Right now I should just come get you. Tell me where you are."

Reality chills my skin, and I realize that my father is not alone. He might have been followed, or he could have alerted someone. I dismiss the second option almost immediately; he's trying to help me. I need to believe he's trying to help me, or I truly have nothing.

"You just give me an address," he says, "and it'll be all right. You can let Marie know it's fine to come home too." My father knows that Marie isn't with me. After a pause he adds, "I'm here for you, Quinlan." He says it in monotone, telling me that he means the exact opposite.

I close my eyes, my fear very real. But I have to be better than my fear. I'll have to be stronger if I want to get through this and find answers.

"I'm scared, Dad," I whisper.

"Good girl."

I open my eyes, steadying myself even through the fog, clearing what I can. I sniffle as I take the phone from my ear, look down at it. Then I click it off and hang up on him. Without a moment's hesitation I go to the closet. When I got the sheets earlier, I noticed an old backpack. I quickly grab it and stuff my items inside.

My father hinted that he was compromised and even mentioned Marie. Was it a warning for her? A hint for me? The department might have tracked my call somehow.

My fingers and lips tingle, and I think that my dad might be right about the drug. I can't pinpoint what exactly it would be—I'm not sleepy. This is mood altering. *Trust*-altering?

I shake my head to clear it and start toward the window, glancing outside. I'm on the second floor. It's dark and I have nowhere to go. The odds are certainly stacked against me. But in spite of everything I trust my father's words. And I have to hope that it's not just because of the drugs that may be in my system.

I push open the window, moving slowly so the noise won't rouse suspicion. I hate to leave Eva. And although I don't think

August has done anything wrong, I can't dismiss the possibility. That would be irresponsible. That would be stupid.

I slip the backpack onto my shoulders and swing my leg out the window until my foot touches the slanted roof. I check to make sure it's not slippery before climbing out. There is a slight creak, but I don't have time to tiptoe. I get to the side where the bannister for the slanted front porch meets the roofline. I make my way to the wobbly railing and then hop down. My boots make a loud thud.

Without looking back, I rush past the stairs and jog up the street, escaping into the night.

CHAPTER FIVE

THE MORNING AIR IS FOGGY, AND EVEN THOUGH it's barely seven, I slip out of the cash-only motel I found near the campus, hair still damp from the shower.

The neighborhood is deserted, and I head toward downtown in hopes of finding an open café where I can blend in and figure out what to do next.

When I woke up, I was able to think about my situation. I did consider disappearing completely, just like my father had asked. But I can't. I can't let it go.

I've decided to find Arthur Pritchard. Only I won't be making a deal with him. A person like Arthur is used to making the rules, so I need to change them.

I'm going to blackmail him.

I'll have to get the upper hand somehow, a bit of leverage

to ensure his cooperation—and I think I've figured out a way. His daughter holds the key to a mystery. My last assignment, Catalina Barnes, killed herself. The circumstances of her death were covered up, but then Aaron's assignment also committed suicide. It turns out that the only connection between these two deaths was that both assignments were in contact with Virginia Pritchard.

Arthur spoke to the families and dismissed his daughter's involvement, never telling them who she really was. He's keeping it from the department. His own dirty little secret. So the question is: What role did Virginia play in their deaths? What is Arthur trying to hide?

Once I have that answer, I'll use it against him. I'll threaten to expose him and his daughter to the department. In exchange for my silence he'll have to give me what I want: the truth about who I am. And I'm ready to do whatever is necessary to get it.

But first I need to find Virginia Pritchard.

As I walk, I try to keep my emotions deadened so that I can continue my journey. I'm not sure if Deacon stayed in town or went ahead to Roseburg without me. Part—okay, *most*—of me doesn't want him to have left. And most of me knows he wouldn't. Despite all that, I need time to figure out what's going on. I need time without Deacon.

Since last night there's been a dull throb in my head, just behind my temple. At first I thought it was a hangover, but now I'm worried that my fragile emotional state has cracked. Like it did last week when I was Catalina. I'm still in shock, and this kind of stress can lead to a break in character. A break in—

The pain suddenly intensifies into a blinding smash: my head shattering like a delicate plate. I stop in the middle of the sidewalk, face downturned as I put my palm over my forehead. I grit my teeth and close my eyes, fearing an aneurysm.

And then . . . A scene plays across my mind, like when you spontaneously remember a dream from the night before. The pain eases slightly, as if the pain has opened the door for a memory to slip out. But it's a memory I can't quite place.

I was with Marie in the small waiting room of a doctor's office, surrounded by hard padded chairs and stark white walls. Marie was seated next to me, casually flipping through a copy of *Psychology Today*. A nurse in pale blue scrubs worked behind a half wall made of glass blocks. I turned and gave Marie such a hateful glare that she must have felt it, because she lowered the magazine.

"We'll fix it, Quinn," she told me calmly. "Just like before. He promised it'll work this time." With that she turned and went back to her magazine, but I immediately reached out and slapped it from her hand, knocking it to the floor. Marie's expression hardened, and just then the office door opened. The sound of it made my insides knot, and I slowly turned.

I take in a gasp of cold air, falling back a step on the sidewalk as the memory ends. I spin and look around the street and find the neighborhood still deserted, but my nerves are frayed. Unsettled. The pain in my head is a dull ache, the memory planted but not connected to an event, a clip from a movie I've never seen. Where had Marie taken me and what the hell were we fixing?

I blink my eyes quickly and try to reorient myself, searching my memories to make sense of the images. Nothing fits. Could that possibly have been real? If it was, I don't think I would have forgotten it. And I would never have glared at Marie like that, slapped a magazine from her hand. Never—she was like a mother to me. At least that was how I saw her.

There's a tickle on my upper lip, and when I lick it, I taste metal. I quickly run the back of my hand over my mouth and see that it's covered in bright red blood. My nose is bleeding.

I spit into the grass to get rid of the taste, but the blood continues to run down my throat. I lean forward, pinching my nose closed. I can't remember the last time I had a nosebleed, but I do remember when Deacon had one while we were sitting outside a pizza place a few months ago. Some self-righteous woman came up to us and yelled at him for tipping his head backward, saying she was sick of everyone always getting it wrong. Deacon didn't like her tone, so he asked if she was the nosebleed police. And then, just to spite her, he unplugged his nose and let the blood run down his face until she got grossed out and left.

I laugh to myself, blood sputtering between my lips. I spit again but keep my head forward, using the technique that I read about in my first aid class. It feels like I stand there forever, and I worry someone will wander out of their house and find me bleeding on the sidewalk. But eventually the rush slows. I straighten, then wait a moment, until I'm sure the bleeding has stopped completely, leaving my nostrils stuffy and only a drop of blood on my shirt.

Well, that was a blast, I think. I'm sure I look like a horror show right now with blood all over my face, so I sneak around the corner of the nearest house and turn on their hose. I rinse off my hand with the ice-cold water and then clean my face until the blood is gone. The faucet squeaks when I close it, and I replace the hose before shaking the water off my hands.

The memory with Marie haunts me, hovering in my consciousness between reality and a dream, and I know I have to talk to her. Fact is, Marie was the one who brought me to my father under Arthur's direction. She's also the person who gave me the truth about Quinlan McKee. My father mentioned Marie when we talked last night. Maybe I'm *supposed* to find her.

Across the street a woman walks out of her front door and slams it shut, turning her back on me while she locks it. I take her momentary distraction to quickly move from the side of the house and walk purposefully in the direction of downtown.

The last thing I need is for someone to think I'm casing the neighborhood. If I get picked up for questioning by the cops, they'll contact my father. No. They'll contact the grief department. Apparently my father is not and has never been my legal guardian.

I speed up my steps, keeping my head turned away when the neighbor drives past in her minivan. I'm going to continue on my trip to Roseburg, but I need to find Marie—to find out what my father wanted me to know. There's only one person left for me to ask for help: Aaron Rios.

Aaron is my best friend. He has always had my back, and as far as I know, he might be the only person who has never betrayed me. But yesterday he was ready to escape from the world of closers with his girlfriend. Then again, he also said he couldn't tell me about the terms of his release from his contract. So it's possible he sucks as much as the rest of them. But I'll have to take a leap of faith here.

If there's anyone who can track Marie, it'll be him. I need a phone.

There's a café on the corner a few blocks down, but I'm reluctant to enter when I see it's not busy. It won't be easy to navigate undetected when I can't disappear into the background. I keep walking. My fingers are going numb from the cold air on wet skin, and the headache still pulses at my temples.

I notice a couple approaching, cups clutched in their hands. I lower my head, shielding my eyes, even though I nod at their hello. I head in the direction they came from and find a coffee shop hidden among the houses. It's a small wood-shingled building with metal chairs and small tables out front. They're all filled, and I see from outside the glass door that the inside is crowded. Perfect.

Even through my plugged nose, the smell of hazelnut flavoring and coffee beans is thick, comforting, and warm. I stand in line. The guy in front is wearing a light spring jacket, his hands tucked inside his pockets. I scan him, but when I don't see an obvious sign of a phone, I lose interest and look around the room. I notice a guy on his computer, his phone perched close to the edge of the table, books spread on the other side as he types quickly. He looks frazzled, distracted. Perfect.

I discreetly keep my eye on him as I get through the line and order a vanilla latte. The cup is gloriously warm on my chilled fingers, and I hover a moment near the stir sticks and survey the area. No one has noticed me. I adjust my hood at my neck to cover my jawline, and I lower the brim of the baseball hat. I wait until I see another person walking down the aisle about to pass the guy's table. I start in that direction, my full backpack over my shoulders.

I time it perfectly. The girl walking down the aisle says "excuse me" and I have to brush along the table to avoid her, our presence crowding the area. The guy continues typing, but leans away from us as his shoulder touches my hip. I murmur an apology just as my fingers close around his phone. It's in my pocket and I'm out the door before he even finishes typing his sentence.

Once outside, I head for a park I noticed earlier. I pull off my baseball hat, reminded of how crisp the morning air is. I fold my hat and tuck it into my coat pocket and shake out my hair. I find a bench that's partially obscured from view under a crooked tree, the leaves bending toward the ground. I sit down and take out the phone to examine it.

SUZANNE YOUNG

It doesn't have a pass code, which surprises me. As a closer, to study the private lives of my assignments, I've had to break dozens of cell-phone codes—some easier than others. Considering this guy has wallpaper of a dog wearing sunglasses, I assume he's sweet and trusting. I mean . . . he obviously loves his dog. And now I feel even worse for stealing it. I hope he has insurance.

Aaron won't have his phone anymore, because he was leaving town and didn't want to be tracked. But since he left before I found out the truth about the lies my father and Marie have been feeding me, he has no idea how dangerous things are. He wouldn't have been as careful as he should have. Neither would Myra.

Aaron always joked that once he was done with his contract, he and Myra were going to run off together to a cabin in North Dakota. They might be halfway there by now. Which is why I assume this will not be well received.

The headache that hasn't left starts to tick up in pain level, and I quickly type in Myra's phone number. A perk of always having to use other people's phones, I guess. I have to actually memorize numbers. Before I finish dialing, I look around the park. There's a man asleep with a newspaper over his shoulder on another bench. A couple walks hand in hand near the roses in the garden area. The woman laughs, and I find myself mimicking her smile.

I stop—alarmed at how easy the habit has become for me. Instead I look down at the phone number and imagine Aaron and Myra sitting by the fire in a cabin. Aaron braids Myra's hair while she talks about how bored she is living in the woods. They're happy, though—free to live their own lives.

I shouldn't ruin that. I should let them get away.

But I'm too selfish, so I hit send and sit back on the bench, watching the fountain across the park. At first the line just rings, and I worry she's left it behind after all, but then there is a click, and Myra's voice rings through clear and aggressive as ever.

"Yeah, who's this?" she says.

A flood of emotions fills my chest, and I steady myself. "I need his help," I say quietly. There's a pause, and then Myra mumbles for me to hold on. I wait, wishing she'd stayed on the line a little longer. Reminded me of what it was like before I knew the truth about myself. But she's getting Aaron, because ultimately she knows how to help me.

"Are you okay?" is the first thing Aaron asks. He sounds distracted, like he's driving, but his voice is urgent.

"I need to find Marie," I say. "She's disappeared."

"I can't believe you tracked me down for this, Quinn. If Marie disappeared, none of us will find her. I told Deacon the same thing last night."

"You spoke to Deacon?" I ask, cold pinpricks running down my arms.

"Wait," Aaron says. "Aren't you together?"

"No," I tell him, and look around, as if Deacon has been just out of sight the entire time. But the park is unchanged. Aaron curses.

"What's going on?" he asks. "First Deacon calls looking for

Marie. Now you? I told you I was out, Quinn. What the hell happened at Marie's apartment yesterday?"

"She wasn't there," I tell him. "But she left me a file." Tears sting my eyes.

"A file? Your closer file?"

"No." I shake my head. "My *life* file. Quinlan McKee was an assignment. I was her closer."

He's quiet for a moment and then, "What the fuck are you talking about?"

"The real Quinlan McKee died when she was six," I say. "Marie and Arthur Pritchard found me and brought me in. Trained me as a closer for Quinn's life. But the assignment didn't end there. They let me stay. They let Quinlan's dad *keep* me. My entire life is a lie, Aaron. I'm not even real."

"So . . . Tom's not your father," he asks.

"Nope."

He's quiet for a long while, and I imagine him sharing a stunned look with Myra from across the seats. "Hold up," Aaron tells me. "Let me pull over."

I wait a minute, and then I can hear Myra's voice in the background asking if I'm all right. It makes me feel good that she asked. But I can't help wondering if she would have been friends with me—the real me—if I hadn't been a closer. I have to question all my relationships now.

"You there?" Aaron asks. When I tell him that I am, he exhales heavily. "Damn, girl," he says, like he can't quite believe what I just told him. "I mean, I've always hated Tom, couldn't understand how you turned out so nice with an asshole like that for a father. Now we know, I guess."

"I guess," I repeat.

"Shit, though," Aaron adds. "Marie, too? They both lied to you?"

"Yeah."

I know the idea of Marie betraying us hurts him just as much as it hurts me. We trusted her with our lives. We were trained to. "So how you holding up?" Aaron asks, quieter. Changed by what I've told him.

"I've certainly been better," I say.

"Understandable. What's this mean to Deacon?" Aaron asks. "What are his thoughts on this mess? I can't believe he didn't tell me."

"He—" I stop, look around the park again. I suddenly feel as if I've been noticed, feel the tickle of someone's gaze on the back of my neck, prickling my skin. I get up from the bench and dart my gaze around, looking for the difference in the setting.

"I hope you're not giving him shit," Aaron says, misreading the concern in my voice. "He said he was leaving town with you and asked for Marie's contact information. I told him I didn't have it. He promised me the two of you were good again."

"Yeah, well," I say, "you should know by now that when someone promises something, it just means they're trying extra hard at lying. Find Marie," I tell him. "And tell her to meet me in Roseburg. I'll text a new number when I get there. But,

Aaron, you can't tell Deacon you heard from me if he calls back. Not this time. Keep this one secret for me."

Aaron scoffs. "You should know by now that when someone asks you to keep a secret, it just means they're about to do something really fucking stupid."

I smile, missing our friendship. All the days of driving around with him, listening to stories and joking about everything. Our lives were never easy as closers, but we had our moments. "Tell Myra I'm sorry for calling," I say. "And tell her I miss her mean ass."

Aaron laughs. "I will. Be in touch soon."

I click off the phone and slip it into my pocket. I'll ditch it soon, but first I have some arrangements to make. I get up and start down the block. The feeling of being watched has faded, and although I'm still slightly unsettled by it, hearing Aaron's voice has given me back some of my confidence. Reminded me of who I am.

I'm a good closer. I can become anyone. And if I want to travel undetected, I'll need to become someone else.

CHAPTER SIX

THE MORNING FOG IS BURNING OFF, AND I WANT TO get to Roseburg before school lets out. I run my hand through my hair, reminded that I cut it short just a week ago. I wanted to look more like Catalina. Now I'll need another look.

I head toward an outdoor mall, and although most of the stores are still closed, there's a small food court in a center building where several groups of people are hanging around the coffee station. I spot a blond, plain-faced girl with a giant bag over her shoulder, which I assume, judging by the size, is carrying all the essentials of her wardrobe. She looks college-age, maybe grabbing her coffee before class.

I watch her a moment as she talks on the phone, laughing at something, crinkling her nose a moment later. I make sure no one is watching, and then I mimic her. The left side of her lip goes crooked when she talks, like it's hitched up on a tooth. It's cute. I imagine it's a quirk her friends like about her.

She flips her hair over her shoulder and sets her bag on the counter. There are other people around her, but not too close. She's talking on her phone, essentially shutting down possible conversations with others. Her hair's longer than mine, so I'll need extensions. Other than that, she will be easy to copy.

I check around one last time and then start in her direction, taking a spot next to her at the counter, pretending to wait for a coffee. She glances over at me, uninterested, and turns away.

"Then he's an idiot," she says into the phone. "Tell him . . ."

I tune her out and use my peripheral vision to make sure no one is looking at me. I lean forward and slide my hand into her bag. For a moment I panic, thinking it's too stuffed with random objects, but my hand touches what feels like a wallet, and I take it out. It's small, black leather, and I close my hand around it. I slip it into my pocket, swing around, and start walking away, all in a smooth movement.

When I get to the other side of the coffee kiosk, I open the wallet and remove her driver's license and a credit card. I won't have much time to use it before she cancels it, so I'll have to make arrangements quickly. When I have what I need, I set the wallet on the counter near the register while the barista is taking an order.

"Someone forgot this," I mumble, not making eye contact. The barista thanks me, and I quickly escape into the main hallways. It's a pain in the ass losing your wallet, and the girl will think she just forgot it at the register when she starts looking for it. Still . . . I feel awful for taking it. If I weren't desperate, I wouldn't even dream of it. Then again, the real me might be a complete kleptomaniac—who knows? I could be anything.

The thought hardens my purpose, and once I'm out of view of the kiosk, I look down at the ID I took. The girl's name is Elizabeth Major, and she's eighteen. It's perfect, really. Well suited for my purposes. I examine her picture and touch my own hair, missing the length I once had. Back when I knew who I was.

I slip the ID and the credit card into my pocket. I use the phone to look up the closest beauty supply store and fine one nearby that's open. It's time for a makeover.

It was just over a year ago that I was sitting in Deacon's bedroom, watching him pose in front of the mirror after his own makeover. He'd shaved his brown hair and dyed it blond. He wore black-rimmed glasses, and he turned his head from side to side, changing his facial expressions. He was going on assignment the next day: Kyle Kelsey, a sixteen-year-old in Springfield who had been killed in a farming accident. Deacon had already nailed down the voice thanks to Kyle's extensive video journaling, but he hadn't figured out his smile yet.

"You look hot in glasses," I called to him. I sat cross-legged on his bed while he stood in front of the mirror that was balanced on his dresser, examining himself.

"Hot, you say?" Deacon looked over, posing again just for me. I was definitely a fan.

I sat up on my knees and motioned for him to come over. He moved like he was about to, but then stopped and held up his hand. "You are an amazing distraction, Quinlan," he told me. "But I have to figure this guy out." He turned away and studied his reflection once again. "And the second I do, I'm going to tear off my clothes and let you ravish me."

I laughed and fell back against his pillows, smiling madly as I watched him. I didn't want to admit that I was consumed with all things Deacon, but it seemed okay because, although he never outright told me, I knew he felt the same.

"I swear," I said, looking up at his ceiling, "I think my father schedules our assignments in a way to keep us apart."

"What are you talking about?" Deacon asked. "We're still partners—we talk during the assignments."

"True," I admit. "But not as ourselves." I look over. "I'll be talking to a version of Kyle Kelsey this weekend."

Deacon let out a deep sigh and finally turned to me. He reached up to touch the corner of his glasses. "On or off?" he asked.

"Off."

He took off the glasses, and his shirt, and came over to the bed to lie down on his stomach. I immediately turned, and I ran my fingernails down his back as he rested his chin on his folded forearms, seeming lost in thought.

"Then let's stop," he said quietly. "How long can we really stand this anyway?"

I leaned in and kissed his shoulder before resting my cheek there and closing my eyes.

"We'll quit after this one," he said.

"You say that every time," I told him. "But we never do. It's a lot easier to say when your father isn't your boss."

Deacon shifted in the bed and moved over. We lay on our sides, facing each other. His soft brown eyes met my gaze. "Your dad may not be related to me, but it doesn't mean he doesn't have the same control. Nothing's easy for a closer," he told me. "Nothing easy but us. This." Deacon leaned in and kissed me.

But Deacon was wrong about us. Eventually we became difficult and complicated. He failed me when I needed him, abandoned me more than once. And worst of all, I'm not sure why. *Why* he would conspire against me. If I get more answers, maybe that one will finally become clear.

As I poke through the different hair extensions in the back aisle of the supply store, looking for the one closest to my color, all I can think about is Deacon. And how much I hate him because of how much I love him.

And when I have to sniffle back my emotions, I brush aside thoughts of him, too. I grab the blond extensions and head to the makeup section. I end up spending another forty dollars in cash on makeup and brushes because Elizabeth Major's face has subtle differences I'll have to create. And although I can't mimic her turned tooth, I can copy the way she compensates for it.

I leave the store and head to the nearest gas station and ask to use the bathroom. Once inside the small, dingy space, I take out the license and prop it up on the backsplash of the sink. I examine the picture. Our eye color is more or less the same, so that's a plus. I didn't buy any contacts.

I open the concealer and cover my freckles first. Once I'm a blank canvas, I begin to change the shape of my features with the stroke of a brush: widen my lips, play down my cheekbones.

I finish the makeup and then take the extensions out of the bag and comb through them with my fingers. I reach under my hair and snap them in, immediately hating how they feel. At least the ones Marie uses are expensive—better quality. I comb the extensions out and change my hair part to match Elizabeth's.

When the transformation is complete, I look at my reflection. Despite the changes, I see a shadow of Quinlan McKee—the girl I used to be—and I grow nostalgic. It must be the hair.

I wait a moment until the emotions fade. Elizabeth probably hasn't noticed that her credit card is gone yet, so I chance it and use the phone to order a bus ticket, which I charge to her credit card. It works. Once that's settled, I swipe the makeup off the counter into the backpack and then walk out into the morning light, popping up my hood.

I'll be on bus number eighty-four to Roseburg. I pull up the bar-coded pass on the phone and head toward the bus station, noticing a decent crowd and immediately feeling eased by it. The buses are already lined up, and I spot number eighty-four in the back.

A car on the street slows and pulls to the curb a few yards in front of me, and when it's apparent it's stopped for me, my heart leaps into my throat and I stagger to a halt.

They've found me.

The driver's-side door of the gray sedan opens, and I put my palm on my chest in relief when August climbs out. He smiles broadly, checking the street before closing the door and walking toward me. "Hey, you," he says, shoving his hands in the pockets of his corduroys.

My momentary relief is quickly covered by my fear of last night. Did he actually drug me? And if so . . . *why*? "August," I say, trying to sound casual. "How did you . . . how'd you know it was me?"

"You look different," he responds. "But you still have the same shape, same eye color too."

"You're very observant," I tell him.

He laughs. "You must be rubbing off on me."

"Must be." My shoulders are tense, and I have to fight to keep my face from reflecting that. I'm growing more certain that I trusted him entirely too much. "You knew where to find me?" I ask, wondering how he'll dodge the question.

"Considering the fact you slipped out my second-story window," he says with a laugh, "I imagined you were ready to leave town. Bus station was an easy choice. I'm surprised you're still here, honestly."

"Me too," I say, tightening my hand on my backpack. "And sorry about that. I, uh . . . I didn't want to wake you guys. I decided to head home," I lie.

He laughs. "We wouldn't have minded if you did wake us. No need to risk life and limb."

"Again, sorry for the scare," I say. In the light of the morning I start to notice things about him that I didn't see yesterday. The roots of August's hair are lighter than the strands hitting his shoulder, as if his hair has been dyed. His irises are slightly larger than normal, his brown eyes the exact color of Deacon's—contacts, I realize. Even August's phrasing is similar to Deacon's.

I swallow hard. My father was right.

"I was worried," August says, taking another step toward me. "You'd been drinking, and then you were off in town alone. I'm glad I found you. You're welcome to stay with us as long as you want, Brooke. It's a safe place."

"Is it, now?" I murmur. I glance behind him to where bus eighty-four has pulled to the front of the line.

August furrows his brow as if he thinks I'm acting weird, but I'm sure he understands what's really happening. He takes another step toward me, hands still in his pockets, feigning relaxation. "At least let me give you a ride home," he offers. "I'm sure your father's worried about you."

I still. I never told him about my father. In fact, I told Eva that I was a ward of the state. That I had no family. And yet here stands this *closer*, thinking I won't recognize him. How he's tried to subtly mimic my boyfriend to provide false comfort and unearned trust. Well . . . he's underestimated me.

"That's super nice of you," I tell him, folding back my hood and smiling. "But I've already imposed so much."

"You kidding?" he says. "Our stray dogs are more trouble than you."

I force a laugh. Yeah, I didn't see any dogs, either. I wonder how real Eva was. If she was a friend or a closer as well. I don't have time to think about it now. I motion toward his car.

"A ride would be awesome, August," I say. "Thank you. Would you mind if we hit up the gas station and grab snacks? My treat . . . for the trip." I start in the direction of his car, noticing the way his hand shifts in his pocket. I can't tell, but I'm afraid he might have a knife.

I quickly tick through my options. I could run, right now, screaming for help. Perhaps I'd find it before he could hurt me. But even so, I would be questioned. Underage, I'd be sent home. Calling attention to myself will have to be my last resort.

August falls into step beside me, chattering away as if he has no idea that I'm onto his ruse. I glance at him and smile, keeping up the façade, all the while watching number eighty-four, waiting until the moment when boarding will be complete and the bus is about to pull away.

I just need another three or four minutes, and then I'll bolt through the crowd, weave in and out, and hop on the bus. Hopefully before August can catch up with me.

When I get to the passenger side of the car, planning to stall, I feel August behind me. I spin, having expected him to be at the driver's side, and find him entirely too close. My plan disintegrates, and my façade falls away.

"What are you doing?" I demand, nearly tripping over my shoes as I back up a step.

August smiles, but it's not the inviting smile he used earlier.

It's lopsided, and I see a flash of his real personality. "Opening the door for you," he says easily, reaching around me to grab the door handle.

My breath is caught in my throat, and I decide that it's time to run after all. I push his shoulder, trying to move past him, but August is fast. He grabs me by my backpack and yanks me backward. He wraps one arm around my waist and lifts me off my feet; his other hand clamps under my jaw, forcing my mouth shut so I can't scream. My eyes are frantic as I struggle to get free.

August spins me around and pins me to the car like we're in an embrace out in front of the bus station. The pressure of his weight is enough to keep me too short of breath to yell for help.

"Just relax," he soothes. "No one's going to hurt you." He reaches into the pocket of his corduroys, and to my horror he pulls out a syringe. I attack with renewed ferocity, shifting from side to side and trying to knee any part of him I can get to. He casts a glance around the street to make sure no one is paying attention. They're not. August flicks off the orange cap with his thumb and looks down at me.

"This is just a sedative," he says as if I'm being dramatic. "I tried the phenylethylamine last night, but I guess you weren't in the mood. Instead you had to be stupid and try to run away."

He has no idea how "stupid" I can be. I have no intention of letting him stick that needle into me. Struggling is pointless at this angle, so just before he's about to inject the sedative into my neck, I stop fighting completely and let myself go limp.

August pitches forward now that the force of me pushing back is gone, and I twist around him, pulling from his grasp.

I ram my palms against his back, sending him chest-first against his car. In the same motion I turn away, set to run, when I hear him yelp. The wounded sound makes me pause, and I look back at him. I wasn't trying to hurt him, and the thought that I did weakens me slightly.

August turns, and I see the syringe sticking into his hip. He yanks it out and tosses it aside, groaning. "That fucking burns," he mutters, wincing.

"I apologize that I don't feel bad that you stabbed yourself," I say, although if I'm honest, I do feel a little bad. "You drugged me last night," I accuse, out of breath.

August laughs, limping over to rest against the hood of his car. The fight is gone out of him now that he knows he won't have time to secure me. "Sure, but it was harmless. Should have made you euphoric."

"Yeah, well, I don't have much to be happy about these days," I tell him. "Now why are you doing this? Who sent you?"

"The grief department requests your return, Miss McKee." He rubs his hip where the syringe jabbed him, the drowsiness already distorting his expression. "They messaged me yesterday and told me you'd disappeared in my town. I studied your boyfriend's records, things he told his advisor. And then, in the files, I saw you'd once had an assignment here. Researched the family and found the bike shop. It wasn't a great choice, Quinlan," he says.

"Obviously," I reply, angry at myself for not having been more careful. He snorts a laugh. "And Eva?" I ask.

"I told you she wanted to be a closer, right?" he says. "That includes being around them—she helps me where she can. She's damn good, too. She did like you, though, if it matters."

"It doesn't," I say. The idea that Eva was playing me stings more than it should. God, I'm so naïve. I'll have to do better if I'm going to survive this.

August pretends to pout. "Poor Quinlan," he says. "But hey, on the bright side, you get to go home."

"Not today," I tell him. "In case you didn't notice, you're over there, all fucked up, and I'm about to run away."

August shrugs sheepishly. "Well, yes, clearly, this"—he holds up his hand to motion around us—"wasn't supposed to happen. I was only charged with monitoring you and earning your trust. Seeing what you were up to. But after you contacted your father, I was instructed to bring you home. You're in breach of contract."

Across the way the bus driver steps off the stair and makes a final boarding call. It's time for me to go. "Do me a favor, August," I say, hiking my backpack up on my shoulders. "Or whatever your name is."

"Roger," he says with a small smile.

"Well, *Roger*. Tell the department that I'm on vacation."

He mock salutes me, his eyelids drooping. I leave him, jogging toward the bus, but I check to make sure he isn't following me. I don't think he can.

I meet the bus driver at the door and let him scan the bar code on my phone. Then, when he steps aside to let me climb the stairs, I slip open the case on the phone and pull out the SIM card. I pop out the battery and dart over to the closest trash bin to toss in the phone parts. I get on bus eighty-four at the last second, earning a dirty look from the driver for making him wait, and find a seat near the back. The bus is mostly empty, and I take a spot near the window, facing the street where Roger's car is parked. I watch as he stumbles and climbs into the driver's seat. I sit up straighter, worried he'll try to drive and get into an accident. But he doesn't even turn on the engine.

As the bus pulls away, Roger slumps over in his front seat and disappears from view. My heart is still racing, but I relax slightly and close my eyes, trying to regulate my breathing. I was stupid to trust him, to go home with him. I'm glad I called my father—he saved me.

After a moment I open my eyes and stare straight ahead toward the front of the bus, knowing there will be no rest for me. The grief department knows where I'm heading. I'm just not sure if they know why.

CHAPTER SEVEN

I'M A BUNDLE OF NERVES WHEN I EXIT THE FRONT doors of the bus station in Roseburg. Once on the street, I slip my hands into the pockets of my jacket and glance around. Whether I mean to or not, I immediately check for Deacon. I'm both relieved and disappointed when I don't see him.

Roseburg itself looks mildly familiar, even though I've never been here. It could be the landscape; it's not much different from Corvallis. I try to find a building or a tree in particular, but it's just a general sense of familiarity. Then again, as Roger proved, I may be searching for a connection that doesn't exist. Surely I accepted him as a friend because I miss Deacon. Now I'm doing the same thing with landscaping. This could all be a symptom of homesickness.

So with that I turn and start down the main street in search of a motel. And once the school day is nearly done, I'll head to Marshall Senior High in search of Virginia. It's not like I can get to her while she's in class.

I see a sign jutting out from a building up ahead. Even though one of the letters has worn off, SHADY PINES OTEL seems like it might fit my criteria exactly. Meaning I can afford its weekly rate in case I need to stay long-term.

I cut across the parking lot toward the front office and see that the building has been recently painted Pepto-Bismol pink with green shutters. It's an absolutely awful combination that gives me little confidence in the room amenities. This is the sort of motel Deacon and Aaron would *want* to stay in just for the story factor. Aaron always jokes that sketchy motels make the best retellings because there is always the possibility of finding blood on the carpet. God, I hope not.

In the front lobby I find a small man with patchy facial hair and a twitchy brow. I use Elizabeth's ID and pay cash for the week. The man only glances at me, uninterested in my appearance. I almost ask for a room with a pool view, but I decide that humor would only make me stand out more.

He slides a key card across the counter. "One person per room," he says gruffly. "Guests pay ten extra dollars."

"Got it," I say, holding up the card. He narrows his eyes as if he doesn't believe me, but then he turns and disappears behind a curtain into a back room.

I sigh heavily, taking one more look around the lobby, hoping for some water. But there is only a plastic yellow jug on a folding table in the corner. I have a sneaking suspicion it wasn't set out today, and I opt to take my chances with water from the faucet.

When I get upstairs, I'm surprised to find that the room is decent, although the smell of cigarette smoke from past tenants hangs in the air. I don't know how long I'll be here, and I don't have any real plan yet, but I hope this will be over soon. More than anything, I just want the truth. And then I want to live my life. Away from the grief department.

I drop my stuff on the bed and take a seat at the small table near the window, too anxious to sleep after all. I push aside the curtain and survey the complex. No one is outside, and in that isolation my fear deepens.

I was nearly kidnapped today. The thought strikes me hard in the chest, knocking the air out of me, crushing my lungs. The helplessness of the moment with Roger strips me down. It tears at my skin, at my confidence, at my person. He almost got me. *They* almost got me.

But why? What does the grief department really want with me? What would they do? The only outcome I can imagine is that they want to silence me—stop me from talking about closers. Or maybe it's because of Catalina's suicide. All I can do is guess right now. And that unpredictability makes them scarier.

I wrap my arms around myself. I'll give Aaron until tonight to find Marie, but if that doesn't work, I'll have to chance another call to my father. No more strangers. Except, of course, Virginia Pritchard.

I glance at the clock on the nightstand and see that it's not even noon yet. So after checking the locks and moving a chair in front of the door, I go to the bed and rest back, staring at the ceiling. I try to clear my head, block out the worry, and put together a real plan.

I'm a little early when I arrive at Marshall Senior High. School is still in session as I stand at the edge of the parking lot trying to be invisible. The school is a modest one-story building with a gated entry and a courtyard just beyond. I imagine that it has a small student population, which must make a suicide (possibly two) a pretty big deal.

The bell rings, startling me, and I walk toward the cars as the doors open and students begin filing out. I swim through the crowd, nothing about me drawing anyone's attention. I get about midway through the parking lot and then stop and discreetly look around. I don't know what Virginia looks like. I scan faces, and after a moment I admit I wouldn't recognize her just because I got a glimpse of her father for five minutes two days ago. I'll have to talk to someone.

I let my facial expression relax naturally, practice scrunching my nose when I laugh. It's nonthreatening. I smile softly—not too eager—and when I see a girl, mousy with brown hair and a cardigan, I walk toward her.

"Excuse me," I call, sounding vulnerable and yet confident—as if I belong here. The girl lifts her head and looks me over hesitantly. "Hi," I say, crinkling my nose. "I was wondering if you've seen Virginia Pritchard?"

I study her face and notice when there's a flash of recognition. "Uh . . ." She looks behind her and then pulls her cardigan around herself. Not exactly the response I was expecting. "Who's asking?" she says.

I fumble for the right words and then finally spit it out. "I'm Liz. I just transferred here, and the front office told me to talk to Virginia to shadow for classes. I couldn't find her, so . . ." I shrug, deciding to go less confident. It works.

"Sorry," the girl says. "There's been a lot of reporters. Someone was here from the *New York Times* this morning asking questions."

"Really?" I ask. "Questions about what?" She flinches, and I quickly explain, "I just moved here from Eugene."

This seems to placate her momentarily.

"I can always catch up with Virginia on Monday," I tell her, turning slowly so that she'll have time to stop me.

"It's club ball season," the girl says. "She and the other volleyball players will be practicing in the gym. They're pretty hard-core."

I glance back over my shoulder. "Thank you!" I smile, warm and affectionate, and then I wave before heading toward the school. The minute my back is turned, my smile fades.

I wasn't entirely planning the "new student" excuse, but it was all I had. I'll go with it, and if I get questioned by the office, I can actually fill out the paperwork as Elizabeth Major. I've heard my father and Marie complain about educational red tape before. I'll use fake numbers, fake school information, and by the time the office requests my records to get more information, which can take up to a week, I'll be gone.

The main hallway of the school is wide and open, lockers on either side. A few bulletin boards are placed outside classrooms, displaying art and poems I don't have time to look over. It's nice, though. It seems . . . safe. Encouraging. Way more encouraging than the talk shows I'd have on in the background while writing essays for my online class. I think I would have liked this.

There is a set of metal doors at the end of the hallway with the word GYMNASIUM in block lettering posted on the wall above them. I continue forward, wishing I'd brought a backpack or something more scholarly so I could have fit in. I feel too much like myself—which feels the same as exposed. But I can't turn back now. I'm just steps away from finding Virginia Pritchard.

I open the doors and slip in, trying not to draw too much attention. I hear the squeaking of sneakers on wood floors, the shouts of players. I don't look at them. I duck my head and start for the bleachers, where a few other people are sitting.

The bench creaks as I climb up a few rows and sit. I wait a beat and then lift my head, relieved when I don't feel anyone watching me. I look out at the court, searching for the face of Virginia.

I realize then that I've never really considered who I'll find here. Do I expect a girl who's drawn and sad because she recently lost two friends in Lake Oswego to suicide? Do I think she's like her father, calculating and cold? Or is she something worse than I imagined?

And yet, as I search, no one sticks out. I settle in and watch the girls on the court. They're in the middle of a scrimmage game, a detail I overheard from the girl in front of me. I've never played a sport, and I'm in awe of how easy it seems for these athletes. One girl actually throws herself forward, hitting the volleyball with the inside of her wrists before her padded elbow smacks the court. She hops up, unfazed, and I smile, admiring her tenacity.

About fifteen minutes go by, and I forget my task, absorbed instead with watching the scrimmage. But then I notice her. She's wearing a uniform, and her muscles are flexed from playing, her brown hair tied back in a ponytail. In an instant I know it's Virginia, although I can't pinpoint exactly how I know. Perhaps it's the way she's apart from everyone. Not in location—she's on the team—but emotionally. She doesn't seem to register the game the same way the others do.

Virginia dives for the volleyball, spinning and landing on her back as she sets up the score for another player. The other girl makes the shot and then helps Virginia up from the floor before slapping her hand.

I'm fascinated, wondering how a person who recently experienced such heavy loss could carry on like nothing was wrong. Then again, I just found that my whole life was a lie, and I still managed to have a burrito on my way over here. I guess even in grief we have to continue to live. Continue to play volleyball and eat burritos.

Which tells me that Virginia Pritchard is an excellent liar.

CHAPTER EIGHT

AT THE END OF THE GAME THE COACH BLOWS HER whistle, and the girls slap hands and laugh together. The group of people in front of me leaves to meet their friends on the court, and I stand up, watching Virginia as she talks to her coach. I never did make a plan. I figured I would seem more authentic if I didn't overprepare, a trick I sometimes used when providing closure. I'm a little wary; I'll need to be damn convincing if I plan to earn her trust and ask her about Catalina.

I hop down from the bleachers and move to the edge of the court, not wanting to appear too aggressive. I wait for a natural pause in her conversation, and then I start forward and call Virginia's name.

She gives a quick look that sizes me up, her brow slightly furrowed.

"Go ahead," her coach tells her, touching her arm. "I'll catch up with you later so we can go over the plans for next week's tournament."

As the coach walks away, Virginia smoothes her damp hair back toward her ponytail before turning to me, her posture rigid. "And who do you work for?" she asks coldly.

My heart nearly explodes in my chest, and I have to do absolutely everything to keep my panic from showing. *She knows.*

"Excuse me?" I ask, feigning confusion. "I . . . I'm actually a new student here."

She waits a moment as if thinking that over, and then she shrugs apologetically. "Didn't mean to be rude," she says. "It's just that you'd be my third reporter this week, and I'm kind of tired of telling them to fuck off." She grins, and I instantly like her.

"I'm sure," I say, smiling like Liz would. "And I'm sorry I interrupted you and your coach."

Virginia waves away the sentiment. "Don't be," she says. "She would have talked forever, so I'm glad you're here. Coach Bryant is a worst-case scenario type of person, which leaves me with the task of being fatally optimistic. And honestly, I'm too tired today."

Virginia walks past me to where a stack of small white towels waits on the bottom bleacher step. I follow, aware of how awkward I feel—like this really is my first day of school. Virginia takes a towel and wipes it across her forehead, around her neck, and even under her arms.

I stand, waiting, and it isn't until she grabs a bottle of water and takes a sip that she sits down and pats the bench as if inviting me to join her. I take a spot, and before I can properly introduce myself, I'm startled by how different she looks up close.

Although I thought her eyes were dark, I see now that their color is actually green or hazel, but her pupils are dilated so large that they nearly crowd out the irises. There are patches of foundation that haven't gotten wiped off, leaving behind streaks of pale white skin. It's unsettling, this peek behind her mask, and I look away from where the makeup is darkest on her jawline.

"Like I mentioned," I start, thinking out each word before I speak, wanting to cause a reaction. A bond between us. "I'm a new student—Elizabeth Major." I turn to her and smile. "My friends call me Liz."

Virginia watches me, seemingly amused, and sips from her water. "Nice to meet you," she says, but she really means *Why are you telling me all of this?* My nonthreatening demeanor is setting her at ease, though, so I continue down that path.

"When I was filling out paperwork this afternoon," I explain, "there was a girl in the office—I'm not sure of her name. Anyway, we were both waiting, and I asked where people around here hang out. She told me to ask you."

Virginia chokes on a sip of water as she laughs. "Really?" she asks, dragging the back of her wrist across her mouth. "Did she give you a reason for her suggestion?"

"She said you're everyone's friend."

My comment is the right choice. I see a slight tint of melancholy in her expression, but in front of that is warmth at the idea that someone else thought highly of her. Seems her self-esteem may be a little on the low side, understandable considering what she's been through.

Seeing the crack, I settle my back against the bench and pull my legs under me, like we're two girls chatting at a sleepover. "I moved from Eugene," I tell her. "Just me and my mom, and she's always working. I was pretty sure my entire social life would take place on the computer, but then there was a small glimmer of hope." I smile, pinching my fingers together.

"Where's your dad?" Virginia asks, catching me off guard and killing the levity of the conversation.

"He died." The minute I say it, I'm struck with guilt. The father I know is alive and well. Okay, maybe not *well*. But alive. But then I have the eerie sense that my real father might be dead—like speaking it out loud makes it possible. There's a phantom pain in my heart for the person I don't know to love, the possibility a blank spot waiting to fill.

"I'm so sorry," Virginia says, making me start, almost like she read my mind. "I didn't mean to press," she continues. "My mother's dead, and now it's . . . it's a point of curiosity for me." She rolls her eyes, embarrassed. "Morbid, I know," she adds. "Imagine my surprise to find that there aren't many kids with dead parents out there. Started to think it was just me."

I murmur my condolences, noting that this is a connection I can exploit later, when she trusts me more. "Well," I say, lightening my tone, "what does everyone do around here? Back home we spend most of our time hiking. Some shopping."

"It's mostly the same here," Virginia says, reaching up to pull the elastic band out of her hair. Brown waves cascade over her shoulders, and she rubs her scalp like it's sore from wearing a ponytail for too long. Virginia shakes her hair out and then loops the elastic band around her wrist. When she's done, she glances at the clock over the doorway and jumps up with a loud sigh. She hikes her thumb toward the locker rooms.

"I have to go," she says. Before I have time to be disappointed, she puts her hand on her hip and smiles at me. "Are you doing anything for dinner?" she asks.

I swallow hard, afraid she's going to invite me to her house. "Uh . . . no," I say, readying my excuses if Arthur Pritchard is going to be there.

"Cool," she says, taking a few steps backward. "My dad's never home, so I grab food at the Mill around seven. It's a diner around the corner. You in?"

"Yeah," I say, relieved. "I'll see you there."

She holds up her hand in a wave and spins on her sneakers, jogging for the locker room. I watch after her, my heart in my throat. Just before she opens the door, Virginia takes the elastic band from around her wrist and ties her ponytail up high. She pulls the threads of her hair through and adjusts her posture. I recognize what she's doing—the façade she's putting up for others.

When she's gone, I'm left to wonder how I can possibly convince her to trust me, and to tell me the secrets she's hiding from everyone else.

The Mill diner is small, with only a handful of tables, most of them taken by what look like regulars. An old man with his hat set beside him in the seat, a club sandwich in front of him. A middle-aged man reading his phone while he spears his pasta salad with a fork. A mom with two kids, smiling when the waitress sets a coloring page in front of the little girl.

I grab a table near the back and order a Coke. The waitress comes by twice to ask for my order before the bells above the door jingle and Virginia appears. She scans the room until her gaze falls on me, and I straighten, folding my hands in front of me. I'm suddenly insecure of my hair extensions and makeup. I feel obviously fake. But Virginia's smile gives none of that away as she comes to join me.

I watch her approach. Instead of her volleyball uniform, she's wearing a crisp white T-shirt with a baby-blue scarf tied in a knot over her chest. Her hair is flowing down over her shoulders, and for a moment I'm struck with the sense that I know her. But of course I don't. I can see how she fit into Catalina's life—how they were friends. Their mannerisms are similar.

Virginia slides into the booth across from me and unravels

her scarf before setting it aside. She looks up at the waitress, who comes over immediately.

"What can I get for you?" the waitress asks in a husky voice.

Virginia puts her elbows on the table, hands folded under her chin. "A Dr Pepper," she says, and then looks at me. "Any objections to pie for dinner?" she asks. "It's really good."

"That sounds perfect," I tell her, although I'm still full from my afternoon burrito.

"Apple, please," Virginia says. "Extra whipped cream." When the waitress leaves, she turns back to me. "The pie is my treat," Virginia says. "Since I was kind of a bitch when we first met."

I laugh. "You were fine. But thank you. And thanks for letting me intrude on your personal life," I say, leaning in to sip from my drink. "I don't usually invite myself into friendships."

"To be honest," she says, "I could really use a friend. So your timing is perfect." She turns to look out the window at the street, letting her smile slowly fade. I want to ask her everything—all about Catalina, about the suicides—but it's not time yet.

"I had to leave my friends behind," I say, more honest than I planned to be. "I miss them."

Virginia looks over sympathetically. "Moving sucks," she says. "I can relate. I was in Washington, and then I spent last summer in Lake Oswego and made friends there. It's amazing how far a few hours can seem, isn't it? Might as well be a different planet."

My pulse kicks to life at the mention of Lake Oswego. "I know what you mean, and Corvallis is even closer."

Virginia tilts her head. "I thought you said you moved here from Eugene?"

"Corvallis is where my ex-boyfriend goes to school," I say without missing a beat. Silently I'm cursing myself for the slip. *Great, Quinn. Why not tell her you live there and work for the grief department?* "But hey," I add, trying to change the subject, "enough about me and my boring life."

"Are you kidding?" Virginia asks. "Ex-boyfriends are my favorite kind. I want to hear all about him. Because by the look on your face, I'm guessing he's not quite as ex as you'd like."

"It's that obvious?" I'm alarmed at how easily she could read my feelings for Deacon.

"Totally obvious," she says. "Now tell me—is he cute? Funny?"

"He thinks he's funny," I say, feeling a sense of relief at being able to talk about Deacon, even if I can't tell her the whole truth about us. I smile. "Okay, he's really funny," I admit.

"Cute?"

"Stupidly so."

"Oooh . . . ," Virginia calls playfully, leaning back in her seat before rolling out her wrists. "Please go on."

I do just that, describing my favorite features, never mentioning his name. When I'm done, she's gazing at me. "What?" I ask.

"You still love him," she says. "Maybe he *shouldn't* be as ex as you want."

"No, he definitely should," I respond, and start to fiddle

with my straw wrapper, tying it in knots. I stop pretending that Deacon is a regular guy and we had a regular relationship. The truth is way more screwed up than that.

"Too bad," Virginia says under her breath.

"Yeah." We're both quiet for a moment, and then I look up at her, daring to get us on course. "So earlier," I say, "you mentioned reporters. What's that all about?"

Virginia stiffens as if I've struck a nerve.

The waitress appears at the end of our table and puts a Dr Pepper in front of Virginia. "Pie is on its way," she says.

"Thanks," Virginia responds, and quickly grabs the drink and sips straight from the glass. We don't speak as the waitress leaves and comes back with an oversize slice of pie, whipped cream piled on top. She puts it in the center of the table and asks if we need anything else.

"No," Virginia tells her. The waitress nods and walks away. Around us the diner is getting busy. Several new customers have come in to fill up the seats at the counter. I'm happy for the distraction, the white noise. I can see that Virginia appreciates it as well.

She picks up her fork and takes the first bite of apple pie, smiling at me after she does. I follow suit, and sure enough, Virginia was right. It's delicious.

We eat quietly; the mood has shifted, and I know that I made a mistake by bringing up the reporters. After the waitress drops off the check and leaves, Virginia lifts her eyes to meet my gaze.

"I didn't want her to hear us talking about it," she says quietly. "She'll tell my father."

Her tone pricks my skin, drawing me in. The paranoia in her words is completely infectious, and I find myself glancing around the room as if we really are being spied on.

I lean forward, hands on the table. "Tell him what exactly?"

Virginia smiles sadly. "I'm sorry you came here, Liz. Sorry you came to me," she says. "Although at this point, I'm not sure it matters where you go."

"Why doesn't it matter?" I ask. "What's going on?"

"I'm not supposed to talk about it. Hell, I'm not even supposed to know about it."

"Okay," I say. "You're starting to freak me out. Talk about what?"

"Death."

Maybe it's the way she whispers it, but goose bumps rise on my arms, a chill over my entire body. I wonder immediately if she's talking about Catalina—if right now she's going to tell me everything I need to blackmail her father. Taking advantage of Virginia is a necessary evil I'm willing to carry out, but I still feel like shit about it.

"Whose death?" I ask, my voice unintentionally hushed.

She pauses a moment, studying me. Then her eyes well up, and when she blinks, tears spill onto her cheeks. "My friends are killing themselves," she says. "And everywhere I turn, it's on the news: gory details and speculation on why. *Why, why, why?* It's all anyone can think about anymore. Obsess about.

But my father told me not to listen, not to speak it—as if it's a contagious thought."

"Perhaps it is," I say. "Behavioral contagion—copycat behavior—is common, especially in teenagers." Virginia lifts her eyes to mine, and I realize I'm showing too much of my closer side.

"Sorry," I say. "I read that in the paper once." I take a quick sip of my drink, feeling Virginia watch me. I'm pissed at myself; I let my disappointment compromise my carefulness. And despite the tragedy of her story, it's not the sort of information I need on Arthur Pritchard. Maybe he didn't tell the grief department about his daughter's involvement with Catalina because he wanted to spare her the details. That's hardly blackmail-worthy.

"Yeah," she says, easing back in her seat, "that's what some of the doctors think." She exhales heavily, checking around once again to make sure no one is watching. When she's sure it's safe, she goes on.

"Brandon Vega and Tracy Thurgood were the first in town," she says. "Both died after ingesting a self-mixed poison. Since them there's been five other suicides."

I stare at her, shocked. "Five?"

"Yes," she says. "And that's just in the past six weeks."

I let the idea wash over me, unable to imagine how a school would be able to overcome such heartbreak. Seven deaths just in Roseburg, and that doesn't even include Catalina and Mitchel.

"People are scared," Virginia says, and looks down at her

fork, twisting it in her hand as she studies the metal prongs. "The media used to keep stories like this quiet for fear of inciting the behavior; they didn't publish details. But now that the public is aware, updates are constantly streaming. We're so aware that it's all we talk about anymore. It's all we are."

She sets down the fork with a clank and leans in. "And then they tell us that we have no right to be depressed. After the deaths, they brought in grief counselors and set them up at the school. They had us journal more often. We had to go through corrective therapy. All in some misguided attempt to *fix* us, when really we just want them to leave us alone."

Her anger comes through, and I think that she's been waiting to confide in somebody, even if I'm a stranger. And yet . . . I don't feel like a stranger. The longer I'm with her, the more I think we could be friends. Then again, I just made that same mistake with Eva.

Virginia continues to blame the doctors, and I start to wonder if she isn't part of a mass hysteria. Could that be the real cause of this outbreak? Of course, I've seen the other side. I've seen the kind of therapy they offer—or, rather, I've felt the threat of it. And how they use it to convince closers to stay in line. Convince clients to seek help with us. Therapy isn't how it used to be; it's not just talking. It's manipulation—at least, that's what happens when ethics are set aside, especially in experimental treatments. Especially when money is involved.

"We did everything they told us to do," Virginia says. "It didn't help, but we tried. And then someone leaked the journals and therapy notes. After that, the doctors closed ranks. They're quiet now, but we know they're working on something. We feel it. We feel their pressure."

"Who leaked the journals?" I ask. It would be horrible to bare your soul to a therapist, only to have it put up for public consumption.

"No one knows," Virginia says. "But it was cruel. Everyone got to see exactly what we thought—our true emotions. Our secrets. It scared our parents, our friends, the public. And then one of my friends, Diana, she . . ." Virginia's posture weakens, and she lowers her head.

"Some of the other students read her journals," she whispers. "And they eviscerated her online, tore her life to shreds. One boy even told her she should kill herself." Virginia's lip hitches up in a sneer, and she glares across the table at me. "Well, she did," she says. "And she won't be the last, either. But the therapists tell us that it's all going to be okay. That *we're* okay. But by avoiding pain, by employing closers, the doctors have taken away our ability to cope. Just because we can put on a happy face doesn't mean we're fixed. No, in fact, I'm pretty sure we're all broken. The system's broken. But who can we tell this to?" she asks. "Who can we trust?"

"You can trust me," I tell her, meaning it. Feeling the ache that's pouring out of her. She hasn't mentioned her involvement with Catalina or how much she knows about closers, but I want to help her anyway. Even if she doesn't have answers for me.

But rather than comfort her, my words seem to snap her

out of the trance she was just in. She brushes back her hair from her face, adjusts the hem of her shirt self-consciously. "Wow," she says, trying to smile away her emotions. "I just dumped that all on you," she says. "I'm sorry."

"I don't mind," I tell her, wanting to continue the conversation. But Virginia reaches for a large scoop of the whipped cream and puts it into her mouth. She avoids my gaze. She's going through the motions of normalcy—a sign of avoidance.

"You're really easy to talk to," she says eventually, her voice shifting up. "I bet you hear that a lot."

I smile. "No, not much. I don't have a lot of friends."

She scrunches up her face like she doesn't quite believe it. If only she knew how much people hated me for being a closer. Then again, she might hate me too if she found out.

We finish our pie, and I listen as Virginia tells me about school, the upcoming volleyball championships, who's dating who—all the stuff that a typical person would talk about. Her words are hollow, though. I can feel that she has more to say— the sort of things I want to hear—but she's not ready.

"Hey," Virginia says. "Want to go to a party after this?"

I'm struck silent. After everything we just talked about, a party sounds like the last thing anyone would want to do. Virginia senses my hesitance.

"You asked what we do around here," she says. "The real answer is we cry in private and party in public. Tonight is a party. You should come." She picks up the bill on the table and glances at the amount before fishing through her wallet for some cash. She sets down the money and turns to me, her eyes pleading.

· *She doesn't have many friends left,* I think. *This is my chance to step into that role. This is my chance to find out who I am.* But even I can feel how unethical this is. The idea of exploiting her misery drowns me in guilt. I'd be a closer—playing a role for *my* benefit instead of hers. But I don't seem to have another choice.

"A party sounds fun," I say, making her smile. I glance down at my clothes, wondering if I look okay, but Virginia quickly waves it off.

"You look great," she says. "Don't worry. Everyone's going to love you. Want to head over now? We don't stay out too late around here." Her expression falls slightly. "Makes our parents worry."

It's possible that Virginia's fears are based in reality, but there's also a chance that this is part of a delusion. That her grief is making her paranoid.

Virginia gets up from the booth, and I take a look around, noticing that the waitress is watching her more closely than she should. Monitoring her. When the woman's eyes dart to me, I lower my head and follow Virginia out of the diner, wondering if I've just gotten caught up in her delusion.

CHAPTER NINE

OUTSIDE THE DINER, THE SKY IS AN ORANGE GLOW.
Virginia and I walk side by side until we pause next to a silver
car with a bundle of unburned sage hanging from its rearview
mirror. We get inside, and the space is fragrant and comforting.
Aromatherapy, I think. We occasionally use it with our clients.

"My dad's old car," she says when she notices me staring at
the sage. "And I hope you don't mind, but I *technically* don't
have a license. But don't worry." She waves her hand. "I'm an
excellent driver."

I remember what life was like before I got my license, and
it definitely involved breaking some permit laws. Otherwise I
would have been dependent on my dad or Deacon to drive me
everywhere.

"Just don't kill us," I tell her with a smile, although I quickly tense at my unfortunate choice of words. Virginia pretends not to hear. I take a moment to glance around at Arthur Pritchard's car, hoping to find some huge clue about my past, which of course is not there.

Virginia slips a CD into the stereo. The music that comes out of the speakers is haunting, itchy. Long whines of guitar strings, a melodic sound of a pained voice. The words are dark and depressing, but when I turn, I see they don't have the same effect on Virginia. She drives, looking over at me with a smile.

But if I'm honest, I'm starting to feel a little suffocated. It's not just the depressing music; I also feel fear. Selfish, personal fear. I'm playing a role: the role of Liz Major, a girl whose identity I stole. I want to be myself—I'm desperate to be myself. But I don't know who she is. I don't know who I am.

The thought of that leaves me lonelier than ever, and I wrap my arms around myself. I turn and stare out the window at the passing houses, thinking about the last time I went to a party—not as Catalina, but as Quinlan McKee.

A memory blooms across my consciousness and I cling to it. I nearly forgot it entirely because it didn't seem important at the time. But now it feels like everything. A tether to who I used to be—who I thought I was.

It was a night while Deacon and I were broken up, a few weeks after one of our ill-conceived hookups. He acted like it had never happened, breaking my heart yet again. After that, both of us were determined to keep our relationship platonic; however, his lingering glances threatened to derail all we were working toward.

SUZANNE YOUNG

Aaron, Myra, Deacon, and I were heading back from some shitty party near the college campus. For the first time in a while, Aaron and I weren't on assignment. We were enjoying a night off, playing pool in some guy's living room until a fraternity showed up and crowded us out. Deacon was driving my car, taking us all back to Aaron's, where I was spending the night because my father was at a conference. Myra was in the backseat with me, more than a little drunk, and changing her clothes without a care that the rest of us were in the car.

Deacon tapped his thumbs on the steering wheel, completely out of time with the smooth jazz he insisted on, as he avoided looking in the rearview mirror. Once Myra pulled her T-shirt back over her head and swiped out her hair from her collar, she leaned back in the seat and turned toward me.

"Much better," she said. "I hate those push-up things."

"I don't hate them," Aaron called out, not even turning to look back at us. I kicked playfully at his seat, and he laughed. Myra flicked my leg with her finger.

"What's up with you?" she asked me. "That boy was all about you tonight, Quinlan. What was his name?"

"Gleason," I told her with a pointed look.

"Yeah, that one." She smiled as if saying it might be good for Deacon to hear all about it. He'd brought dates around me since the breakup, something I pretended not to care about.

"Not my type," I told her. And he wasn't. He was just another dude at a party who thought teaching me how to play pool would end with him teaching me a few other tricks involving balls. "He wasn't horrible," I said. "But he wasn't for me."

"None of them are ever your type," she said under her breath. "Well, almost none of them." She nodded toward Deacon.

Although he didn't catch her comment, Deacon lifted his eyes to the rearview mirror. "I hope you're not giving Quinn advice on how to use her closer party skills to manipulate unsuspecting young men, demolishing all the lies I've told myself about true love and soul mates."

I hold Deacon's amused gaze for only a second before looking out the window into the dark night. "I never use my skills for evil," I told him. "Not even when you call me at three in the morning begging me to tell you good night so you can sleep."

"Ohhh . . . ," Aaron sang, and pointed at Deacon.

"Demolished," Deacon muttered.

"You'll get over it," I told him, fighting back my own smile. Myra did a dramatic double take between the two of us and then made a sound like *mm-hm* and crossed her arms over her chest.

"Calling at three a.m.? Good thing you two are broken up," she said sarcastically, and exchanged a look with Aaron, who had turned around in the seat to grin at her like an idiot. "What happened to Reed Castle?" she asked. "The closer from Tillamook. I saw you two talking the other day. He's hot. Pretty sure he was his school's quarterback once upon a time."

"Tight end," I corrected.

"I bet."

"Hello," Deacon said with a wince as he pulled into the

parking lot in back of Aaron's apartment complex, his knuckles white on the steering wheel. "Self-censor, please. I actually know Reed—we used to hang out before he moved. So I'd rather not listen to the two of you rate his body parts."

I turned to Myra. "I'd give it an A," I told her.

"No," she responded seriously. "Easily an A plus. Maybe A plus plus?"

Deacon snorted a laugh, shaking his head.

In reality, I'd met Reed only a handful of times, and none of them had involved seeing naked body parts.

Deacon parked my Honda near the back of the brick building and yanked up the emergency brake. When he got out, he opened the back door for me, standing over me as he pretended to pick casually at his fingernails.

"So Reed, huh?" he asked, not looking at me.

"Maybe," I said as I reached back into the car to grab my bag from the floor. Part of me wanted to hurt him. At least a little bit.

"I'm just trying to be friends," Deacon said offhandedly. "Thought that was the plan."

Now I was the one who was hurt. I pushed past him, hooking my backpack strap over my shoulder as I headed toward Aaron's apartment. "You should go home, Deacon," I called, turning to walk backward so I could see him. "It's nearly three and you need your beauty sleep."

"Me? Quinlan, I'm the most gorgeous thing out here."

I laughed. "That's a bit of a stretch."

Deacon slammed my car door shut and then jogged over so that he could walk beside me. "You're right," he said. "*You're* the most gorgeous thing out here. But I'm a close second."

My smile faded slightly, and I looked sideways at him, finding him staring straight ahead as if he hadn't spoken at all. Our pace slowed—stretching out every moment together. Every second was precious. Myra passed us, glancing back at me and smiling before disappearing inside behind Aaron.

Just before we got to the door, Deacon reached to take my elbow. Without hesitation I turned and stepped in to him, burying my face near his neck. My entire soul ached for his. We stayed like that for a long moment, breathing against each other. And then Deacon leaned down, his lips near my ear as his fingers slid under my hair.

"I'm still crazy about you," he murmured so quietly it was like a secret. And I closed my eyes and let the thought consume me.

The sound of Virginia cursing draws me out of the memory, though the feel of Deacon's arms around me takes longer to fade. But it does, and I'm pulled back into this world that Virginia has painted for me.

"What's wrong?" I ask her, my voice slightly hoarse. She clicks on the windshield wipers as rain taps the windshield and then out-and-out pours down.

"The rain," she says, glancing over at me. "I'm so sick of it. I swear there won't be a summer this year. It's like every season the rain stays longer and longer."

Although I'm not sure that's technically true, I understand what she means. I've always assumed it was perception: When we're in the middle of it, the rainy season can feel like years.

The music is still on, moody and dark, and all I can think about is how much I miss Deacon. Miss my life. I even have a quick thought that maybe I could go back—we all could. What if we just pretended it never happened, lying to ourselves so things could be easier?

I blink quickly, trying to right myself. I'm losing perspective. That wasn't my life—not my real life. This is my chance to find out who I am, who I was meant to be. I can't let anything get in the way of that.

I'll go to this party with Virginia, and then later I'll figure out her role in Catalina's death. I'll use that—use her. Even if it makes me feel like shit. Arthur Pritchard has my identity, and I'm going to get it back. I'm going to find my family. I'll find where I belong.

"Here we are," Virginia says, pulling in front of a four-story apartment building with a rickety-looking iron fire escape on the front. The place is a bit worn down and appealing because of it. I realize how much I want to be around other people in this moment. How much I crave interaction to distract me from myself.

Once she's parked, Virginia switches off the engine and reaches into the backseat to grab a cute jacket. She puts it on and then checks her hair in the rearview mirror. I don't have anything else with me, so I sit as she applies pink lip gloss and some powder to her cheeks.

When she's done, she flashes me a smile. If I didn't know how she felt in the diner, I wouldn't imagine anything is wrong with her. She seems happy and well-adjusted. But, of course that's not the case. Still, I match her smile, and we both climb out of the car.

The rain has lessened to barely a drizzle, but the cold clings to it, and I shove my hands in the pockets of my sweater. Virginia walks around the car and pops open the trunk. She pulls out a liter bottle of vodka and then comes to stand next to me, facing the building. She points to a window on the fifth floor, the lights blazing behind the sheer curtain, silhouettes moving.

"Roderick lives here," she says. "He's a sweet guy and his parties are fun. Nothing stupid happens."

I laugh. "Let's have some fun, then," I tell her. She nods like she appreciates my attitude, and together we walk inside and head up the flights of stairs.

The air in the apartment is sticky. The heat is cranked up, and both Virginia and I have to take off our jackets about three seconds after walking inside. The party is crowded, but not overly loud or obnoxious. Virginia leads the way to the small kitchen, where three guys sit at the table playing cards, barely registering our presence. When Virginia thunks the bottle of vodka down on the counter, one of the guys offers a head nod of appreciation before going back to his game.

I take the moment to survey the party supplies, seeing half-empty bottles of liquor lining the side of the sink, and a knocked-over stack of plastic cups. Some spilled red juice on the white counter, which I doubt will wash off. Virginia taps my shoulder.

"Here," she says. "Give me your coat."

I hand it to her, and together we walk through the dining room past the sliding glass doors that lead to the balcony. She says hi to people as she passes, but she doesn't stop to talk with any of them. When we get to the living room, Virginia tosses my jacket, along with hers, onto a pile of coats already on a papasan chair.

The bulk of the party is crammed in this space, where the lights are dimmed. Four girls dance with each other in the center of a circular woven rug. The music pumping from the iPod dock near the television is moody, much like the song in Virginia's car. But the bass is deeper, and the girls sway to the music, laughing and grabbing each other by the arm as they talk. There's a couple sitting on a love seat near the window, all in each other's mouths. Judging by the way the guy spills his beer each time he switches his head tilt, I guess that they've been drinking for a while.

A cute guy is alone on the cracked leather sofa, scrolling through something on his phone. His black hair is shaved short, much like Aaron's, and he has on a pair of lemon-yellow sneakers that nearly glow in the dark. He's hot. As if sensing my gaze, he lifts his eyes in my direction. He looks next to me and holds up his hand to Virginia. She returns the wave and then leans sideways to press her shoulder against mine, her voice low.

"That's Micah Thompson," she says. "He's my favorite."

"I can see why."

Virginia sighs, and when I check her over, she seems better. Her earlier admission of her fears is seemingly forgotten. I think maybe this is what they all need. Time to live. Time to be free.

"Go talk to him," I tell her, knocking her gently with my elbow. "He looks pretty happy to see you."

She can't hide the smile that immediately creeps over her lips. She turns, and Micah laughs, as if he just got caught staring. "We're not like that," she tells me, although the words sound like a repetitive verse. "We're just friends."

"Hmm . . . ," I say in mock consideration. "Yes, I've said something similar myself. Just before I'd make out with said friend."

Virginia closes her eyes and chuckles. Then she motions around the party. "Don't you want me to introduce you to people? I thought I was the *person to know* at Marshall Senior High," she jokes.

"I can introduce myself. You go have that fun we talked about."

She hesitates, checking with Micah once again, and then, as if I've twisted her arm, she breathes out dramatically. "Why not?" she says. "Life is short, right?" And before I can think about the irony of her statement so soon after talking about teen suicide, she's walking through the crowd and dropping down on the sofa next to Micah.

Once she starts talking to him, I head back toward the kitchen to get a drink. I'd be lying if I said these people didn't all fascinate me. I observe everything—absorb it, even. As I pour a vodka cranberry, I listen to the guys playing cards.

"Has anyone seen Roderick?" a guy in a blue Nike shirt asks, picking up his just-dealt cards. "You heard about his girl, right?"

"Naw, what happened?" the kid across from him says. He's wearing a U of O hat with a straight brim, his eyes shaded.

The guy in blue tosses his cards in front of himself, face down. "I'm out," he says. Then to the kid in the hat. "She got locked up. They committed her, I think. My parents told me about it earlier. Can't believe Roderick's even having a party tonight. Those two were close."

My hand tightens around my cup, the reality of their world in contrast with the party around them.

"Oh, shit," the kid says. "Ari's in the hospital? That's too bad. She was cool," he adds, as if she's dead. He puts his cards down and leans back in his seat, stretching his neck to look in the other room, presumably for Roderick. "There he is," he says. "In the corner. Poor dude."

I can't see from this angle, but the sympathetic expression on his face tells me that Roderick must be pretty distraught. So why did he throw a party? Just to go through the motions?

The dealer takes the pot of poker chips and starts shuffling for the next game, the conversation quieting now that they've darkened the mood. I take a sip from my drink, barely able to swallow it down since it's warm. I head back toward the living room to join Virginia, and I find her and Micah talking in the corner of the sofa, another guy having taken up space on the other cushion.

Virginia doesn't notice me, so I decide not to interrupt. I find a spot against the wall, still with the party but far enough aside that I can have a moment to think. I sip from the cup, watching everyone. I wonder how I fit in. If Arthur and Marie hadn't brought me to Tom McKee, could I have been one of them? Could I have lived a normal life?

I take another drink. Would I have really wanted another life?

I think about Catalina Barnes—the girl I thought I wanted to be. But look what happened to her. She killed herself, despite how perfect her life seemed. What could have driven her to that? I feel like I'm missing something in her story. A missing chapter of a book. One that involves Virginia.

Virginia hasn't mentioned Catalina directly, but they knew each other. And although I don't think Virginia herself is a threat . . . maybe her words are. Even during our short talk, I felt pressure closing in, helplessness. Is that what she fed Catalina? Is that what—

I stop, frozen in place, when I notice the guy in the corner of the room. *Roderick,* I think. He's tall with shoulder-length red hair. His freckled skin is impossibly pale, especially against his navy T-shirt. I'm not sure why he stands out so much. Maybe it's the rigidity of his posture or the fact that he's all alone at a party, his party, staring straight ahead toward the sliding glass doors.

But I notice him.

I immediately assess his condition, see all the signs of complicated grief—only worse. And I've seen some pretty devastated people. Roderick is so still that it's eerie, the way he doesn't sway in a room full of moving bodies. A line of drool begins to slip from the corner of his lip, down his chin.

My stomach registers my panic, and I quickly dart my eyes over to Virginia to get her attention. She's still talking, laughing, when suddenly there is movement from the corner. I swing back and find Roderick walking toward the balcony.

I stare, wondering where exactly he's going. He bumps a few shoulders on his way, but it doesn't deter him. Is he about to be sick? He doesn't speak a single word to anybody.

He comes to the glass doors and slides them open. He walks onto the balcony without bothering to close the doors behind him, and then, without even a pause, he continues to the edge and puts his hands on the railing. The rain has started to come down hard again, and it soaks his hair, matting it to the sides of his face.

My heart jumps up into my throat. I'm transfixed, and then Roderick pulls himself up onto the railing. My eyes widen.

"Wait!" I call over the music, the cup of red liquid falling from my hand and splashing on the carpet. I start forward, but it's too late.

Without a backward glance Roderick jumps headfirst off the fifth-floor balcony.

CHAPTER TEN

THERE IS A SCREAM SOMEWHERE IN THE ROOM. I
rush for the door, but the three guys from the kitchen are
already out there, leaning over the railing and looking down.

"Holy fuck!" one of them yells. "Holy shit." He continues
swearing, running his hand through his hair, blinking against
the rain.

Music still plays, but no one is dancing anymore. The sound
is haunting amid the cries, like the ghost of a nightmare that still
clings to you after you wake. I stare around, wide-eyed, my body
shaking as I go into shock. Several people have their phones out,
frantically calling 911. One kid runs into the kitchen and sweeps
all the booze bottles into the trash can, but his attempts to hide
the party are only halfhearted. He knows it doesn't matter. Pretending it does helps him deal with the brutality of this moment.

We are all horrified, terrorized, wrecked.

Virginia suddenly appears next to me, our jackets in hand, and I look at her without fully grasping who she is. "We have to go," she says. When I don't move, am unable to move, she pulls my arm. Her expression is stoic, and her nails dig into my skin through the cloth of my shirt. "We have to go now, Liz," she says more forcefully.

People have begun to crowd onto the small balcony, gathering in the rain. A girl wails from outside. Virginia's steady gaze is not shocked, though. It's fearful. I blink quickly, trying to sort myself out as Virginia shoves my jacket into my arms. I slip it on soundlessly and follow her to the front door.

People are talking and crying on each other, and we manage to zigzag through the crowd and get to the landing of the stairwell. We run down the steps. No one calls to us, asking where we're going. We're invisible; everyone is steeped in tragedy instead.

Virginia pushes open the door to the outside, and the metal handle smashes into the brick of the outside wall with a loud clank. I stop in my tracks, making Virginia lose her grip on me. I slap my hand over my mouth to muffle my screams.

Just down the sidewalk is a broken body. Blood has made a pattern on the sidewalk, sprayed on the car parked at the curb. Roderick is far enough away, and facedown, so I can't see the details of the gore. *It's just a heap of clothes,* I tell myself. But my mind tries to make sense of what I saw upstairs and begins to fill in the blanks. To form the shape of the broken arm, turned neck, broken hip.

"Liz," Virginia snaps. "Don't look!" She grabs me hard around the wrist, and then we're running again, rain whipping our faces. We get to her car, and she opens my door and pushes me inside. When she slams it shut, I'm engulfed in heavy silence.

I've never seen anyone die before. I've spent my life playing dead people, all without ever seeing their bodies. I don't know how something as natural as death can feel so jarringly unnatural.

The driver's door opens, flicking on the overhead light again. Virginia asks where I live, and I tell her the name of the motel. She turns over the engine and squeals her tires as she pulls out into the road without checking the mirrors. Rain sprays the windshield. The wipers provide a timed scrape, then click before doing it again—like a damaged heartbeat.

"He just jumped," I murmur. "He did it on purpose." Tears sting my eyes, and I turn to Virginia. "Shouldn't we tell the police or something?"

"There were other people there," she says. "They won't need our statement." Her jaw is set hard, and her knuckles are white on the steering wheel. I can barely catch my breath.

"But I watched him do it," I tell her. "I didn't know he was going to jump. I—" My voice cracks.

"Listen to me," Virginia says, looking over. "You didn't see anything. We weren't even there tonight. Do you understand?"

I stare at her, the first tears falling onto my cheeks. "What?" I ask.

Virginia doesn't falter in her steady gaze. "You have to stay away from this, Liz. Stay ahead of it. It's like I told you: Most people aren't equipped anymore. We've been stripped of our coping mechanisms. We've been left vulnerable. The reporters will come tomorrow. Don't read about any of it. Forget Roderick even existed." But this time there is a flash of pain in her eyes, and she quickly turns back to the road.

She eases to a stop at the next red light, and when she looks at me again, tears have run through her makeup. "Don't you see?" she says. "It's hopeless." Her expression goes slack. The light switches to green and the car moves forward. Virginia's shoulders are slumped. Her grip on the steering wheel weakens.

I am stunned silent by the way she's made me feel. Her words have scared me, because I almost believe them. Right now . . . I do feel hopeless. And it's a dark place to be.

My thoughts turn back to Roderick, retracing my steps at the party to see if there was a point when I could have interacted with him. Stopped him. What if I had just talked to him? Maybe that could have been enough.

I'm nearly swallowed up by survivor's guilt, and the next time I look outside, I see that we're pulling up to the Shady Pines Motel. Virginia parks near the office, and when I reach numbly for the door handle, she calls my name.

"Can I ask you a favor?" she says. "If the next time I see you, I don't remember this . . . remind me, okay?"

I furrow my brow and stare over at her. But it's like I don't have the ability to question anymore. To know any more.

Virginia presses her lips into a sad smile. "Please?"

I nod, although I don't see how she could forget what happened tonight, no matter how deep her denial runs.

I exit the car and start across the lot, letting the rain soak through my clothes. I'm shaking in the cold, and my teeth begin to chatter. I hear Virginia's car pull away, but I don't turn around. I'm desperate to get out of my head.

I walk up the exterior stairs of my hotel, each step more exhausting than the last. I'm weak—nearly too weak to make it up to the next landing. If Marie were here, she'd tell me I'm in shock and that I should start with a hot shower. A cup of tea. It would be peppermint, of course, and then I'd tell her everything. All the truth. I'd tell her how much my heart hurts. My soul.

I wrap my arms around my chest when I get to the second-floor landing; my body feels like it's collapsing in on itself. The image of a dead boy crowds my thoughts. I can't push him away. All I can see is the splatter of the blood. All I can hear are the cries of his friends.

I pause, putting my hand flat against the exterior wall, choking on my sobs. My mind is like a black spiral pulling me toward darkness, making me obsess about the pain. Dig into it. I want to feel Roderick's pain. My pain.

"Stop," I whimper, squeezing my eyes shut. I'm slipping away.

Just make it inside, I think. I force myself off the wall and take the key card from the back pocket of my jeans, my fingers shaking. I get to my door, and the first time I swipe the card, there's only a red square. I sniffle and then take a steadying breath.

You'll get through this. You always get through.

I swipe the card again, and the door lock turns green. I shove the door open, turning my back on my room as I close it and throw the security latch. I lean my forehead against the door, letting the card fall from my hand to the floor with a quiet thump.

The temperature in the room is warm, but my wet clothes keep me chilled. My heart hurts too much. *You could have saved him,* it says. Maybe I could have.

There is a sound behind me, the high-pitched creak of my mattress springs. Fear snaps over my skin like electricity, and I spin around, my breath caught in my throat. I see a figure across the room. I slap my hand along the wall until I find the light switch and flip it on.

Deacon sits on the edge of my bed, his eyes downcast as if he can't bear to look at me. His brown hair is disheveled, sticking up like he's been pulling his hand through it. His clothes are wrinkled, and I imagine he spent last night on the streets. But it's him. He's here, exactly when I need him most.

I stumble forward a step, my palm over my heart at the absolute relief. "Deacon," I breathe out.

He lifts his head, and when he catches sight of my condition, his sorrowful expression falls away, and he jumps to his feet. I walk over and immediately wrap myself around him. My comfort. My tether to reality.

"I could have saved him," I sob, burying my face in Deacon's neck, my fingers clutching his shirt. The smell of his skin pulls me back from the darkness. Takes me away from the death.

And I don't even realize how desperately I need him when he tentatively puts his arms around me, laying his cheek on the top of my head, and whispers, "Quinn, I have to tell you something."

PART II
HOW NOT TO DISAPPEAR COMPLETELY

CHAPTER ONE

THE FIRST TIME I REALIZED I WAS IN LOVE WITH Deacon was after we'd been dating for three months. The discovery was purely accidental—shocking, really, since I'd never been that close to anyone. But something about us just clicked and locked in place.

Deacon and I had already been working together for a while, so when we started dating, we did so carefully, neither of us going all in from the start. We were closers—we had to be cautious. Our entire livelihood revolved around not getting too attached to the families we helped. That easily bled into our personal lives as well.

But Deacon was everything back then: funny, smart, gorgeous. More than that, he was kind. I hadn't known another closer who cared as much as he did. As much as I did. His compassion drew me to him more than anything. His ability to predict what others needed to hear.

We were in my backyard, contemplating the best way to get out of cutting the long-neglected grass, when I play tackled him to the ground, burying us in the knee-high blades. He laughed, and we rolled around until he bested me and got to his knees and straddled me. Once there, he smiled and leaned down to kiss my lips quickly.

He was about to climb off when I grabbed him by the bottom of his T-shirt and pulled him to me. I'm not sure what brought it on, but I had this sudden loneliness that only he seemed to fill. Maybe it was that he accepted me as myself, as a closer.

Deacon read the expression and hummed out his mutual feelings as he lay down next to me, propping himself up on his elbow.

"Love this face," he said adoringly, tracing his finger over my lips before kissing them.

I closed my eyes as his hand trailed over my jaw, down my neck. It was the heat of the day, the smell of the grass, the feel of his touch—they all conspired to cloud my better judgment.

I love him, I thought dreamily. The words startled me, and I turned to Deacon, feeling vulnerable and stripped down, like he knew what I was thinking. And maybe he did. Because he stilled, his expression unreadable. And then he leaned over and kissed me fiercely, the kind of kiss that made me moan into his mouth, clutch at his clothes.

To this day Deacon has never said that he loves me. But he shows me sometimes, like now, when he holds me in this dingy motel room and lets me fall completely apart in his arms.

"I have to tell you something," he whispers against my hair.

And all at once, the safety of his arms feels anything but safe. I stumble back, slapping his hand away when he reaches for me. My vision is blurry with tears, but my grief and horror are set aside for rage.

"Quinn, calm down," he says.

"Don't tell me to calm down!" I snap, pointing at him. "Don't you dare."

He lowers his eyes to the floor. I haven't even started to process tonight, but I'll have to face my own problems before I can do anything else. And standing in front of me is my biggest problem of all. One that's been trained in the art of manipulation.

"You have no right to be here," I say. "How did you even find me?"

"I told you before," Deacon starts in a low voice. "You take up my whole world, Quinlan. It makes you easy to spot." He moves to sit in the chair by the window and leans forward with his elbows on his knees. "I went by the school," he continues. "I figured that was where you'd go, and I saw you in the parking lot."

I curse myself for not being more aware that I was being watched. I shouldn't have underestimated him.

"And once I knew you were in town," he says, "I saw that

you looked different, noted the changes, and checked the local motels. This was my fifth stop. The guy at the front desk was more than happy to tell me you were his tenant and that it would be an extra ten dollars a day if I planned on staying here."

"You broke into my room?" I ask.

"No. I gave him seventy dollars for the week and got my very own key card." Deacon pulls a card out of his back pocket and sets it next to him on the bed. He offers a smile, something small and private, meant to melt my frosty exterior. Now he's the one underestimating me.

"You can't stay," I tell him, watching him crumble under my words. He's not the only closer who knows how to manipulate. I have every reason to think Deacon is playing me, and there is only one misguided-reason—love—to trust him. I think I'll go the safer route. "I want answers, and then I want you gone."

"I tracked you down because you left me without a word," he says, his voice scratchy and raw; it sounds like pure devastation. It's too real, and I flinch against it. "You destroyed me, Quinn, so don't stand there as if I'm the one running away this time."

I'm rattled by the truth in his statement, even if it's framed in lies. "I left because I needed to think," I tell him.

"And you can't think when you're with me?" he asks, clearly hurt by the statement.

"No," I say simply, and sink down onto the bed across from him. "I can't trust you anymore. I saw the text, Deacon. You've been working against me."

He lifts his eyes, and then his lips part, guilt painting every corner of his expression. Oh, God. It's true. White-hot anger burns my face, and my attempt at a reasonable interrogation falters. I'm all hurt.

"You fucking asshole," I say, a cry threatening to break through. "You betrayed me!"

Deacon leans forward suddenly, his hands folded in front of him like he's begging. "Never," he says. "I was on that bus with you, Quinn. I was running away too. How could you think—"

I hold up my hand for him stop bullshitting me. "This is all easy to say now."

"Oh, believe me," Deacon replies, "I have no expectation that you'll make this easy. And you shouldn't. You're right—I *am* a fucking asshole. But not because of this. That text was from Arthur Pritchard," he says. "He was worried about you."

The name is a shock to my system, and panic crawls up my throat. "Even if that was the case, why the hell would Arthur Pritchard contact *you,* of all people?"

Deacon stills, holding my gaze. "Because I work for him," he says miserably. "And I have been for the past eight months. Eight and a half."

It's a slap in the face, one I wasn't expecting. One that makes the entire room tilt. Eight and a half months ago Deacon and I broke up. It was devastating for me, but our lives since have been almost worse. The back and forth of our relationship, the hot and cold. Deacon was working for the person who stole me from my life.

It feels like every word Deacon has ever spoken to me has

been a lie. He *works* for Arthur Pritchard. My arms fall help-lessly to my sides as I stare at him, heartbroken. "What have you done?" I ask, shaking my head slowly from side to side.

"I promise I never did anything—"

"No more promises!" I shout, making him jump. "The truth, Deacon. For once just tell me the truth. What are you doing for Arthur Pritchard?"

"I thought I was protecting you," he says earnestly. "He told me there was no other choice."

"Protecting me from what—the grief department?"

"No," he says. "From yourself. Arthur wanted me to be your handler; he said I was the best person because of our rela-tionship. I was supposed to monitor you for any changes, any breaks with reality—like what happened when you were Cata-lina Barnes. I was supposed to inform him so he could treat you if necessary." He straightens to sit back in the chair. "He told me you could die."

A thought dawns on me, twisting my stomach. "Are you the one who told him I left my assignment and came to you? Is that why he went to the Barneses' house?" I ask. "Jesus, Deacon—did you call him because you were jealous of Isaac?"

He hitches up his lip in disbelief. "No," he says. "I mean, yes, I was jealous, but I didn't call him. He must have been watching the house." Deacon quickly gets to his feet, staring down at me. "Don't you understand?" he starts. "This isn't about jealousy or selfishness—I would have never turned you over to Arthur, not for anything. I sold my soul to the devil to keep him *away* from you. I didn't trust anyone else to be your handler. I didn't want him to find another person. It had to be me."

It's a great sentiment, but I'm not so easily convinced. He's been lying to me—I can't let myself forget that. "And you weren't my handler when you came to the bus station to run away with me?" I ask.

"No. After you called from Marie's and told me she was gone, I knew Arthur and the grief department would come for you. Something had to be wrong for Marie to just disappear. I called Arthur's office and I told them I was out. Done. It didn't matter what I'd signed to the contrary."

Arthur Pritchard is not the kind of man you make deals with, my father told me last night. It's entirely possible that Deacon is in more danger than I am right now. And if that's true . . . it's because of me. "What have you gotten yourself into?" I ask him.

"A contract," he says, sitting next to me on the bed. His weight shifts the mattress and tips me closer to him. "It states that if I expose my purpose, they can take me into custody," Deacon says. "Indefinite therapy. I'd be committed, and I'm not sure what would happen after that."

My resolve to be angry with him weakens. We're closers. We're not your typical patients, and we don't receive your typical care—therapy for us is a looming threat, a well-known treatment that worms its way into our heads, disrupts us, changes us. We avoid it at all costs. So Arthur's threat of indefinite therapy could very well kill who Deacon is. That certainly would be definite.

I look sideways at Deacon and find him watching the floor. He's defeated, desperate. He'll leave if I ask again, and that question ignites a battle between my head and my heart. "Tell me one thing," I say, drawing his gaze. "Did you know about Quinlan McKee? Did you know I was a closer for her life?"

"No, of course not," he says. "I wouldn't have kept that from you."

"You kept this from me."

"*This* is different," he says. "And I'm telling you now. Yes, I'm your handler; I've monitored your behavior. But I didn't tell Arthur Pritchard a damn thing other than to say you were fine, even when I suspected that you weren't. I always had your back. Always."

"Is that why you broke up with me?" I ask.

"Yes. I wanted you to be able to move on—to try for a normal life." Deacon runs his palm over his face. "I wanted you to escape all of this—especially me. I tried to stay away. I failed, but I tried really fucking hard. And that's why I'm an asshole."

As far as handlers go, Deacon was a terrible choice for Arthur to make. Sure, he had access to me, access he tried to limit when he could, but the truth is obvious now. And I think I've always known it. I think it's why I love him so madly.

Deacon's loyalty lies with me. It always will. Not even Arthur Pritchard could break it.

I'm not going to make him leave. Deacon's a good closer, but he's not as good as me. We know each other too well, and I can see that he's not playing me; I don't think he can. Instead he's baring his soul, leaving himself vulnerable. It's what I've always wanted, but now . . . I don't know that it's enough. And it might never be enough. Not when neither of us can seem to tell the truth.

But right now I need him more than I need to punish him.

"Something happened," I say, feeling the grief scratching its way to the surface now that my anger has (partially) subsided. "Something horrible."

Deacon must sense the flood of emotion coming, because he moves to kneel in front of me on the threadbare, burgundy carpet. "What is it?" he asks, his voice the perfect pitch of calm and tender. He's such a closer.

"It was a pile of clothes," I say out loud, breaking my own heart. Because, of course, they weren't just clothes. They were part of a life. And now they're death and blood and gore. I imagine Roderick's body on the sidewalk, broken. Chills stretch over my skin and I start to shiver. A headache starts, and all I want is to slip away and get some distance so I don't die too.

I start to cry. I can barely see Deacon through my blurry vision, and he reaches to brush his palms over my cheeks to clear the tears. "I'm going to get you some water, okay?" he says softly.

He doesn't leave until I nod, and rather than turn on the faucet, he pulls a water bottle from the duffel bag he has stashed in the corner of the room. He brings it back to the bed and sits next to me, his thigh touching mine.

I take the bottle from his hand and sip, but my throat feels thick from crying, and I choke. I drag my hand across my mouth to wipe away the water. I need to calm myself—Marie would have told me as much—but I can't seem to. My eyes have gone dry, painful and sore from crying. Deacon doesn't ask me to talk or explain. He's always known when not to.

I set the water bottle on the table next to the lamp and curl up on the bed, shoes and all. I sporadically twitch, like a full-body hiccup, and I feel half out of my mind. Deacon goes to the other bed and pulls off the comforter. He drags it to lay over me rather than asking me to get under the covers. He tucks the blanket all around me, and I look up at him. It buries me to see how much love is there, how much guilt.

"I'm sorry, Quinn," he whispers.

I know he is. He's sorry for now and for all the things he hasn't told me yet. He's sorry for my pain. But tonight I just want it all to go away. I don't want to be alone. Not after everything I've seen.

I reach for Deacon's hand and pull him toward me. He comes to lie beside me, the heat of his body close to mine although he doesn't touch me. I hear him exhale heavily.

"I've missed you," he says, sounding a million miles away.

He's the only comfort I have left as I start to drift asleep. And as my eyes close, I murmur back, "I always miss you, Deacon."

CHAPTER TWO

BRIGHT SUNLIGHT ROUSES ME FROM MY SLEEP, and my eyelids flutter open. I put up my palm to block the light streaming in the window, and I slowly sit up. My head is stuffy, and my face feels swollen from crying. I'm exhausted and drained.

But at least I'm alive.

I turn and see Deacon sitting at the small table, a drink carrier in front of him with a tall coffee cup, another cup near his left hand. His head is down as he sketches on the back of a receipt, a picture I can't see from here. He picks up his drink and takes a sip. He notices me then, and sets down his pen and motions toward the other cup.

"It's hot chocolate," he says. "I can go get you something else if you want."

"No, it's fine," I say, trying to put together everything we talked about last night. Slowly things come back to me. I peel off the comforter and swing my legs so that my feet touch the floor. I stare down at my socks. I don't remember removing my shoes.

I get up and cross to where Deacon is sitting. He watches me carefully, waiting to see if I've forgiven him. If I'll let him back into my life. I pause at the end of the table and reach out to take the hot chocolate.

My heart aches a little when I see the picture he's been drawing. It's still just a sketch, but I can tell already that it's me and him, side by side. Only we're rigid and empty. It's the loneliest picture I've ever seen.

I take a sip, chocolate-flavored sugar coating my tongue.

Deacon's chin has the shadow of a beard, and his eyes are red and weary. The anticipation of my answer must kill him, because he leans to rest his forehead against my hip and closes his eyes, apologetic and broken.

I can't help it—I thread my fingers through his soft hair like I've done a million times before. Run them down his neck. I feel his warm breath through my clothes, his hand on the back of my calf. When he looks up at me, he doesn't smile.

"I love you," he whispers as if he's been trying to say it his whole life.

My entire world stops spinning; I'm completely stunned by his confession. I honestly never thought he would say the words.

"I've loved you since the first day I showed up at your house and gave you a hard time," he continues. "I loved you when I broke up with you because I was too scared to love you anymore. I wanted you to find better than me. I wanted you to have everything." His throat clicks when he swallows, as if he's overcome. "I love you so much that it might just kill me, Quinn," he murmurs. "But I'll go ahead and keep on loving you until it does, because I don't know any other way to be alive."

I gave up hoping Deacon would ever say the words, but now that he has, I don't know what to do with them. So I give him the only response I'm able to.

"I love you too," I say quietly. "But that doesn't change a thing."

I turn away and sit on the bed across from him. Deacon may not have gotten the answer he wanted, but he does look relieved to have admitted his feelings. And he knows I'm right about it not changing our situation. At least we're finally being honest with each other—not exactly a strong point in our relationship.

Although I'm sure Deacon's still waiting for me to decide his fate one way or another, I'm not prepared to make that decision just yet. But I need his help on something bigger than both of us.

"There's something else we have to talk about," I say.

Deacon picks up his cup to take a sip of his drink, more at ease than he'd been earlier. More focused now that the biggest burdens are off his conscience. "Is this about last night?" he asks.

"Yeah," I say. I couldn't talk about it then; it was too near my heart. But now my emotions are at bay, pushed aside as if I'm closing. "There was a party," I tell Deacon. "And I went there with Virginia Pritchard. There was this guy . . . he killed himself. At his own party in front of everyone."

Deacon pauses midsip and turns to me. "You saw him?" he asks, pulling his eyebrows together in concern.

"I witnessed the whole thing," I say, sickness bubbling up in my stomach. I begin to wring my hands in front of me and slowly recount every horrifying detail for Deacon, every second of thought. He doesn't say a word, but it doesn't mean he isn't thinking. He's always thinking.

When I finish, I look up and find him watching me intently. He licks his bottom lip before he talks, his words measured.

"What you saw last night," he starts, "it's not the first time. I did a little research on the school when I saw you there yesterday. There have been over a dozen articles just this week." He pauses at the weight of his next words. "The students there are killing themselves, Quinlan. And nobody can figure out why."

Deacon and I hold each other's gaze, each of us assessing the situation in our own way. Getting a grip before making a plan. This is how we manage our assignments, too. This is the Deacon I know more than any other. This one I can trust.

"How bad is it?" I ask. "I only know what Virginia has told me, and I worry that her perspective is skewed."

"They're calling the deaths part of a suicide epidemic," Deacon says. "The last article I read was from the Oregon Health Authority. Several officials are demanding mandatory therapy for everyone in Douglas County who's under eighteen."

"Mandatory?" I repeat. The word "mandatory" is a scary one. A controlling one. "How could they enforce something like that?"

"There's a meeting next week at city hall. That's probably what they intend to discuss."

I look around the room, thinking over this development. "So . . . they're going to round up everyone under eighteen. Virginia said they had been bringing in grief counselors. Do you think it's more of that? I mean, what sort of therapy are we talking about here?"

"I have no idea," Deacon says. "Chances are it'll be much more invasive than anything we've seen before, though, especially since it comes with a mandate."

I consider that statement. "But will it help?" I ask, even though I realize how double-edged the question is. "Because I saw Roderick die, and I have to tell you, Deacon . . . I'm not sure what can be worse."

"It can always be worse," he murmurs. "He might have triggered more."

And the truth is, I think Deacon's right—his actions have triggered something. I felt it, and I'm trained to control emotions.

To temper them. I may not have loved being a closer all the time, but I can see the benefits. It certainly hurts less this way. But what about Roderick's friends at the party? How will they process what happened to him?

"Virginia," I say, mostly to myself. She handled the devastation like a pro, like someone who's been through it a million times. There's no way it hasn't affected her, though.

"About her . . . ," Deacon says. "I know you feel loyalty to the Barnes family. And although finding Virginia's connection to Catalina's death is important, and you're a good person for wanting those answers, I don't think—"

"It's not just about Catalina," I interrupt. "I'm going to use Virginia to blackmail her father." As soon as the words are out, I'm stunned by how callous they sound. The way Deacon rocks back in his seat, I can tell he feels the same way.

He lowers his eyes to his cup, speechless. It occurs to me then that I'm not an entirely good person—maybe I never was. I've been playing a part my whole life. Maybe Quinlan was the good one. I don't know what I am anymore.

"Regardless of your plan," Deacon says in a quiet voice, "my vote is to leave town. Before someone from the grief department finds you and brings you back to Corvallis."

"Someone already found me," I say. Deacon's head snaps up. "I thought there was a doctor or a therapist on the bus with us. I . . . I thought you were working with her."

"What?" Deacon says, screwing up his face. "First of all, no. Second, I didn't notice anyone out of place. Your distrust in me might have been . . . skewing your perception."

He's probably right, but he's not in a position to call me paranoid. "Yes, how crazy for me to be distrustful." Deacon takes a sharp breath at the dig, but then nods respectfully for me to continue.

"In Eugene," I tell him, "a closer named August—Roger, actually—attacked me. He drugged my drink, and when that didn't work, he tried to physically inject me with a sedative and drag me back to the grief department."

Deacon's eyes flash rage, but I hold up my hand to tell him that the time for that has passed.

"I can take care of myself, Deacon," I say. "He ended up passed out in the front seat of his car. But he told me that the grief department considers me in breach of contract. My father said they want to 'transition' me. Any idea what either of them is talking about?"

He furrows his brow as if thinking, and then his face clears. "When I met with Arthur eight and a half months ago, he told me your memory had been manipulated. I assumed it was after your mom died." He winces. "After Quinlan's mom died. Now I realize it was probably when he brought you in to close for her. But . . . he told me he needed to monitor you to check for a break with reality.

"He called you his case study," Deacon continues. "He said . . ." He shakes his head like he's figured it all out. "He said there was an epidemic starting, one he couldn't stop. And he needed to know if whatever he did to you was a viable treatment. Quinn, that's the mandatory treatment—memory manipulation. I'd bet my life on it."

"Sounds like Arthur bet my life on it," I say, feeling used. Violated. "So he stole my life, my memory. And now he plans to do that to other people. He's a bastard," I say.

"He's a total asshole," Deacon agrees. "And yet . . ." He pauses, reaching to take my hand. "I still don't want you to manipulate Virginia for blackmail," he says gently. "That's just not you, Quinn. You would never—"

"We don't know what I would do," I correct, pulling my hand from his. "I've been pretending so long, there is no telling what I'm capable of."

Deacon swallows hard, his Adam's apple bobbing as he sits back in his seat. "I do know you," he says. "I know who you are."

"Well, then, you're the only one," I say.

I want him to be right. I don't want to be a stranger, not to him, but mostly not to myself. I don't know how to reconcile this, though. I'm nobody—I'm a lie. How can I be sure of anything about me?

"Tell me more, then," Deacon says. "What exactly are you looking for and how do you plan to use it against Arthur?"

He doesn't agree with me, but he's willing to fight with me anyway. I can appreciate that, and I hope he sees that this is the only option I have. "Virginia is tied to these deaths somehow, right?" I start. "At least the ones in Lake Oswego—we know that from Catalina's family, boyfriend, and diary. Arthur sent closers in and tried to cover up the suicide. He talked with the family to cover up his daughter's involvement. He doesn't want the grief department to know about her, but why? What has Virginia done that her father wants to hide? Once I know that—"

"You'll use it as leverage for your identity," he finishes for me. I nod. "Well," he says, locking his hands behind his neck like he's settling in for whatever fucked-up mission we're about to embark on, "what have you gotten so far?"

"Not much," I tell him. "And after last night, after Roderick jumped, she should have let her guard down and told me everything, even if I was a mess myself. But instead she told me to forget what I'd seen, to avoid thinking about it. Avoid reading about it. She said the coverage will be relentless."

Deacon narrows his eyes. "She's right about the coverage, but why avoid talking about it?" he asks. "Did she give a reason?"

"She said most people weren't equipped to handle the news. Earlier she mentioned closers, and, big surprise, she's not a fan. Luckily, I'm operating under my false identity."

"I still don't see her connection," Deacon says. "So she knew the people who died? What is that other than tragic? Any chance she has dirt on her father? Are they close?"

"Uh . . . doubt it," I say. "She was worried that a waitress was spying for Arthur, so he doesn't exactly sound like father of the year."

"I'm so surprised," Deacon says sarcastically, and I snort a laugh.

"Virginia has some serious dad issues," I say.

"As bad as you?" Deacon asks, lifting one eyebrow.

"The fact that she's even in the running tells us a lot."

Deacon laughs, but then straightens his face. "That's actually not funny."

"If we don't laugh, we'll cry, right?" I ask.

"I don't like that those are our only two choices."

I press my lips into a sad smile, our situation certainly not a good one. I cross my legs at the ankle and lean back on my arms. Talking to Deacon has been good for me—it's brought things into perspective, refocused me. I don't forgive him for not telling me about Arthur, but right now we have bigger problems. And for once they're not about our relationship.

Deacon must notice the change in my attitude, because he watches me, looking thoughtful. He stands from the chair just in front of me, and his knee brushes my outer thigh. The touch is fire, and we stare at each other, my breath held. My skin alive and electric. For a moment I think he's going lie on top of me, kiss me passionately—part of me even wants him to. I want him back completely. I want me back.

But instead Deacon runs a shaky hand through his hair and backs away before crossing the room to his duffel bag. "We should move," he says. "This place sucks for security. And I need some supplies. Are you . . . ?" He pauses and looks back over his shoulder at me, the vulnerability passing over his features once again. "Are you coming with me?"

"Yeah," I say as coolly as possible. I'm apprehensive, I'm not going to let my guard down, but yes . . . I'll go with him. And when I stand, I see his lips hitch up in a smile, even if he turns away in hopes of hiding it.

But I have Deacon figured out now. And I'll never let him lie to me again.

CHAPTER THREE

I STAND IN FRONT OF THE FOGGY BATHROOM mirror on Monday morning and swipe my hand across the glass. I finger-comb the blond extensions before snapping them into my hair, pulling the longer strands over my shoulders. A towel is wrapped tightly across my chest, and I apply my makeup, changing my features only slightly, but enough to match my ID. Elizabeth's credit card is useless, but the ID will work as long as no one calls to verify it with the Oregon DMV.

Deacon and I used the weekend to find a new motel, a nicer one, forfeiting the weekly payment we already gave Shady Pines. Deacon had emptied his bank account before leaving Corvallis, so he paid for the hotel in cash and used a fake ID of his own to register. After that, he went out and bought a piece-of-shit car, reminiscent of my piece-of-shit Honda back in Corvallis, and we tracked down Virginia's home address. We covertly staked it out, but no one came or went for the entire weekend, not even her father.

Deacon appears in the doorway of the bathroom and leans against the frame. I glance over, and I smile when I get a peek of him shirtless before he pulls on a clean white T-shirt. I turn away before he notices my admiration. We're back to being partners, friends, for now. I decided that although we love each other openly, I need time. I can't just pretend the last eight and a half months never happened.

"So what's the plan?" Deacon asks. "Are we going to school?"

"No, *I'm* going to school," I tell him. "You're going to do Deacon things on your own while I try to catch Virginia before she heads into class. I want to know what happened Friday at the party and what she's been doing since." I turn to him, leaning against the sink. "At least, I hope she's at school."

"I'm just worried about you going alone," Deacon says.

"I'll be fine."

Deacon comes into the bathroom to stand behind me, and we meet each other's eyes in the mirror. I'm acutely aware of how naked I am under my towel. Deacon doesn't touch me, even though I'm sure we both want him to.

After an agonizing moment he moves next to me and leans against the sink, facing forward. From separate beds Deacon and I have talked about everything over the last two days. I told him about the nosebleed and the memory with Marie. We added it to the long list of things we'll have to ask Marie about.

Deacon and Aaron have been talking, and Aaron is thrilled that we're together again, although we've kept him out of the details. He still hasn't turned up anything on Marie's whereabouts, which is concerning. At this point, all any of us want is to get answers, get my identity, and get the hell out.

"I know we've promised before," Deacon says, looking over at me, "but once this is over, we really are running away. We'll go someplace where we can be ourselves all of the time. No more pretending."

"Pretending is the only thing I know," I say, feeling a little sorry for myself. Deacon's bottom lip juts out in concern, but I wave it off. "I want to believe it," I say, "I want to think we can get away from this, but even if we do, I have no idea how to be myself. What if I hate who I'm supposed to be?" I ask. "What if I find my parents and they're terrible people?"

Deacon straightens, surprised. "Your parents . . . I hadn't even thought about that."

"Even ghosts have parents," I say. "And I've been Quinlan's ghost for too long. To be honest, the only possible memory I have is of a woman in a hospital bed. I think . . . I think she died." Although I don't know her, the loss stings a bit. "What if she's alive and looking for me, too? And then there's my father—my real one. Maybe he's not a total asshole."

Deacon's eyes soften. "That would be a nice change for you," he says, and smiles sympathetically. I don't go on, making up stories of my dream parents. I'm not that optimistic; I'm too much of a realist.

"You know I love you, right?" Deacon says. "Because I can keep saying it if you need me to."

"Yeah, keep telling me," I say, my cheeks warming. "I figure you owe me a few."

"I love you, Quinlan," he says again. "I love you." He pauses dramatically and tilts his head. "Or is it Liz?"

I laugh. "Yes, we should switch to Liz for now."

He crinkles his nose and then moves to stand in front of me, looking me over. "Why Liz? Why not Beth?"

"I don't know. I like Liz."

"I think I like Beth better."

"Uh, does it matter considering my name isn't even Elizabeth?" I say, gripping my towel and then pushing him aside to walk back out into the room. I grab the clothes I laid out on the bed earlier, but I look at Deacon as he comes out of the bathroom. "At least, I don't think my real name is Elizabeth."

Deacon flops down on the bed, arms spread out at his sides as he stares up at the ceiling. I get dressed, and when I'm done, I sit on the opposite bed to put on my shoes.

"Well, if it turns out you're really an Elizabeth," Deacon says, "I'm calling you Beth."

I crack up and grab the towel from the floor and toss it at him. Deacon swats it away before it can hit him.

"I've got to go before school starts," I say, grabbing one of the phones from the pair Deacon and I got this weekend. I slip Liz's ID into the back pocket of my shorts.

"I'll be waiting," Deacon calls as he watches me walk out.

The sky is covered in heavy gray clouds as I drive Deacon's car to school, missing the bulk of morning traffic. When I arrive, I park in the back of the lot, closest to the exit. I do it for convenience when leaving, not because I have to. There is an unusual amount of empty spaces. I wonder if this weekend's suicide kept some of the students home.

News trucks line the front entrance of the building, giant antennas perched on top of the vans. A man in a suit keeps leaning forward with a mic as students rush past him into the school. None of them stop to talk to him, and he looks frustrated, although he smiles when he turns to the camera.

What does he want them to say? Why is he even here? It seems tasteless, trying to cash in on a tragedy. Then again, that's what some people think closers do. I don't believe that—I never have. I wanted to help people. And I think . . . I did. I gave them closure. So, yeah, I'm better than an opportunistic newscaster.

I scan the lot for Virginia's car, and when I finally find it, I'm disappointed to see that it's empty. She must already be inside. I check the time on my phone, and realize school starts in just a few minutes.

I glance back at the large building, considering my options. I'd be lying if I didn't admit that part of me wants to know what it's like to be within those walls, to be one of them. A few students walk in the back door, and just as the bell rings, I know I have a decision to make. I can leave and come back at the end of the day or . . . I can go to school. Attend classes and track Virginia down, maybe get a peek at the rest of the student body. My fake ID is good enough to pass for, and I've filled out my share of paperwork. I'll even mention Virginia to see if I can get into her PE class or something. I'll be persuasive. I'll be . . . totally stupid and irresponsible.

And yet I smile to myself, wishing I'd bought supplies—backpack, folders, and pencils. Hell, I would have even gotten a highlighter. My stomach churns with a nervous excitement, and I start toward the back entrance of the building.

I'm going to school.

With only a few weeks left in the school year, I get a shortened version of the usual paperwork. I've helped my dad fill in this type of information before for his closers. Since they were wards of the state, he'd help them with the details. I even filled out Deacon's school paperwork when he first came to Corvallis.

The office will send a fax request for my—or rather, Liz's—grades from South Eugene High School. Of course, I have no idea where Liz went to school, but it doesn't matter. Neither her grades nor her vaccination records will ever arrive.

The office staff look dazed as they hand me a schedule, as if still reeling from the death of yet another student. On the desk the phone rings, but no one picks it up. It's probably a reporter.

I feel sorry for the secretary as she wipes at her watery eyes and slides a schedule in my direction. She looks helpless in her sorrow; the pain is written all over her expression.

When I'm done, she sends me along to second period. I'll be gone before they find out my name isn't Elizabeth Major.

I'm early when I arrive at room 117, so I wait outside the door for the first-period class to end. Once the bell rings and the students filter out, I slip inside the room and look around.

The desks are arranged in five even rows—perfect for math, I guess. I know enough social etiquette to not just sit down in someone else's seat. The teacher hasn't arrived, so I stand awkwardly at the back, fading successfully against the posters so as to not be noticed. My closer skills would have definitely come in handy in high school. I still can't believe I'm here.

For a moment I imagine I could have always had this if Arthur Pritchard hadn't stolen me away. I'd be your typical student, complaining about homework . . . or whatever it is students do. But then I remind myself that I don't know the details of my before life—I may not be stolen at all.

I look up and accidentally lock eyes with a tall, long-haired boy. I'm quick to dart my gaze away, but not soon enough. He sits down and leans toward another guy. Both look at me. I lift my eyes to the ceiling and twitch my mouth to the side as I wait impatiently.

The bell rings, and the teacher still isn't in class. But with half of the room now checking me out, I decide to move forward and slip into one of the empty seats nearest the back. I'm starting to regret thinking school was a good idea.

But at least now that I'm seated, the other students must feel more comfortable, because most go back to chatting among themselves. The boy in front of me turns around and smiles, wide-mouthed. His hair falls over his left eyes in a goofy yet endearing way.

"Mr. Roth's been late a lot lately," he says. "But he eventually makes it."

I nod and smile as if this is a conversation I've had before. He turns back around, and I take the time to look around the room, analyze the students who are in here.

I notice a girl on her phone, texting. At that moment another girl pulls her phone out of her backpack. And they're not the only ones. I assumed phones weren't allowed, but I guess it doesn't count if the teacher isn't here yet.

I take out my phone and text Deacon. IS IT NORMAL FOR THE TEACHER TO BE LATE TO CLASS? I ask.

UH . . . NOT USUALLY. NO.

I look up again and check the time. The teacher is five minutes late into a fifty-minute period. No one else seems to care, but I find it strange.

YOU DECIDED TO ACTUALLY GO TO SCHOOL? Deacon writes. SO HOW'S THE FIRST DAY?

WELL, NO VIRGINIA YET. AND I'M THE WEIRD NEW KID.

HA! he writes. THINK ABOUT HOW THEY'D REACT IF THEY KNEW WHO YOU REALLY WERE AND THEN ENJOY BEING THAT WEIRD NEW KID.

GOOD POINT.

The door at the front of the room suddenly opens, and I watch my classmates scramble to put away their phones. The teacher walks in, and I'm surprised by how young he is—early twenties. His hair is disheveled, and his tie isn't quite knotted correctly. He holds a stack of papers, and, without making eye contact with any of us, he hands some to the first person in each row to pass back.

"Answer these questions," he says in a low voice. "When you finish, just turn them over on your desks. I'll collect them after you leave." He doesn't notice me at all.

A few students exchange looks, and I read that this is out of the ordinary for Mr. Roth. He sits at his oversize desk and stares at an empty desk near the front. After a moment he puts his head in his hands. I see a boy next to that desk sniffle. A girl wipes her eyes.

I bet Roderick was in this class. That was his seat.

The guy in front of me passes back the paper and, to my relief, asks if I need to borrow a pencil. I thank him when he hands it to me. When I look down at the paper, I'm surprised that it has nothing to do with math.

> *In the past day have you felt lonely or*
> *overwhelmed?*

Unease crawls up my arms at the invasiveness of the question. *What sort of quiz is this?* I turn to look at the other students, each of them also seeming perplexed and uncomfortable. One boy raises his hand, but the teacher ignores him.

"Uh, Mr. Roth," a girl toward the back calls. When he lifts his head, his eyes are rimmed in red, and he seems to stare right through her. I hear the boy in front of me curse under his breath.

The sound of the fire alarm blasts through the room, and I jump so hard I bang my elbow on the corner of the desk. It's enough to break the spell in the room, though: Mr. Roth gets up from his seat and tells all of us to head outside.

So much for the normal high school experience. This place is messed up. They have no right to ask those questions. And more importantly, who gets to interpret the answers?

I pass through the doorway where Mr. Roth is standing, lost in his head. His eyes drift to me, but he doesn't register that I've never been his student before. I wonder if all the teachers and staff are like this. I wonder if they're all feeling completely helpless to stop their students from dying.

I follow the line of people through the hall and out the side door to a large field on the side of the building. I glance around for Virginia but still don't see her. If it weren't for her car, I would assume she wasn't here today.

The shrill ringing of the fire alarm cuts off, leaving its echo hanging momentarily in the wind. The crowd is silent around me, but as I look around, I start to realize why. They're not confused, worried. They're shocked. And yet they've obviously done this before.

A new siren starts, and I feel a sick twist in my stomach when I see the ambulance pull up. A dark-haired girl standing next to me begins to cry.

"It's Micah Thompson," she sobs. "He's dead."

I immediately turn back to the building, panic and horror washing over me. Micah Thompson—the guy that Virginia talked to at the party. Her *favorite*.

I watch the paramedics rush in, the lack of police involvement. The devastated and subdued faces of the teachers. And I realize that Micah committed suicide—right now. Right here. That was the alarm.

CHAPTER FOUR

AS WE WAIT IN THE EMPTY SPACE NEAR THE BUILDING,
a tall black man in a steel gray suit and a lemon yellow tie
approaches. He stops in front of the crowd of students and
holds up his hands, waving them to get everyone's attention. By
his authoritative stance, I assume he's the principal.

"Students," he calls. "Please, quiet down." When he's mostly
got everyone's attention, he adjusts his tie; his other hand is
balled into a fist at his side. "Due to a medical emergency, classes
are dismissed for the day. We ask—"

There is an immediate murmur in the crowd, and the principal holds up his hand once again to silence them, raising his
voice. "We ask that you head directly home. Your parents have
been notified of the shortened school day and will be expecting you. Now please, gather your belonging and leave campus

immediately." I see him flinch. "And please avoid the English wing for now," he adds. "For students who need to retrieve their items from those classrooms, the teachers will bring everything to the front office momentarily."

The world is dazed, and the scene outside the school is somber as people make their way to the parking lot or start walking home. There are murmurs of details of Micah's death, but they vary wildly, and I know I'll have to wait for the real story. I'm just sorry that it happened. I'll need to find Virginia and make sure she's okay.

As I walk, I'm grateful that the news trucks are temporarily gone. I imagine that a producer, upon hearing the news, will curse for missing out on this *story*. Bloodthirsty media.

I take out my phone, ready to text Deacon, and nearly bump into two girls who are hugging and crying. I apologize, but they don't seem to notice through their haze of grief. I sidestep them, and as I cross onto the blacktop, the stillness of one person among all the moving parts catches my attention.

My heart seizes, and I do what I can not to react, but he must read my pause. The guy leaning against the hood of his red sports car like a goddamn *GQ* model meets my eyes and then turns away as if I don't interest him. But a small smile tugs at his lips.

I recognize him, of course—he looks exactly the same. Reed Castle, a good-looking closer who's good at his job, too. A closer who I know. But more importantly, a closer who knows me. He used to be one of Marie's.

After what happened with Roger back in Eugene, I can't be sure of Reed's motives: if he's here on a normal assignment or if he's here to pick me up for the grief department. But now that I know the options, I'm not about to be scared away.

I straighten my back, trying to look unrattled, and head in his direction. I'm not granted his attention again until I stop next to him, resting my hip against his car. Reed looks over at me, and his striking blue eyes catch the sunlight, making him squint. He's classically handsome with black hair and an ultrasharp jaw. He's always been just a little too perfect.

"Quinlan McKee," he says, drawing out my name, "you're more beautiful than ever." He crosses his arms over his chest, his biceps straining his sleeves, and smiles as he looks over.

"What are you doing here, Reed?" I ask pleasantly, although I'm sure he can hear the hostility underneath it.

He snorts a laugh. "Uh . . . not going to school," he says, nodding toward the building in amusement. "What the hell are you up to? And don't tell me it's calculus."

"This isn't a good time for jokes," I say.

"I gathered that," he responds seriously. "But maybe that wouldn't be such a bad thing. This place is falling apart. That why you're here?" he asks.

"It doesn't matter why I'm here," I say. "I don't work for the grief department anymore." This seems to surprise him, and he turns toward the school to hide his expression. "But you,"

I continue now that I know I have the upper hand, "you work for Christopher, right?"

"Dr. Levi," he corrects, as if I'm being rude. "Yep. Ever since I moved to Tillamook. I'm here to check on a girl." He turns back to me, and I hitch up an eyebrow. "A client, of course," he clarifies. "Keep your scandalous thoughts to yourself, McKee. I'm researching."

"This might sound weird," I say, appreciating a moment of honest conversation, the kind I can have only with another closer, "but I randomly thought of you the other day."

"Weird that it was random," he says.

I laugh. "Sorry you're not always on my mind, Reed. I've been kind of busy."

He nods, watching a group of students round the building. "I think we've all been busy," he says, his eyes searching for someone in the crowd. I realize that I should be doing the same. I push off his car.

"How long are you in town for?" I ask him.

"Few days," he says. "You?"

I smile my answer, making him chuckle and turn away. He knows I'm not going to tell him my plans. Even if I had an assignment, closers are usually private, even secretive. It's how we maintain our sense of self. There's a twist in my stomach. Even when we're not sure who that really is anymore.

"See you around," I tell him.

"Probably," Reed says. He must know that I'm involved in something bigger than a typical school day. I'm the best closer the grief department has ever had—it's not like I can just start a normal life, not without some fallout. But he hides his suspicion well.

I say good-bye and leave, seeing Virginia's car still parked in the same spot. I head in that direction to wait, hoping she'll be here soon. As I pause near the driver's door, I take out my phone and text Deacon.

I RAN INTO A CLOSER AT SCHOOL JUST NOW, I write.

WHO? he asks.

REED CASTLE.

YOU OKAY?

YEAH, I write. HE SAID HE'S RESEARCHING AN ASSIGNMENT. INTERESTING TIMING.

TRUE. WE'LL KEEP AN EYE ON HIM. SO . . . HOW HANDSOME DID HE LOOK?

I laugh. VERY.

FIGURES. ARE YOU ON YOUR WAY BACK?

THERE'S MORE, I type, gnawing on my lip. THEY CANCELED THE REST OF THE SCHOOL DAY.

WHY?

THEY SAID IT WAS A MEDICAL EMERGENCY, BUT PEOPLE AROUND ME SAID IT WAS THIS GUY MICAH, I tell him. HE'S ONE OF VIRGINIA'S FRIENDS. I THINK IT WAS A SUICIDE.

WHERE'S VIRGINIA NOW? Deacon asks.

My heart stops dead in my chest. What if it wasn't just Micah? What if . . . ? Oh, God. Virginia might have needed help, and just like with Roderick at the party, I could have let her walk right past me.

I lower the phone, about to run back into the building to

find out if it's true. But just as I look up, I see Virginia walking in my direction. My entire body sighs with relief.

FOUND HER, I type quickly, and then slide my phone into my back pocket and rush ahead.

"Hey," I call, slightly out of breath. "Are you okay? I heard it was Micah?"

She slows her steps and stares at me for a moment, her eyes slightly narrowed as if she's trying to place me. Her hair is perfectly straightened; her clothes look new and stiff. And there isn't even a flicker of recognition in her expression.

"Micah?" she asks, as if she's never heard the name before. She holds out her key ring and unlocks her door. "And who are you again?" she adds. I'm at once offended and concerned.

"I'm Liz," I tell her, pointing to myself awkwardly. "We . . . met Friday. We had dinner and went to a party together."

She turns suddenly, nearly dropping the books in her hands. "We were there?" she asks. "The party on the news?"

Now it's my turn to look perplexed. "Yes," I say. Then I think of the ride home and how she told me to remind her if she forgot about the night. *How could she forget?*

"Virginia, what's going on?" I ask. "You told me you might not remember, but . . . wait, *do* you remember?"

Two news vans turn onto the street, pull into the school lot, and park near us. Quickly, several reporters and people with cameras jump out and begin to set up their equipment.

Virginia opens her car door. "Get in," she tells me, and drops down on the seat and slams her door shut. She starts the engine, and I jog around the car, hoping she won't leave without me. I'm completely taken aback by her behavior, and I don't want her off on her own.

I climb in the passenger side, and without a word Virginia drives away from the school, speeding through a yellow light as we head west. I think about texting Deacon to let him know what's happening, but after the way Virginia thought the waitress was spying on her, I don't want to feed into her paranoia.

I look sideways at her and see how she's paled, even beneath the perfect veneer of her hair and clothes. She's falling apart, no matter how well she tries to hide it.

"You really don't remember Friday night?" I ask as gently as I can.

Virginia shakes her head but keeps her eyes trained on the road. "What exactly did I tell you about my memory?" she asks.

"Nothing. You just told me to remind you if you forgot."

Virginia presses her lips together, and I worry that she's about to cry. But instead she glances over at me. "Will you tell me?" she asks. "Tell me everything about that night. That day. I've never even seen you before, Liz. Never heard of any Micah. So start with one of those."

"Why can't you remember?" I ask, a sudden thought occurring to me.

"I don't know."

Seems Virginia and I have some things in common: memory loss and her father. I doubt it's a coincidence.

Virginia takes the exit onto the freeway, and I see by the

signs that she's heading toward the coast. "Where are we going?" I ask, a little frightened, although not exactly of her.

"Out of town," she says. "It's about an hour away, if you don't mind." She turns to me, seeming concerned that I don't have the time. But she doesn't know that she's the reason I'm here.

"I don't mind," I say.

"Great," she says, and turns back to the road, speeding up. "Now," she says. "When did we meet?"

CHAPTER FIVE

I TELL VIRGINIA ABOUT FINDING HER AT HER VOLLEY-
ball scrimmage, reusing the line about being a new student.
I'm careful with the details, making them seem less important
than they are. My existence in her life should be a red flag, a
random stranger showing up and inserting herself in her social
circle. But Virginia only seems interested in hearing about the
party. She grows quiet when I mention Micah again. She has no
recollection of him at all—like he never existed. It's a shocking
thing to witness.

When I finish telling Virginia about Roderick's death and
the way we ran out of there, she's stoic, looking unmoved—
much like she was after the suicide.

"And that's what happened," I say, studying her for a crack
in her character.

"Thank you," she tells me, watching the road. "This isn't the first time, you know. I'm just lucky you were there. Other people have stopped filling in the blanks for me."

"How often does this happen?" I ask.

"Lately?" She looks over. "I think it's been every other week. My father's a doctor, and he says these are memory blackouts, but nothing to worry about. He claims they're stress-related. But if it were something to worry about, I doubt he'd tell me. He deals in denial."

"What do you mean?"

"Closers," she says with contempt. "Ever hear of them?" She doesn't wait for me to answer. "They're my father's creation. People trained to absorb grief—perpetrate denial. It's predatory and disgusting, even if it started with good intentions."

I want to jump to defend myself, tell her about all the people I've helped, but I can't compromise myself. She obviously doesn't remember that she already mentioned her father to me.

"That denial is killing us," she continues. "But my father thinks otherwise. He's not listening to me." She rubs her face roughly, seeming frustrated. "I keep forgetting things— important things. And I think my father is somehow behind it.

Arthur Pritchard made me forget my past, but could he really have induced her memory loss too? *Would* he do that to his own child?

"What makes you think it's your father?" I ask, prying deeper into Virginia's life.

"My mother died when I was little," she says quietly. "Cancer, they say. But I can't remember much about her, and it bothers me. I know that her death changed my father. I think he's lied to me every day since."

"Lied how?"

"He's taken some of my pictures, switched others around," she says. "I have one photo of my mother, and it's cropped from a larger photo. He says no, but I'm smarter than he thinks. I'm going to beat whatever system he's put in place. I'm going to beat him."

And I know now that I have my opportunity. I don't need to betray Virginia's trust to blackmail her father if she'll help me willingly. I open my mouth to ask if she has anything I can use against her father, when Virginia takes her hand off the wheel and points.

"There it is," she says, nodding ahead. She eases her car to the side of the road in front of a DEAD END sign, and it takes me a moment to find any reason why we're stopped in what looks like the middle of nowhere.

I squint; the weather is foggy out here, this close to the ocean. I notice a small lighthouse. It's not facing the water, though, only a marshlike strip of land.

"Come on," Virginia says, opening her door. "I have to show you something."

I reluctantly climb out of the car, take a look around, and get my bearings. The air is thick, a mixture of salt and seaweed smell. I step over rocks into tan sand, spits of grass popping up throughout.

I follow Virginia and come to stand next to her where she's paused outside the lighthouse. The white paint on the exterior of the building has chipped away, leaving the gray metal to rust in the salty sea air. It's nothing they'd use for tours, but it is a lighthouse. A small, decaying one.

"We call this the End of the World," Virginia says. "A bunch of us used to come here to hang out. Now it's just me. The place was abandoned years ago after a jetty was put up to create the bay. No one even knows it's here anymore. It's not on any maps."

"What happened to the people you'd come here with?" I ask.

"They died."

I widen my eyes, alarmed, even frightened. Virginia walks ahead and climbs the steep steps to the front door. I touch my phone in my pocket for reassurance. I should tell Deacon where I am in case this place is cursed or dangerous. But again I wait, unwilling to break Virginia's trust when I feel like I'm close to getting her help.

The white door has a big bolted padlock, and Virginia fishes through her keys until she finds a small one and slips it into the lock. She glances over her shoulder at me and shrugs guiltily.

"We put this lock on," she explains. "We didn't want anyone else finding it."

"Makes sense," I respond, although I'm scared of what's inside.

Virginia works off the lock and then hooks it on the frame

before using her shoulder to push open the door. From out here it looks pitch black inside, and I'm in no rush to walk into spiderwebs or step on mice.

Virginia notices my reaction and laughs. "It's not bad," she says. "Promise."

"No offense," I say, making my way up the steps cautiously. "But maybe you can go in first."

She smiles, amused, and then walks inside, disappearing from view. I cast an anxious look around the deserted area, suddenly wishing I weren't alone with her—this girl who's connected to so many deaths. But I am here. I am alone. And so the only thing left to do is follow her inside.

I step in the doorway and wait. Once my eyes adjust, I find that Virginia was right. The inside of the lighthouse is small and cramped but relatively clean. There is some sand buildup in the corners, but light filters in from the top of the spiral staircase, where there's a circle of windows. Virginia stands on the first stair as she rummages through her purse until she pulls out a Sharpie. Then she starts up the stairs toward the top.

There is an eerie sense of calm to this place. It doesn't feel abandoned, it feels claimed, and as I make my way up the stairs, I see why. There is writing on the walls—literally. Something like journal entries written in different-color markers and pens. They're dated, going back to last year. I pause midway up the staircase when I notice the handwriting of one of the entries.

My breath catches, and I reach out to run my finger over the penmanship. I recognize it. It's from Catalina—she was here. I look accusingly at Virginia, as if my entire life is all somehow her fault. I find her on the top landing, scribbling notes on the wall. While she's distracted, I turn back to Catalina's note and read.

> Isaac wants to help, but he can't. I feel it now, just like Virginia said I would. She was right. It's almost like a virus, the way it's infected me. The way I've become obsessed with it. It's like I'm twisting the knife in my chest to feel more pain. I invite more pain. I'm addicted to the pain. But what scares me most of all is that the more I feel, the more I want of it.

There's a catch in my throat as I read the dying words of the girl I closed for. I feel the loss her family felt. What Isaac felt. Catalina was here, alive. Asking for help. When I turn to Virginia again, tears are stinging my eyes.

"You knew she was sick," I say, my voice echoing. Virginia looks down at me, surprised, and I motion toward the writing. "You knew Catalina wanted to kill herself. Why didn't you stop her? Why didn't you tell anybody?"

Virginia lowers her arm that's holding the Sharpie, her face going slack. "I don't know who Catalina is," she says. "But I've read that note a million times. I've forgotten her, Liz. Just like Friday night. She's part of my empty space." She pauses and looks around at the words on the wall. "Just like all of these." She tilts her head, examining me. "But . . . how do you know her? Who is she?"

I can't tell her the truth, so I sidestep it. I glance around at all the notes. These would be pages and pages of journal entries, but with different handwriting, from different people. "What is this place, Virginia?" I ask her.

She straightens her posture defensively. "This is where I keep what's left," she says. "When I forget, I come here to read and remember. But it's not enough. Can you imagine . . . ?" Her voice cracks. "Can you imagine what that's like? I'm *disappearing*, Liz. Soon I won't even know who I am anymore. I won't even exist."

Her words wound me, not only because they're terrifying, but because I don't have to imagine them: I've lived them.

Virginia points to the spot where she was writing. "This is about the party, the story you just told me. I'm going to keep it here so I won't forget."

I swallow hard and go up the stairs, keeping my distance from Virginia to glance at the writing. She has, indeed, written nearly word for word what I told her in the car. It feels suddenly strange, as if I'm the one on the wall. A ghost, like Catalina. I turn away to scan the other writings, all of them bleak. These are just memories—they're horror and sadness. They're desperation.

The walls surrounding me begin to take on a life of their

own. All at once I'm having trouble breathing. I put my hand on the railing to steady myself.

"Are you claustrophobic?" Virginia asks, concerned.

I shake my head no. At least, I didn't think I was.

She comes over to where I'm standing and puts her arm across my shoulders. "There's more room at the top," she says, leading me up the stairs. "This place can be overwhelming at first."

We get to the top, and I'm flooded with light. All around the circular platform are windows, and even on a misty Oregon morning the light shines through this small space. I take a breath. Virginia leans against the wall. Strangely, there's no writing up here.

"I come to the End of the World when I feel like I'm missing a piece," she says. "And when I see them all together, I realize I'm missing a lot. Half of these don't make sense." She points to the writing below. "They're only a piece of a larger truth."

She notices me scanning the bare walls around us.

"I don't write up here," she says, running her palm along the paint. "This is where I find hope." She smiles, and turns to face out the window. "It's a blank slate here, filled with possibility."

The observation deck overlooks the dried-up land that used to be part of an ocean, a pile of huge rocks on either side redirecting the water. But this high up, it's almost like we really are at the end of the world. Not a car or a person in sight. It's lovely.

I turn to Virginia, seeing the hope she mentioned reflected

in her expression. And I can't do this anymore; I can't deceive her. I see now that she's being put through something horrible, something cruel. I'm no better than Arthur Pritchard if I continue to lie to her. We can work together; we have the same goal. We want answers to our pasts.

"I'm sorry," I say in a quiet voice. My heart begins to pound at the threat of my impending confession. Virginia's eyes flick to mine.

"For what?"

"Lying to you."

She flinches and takes her hand from the wall. She clenches it into a fist at her side. It's an unexpected reaction that alarms me. "About the party?" she demands.

"No, that was all true. It's me. My name's not Liz, and I'm not from Eugene." I swallow hard. "Last week I was in Lake Oswego, and I knew of Catalina because—"

"Lake Oswego?" Virginia repeats, taking in a sharp breath. "Did you know Mitchel Caprice?"

I'm stunned at the mention of Aaron's last assignment, stunned that she remembers him but not Catalina. "Sort of," I tell her.

"Do you know what happened to him?" she asks.

"Yeah. He . . . he killed himself."

Virginia's lips pull taut as she holds back the start of a cry. "I knew it," she whispers. "Of course I knew it." She shakes her head. "I just didn't want to believe it."

"You remember him?" I ask.

She nods. "Yeah," she says miserably. "I do. I met Mitchel in Lake Oswego. We were dating, but I kept it from my dad. But then . . . Mitchel disappeared. Didn't return my calls or texts. I suspected, but . . . now I know for sure."

"I'm sorry to be the one to tell you," I say, feeling guilty. As if she hasn't been through enough today.

"I already knew," she repeats. "Last week I had a feeling, a terrible feeling. I searched my father's files and found his name. Saw that a closer was attached to his case. That's how I knew he was dead. But I couldn't show even an instant of pain. I was scared I'd forget him if I did. I was scared of getting the memory of him taken."

She studies my expression, and I feel her grief. Hiding your pain—it'll wear you down. Wear you away.

"But now," she says, her voice taking on an edge, "I'm wondering what role you have in this. You knew Mitchel and Catalina." She points to the note on the wall. "Did you know me?"

"No," I say simply.

It only takes a second, but my heart pounds as I watch the reality fall over her.

She gasps in a breath and backs into the wall. "You're a closer, aren't you?" she asks. "That's why you're here. Did they send you in to close out my life? My father thinks I'm going to die, doesn't he?"

"No," I say, holding up my hands up in front of me as I take a step toward her. "The grief department has nothing to do with me being here. Your father didn't send me. But he *is* why

I'm here. I came looking for you first, but not to close out your life. And honestly, that's not how closing works."

"I know how closing fucking works," she snaps.

"Then you'd know that we never meet our assignments while they're alive."

"Maybe your advisor considers me a lost cause." Her eyes have gone wild, and although I understand why she's upset, it suddenly occurs to me that Virginia might be dangerous. People do unexpected things when backed into a corner like this.

"No," I say, trying to reassure her. "I don't have an advisor. I'm not a closer anymore. I swear it."

Virginia crosses her arms over her chest, her anger turning to bitterness, as if she doesn't believe a word I'm saying. "So you get out of my father's employment and then come to where he lives? If that's true, then I wouldn't say you're very smart, Liz— or whatever your name is."

"My name's Quinn," I tell her. "And you're probably right. But your father took something from me, and I can't move on until I get it back. I don't know *how* to move on." She lowers her arms, my confession seeming to ease her fear slightly. Her face pales, and her eyes drift past me to the stairs.

"I want to leave now," she says in monotone. "I want you to leave. Please go outside. I need to write something first."

I debate asking her what she's about to write, but ultimately I figure I've wrecked her day enough. Besides, she's most likely writing the truth about me—that she shouldn't trust me. The least I can do is give her some privacy.

Feeling ashamed, I start down the stairs, reading the writing as I pass. Nothing new jumps out, just more of the same. I touch Catalina's handwriting one last time before I get to the bottom. I'm sure Virginia's father has no idea this place exists. All her inner thoughts are hidden. It seems to me like Virginia is finding a way to beat the system. And that I can admire.

CHAPTER SIX

THE MINUTE I'M OUTSIDE, I SEE THAT THE FOG HAS burned off, and the first bits of true sunshine in a while beam down on me. I take a second to tilt my face toward the sky, absorbing the warmth on my cheeks. It feels good—pure. It centers me.

I check over my shoulder to make sure Virginia is still inside and then I take out my phone to text Deacon. With my back turned to the lighthouse, I glide my thumbs quickly over the words.

THINGS ARE NOT EXACTLY GOING TO PLAN, I type.

As if he's been waiting for me, he responds immediately. YOU HAD A PLAN?

FAIR POINT, I write. WELL, I'M CURRENTLY IN THE MIDDLE OF NOWHERE WITH VIRGINIA. AND THIS SITUATION IS FAR MORE SCREWED UP THAN I THOUGHT. I THINK HER DAD'S BEEN ERASING

HER MEMORY. I pause. AND I SHOULD PROBABLY MENTION THAT SHE KNOWS I'M A CLOSER.

The text bubble pops up before I even finish typing. YOU TOLD HER?!! Deacon asks.

I DIDN'T WANT TO BE A LIAR.

OUCH, he writes back. Although I didn't mean the line to hurt him, I can see why he feels the comment was directed at him. It might be a long time before we can get past that.

I'M NOT SURE WHERE TO GO FROM HERE WITH VIRGINIA, I tell him, getting back on topic. IF SHE CAN'T REMEMBER HER ROLE IN CATALINA'S DEATH, THEN I'M NOT SURE I CAN LEVERAGE HER AGAINST HER FATHER. I ALSO DON'T WANT TO MAKE HER WORSE. WHAT SHOULD I DO?

COME HOME.

My lips twitch with a smile. He said "home," as if that's a real place. As if he's my home. But it still isn't much as far as advice goes. BE BACK SOON.

I turn off the phone, slip it back into my pocket, and walk to the car. I've exposed myself to one of the most dangerous people in town. All Virginia would have to do is mention my name to her father. He could bring the entire grief department down on me. He could hand me over, and then who knows what would happen. I wasn't thinking clearly. I should have just kept picking until I found something I could use—but I let my conscience get the better of me. Now I might have lost my only chance at finding my identity.

Virginia appears in the doorway of the lighthouse and

closes the door behind her. She sets the padlock back on and then walks in my direction. She's clearing tears from her eyes, and I feel terrible for putting her in this state. She would have been better off if I hadn't shown up at all today.

Virginia unlocks the car doors and we both climb in, silent. She turns on the engine and looks over her shoulder before backing up and making a wide U-turn. Her jaw is clenched, and she acts like I'm not in the car. When we're back on the freeway, I look sideways at her.

"I didn't mean to upset you," I say.

"I'm sure you didn't," she replies, "but you'll understand if I decide not to speak to you anymore. I'd rather not give you easy access to my life."

"Virginia," I say, frustrated with our misunderstanding. "I'm not here to close for you."

"Maybe you should be," she says quietly.

My lips part in alarm, and I fear that she's finally breaking. And if she is—it's my fault. "If you need help, I can—"

"What I need," she interrupts, "is for everyone to *stop* helping me. I want to deal with my life. I want to live my life. But I'm losing control over it. I'm losing pieces of it, and I want them back. I want to be whole."

And then, suddenly, I have my first real plan. A way for both of us to get what we want. A way to do it without hurting Virginia any more than I have to. I watch the side of her face, hope building in my chest. "What if I can help you find out what happened?" I ask.

Virginia turns to me, her eyes wide but untrusting. "How?" she asks.

"I think your father really is behind your memory loss," I tell her. "If we can figure out why, then maybe we can find out what he's taken. My partners and I are great at finding information, and we'll—"

"Partners," she repeats, and then turns away, disgusted. I'm quick to try to reel her back in.

"None of us are closers anymore," I say, "and we don't plan to stay here. It's just . . . I need something first."

Virginia sniffs her discontent. "Of course you do. What is it? What do you want in return?"

"Once we figure out what he's done to you . . . you have to let me use it. I need it as leverage to convince him to give back what he's stolen from me."

Virginia looks over. "What does he have?"

"My identity."

Virginia turns abruptly back to the road, the lines on her forehead deepening as she seems to think it over. "So you don't remember either?" she asks. "And it was him? *He* erased you?"

"I don't know what was done, but yes, he admitted to manipulating my memory. I don't remember who I am . . . who I *was*. He placed me in a home when I was a child, and I was raised there under a different identity. I only found out the truth last week. That's part of why I ran away from the grief department. I can't trust them, Virginia. The grief department, your father, *my* father—they all conspired to hide the truth from me. I want to know who I am."

She's quiet for a long moment, probably absorbing the fact that her father might be more of a monster than she thought. "How do you suggest we find that information?" she asks, her voice low.

"You mentioned earlier that after Mitchel disappeared, you searched your father's files and found a closer attached to his case. I need access to those files. All of his files." She looks at me like she thinks I'm crazy, but I keep talking.

"Get us a way in and we'll find your memories—the real ones," I say. "I just need a pass code, a key to an office—anything can help. We can take it from there."

Her expression has softened, and as she turns away, I think that maybe she doesn't believe that we can help her.

"Please," I beg, my voice hitching with desperation. "Please help me get my life back."

And it could be out of the kindness of her heart, or it could be the fact that our shared amnesia seems to comfort her, but Virginia takes one of her hands off the steering wheel and reaches to grip my fingers. She holds my hand like that, and for a moment there's a surge in my heart. A bond. She doesn't speak a word.

When she unclasps my hand again, staring straight ahead, I think we've agreed upon an unspoken mission to help each other. The loneliness in my soul abates slightly—the promise of our friendship a bit of hope in our otherwise dire situation.

*　　*　　*

After picking up Deacon's car at the school, I go back to the hotel room, Virginia's number programmed into my phone. I open the door and find Deacon sitting at the table, a bunch of papers scattered in front of him and his phone pressed to his ear. Just the sight of him relaxes me, covers up the fear I came in with. Deacon holds up his finger to let me know he'll be another second; his eyes study me before he turns back to his papers.

"Yes, I'm still here," he says into the phone. "That would be amazing, Martha. I really appreciate your help." He chuckles, and I recognize the charming and oh-so-fake tone. Rather than annoy me, it makes me miss our easy banter. It makes me miss us. "Well, that's kind of you to say," Deacon tells the woman. "I think you have a nice voice too."

I lift my eyebrow, letting him know he's laying it on a little thicker than necessary, but he just winks at me. I play along and blow him a quick kiss, and without missing a beat, Deacon snatches it out of the air and pretends to eat it. I laugh but then cover my mouth when he frowns at me, turning away with the phone still at his ear.

"All right, Martha," he says. "You have a—oh . . . sure. I'm free. I'll stop in. See you then." He hangs up and then exhales heavily and looks over at me.

"Did you just make a date?" I ask.

"It's only lunch," he says, and then shakes his head like he can't believe I thought he'd actually go.

"I'm just saying it's not the most ethical way to get information."

"Oh, yes." He rolls his eyes. "Our ethics." Deacon sets his phone on the bed and comes to a stop in front of me. "I've had a terrible day," he says, and when I reach to touch his arm out of concern, he tries to smile. "I didn't even get to finish my hot chocolate."

But he can't keep the mixture of fear and relief out of his expression, and his smile breaks. "I've been out of my mind with worry," he whispers, dropping all pretenses. "Are you okay?"

I nod, and Deacon immediately pulls me into a hug, wrapping me up. I close my eyes, my cheek against his chest. I wanted to forget the darkness of the day, but I realize I can't. It's always with me, screaming to be let out.

"The incident at the school has been all over the news," Deacon says, his breath warm in my hair. "That kid Micah . . . he was in tenth grade. He's dead."

I'm glad I didn't witness his death, and just as soon as I think that, I'm attacked by guilt for being grateful. It's selfish. I really am a coldhearted closer.

Deacon runs the back of his hand over my hair and then straightens, gazing down at me. "How did it end up with Virginia?" he asks. "How fucked are we?"

I step out of his arms, immediately missing the heat, and go to sit on the edge of the mattress. "I told her everything," I say.

Deacon stares at me. "Okay," he breathes out. "Everything everything?"

"I told her I was a closer and that her father brought me to the grief department and helped fake my life for the past eleven years. I asked for her help in return for us helping her."

Deacon tilts his head. "Wow—so yeah. All the everythings. Now, what did you promise her exactly?"

"She's having blackouts. Big pieces of her memory have been wiped out. So I promised that we'd find out what her father has done and retrieve her memories for her."

"Wait, what?" Deacon asks. "How are we supposed to do that? You think Arthur is just going to tell us? You can't promise someone a thing like that."

"I had no choice. She was ready to cut off ties with me. But she has a clear way into her father's files; she's gotten into them before. She agreed to try to get us that access."

Deacon folds his hands and locks them behind his neck as he looks at the ceiling, thinking it over.

"But there's more," I tell him. At this, Deacon meets my eyes, concern painting his features. "She's not well, Deacon. Whatever her father is doing, it's breaking her. And it scares me."

Deacon drops his arms to his sides and comes to sit next to me on the bed. "Tell me about her memory loss," he says. "Any specifics you can think of?"

"The missing pieces seem to be tied to the times around traumatic events. Deaths. She didn't remember the party on Friday, didn't remember Micah—maybe because he was at the party too? I'm not sure. And she doesn't remember Catalina at all. She keeps notes of her memories so that she can revisit them, but she can't recall them on her own."

"Quinn," he says. "That reminds me of . . ." He pauses, furrowing his brow.

"Of what?" I ask.

"Well . . . of you."

"I guess, but it's hard to compare. I was only a kid, so Arthur couldn't have erased all that much."

"No, not that," Deacon says. I can see that he's putting something together in his head, figuring out a puzzle. His seriousness makes my heart beat faster with anxiety.

"Are you talking about my last assignment?" I'm embarrassed by how I completely lost touch with reality when I was Catalina. I couldn't remember which identity was mine. I believed I was Catalina Barnes, and then I believed I was all of them—all the girls that I'd portrayed. It terrifies me that I got to that point, and I'm ashamed that I wasn't stronger.

Deacon winces, knowing it was a terrible time—for both of us. But he did help me through it. He reminded me of who I was, or at least who I thought I was.

"I hate to bring this up," Deacon says, leaning forward. "But I'm talking about the day we broke up."

There's a twist in my stomach. He hurt me that day; he broke my heart. And even though I know about his deal with Arthur Pritchard now, it *still* hurts me. I cross my arms over my chest, trying to shield myself from the wound it reopens.

Deacon watches me a long moment, his eyes slightly narrowed. "I can't believe I didn't realize before. I thought maybe you just didn't want to talk about it."

I lower my arms, a rush of adrenaline flooding through me. "What do you mean?" I ask.

"Do you remember coming to my place?"

"Of course," I say. "Do you think I could have forgotten? Because I'm pretty sure I've obsessively thought about it for eight and a half months."

Deacon swallows hard, like he's already figured out the answer. "Do you remember your nosebleed?" he asks.

There is a horrible and sudden reaction under my skin, as if I've been touched by dry ice, dissolving me away. I quickly go over the day in my mind, but . . . no. I *didn't* have a nosebleed. I went to Deacon's apartment, and he told me he didn't want to see me anymore. I begged him not to do it, not to break up with me. He shut the door in my face.

"Are you sure *you're* remembering correctly?" I ask.

Deacon glances down at the floor, looking guilty. "I can't believe I didn't see it," he says in a quiet voice. "Arthur told me—"

I scoff at the name, and Deacon gives me an apologetic glance before continuing.

"Arthur told me that you were becoming too attached to your assignments and that I had to look out for erratic behavior. I told him you were fine. But . . . that day . . . you showed up at my door, frantic. You said we were running away, and then you started grabbing my clothes out of the drawers. You weren't yourself, and I was worried that you'd found out about my meeting with Arthur. I felt like a fucking monster. That was when I knew I had to step back from you. I told you we should stop seeing each other, but you argued with me, saying I didn't understand. And then your nose started bleeding. Next thing I knew, you were hysterical. I had to call your dad."

My face stings with the absolute lies he's telling me. At least, they sound like lies, because that's not the way I remember it at all. But he wouldn't lie to me now, not about this. "And then what?" I ask.

"Your dad showed up. He told me it was my fault, that I was doing this to you—he didn't know about my arrangement, but it proved what I was worried about: I thought I was hurting you.

"You didn't want to leave with your dad," Deacon continues, "but he told me he could help. I had no choice but to believe him. At that time, I thought he loved you."

I flinch involuntarily, and Deacon apologizes. "I didn't mean it like that," he says quickly, but I tell him to go on with his story. The question of my father's love isn't even the worst of my problems.

"Then he ordered me out of the room," Deacon says. "I . . ." His expression crumbles, and he bites hard on his lip to keep himself together. "Your dad told me that if I really wanted to help, I needed to get away from you. He said I would end up killing you. So I left the room. I shut myself in my bedroom, and then you stopped screaming. I thought he was right—I thought it was me. The next time I saw you, a few days later, you hated me."

"I've never hated you," I say.

"It felt like you hated me," he replies. "But at least you seemed better. So I knew I had to stay away . . . at least in some capacity. I couldn't stay away altogether. You and I have never talked about that day, and I realize now that it's because you don't remember it."

I look at my hands clenched into fists in my lap. I search for even a tiny glimmer of the moments he mentioned, but they're not there. I remember going to Deacon's door. I remember him telling me we were over. I remember crying and calling my dad. But as I sit here, I'm beginning to doubt the memories at all. Something about them feels hollow the more I inspect them.

"They've manipulated my memories," I say without looking up. "Not just when I was a child, either. It's the same thing they're doing to Virginia. And that means . . . that means, the other day, that memory I had of Marie—it was real." I lift my head, betrayal striking me in the chest. "Marie knew all along, Deacon. She was helping him erase me."

CHAPTER SEVEN

DEACON CONTACTS MYRA AND GETS AARON'S NEW number and then tells Myra to ditch her phone. Deacon and Aaron talk, making plans for how to track down our former advisor.

Marie is a liar, an accomplice. But if anyone has the goods to blackmail Arthur, and possibly save both me and Virginia, it's her. We need her help, even if she's part of the reason I'm in danger in the first place.

Deacon paces the motel room, occasionally giving me encouraging looks, as if he's worried about my emotional state.

He pauses and turns away. "What do you mean, 'nothing'?" he says into the phone. "Can't you trail her from when she left the apartment? Uh-huh. No." He glances over his shoulder at me. "No, Tom didn't mention where she could be. Yes"—he smiles a little—"he is an asshole."

Deacon cracks his neck, listening on the line a little longer, even though I can tell that Aaron has had zero luck tracking down Marie. She's probably better than any of us at disappearing. She's definitely better at lying.

"All right," Deacon says into the phone with a heavy sigh. "Do what you can. Yeah"—a little laugh—"love you too, man."

Deacon takes the phone away from his ear and clicks it off, tossing it onto the bed. He puts his hands on his hips, looking frustrated. "He says she doesn't want to be found— that he thinks she's actively hiding from us. He's trying everything, but he's not hopeful. He also said he thinks we should disappear too."

"He's right," I say. "But we're not nearly smart enough to do that."

Deacon groans, running his palm over his face. "We *need* Marie," he says, sounding helpless. "Why is she doing this to us? Why won't she help us?" He sits on the bed across from me, looking betrayed. And it's in his hurt that I can recognize my own. I never had a chance against the grief department— there were too many people working against me. The thought is heavy and hard to take, and I'm losing myself in the hopelessness of it.

"Hey," I call out. Deacon slowly lifts his eyes to mine, his expression stricken. "Hey," I repeat more softly, and stand up.

Maybe if I take away his pain, it will lessen my own. I cross to the other bed, stopping between Deacon's knees. He leans in to me, wrapping his arms around the backs of my thighs, gazing up at me.

"I failed you," he says. "I could have stopped this; I should have seen it. And now we don't even know what they were doing to you. I let them. I let them experiment on you."

"You didn't know," I say, moving to sit next to him, the side of my thigh pressed to his. He's right—he did fail me. But I can't blame him for this. The most trusted people in my life manipulated me. Erased parts of my past. I hate the vulnerability that they've left me with.

Deacon sinks down as if ashamed and rests his cheek on my shoulder, his hand casually on my leg. His fingers brush the skin just inside my knee, and it sends a shiver up my body. I close my eyes. Although he didn't mean to, Deacon has brought a new feeling to the surface.

I want to feel powerful. I want to be in control of my life. I turn so that our mouths are closer, and I reach up to place my palm on his cheek. His hand slowly glides over my thigh, and I pull back to look at him.

Deacon's eyes are heavy-lidded, and he licks his bottom lip before he breathes my name. His fingertips dig into my thigh, and at the sudden pressure I lean forward and press my mouth hungrily to his. His lips are soft, even as I'm rough against him.

I pull off his shirt and kiss him again, his skin hot under my hands. I'm completely lost in a moment that is everything—and nothing. It's easy. No thoughts can break through the absolute desire burning me up. Soon we're falling back on the bed. Deacon kisses my neck, my jaw. He murmurs how much he loves me over and over.

And then it's just us—naked and alone. Then it's just him holding his weight above me.

We're careful like always, but our hearts are threadbare as we give in to each other. Broken and honest. Both of us with regrets and old secrets. A terrifying future ahead of us.

But just like I'd hoped, the desire consumes me and blocks out the fear, sending it to the edges of my consciousness, where it will wait for later.

For now I let myself love Deacon recklessly, stupidly, and completely.

I turn my face in to Deacon's shoulder, kissing it, before snuggling up against him. I slide my thigh over his, closing my eyes. I listen to the beat of his heart—slow and steady.

"Well, we made up pretty quickly," I say, and laugh.

"Uh, it was two full days," Deacon replies, his voice scratchy. "Believe me."

I run my fingers down his chest. Surely our friendship could have continued platonically, but in the face of everything we're seeing—why? Why force ourselves apart anymore? I'm tired of holding back, of always doing what's right for other people. I'm going to take what's mine. I'm going to save my damn self.

And I'm going to have sex with my boyfriend if I want to.

The phone buzzes and Deacon glances at the side table, but it's not there. He curses and starts looking through the bedding as I tuck the sheet under my arms. He jumps up and checks under the bed, lifting the phone up to me triumphantly when he finds it.

He answers, scanning me playfully as if he's thinking about coming back to bed instead. But then his eyes snap away in response to something said on the other end of the phone line. He stands.

"Yeah, I'm here," he says, bending to grab his clothes from the floor. He dresses, balancing the phone on his shoulder as he pulls on his pants. "When?"

I want to be one of those annoying people who asks questions while he's still on the phone, but I wait, my heart in my throat. I quickly put on my clothes and smooth back my hair. My nail catches on an extension and tears it out. Frustrated, I unsnap all the clips and toss them aside, enjoying the freedom of my short hair, the cool air on my neck. I don't want to be Liz Major anymore.

Deacon hangs up the phone and lowers it to his side, turning to stare at me. "That was my contact at city hall," he says. "They're moving up the meeting to tonight. She says it's going to get passed. They're going to start a mandatory evaluation of all of the teenagers in the district."

"What?" I ask. "On what authority?"

"Seems there's precedent. The council cites a court case

that upheld mandatory vaccines in order to stop the spread of infectious diseases. To support the connection, they have a doctor claiming that this suicide cluster has mutated. He's says it's infectious."

"Is that possible?" I ask. A behavior that influences copycat behavior is not the same as an infection. There can't be a true link. Can there?

Deacon rubs his chin like he's thinking. "I don't know," he says. "I guess we'll have to ask Arthur Pritchard. He's their medical expert."

My head spins, all the coincidences and information colliding together to make a jumbled mess of my brain. Everyone could be lying. Everyone could be trying to help. I don't know which is true—maybe it's both. But as I watch him, I know that I'm all in with Deacon now. We're in this together. And I'm about to ask him to help me with a really, really dumb idea. That's love.

"You said the meeting is tonight?" I ask Deacon, pulling on my sneakers.

"Yes," he says slowly. "But we're not going. I was being sarcastic when I said we should ask Arthur."

I walk over to the table and pick up my phone, then quickly find Virginia's number. She agreed to help us earlier, so long as we helped her. I hope she meant it.

"Hello?" she answers.

I'm immediately struck with panic, afraid I'm asking too much too soon. But we can't miss out on this chance.

"It's Quinn," I say, not reassured when her end of the phone line goes completely silent. Deacon has his hands on his hips as he waits to see what I'm planning. "Look," I tell Virginia, feigning confidence, "I know I've lied to you, but I meant it when I said I wanted to help you. But we have to move tonight. Are you in or not?"

She pauses so long that I pull the phone from my ear to check that the line hasn't gone dead. Then I hear her clear her throat. "What do you want to do?" she asks.

I smile. It's a small victory even if I don't know the bigger implications. "Does your father keep any files at home?" I ask. I think back to the mess I found in Marie's apartment, files spread everywhere.

"He has a home office," Virginia says cautiously. "I'm not sure how much he keeps in there, but it is where I found the closer information for Mitchel."

"That's good," I say. "Does he access his work e-mail from there?"

"Yeah, I guess."

"Then this is important: Is there any way you can find out that e-mail password? Set up a camera or something?"

She laughs as if she thinks I'm joking. "Uh, I could try," she says. "I mean, I'm not going all 007, but I have a good idea of where to start."

"Perfect." I take a deep breath and sit down at the table. I look over, and Deacon flashes me a small smile as if he can sense how deranged this plan will really be. I sometimes forget how well he can read me. I turn away, cradling the phone to my ear.

"There's just one other thing," I tell Virginia. "We're going to break into your house tonight."

Surprisingly, Virginia was more than accommodating. She agreed to leave the side door to the garage unlocked while she went to the city hall meeting with her father. She also texted me the password to his office e-mail, although she didn't say how she got it.

Deacon and I grab a couple of sandwiches and then head over to the other side of Roseburg, where the Pritchards' modest two-story house is located. Deacon parks down the street and plays a game on his phone while we wait for Arthur and Virginia to leave. I bite my thumbnail, watching the garage nervously. It's crossed my mind a few times that this could be a setup, but there doesn't seem to be much point if it is. Then again, I have no idea of Arthur's true intentions. But I hope to solve this mystery tonight. This might finally be it.

"I love you," Deacon says, not taking his attention from the game, "but you're being incredibly annoying right now." He smiles and then glances over, motioning to my thumb. I realize that the clicking of the biting must have been driving him nuts, and I lower my arm.

"Aren't you nervous?" I ask. "What if they don't go to the meeting? What if they do, and we break into this guy's house, get caught, and go to jail—or worse, go home?"

"Now, how can we fail with your brand of optimism on our side?"

I swat his shoulder and he laughs, abandoning his game and setting his phone in the cup holder.

"We're going to be okay," Deacon says a little more seriously. "And I hope none of your concern is guilt, because you have every right to break into this asshole's office. He owes you."

"How can I feel guilty when you have such a moral conscience?" I respond. Deacon hums out his lack of caring and leans over to kiss me. I put my hand on his cheek and kiss him again.

Movement steals my attention and I turn, making Deacon's kiss land on the corner of my mouth instead. The white garage door at the Pritchard house goes up, and both Deacon and I instinctively sink down in our seats, watching Arthur back out of the driveway. There are two heads in the car, so I assume Virginia is with him.

We sit silently until we're sure they're gone, and then Deacon turns to me, a flash of absolute exhilaration in his eyes. "It's—" he starts.

"Don't you dare say 'it's go time.'"

He snaps his jaw shut. I smile at him, glad he's here to help temper my nerves. I wish I weren't scared. Deacon's right—Arthur owes me. I'm not just afraid of getting caught. I'm afraid of what I'll find.

CHAPTER EIGHT

DEACON AND I WALK DOWN THE BLOCK, DOING WHAT we can to be completely unnoticeable, to dissolve into the background. There isn't anyone outside that we notice, but we don't want to turn and check more thoroughly because that would draw suspicion.

We slip around the side of the house and find that the garage door is indeed unlocked. So far so good. With one last cautious look toward the driveway, Deacon and I enter the garage and find our way inside the house.

Although I have lived with a doctor most of my life, our home was mostly normal-looking. But this house . . . it's like being in a doctor's *office*. And I'm not the least bit surprised.

We enter through the kitchen. It looks recently remodeled, with white marble counters, whitewashed cabinets, and white tiled floors. I'm struck immediately by the smell of cleaning products; the place is immaculate. I lean over the sink in hopes of finding a dirty dish to prove he's human. Nothing. It's creepy.

"Holy shit," Deacon says, looking around. "Do you think they have a house cleaner, or is Pritchard an uptight prick?"

"Not sure," I say. "But if he's this meticulous, I bet he keeps great files."

"And possibly a body wrapped in plastic in the basement," Deacon replies with a pointed look. I laugh and head toward another part of the house.

Virginia didn't mention where the home office was, so we start opening and closing doors, discovering a bathroom and two bedrooms before finding the door that leads into a modest-size study with a massive wood-carved desk near the window.

This room isn't white. It's rich and full of books, even a bit crowded. Interesting that his own personal space is so rich, while the world he has his daughter live in is completely sanitized.

I quickly check the desk drawers while Deacon checks the file cabinets. Neither of us finds anything out of the ordinary. I sit in the wheeled desk chair, and Deacon grabs a second chair from the corner of the room, and we both sit at the computer.

"Here we go," Deacon mumbles.

I shake the mouse to bring the monitor to life, and the screen bathes both of us in blue light. Deacon sets a timer on his phone, counting down an hour, an agreed-upon deadline. I take out my phone, and while holding it in one hand, I type in the password Virginia sent.

The screen unlocks, and both Deacon and I breathe out a relieved sound. I imagine that the password is a combination of a nickname and a birthday, and I wonder how Virginia feels being the key to the memories her father locked away.

I look sideways at Deacon and he flashes me an *I can't believe it fucking worked* smile. I turn back to the computer and begin to scan through Arthur's folders, trying to find one that might be related to us.

"What about that one?" Deacon says, pointing to a folder icon labeled SC STUDIES.

I double-click it, and at first the documents are hard to read, some of the words redacted. Luckily, the complicated terms relate back to my training in the grief department, so after a slight learning curve the sentences start to make sense.

These are studies from outbreaks of suicide clusters in the past, from the United States, Germany, Russia, and Finland. The studies are from ten years ago and list suicide as the number one cause of death in people aged fifteen to forty-seven in developed countries. But always, seemingly with no cause, the clusters would fade away. Life returned to normal. There hasn't been another outbreak in years.

Until now.

Deacon scoots closer to read the screen, giving me a wary look. The last file describes a suicide cluster right here in Roseburg, but that's not the whole picture. The study reveals that the Pacific Northwest is only a high point of a problem spreading across the country. Just here in Oregon, the latest numbers show that the rate of death in persons under eighteen has increased to one in five.

I draw back from the computer, stunned by the statistic.

The idea is horrifying. Impossible. How have they kept it so quiet? Virginia was right about all of her friends dying.

I hear Deacon's throat click as he swallows, and he turns to me. "So this really is an epidemic," he says in a low voice. "This really is happening."

The validation of it is heartbreaking. As closers, we understand death; we know what's at stake and how it affects families. "This is the worst thing imaginable," I say. "Maybe that's why Arthur wanted closers to help. We'd want to stop this too."

Deacon nods slowly, his skin tinted from the light of the screen. In silence we continue clicking through more files. We find several studies from the CDC, a few on past treatments—including lobotomies, the pros and cons. Surely, that's not Arthur's plan. Despite society's previous failing on mental health care, I refuse to believe they'd go back to that archaic practice.

And then I find a subfolder labeled THE REMEDY.

The world goes into slow motion, my finger frozen on the edge of the mouse. This could be it, could be everything, or nothing; I could walk away and avoid both options. I can choose to not go any deeper into the rabbit hole. I feel Deacon look sideways at me, but he doesn't say a word. It's time for some truth. I dive headfirst and click.

The first file is a list of closers throughout the Pacific North-west, leading all the way up into Washington. I find my name still listed as active, but there is no notation to signify that I'm not Quinlan McKee at all. No notation that I was ever anyone else. I'm flooded with disappointment, but I continue on. I check for Reed's name and find him listed as an active closer in Tillamook. There's nothing to make me think he was lying when I saw him in the school parking lot. Deacon's and Aaron's names are both labeled inactive. I find Roger's name in a column for Eugene, but there's a notation that reads "special assignment only."

Of the thirty-five names listed, two of them are ruled sui-cides, one unknown. An annotation mentions that the rate of suicide in closers is much lower than the general population.

The next file is a transition plan that details the position of a closer and the additional training needed to become a han-dler. There will be more therapy courses, but mostly the addi-tions are minor compared to what we went through to become closers in the first place. I was right: We're the best choice to help Arthur. We're overqualified. And we're unaffected by the epidemic—at least not at the same staggering rate.

I read over the purpose of the handlers, slightly uneasy with Deacon next to me. I wonder how many of these apply to him. "'Handlers help facilitate the role of the counselors, and in some cases forge bonds with patients to help break the cycle of self-harm. They monitor the public, looking for signs of erratic behavior, trying to predict where the next outbreak will happen.'"

I sit back in the chair, thinking that it's unethical to fake relationships with people, but of course it's not any less ethical than what we do with the grief department. I'm a total hypocrite. But I take some solace in the fact that clients willingly signed up. It doesn't seem that handlers give that same option to their assignments.

Deacon rolls his shoulders and cracks his neck, clearly uncomfortable. When I glance over at him, he's apologetic. "I didn't do all that," he says. "I monitored you, but there was no extra training. No faking bonds. I didn't pretend to love you. I just did."

"I know."

He smiles at this, and we both turn to the computer. This isn't what I was looking for. Deacon takes the mouse and starts clicking through faster.

"Let's see if we can find something about you," he says, sounding impatient.

I let him search while I glance around the room. Books on psychology, psychotherapy, and the classics—including *Frankenstein*—line the bookshelves. It's not a stretch to imagine that I'm a lot like the creature in the book, coming after the person who made me. It remains to be seen if I'll want to destroy him, though.

Other than handlers, I have no idea what Arthur's solution is to the suicide outbreak. A mandate for therapy is irrational, but if I've learned anything in the past week, it's that rationality seems to be out the window in the face of fear. And this epidemic has everyone scared.

When I hear Deacon cuss, I turn back to the screen.

"There's nothing here," he says. "How can you be completely off the books? How did he hide you so well?"

"I guess he knows how to keep secrets," I say. Deacon looks at the time on his phone—we're down to twenty minutes—and stands up from the chair.

"I'm going to check the other rooms," he says. "But then we should go. The last thing I want is to run into Arthur Pritchard in the middle of his spotless kitchen."

"Okay," I say, and click into the trash files, looking for more information. "I'll be there in a second." Deacon runs his hand under my hair and kisses my cheek before walking out.

From the other room I hear Deacon open a door, and then shut it, moving on to the next. I continue going through the files.

I must have missed something. I haven't even found anything about Virginia, and I owe her. I promised I'd help get her memories back. I'm about to click out of the trash when I notice one file labeled with only numbers. I lean forward and click it open.

My breath catches. At the top is the name Marie Devoroux. "Deacon," I call, but I'm too busy reading her personal file to call for him again when he doesn't answer. There's a list of her infractions. The descriptions are vague, mostly reports of insubordination—five of them altogether—and a dismissal. But the dismissal was actually dated today, and Marie had disappeared on Thursday. They didn't fire her, which means they're likely just covering their asses.

SUZANNE YOUNG

It's in the notes that I find the most interesting information. There's a listing for Desiree Richardson typed in a box at the bottom, along with a number and an address in Albany. It's only twenty minutes from the grief department, from my father. So if this is Marie's alias, she sure didn't go far. Then again, Marie doesn't have any family; hell, I don't even think she has any friends other than my father. Maybe she couldn't bring herself to completely leave it all behind.

Like I do with all names, I immediately check through my memory to see if it's familiar—someone I've role-played. But I've honestly never met a Desiree, and weirdly, that unsettles me. Even though I'm sure it's just coincidence, it makes me feel completely cut out of Marie's new life, reminds me that maybe I didn't matter to her at all.

I take out my phone and snap a picture of the page, zooming in to make sure I get a clear shot of the phone number. It's Marie—it has to be. Arthur must have found her. What he plans to do with that information, I don't know. But I hope I find Marie before he does anything.

I close out the file. There's nothing else to check, so I turn off the monitor. I have no idea what I'm going to tell Virginia. She got us in here, but I don't have a way to repay the favor. I stand and push in the chair, double-checking that I haven't left behind any sign that I've been here. I don't know how observant Arthur Pritchard is, but if I were to guess, I'd say he's quite perceptive.

I slip my phone into my pocket and peek into the hallway,

trying to guess which way Deacon went. The house is dead quiet, and I'm not sure how much time we have left. "Deacon," I call, but there's no answer.

Uneasy, I go back out into the kitchen to make sure he hasn't left. But the minute I step on the white tiles, the door leading to the garage opens, and my heart stops dead in my chest.

CHAPTER NINE

"VIRGINIA?" I SAY, DARTING A LOOK BEHIND HER. Fear shakes my knees, and I stumble back a step, grabbing on to the edge of the marble countertop to keep myself upright. A quick glance out the window shows the sky has darkened. *We took too long.*

"It's okay," Virginia says quickly, holding up her hands. "It's just me. I called a cab while the council was wrapping up. My father will be here in about fifteen minutes—you have to go."

My heart is pounding so fast, and my voice is barely a whisper. "Holy shit," I say, clutching my chest. "I . . . I . . ."

There are footsteps behind me, and I swing around, still panicked, and see Deacon come in from the hallway. He smiles questioningly as if asking if everything is all right, and when he looks up and notices Virginia, he stops abruptly.

But my heart is still racing—the fear so real that I can't catch my breath. The staggering numbers of the epidemic, the panic that I'd been caught: I'm suddenly and completely overwhelmed.

A shadow passes over my vision. At first I think someone else has entered the room, but then another shadow, and another, begin to cloud my vision. A sharp pain cracks across the side of my head like a baseball bat.

I tip forward, hearing Deacon call my name, feeling the floor rush up to meet me. And before I can hit the tile, a memory slams into my consciousness.

I was at Deacon's house, curled up on the floor and pressing my forehead to the wood slats, trying to block out the pain of another headache. The doorbell rang, and Deacon jogged past me, his voice frantic as he led my father inside. I forced myself upright just as *Tom* entered the room. Anger raged inside me because I knew he wasn't my father. I knew why he was there.

"Don't," I said, sliding back along the floor until I hit the couch. But my vision was blurry—memories crashing back at once, unraveling me.

Deacon flashed a concerned look in my direction, but then he went on to tell Tom about my nosebleed and headache. I felt betrayed, even though he didn't know what he was doing.

"Get out, Deacon," Tom told him calmly, although his eyes were trained on me. "I've got it from here. I need to get my daughter home."

Deacon looked conflicted, and as Tom stepped toward me,

Deacon grabbed his elbow and demanded to know what was going on.

"This is what happens when a closer gets too involved," Tom told him cuttingly. "I warned you. I warned you both."

Deacon lowered his arm and turned to me, devastated as he studied me. I understood how I must have looked to him: face soaked with tears, blood from my nose running fresh again. He thought I was having a psychotic break. He thought it was his fault.

"Get out *now*, Deacon," Tom demanded. "I know what's best for her." He leveled his gaze on me, and I clenched my jaw, ready to fight my way out the minute I was strong enough.

Deacon left me in the living room with that liar. And the minute he was gone, Tom McKee pulled out a syringe and stuck it into my arm. The stick hurt, but the burning sting after was even worse. Although I knew Tom wasn't my father, even though I knew he and Marie had done this to me, the moment of betrayal was enough to break my heart. I gasped in a breath—feeling like a child. Feeling alone and scared.

"Please don't," I whispered to him as the world began to tilt. "Not this time."

Tom furrowed his brow, a moment of sympathy passing over his features. "I don't have a choice, honey," he said.

Deacon catches me by the elbow just before I hit the kitchen floor of Virginia Pritchard's house. I swoon, nearly unconscious. He steadies me, his palm on my cheek as he tries to rouse me; I come back to myself. I gaze a moment into his soft brown eyes, forgetting where we are. And why we're here.

But the memory sticks, and I inhale, the same betrayed breath I took that day eight and a half months ago. "I knew," I whisper to Deacon, my eyes welling up. "I knew he wasn't my father."

Deacon's grip on my arm tightens involuntarily. "What?" he asks.

"That day I came to your house, when you called my father to pick me up. My breakdown," I say. "It was because I was remembering. I was remembering that I was a closer for his daughter's life. There must have been more to it, because I was *so* angry. I'm not sure why. He made me forget."

There's a clatter of a dish as Virginia backs into the kitchen table, rattling the perfectly placed table settings. She's wide-eyed as she stares at me. "What did he do?" she asks. "How did he make you forget?"

"I'm not exactly sure," I say weakly, my head still throbbing just above my ear. At least my vision has cleared and I'm feeling steadier. "But it's probably the same thing they've been doing to make you forget."

"Do you know what happened to me?" Virginia asks, her voice pleading. "Did you find out what they erased?"

I feel Deacon tense. He knows I didn't, but in this moment I can't bring myself to break Virginia's heart. I can't deal with the fallout of that, because I just got a piece of my own puzzle. What helps me can help us both, I hope. But I'm not sure she would understand that right now.

"I have a lead," I tell her. "We're going to check it out now."

Deacon turns to me, and I offer an apologetic look. Across from us Virginia smiles, and I feel like garbage for lying to her, pretending it's about her.

"So what's this lead?" she asks. "Maybe I can—" Headlights from the driveway shine in through the window and illuminate the living room.

We all duck down behind the counter, and I hear the garage door opening.

"That's my dad," Virginia says, darting to the sliding glass door that leads to the back patio. "Quick," she tells us, "go around the side of the house. The gate has a padlock, so you'll have to climb it."

"Fantastic," Deacon mutters, one arm around my waist. I find my footing, and then we dart across the room and slip out the door. "I'll call you later," Virginia whispers after us. She slams the sliding door shut, and just as we get off the last porch step, the overhead lights in the kitchen flip on.

Deacon and I stop just out of view and see Virginia backed up to the glass, gesturing as she talks. She's smart enough not to look in our direction, because within moments Arthur appears in front of her.

"Go, go, go," I whisper, pushing Deacon's shoulder. We quickly round the house and move past the trash cans to get to the side gate, a thick padlock blocking an easy exit.

Deacon gives me a boost, and I put the heel of my shoe on the top of the gate and then jump for the other side. I land deftly, with a little rattle in my knees. Deacon hits the ground next to me and reaches out for my hand. He grabs it and pulls me toward our parked car. We disappear in the shadows of the streetlamps before Arthur can come searching for us.

We get in the car, and Deacon quickly turns the ignition and starts down the street, waiting until we're past Arthur's house before turning on the headlights. We're both panting, our adrenaline spiked from the near miss with the doctor. Just around the block, Deacon drifts to the side of the road and parks at the curb between houses.

It's quiet for a moment, and it gives me a chance to think about what I remembered, think about how betrayed it makes me feel. I knew my memory must have been manipulated, but now . . . now I know it's so much worse. They didn't do this for my safety or my benefit. It was for control.

"I'm scared," Deacon says in a low voice. The honesty of his words speaks for both of us. "In there," he continues, "I didn't know what was happening to you. I'm not enough. We need help, Quinn. And we need it badly."

Although Deacon and I are both good at taking care of ourselves, this is beyond us. At this point I'm not sure how reliable I am. If my memories have been manipulated, I truly don't know who I can trust. Everyone I've ever met might have betrayed me, only I wouldn't know because that memory could have been stolen.

"I know who to call," I say, and take out my phone. But my bravado falters as I stare down at the screen. Grief crawls up my throat and steals my voice, and I fear I may be growing close to another psychotic break. Too much has been happening; maybe I'm not equipped to handle it. Maybe I'll be the next victim of the epidemic.

"Quinn?" Deacon says, like he's worried.

I squeeze my eyes shut. I have to drain away my fear if I hope to continue. I have to be a closer—the best closer. I have to learn to be numb.

"I'm okay," I tell Deacon, opening my eyes. I click through the photos on my phone and zoom in. I switch over to the number pad, feeling desperate, and begin to dial. I put the phone on speaker, my heart beating faster with each ring that echoes through the car.

"Who are you calling?" Deacon asks.

"Marie," I tell him in monotone. "I think I found her." His breath catches, and he turns in his seat, watching the phone intently. He doesn't say a word.

The memory of that day with my father is a pain in my head, and I need to track down the one person who can help fill in the blanks. No matter what, after all we've been through, I know I need to talk to her. I might not get another chance.

CHAPTER TEN

ONCE UPON A TIME, MARIE WAS THE PERSON I turned to for advice. Before Deacon or Aaron, there was Marie and my dad. In fact I'd sometimes wish they would get married so she'd move in. But they were only friends, confidants. Conspirators.

There is a loud click.

"Hi, Marie," I say coldly.

"Now, that didn't take you very long," Marie says in her deep, loving way. Despite my preparation, her voice touches me down to my soul. And before I can say a word, tears are streaming down my cheeks. "I know, baby," she murmurs. "I'm sorry I didn't tell you sooner."

She lets me cry for a moment, and next to me I hear Deacon sniffle. We're both tough, both hardened by our jobs. But when it's *your* parent, *your* loved one—it's not that simple. We default to loving her. It's what we know. And it makes every question I have to ask all the more painful. I fight to get back my composure, and I wipe the tears roughly off my cheeks.

"Don't do that, Marie," I say. "Don't pretend to care now. I want answers. And I want all of them."

"You're letting your anger cloud your judgment, and I've trained you better than that," she says. "We can lie *and* still care about someone—those things are not mutually exclusive. You should know that by now."

Her words are sobering and not entirely untrue. I straighten in the seat and look over at Deacon, who's hanging his head as he listens to her on speakerphone. I want to rage at Marie, scream and cry. But that would be childish and weak. I need to be strong.

"You've lied to me all these years," I tell her, keeping my voice steady. "How could you? What kind of person are you?"

"Whatever kind of person I am," she says, "it doesn't change who you are."

"And who am I?" My heart speeds up at the question.

"I don't know—at least, I don't know where he found you."

The "he" being Arthur Pritchard. I'm devastated—maybe part of me thought it would be an easy answer. That hope vanishes with Marie's plain words.

"Fine," I say. "Then how about we start from the beginning? Quinlan McKee died, and you went to Arthur. What did he tell you? Why did he help you, because I'm sure it wasn't out of the kindness of his heart?"

"You have to understand that we were all grief-stricken," Marie says. "After your father's daughter died, our lives were ruined. I loved Quinlan like she was my own."

There's an irrational moment of jealousy, the idea of Marie loving the other Quinlan more than me. But I bury that, knowing I can't be jealous of a dead girl.

"I didn't have any children, and your father . . ." Marie pauses. "Quinlan's father was a close friend. I was part of the family. And then that little girl and her mother were gone, and we were stripped down and broken. So I went to Arthur Pritchard and begged for his help. He had lost his wife not long before, so I thought he would understand. Make an exception."

I grip the phone harder in my hand. "What kind of exception?"

"I didn't want a temporary closer. I wanted my Quinlan back," she says, her voice cracking. "I wanted my baby girl."

"You planned it?" I ask. "All along you *planned* to keep me? I thought that was Arthur. I thought he was the evil one. But I guess it was you."

Marie sniffles hard but doesn't deny anything. At least she's giving me that bit of honesty. Deacon reaches to put his hand over mine on the seat. My fist unclenches, and I rest my other hand with the phone on my lap.

"We tried two other girls first," she says, her voice growing hard. "But at the time there were no young closers—it was an ethical question of whether to put a child through that."

I scoff at the sentiment, because that is exactly what she and my father put me through, ethics be damned.

"So the girls were older, nearly ten. They cried after just a few hours in my care—they couldn't detach. I asked Arthur if there was a solution to that."

My stomach turns; the clinical way she's describing how they essentially kidnapped me is too much. "Where did he find me?" I ask.

"I told you I don't know where you came from," she says. "What I can tell you is that you were already a ward of the state, but Arthur had custody of you."

I flinch and turn to Deacon, his face registering shock. I look down at the phone. "What does that mean?" I ask. "Why would he have custody?"

"He said he'd been working with you personally," Marie responds. "And that you were the hope for future closers—a perfected version. He told me he'd bring you by, and for me to have Tom ready to meet you. He said he would prepare everything."

My mind spins, and I try to figure out what this means. Did I live with him and his family? Did he keep me in some lab and experiment on me? Maybe I really was like Frankenstein's creature.

"Did he know my parents?" I ask.

Marie exhales deeply. "I truly do not know," she says. "I should have asked more questions—I'm sorry for that," she says. "But I was heartbroken. I was sick with my grief. I would have done anything to make it better. And then, after we took you in, the grief department, under the direction of Arthur, made us sign an agreement to never search out your history. An agreement that would destroy us if we broke it."

"But you did break it," I say.

"Yes. I left you that file, disrupted their plan. And that's why the department is looking for me now—I assume that's how you found me?" she asks.

"You're in Arthur's files," I tell her.

She sniffs a laugh. "I'm sure I don't want to know how exactly you got into those. But I'm glad you did. The grief department will find me shortly," she says. "I've messed up too many times. Now that I'm in breach of contract, they plan to erase me. They won't kill me, Quinlan—they'll just take my life."

Deacon clenches his fists, and I can relate to the fierce protectiveness that comes over us. Marie, despite everything, is still ours. And we protect our own.

"Can't you talk to my father?" I ask her. "Maybe he can help. Or Arthur—"

"The board of directors doesn't want any loose ends at this point," she says. "We're all in danger now. Every closer, every advisor. If we're not part of their big picture, we're part of the problem. They want to move forward with some grand plan that Arthur has begun. He's going to use handlers, and if he can't transition you into one, then he will strip you of your identity."

Deacon looks guilt-stricken, and I have to turn away from him, "handler" still a bit of a stinging burn on my heart.

"Again," I say to Marie. "You mean he'll strip away my identity again. But the thing is, I'm starting to remember." I confide in Marie the way I used to. Perhaps it's habit or even training, but God, it feels good to tell her. "I've been having flashes," I continue. "Headaches and nosebleeds. My memory is coming back, and not from when I was six. It wasn't just once, was it, Marie? Exactly how many times did you let Arthur Pritchard erase my memory?"

She's quiet for a painfully long moment. "Five," she says. "Five more after the time we made you Quinlan."

It's a punch to my chest, and I cover my mouth with my hand. It feels like my greatest fear realized: None of me is real. I am absolutely nobody, rewritten so many times that I've never lived at all.

When Marie continues, she employs comforting techniques: calculated pauses in her sentences, a softer but authoritative tone. I don't reject her manipulation. Just like my former clients, I recognize that I need it. It's too difficult to have this conversation without it.

"Arthur repeatedly warned us," she says, "that resurfaced memories could cause a meltdown. He said it would leave you with permanent damage. But the memories kept coming back, and your father and I started to figure out that it was the assignments—emotional stress did the triggering. We tried to ease up on you—I even stopped drugging your tea. But then your last assignment came up, and Arthur strong-armed us into sending you too soon. I don't know why. My guess is because of your success rate. And now here you are, on the verge of remembering again."

"How much did I remember?" I ask her. "Did I remember my real parents?"

"What *exactly* you remembered, we're not sure. You didn't trust us enough to tell us."

"Then how did he make me forget?" I ask, desperation creeping into my voice.

"I don't know how Arthur did it," she says. "We took you to him like we were advised, and when you came back, you were better, as if the preceding days had never happened. Tom and I thought we were doing the right thing, keeping you safe. Keeping you our Quinlan."

"I was never your Quinlan," I say sharply. "And, as if I needed further proof of Arthur Pritchard's depravity, it turns out I'm not the only person he's done this to."

"What do you mean?" she asks. "Who else?"

"His daughter, Virginia," I tell her. "Bits and pieces of her memory have been wiped out. It's driving her insane. What kind of man does that to his child?"

"The same kind of man who makes us sign agreements to have our memories erased if we go against him," she snaps. She seems alarmed, her composure faltering. "I'm sorry, Quinn," she continues. "You have no idea how long I've wanted to tell you, and your father has too. It wasn't until recently that I realized it wasn't keeping you safe anymore. And when I knew that . . . I let you go. I gave up my life for you."

Although she can wield these words as emotional blackmail, it doesn't lessen the guilt I feel over her predicament.

"What now?" I ask her. "Arthur's found you. And he might have gotten to my father, too. Have you talked to him?"

Marie is quiet, and I picture her looking around the surely cluttered room of wherever she's staying, making certain that she's alone. "No," she says. "I'm sorry. I haven't heard from Tom. But if they've gotten to him . . ." She doesn't finish the thought.

I fight back my panic. I can't even call him, can't even find out for myself. "If they're just rounding us up," I ask her, "what do we do?"

"You can always run," she says.

Deacon looks over at me, and I know if he could, he would convince me of the same.

"And let Arthur get away with it?" I ask Marie. "Get away with manipulating me and his daughter? Let him keep my life from me? No, I won't do that. I want the truth. Besides, what about the other closers? Are you just going to leave them behind?"

Marie quiets, and when she talks again, her tone is filled with sorrow. "I've spent my life helping families," she says. "Protecting my closers—or at least trying to. But I let my self-interest ruin everything. The department is now corrupt and my kids are in danger.

"You see, Quinn," she continues, "it doesn't matter who you come from, not in this life. It matters who you become. And I think I've betrayed you, *all of you*, enough. That's not the kind of person I want to be. I'm going to set things right—as right as I can."

"How?" I ask.

"We'll get your identity, but first we need to warn the other closers about the department. Give them the same choice: to run or to help. But we have to do so without arousing the suspicion of the people who have already been transitioned—we won't know what side anyone is on. Once we have a group that we can trust, we'll figure out what to do next. Ultimately . . . we have to stop Arthur Pritchard. And hopefully that will be enough to take down the grief department too."

Her impassioned speech wakes up my courage. Although I want to know who I am; although I want to give Virginia back her memories, right now my loyalty lies with the other closers first. I have a chance to protect them, to have their backs.

"I'm in," I say. I turn to Deacon, waiting to see if he's with me on this. It takes him a moment, but then he lifts one corner of his mouth and shrugs as if saying, *We've done stupider things, so why not?*

"Now," Marie says firmly. "I assume you're with Deacon?"

I smile at how well she knows me. "Yeah."

"Hello, Marie," Deacon responds with little warmth.

"Deacon," she says, "I need you to contact Tabitha for me. Do you still have her information? She's off the grid."

"I do," Deacon replies. "I left her file with . . ." He pauses momentarily. "I left it with my brother."

My heart stops dead in my chest and I look at him accusingly. Although I'm sure he can feel my stare, he doesn't meet my eyes.

"Good," she says. "Get it. Now, Quinlan, I want you to leave Aaron out of this, do you understand?"

"Wait," I say, turning back to the phone, "why? Shouldn't he—"

"Aaron isn't part of this," she says curtly. "He had his choice, and he chose to run. Don't use his affection for you to drag him back in. We need to help the ones who are still at their positions. The closers."

"Fine," I tell her, although I have no intention of leaving Aaron out. He at least deserves to know what's going on. I don't look at Deacon, but I feel him watching me, waiting to explain about his brother.

"Let's meet tomorrow," Marie says. "There's a diner called the Hash House out in Myrtle Creek. I'll text you the address. Say ten a.m.?"

My mind can't keep up with our conversation when I'm worried about Deacon and Aaron and just about everything else. "Yeah, that works."

"Good," she replies. "I'll see you both then."

Marie hangs up, and I set the phone next to me on the seat, my heart thudding loudly in my ears. My problems continue to add up.

I turn slowly to Deacon, heat rushing to my face. I was told he'd been in foster care when my father found him. I thought his parents were dead. In all our time together, Deacon has never once mentioned a family, a brother. And the casual way Marie said it made it sound like a known thing. Deacon's been keeping this from me too.

"Your *brother*?" I ask.

Deacon studies my expression, and then, without giving away his thoughts, he turns to stare out the windshield.

"It's complicated," he answers.

My jaw falls open, and it takes everything I have to not grab him by the shirt and force him to face me. I hate having to jump to conclusions—I want to trust him completely. But he continues to prove that that's a terrible idea. "Have you ever told me the truth about anything?" I demand, glaring at him.

"Yes," he says, and turns to me. "I told you the truth about us, and about Arthur. I just didn't tell you everything about *me*." His tone startles me. It's not defensive or hard. It's not apologetic. It's just fact.

My skin is electric with betrayal, even if he's twisting his words so I'm not sure which part he's lying about anymore. "I can't keep doing this," I tell him. "I need to know everything. Every detail. We can't keep things from each other anymore. We won't survive that way."

Deacon doesn't agree or argue. Instead he turns on the car and shifts into gear, checking his mirror before pulling onto the road. He's shutting me down. I can't believe he'd do this. I'm ready to beg for him to let me in this last door.

"I need to show you something," he says quietly, not looking over. "You say you want to know me? I'll give you everything, Quinn. Every single piece."

His hands tighten on the steering wheel, and I watch him from across the car. He's deadly serious right now. Suddenly I'm scared of all of his pieces, scared of the picture they'll create. Scared they'll scatter in the wind before I can put them together.

But this is Deacon. And for him I'll take the chance.

Deacon gets on the freeway and heads south, the opposite direction of our motel. After twenty minutes of quiet, my initial anger tempers. The betrayal eases. He said this was about him. Not us.

"Where are you driving?" I ask. "I thought we were going to talk?"

"No, I said I had to show you something. It's easier that way."

"I hope you're not planning to show me a shallow grave," I respond, and then laugh when he looks over. Of course I don't think that, but I want to shock him into responding. He bites hard on his jaw, but I see a flicker of a smile there for just a moment. Sure, I can hate him every second until he gives me a reason not to, but that's just not us.

If we were normal people, a regular couple, this alone could be enough to destroy our trust. But we impersonate dead people for a living. We live our lies every day. We keep secrets, and we hide our pasts. Sometimes our pasts are hidden from us.

But it's in rare moments when we get to live in the present that the real us comes through. So I shouldn't have expected Deacon to tell me everything about himself. It just hurts a little that he didn't want to.

"Joking aside," I say, "we can go back to the motel and talk. We have to meet Marie."

"Not until the morning, and this can't wait," he says. "We need to trust each other, and I need to prove to you that I'm trustworthy." He pauses, and I hear the hitch in his voice. "I need to give you a reason to stay."

"I won't leave you," I say truthfully. I'm not sure what the breaking point is for us. I'm not sure we have one.

"You've left me twice in the past week. I don't think I'm being dramatic here."

I don't tell him that I do trust him—deep down I do. Despite everything I always will. Instead I relax back against the seat, and Deacon turns on the radio. And when he takes his hand off the wheel and rests it on his thigh, I reach over and thread my fingers through his, destined to repeat the same mistakes over and over. But willfully deciding to do so.

CHAPTER ELEVEN

DEACON TAKES US ABOUT AN HOUR AWAY TO AN old neighborhood just north of Grants Pass. The houses have chain-link fences in the yards and there are stray dogs loitering along the curbs. Deacon parks in front of a small bungalow with missing slats of siding, crooked black shutters on the window, and a porch pitched heavily to the right.

Uneasy, I get out of the car and wait on the sidewalk. Deacon walks around the front of the car and comes to stand next to me. I look sideways at him as he surveys the house.

"So . . . ," I say. "Whose house is this?"

Deacon smiles to himself, something sad and lonely. And then he shrugs one shoulder as if he's resigned to tell me. "This is where my mom lives," he says, and starts up the walkway toward the porch.

Speechless, I jog to catch up with him. He knows his mother. I have no idea how he could have kept that fact from me—that's a heavy secret to carry. Once on the porch, we stand together underneath the bald hanging lightbulb.

"So you know your mom?" I ask quietly, not looking at him. "Your family?"

He leans forward to knock on the door, staring straight ahead, his body stiff. "Yeah," he says. "But it doesn't matter. I chose another life."

"'Chose'?" I turn to him. "You were a ward of the state. My father said he found you in foster care. Have you been lying about that this entire time?"

"Your *father* lied," he says. "You never asked me."

"You—"

The inside door opens. Deacon rocks back on his heels before plastering a pleasant smile on his face, staring at someone I can't see through the mesh of the screen door.

"Hi," Deacon says simply. There is a tug on my heart, because despite his comment about it not mattering, the vulnerability in Deacon's tone hurts me to my soul. I turn to the screen, waiting for it to open so I can get a look at whoever would have given him up—or whatever it was that happened here. And with that want comes a fierce need to protect Deacon. Where he's leaving himself defenseless, I'm solidifying my courage and wrapping us up to keep us from harm.

"Well, isn't this a big fucking surprise," a gruff male voice says. Deacon wilts slightly, and it's all I need to spring into action. I step forward and open the screen door, unable to talk to a faceless entity.

I startle the guy standing there, and he takes a step back into the shadow of the house. He's wearing a white undershirt and khaki pants, and I guess he's in his twenties. His hair and beard are blond, but his brown eyes—they're the exact shade and shape as Deacon's. This must be his brother.

The guy quickly runs his gaze over me and then turns back to Deacon. Behind him I smell stale cigarettes and musty air coming from inside. He crosses his arms over his chest as if waiting for Deacon to ask permission to come in.

"I need to talk to you, Brandon," he says.

His brother laughs, shaking his head. "Are you kidding?"

"It's important," Deacon says. He stops, and swallows hard. "Is Mom home?"

"Oh, let me go fetch her for you," Brandon answers in mock graciousness. He steps out onto the porch instead, and closes the door behind him. He walks up to Deacon, slightly shorter, and for a moment I'm scared I'll have to break up their fight. Deacon holds his ground, though, staring down into his brother's eyes.

"I gave you a file a while back," Deacon says. "Do you still have it?"

"Probably."

"Look, this is important," Deacon says. "Do you have it or not?"

Brandon exhales heavily, rolling his eyes. "Yeah, it's still here," he says.

Deacon nods stoically, hiding how appreciative he really is. Reading the situation, I'm guessing Deacon is afraid his brother would use the whereabouts of the file against him—exploit any weakness. It makes me toughen my stance.

Deacon glances at the night sky and then steadies his eyes on his brother again. "I want to see her," he says as if expecting an argument.

"It's not a great time," Brandon says.

"Is it ever?" he asks.

For the first time I see a small bit of sympathy in Brandon's expression. There's another moment of silence before Brandon turns and pulls open the screen door.

"We need a place to stay tonight," Deacon adds, surprising me. Brandon looks back at him and scoffs.

"This isn't a hotel," he says.

"I know," Deacon responds. "I paid off the mortgage, remember?"

Brandon stops, crowding the doorway. "So now we owe you something?" he asks, tilting up his chin defiantly.

"Yes," Deacon replies simply. "And you know she owed me long before I paid off her house. She's owed me my whole life, but I'm not here to collect, Brandon. I just need that file and a room for the night. Also, this is my girlfriend," he says, hiking his thumb in my direction. "Be nice to her."

Brandon huffs a small laugh, clearly unable to hate Deacon as much as he wants to. He tells us to come inside but lets the screen door slam before Deacon can catch it.

Deacon looks at me, apologetic, but I can't even manage a smile. I'm too shocked—my mind is spinning as I try to understand this situation.

"Sorry," he whispers, holding the door as I walk past him.

"For which part?" I murmur back.

The inside of the house is dimly lit, the smell of cigarettes thicker inside. The fabric on the arms of the plaid couch has worn off, but the living room is tidy enough. I close the door and follow Deacon as he and Brandon walk toward the kitchen.

Once there, the light improves slightly, and I find a small gray-haired woman sitting at the kitchen table. She's smoking a cigarette, and there's a beer can resting next to her ashtray. She's older than I expected, well into her fifties, and she looks as worn as her couch.

She lifts her watery eyes to me first, and then she turns to Deacon. She takes a long drag of her cigarette so that the ashes fall to the table, burning a new tiny hole in the plastic tablecloth. She swipes at the area and blows the smoke out of her nose before she smiles. One of her front teeth is missing.

"It's my boy," she says in a smoker's voice. "Look, Brandon." She turns to him. "It's your brother. Little bastard's come home." She says it with humor, and Brandon nods, looking incredibly uncomfortable in the small room.

"Hi, Mom," Deacon says. He studies her, his expression betraying how her condition hurts him. Hell, it hurts me.

I see little resemblance between Deacon and his mom. Her skin is jaundiced, and she has swollen black circles under her eyes. A quick look around the room shows at least a dozen empty cans and a liter bottle of Jack sitting on top of the trash.

Deacon pulls out a chair to sit next to her, and his mother drops her cigarette into the ashtray and immediately puts her small hand over his, gazing at him.

"You look real nice," she says, nodding. "Real nice."

Deacon bites down on his jaw and looks at her hand, her skin spotted and weathered. "Thanks," he says. "Although Quinlan may not think I'm so nice right now." He glances over his shoulder, giving me a sad smile. His mother examines me, but I'm not sure how well she can see; I think she may be drunk.

"Oh, is this your girlfriend?" she asks, waving me over. I go and sit on the other side of her, and up close I see the deep ridges of wrinkles above her lips, the yellow tint to the whites of her eyes. She seems unwell. "You're so pretty," she tells me, reaching to touch my chin. Her fingers are dry and rough against my skin. "I hope Deacon's good to you. Better than he was to me. Little fucker." She cackles.

I hear Brandon exhale behind us, like he's embarrassed by her words. Deacon doesn't even flinch, but my stomach is knotting up. I'm boiling over with anger and, at the same time, sympathy.

Their mother sniffles and picks up her cigarette from the ashtray, alternating puffs and sips from her Miller Lite. After a moment she looks at Deacon and smiles, as if she's already forgotten her harsh words.

SUZANNE YOUNG

"Run out and get me some more beer, will you, doll?" she asks. "I don't have any money, so you'll have to—"

Deacon lowers his eyes. "Yeah, I know," he says. "I'll take care of it, Ma." He pushes back from the table and motions for me to follow him.

I do, wondering if I should say good-bye to his mother. But when I look at her, she's gazing out the window like we were never here. I pause at the door, wishing she would call for Deacon and say something kind—he seems to need it. But she doesn't.

Deacon takes us back through the living room, and although he tries to hide it, I see him wipe at his eyes. We walk to the staircase with the missing bannister, but Brandon jogs after us.

"Deacon," he calls. I'm afraid he's going to start an argument with Deacon, but instead he leans against the wall, fighting back the emotion in his voice.

"You know she doesn't mean it," he tells Deacon. "It's just . . . her health has gotten worse."

"I noticed," Deacon says, his teeth clenched.

"New hospital bills just came. They told her to quit drinking, but—"

"I'll take care of them," Deacon says, keeping his head down. Brandon shifts uneasily, and his guilt is evident.

"Yeah," he says. "Model son, right?"

Deacon lifts his eyes, silencing Brandon with the look. "You could have left too," he tells him. Brandon sneers.

"I was never as good a liar as you," he says.

"You sure about that? Because you're still making excuses for her."

Brandon holds Deacon's glare, and after a moment he nods up the stairs. "The file's in the closet in your room," he says, like he knew exactly where it was all along.

"Thanks," Deacon says. He takes my hand, and we're halfway up the stairs when Brandon says his name again.

"You in trouble?" his brother asks.

"Yeah," Deacon says, not looking back. "I guess we are."

Brandon considers this, and then turns away. "Well, then don't stay too long," he mumbles, and heads into the kitchen.

I let go of Deacon's hand when we get upstairs, and he stops at a closed door at the end of the hall. The carpet runner is worn so thin it's to the wood, and there's only one dusty frame on the wall. It breaks my heart when I realize that the child in the picture with the messy hair and ill-fitting clothes is Deacon. His expression is solemn, and his limbs are frightfully skinny. He notices me staring and follows my line of sight to the picture, flinching when he sees it. He turns away and opens the door, peering in first as if scared there will be someone there. He pushes it open all the way and goes to sit on the bare mattress.

The room is sad and dreary. There is a small metal frame with a full-size mattress, a tall dresser with one of the drawers missing, and peeling paint along the window frame. There are several fist-size holes near the closet door.

SUZANNE YOUNG

Deacon leans forward, his elbows on his knees, as he watches me study his room. He understands what I'm doing. As closers, we've been in dozens of bedrooms, and we know how the little details add up—the things we take for granted. All the damaged pieces in this room reflect his broken life. His neglect.

"Why didn't you tell me?" I ask, thinking back to all the times he and Aaron would say that kids without parents made the best closers. Although I never asked, I assumed Deacon didn't know his family. He certainly never mentioned them.

"Because these are my demons," he says.

I can see them on his face, a dark cloud of pain that haunts him. I have a moment where I can decide just how much I want to know. Is it my right to ask? Do any of us have the right to other people's secrets just because we're in a relationship?

I walk over to the bed and sit down next to him, both of us quiet. I wonder if part of the reason we're here is because Deacon wanted to see his family. Or maybe he needed the reminder of where he came from.

"You said you chose to leave," I start, not wanting to press too hard. Deacon turns his soft brown gaze at me.

"Did he ever tell you how he found me?" he asks. I know he's talking about my dad.

"No," I say. "Only an offhand mention of foster care." It would have been rude to ask for details beyond that.

"I was never in foster care," he says in a low voice. "I was a runaway. My mother's an alcoholic. It can make her mean, but mostly just negligent. I'd like to say she's better when she's sober, but I could count those moments on one hand."

"What about your dad?" I ask.

Deacon shakes his head, lowering his eyes. "My father left before I formed any lasting memories of him. I try to imagine he's dead, because otherwise he's worse than her. Leaving us here, no money, no food. What kind of person does that?"

I swallow hard, wanting to reach for him. To tell him I'm sorry for what happened. But he already knows that, so I let him continue. He wants to get out this poison.

"When I was a baby, we had a neighbor who'd come by and make sure I got fed. She was no saint, but when she moved away, things got worse. My brother did what he could. Brandon's five years older, and he got a job working off the books. But my mother would drink up the money. And when that was gone, she'd have us steal the alcohol—said no one would suspect a kid.

"But Brandon got caught. He did some time, and when he was released, he moved out. I was eleven, and he left me here alone with her. There was never enough food. No shoes that fit." He looks up, and shrugs. "It's how I got this way. I had to learn to watch people, see what they liked, see *who* they liked. Because then I would become *that kid*—the one they would help without a second thought. The one they could trust. I didn't have to beg for anything.

"When I was fourteen," he continues, "Brandon came back, nursing a healthy drinking habit of his own. He was right earlier tonight when he said he wasn't as good of a liar as me. He couldn't get a job with his record, which had gotten longer during his absence. Soon the little bit of food I brought home wasn't enough. I realized how much easier it would be for our mom with one less mouth to feed. How I should be that mouth."

I think back to the day my father first brought Deacon home and fed him. I recognize the boy he's talking about. He was hungry, distant. Watchful.

"I'd read a short article about closers on the Internet at school," he says. "It was taken down the next day, but I remembered your father's name: Thomas McKee. I hopped a bus to Corvallis with nothing but the fare and an address scrawled on a piece of paper. I tracked your dad to his office and marched right in and told him I was a ward of the state and I wanted to work for him. He laughed, looked around like it was a joke. But then he took a minute to stare me down and figure me out. He asked me a few questions, and every time I lied, he could tell. He was the first person who had been able to do that." Deacon looks over at me, a hint of respect in his eyes.

"He's the best liar out of all of us," I say with a small bit of hurt in my voice.

Deacon nods his agreement. "I was fourteen, and Tom said I could learn," he continues. "I told him the truth about where I was from, about my mom. I told him I hadn't eaten in three days. Tom pulled the strings necessary to bring me into the grief department. He gave me a chance at a new life. He also never let me forget it." Deacon glances over. "Your dad can be a real dick."

"Yeah, I know," I say. "But he knows how to spot a good closer. You were probably a gift."

Deacon sniffs a laugh, and then reaches to take my hand. He slides his fingers between mine, studying the way we fit together. Sadness rolls off him.

"And the mortgage?" I ask.

He nods. "I thought . . . I thought if I paid the bills, it would take away the stress. I thought she'd get better. But she doesn't. I've finally figured out that she'll never get better. She'd rather die this way."

"Then why do you come back?" I ask honestly. "Why do you keep helping her?"

Deacon looks up at me, surprised by the question. "Because she's my mother," he says simply.

His words unexpectedly hurt me, reminding me that I don't have a family. I don't have someone to love just because they're related to me.

"Is that why we're staying the night?" I ask. "You're worried about her?"

He shakes his head. "No, we're staying because I needed to remember how to be stronger. I couldn't protect my mother or my brother, but eventually I saved myself from this life. I love you, Quinn. I love you as much as I love myself, maybe more. Having survived this proves to me that I can keep us safe."

"We protect each other," I tell him. "We have each other's back—that's how closers work. We're in this together."

Deacon smiles, adoration clear in his expression. "You sound like a motivational poster. Should I type that up and put it over a picture of a baby sloth, or maybe—"

I laugh. "Shut up," I say, slapping his thigh. "Now, where is this file you're looking for? And how exactly do you know Tabitha?"

Deacon stands and walks over to the closet, opening the door and scanning the space. "I don't, really. I've only met her once. Marie's worked with her." Marie occasionally consults with other advisors and their closers when they need help with an assignment. I've heard Tabitha's name before in the department. Marie must have worked with her, liked her. She must trust her now.

Deacon reaches up and slides his hand along the top shelf. He pauses and then pulls down a black file. He turns to look at me, holding it up. "Got it."

He comes to sit on the bed and slides his finger under the lip of the envelope to open it. "Anyway," he continues, "last year Marie told me that Tabby went off the grid, so she asked me to make sure she was okay. I gathered her contact info, put it in a file. But when I brought it to Marie, she asked me not to tell her the details. So I left it here. Honestly, I forgot until she mentioned it. It wasn't a huge assignment or anything."

"I wonder if there were people keeping tabs on me," I say. "I mean other than you."

Deacon scrunches his nose as if he hates the reminder. I lean back on my arms, watching as he takes out a paper and reads over the handwritten notes. He grabs his phone and dials a number, setting down the paper before standing up. He paces the room, the phone at his ear. I can tell when Tabitha answers, because he stiffens.

"Hey," he says. "Is this . . . is this Tabitha?" He stops to stare out the filthy window toward the street. "Deacon Hatcher. Yeah," he says with a laugh. "That one. I know. I hoped you'd never hear from me either."

He listens, nodding along. Then, "She wants you," he states. "And it's not bullshit, either. We've got some big things happening here, and she trusts you. You up for it or not?" He smiles and looks over at me, giving me a thumbs-up. "Cool. Yeah, tomorrow at ten a.m.," he says into the line. "A place called the Mill in Roseburg. See you then." Deacon clicks off the phone and puts it in the back pocket of his jeans.

"That's done," he says, and comes to stand in front of me. "Hopefully we didn't just ruin her life."

"It's sad how often we have to ask ourselves that about the people we meet."

He reaches to put his hand on my hair, all loving and tender. "It is," he whispers, and his fingers slowly thread through the strands. He turns and walks back to the closet to get some sheets for the bed. When he finds one yellowed white sheet, dusty from time in the closet, and a thin blanket, I help him make the bed.

Once we're done, he spreads out on the mattress, sighing heavily as he stares up at the ceiling. I shut off the light and go to lie next to him, my thigh over his, my cheek on his shoulder.

Before we drift off, I have one last question. "Is there anything else, Deacon?" I ask, closing my eyes. "Anything at all?"

"No," he says. "This is all of me. You have all of me, Quinlan."

CHAPTER TWELVE

DEACON AND I SPEND THE NIGHT IN HIS CHILDHOOD home. I don't sleep well; the creaks and groans of the dilapidated house set me on edge. But I notice how well Deacon sleeps. Whether it's because he's home, or because his conscience is finally clear, I'm not sure.

The house is quiet in the morning. I stand up and stretch, and when I look back at the bed, Deacon smiles at me. I can see that his nerves have twisted him up. He checks the time and says we should leave.

As we get downstairs, ready to slip out like we were never here, the sound of a thick cough comes from the kitchen. Deacon flinches at the sound. He hesitates a moment, and after an apologetic look we both head toward the kitchen.

We find his mother at the same spot at the kitchen table,

her short hair a bit more askew, her dark circles deepened. She looks up when we enter.

"Deacon," she says, as if relieved to see him. Deacon starts to smile, but his mother picks up her drink and sloshes around what's left in the beer can. "Your son-of-a-bitch brother stole my beer again," she says.

Deacon's smile fades, his shoulders slumping slightly. And it feels like a knife twists in my heart for him.

"There's none left," his mother continues. "Go get me some from the market. They've been open for an hour, but you know I can't walk down there." She rubs her knee, her mouth in a sneer as if Deacon asked her to go for herself.

"I don't think Brandon stole it, Ma," he says, his voice far away. "And Quinlan and I have to leave right now. But it was good to see you."

She casts her eyes in my direction and then looks at Deacon. She picks up her cigarette from the ashtray, taking a long drag until it reaches the filter, and talks through the smoke. "You can be an asshole," she says, putting out her cigarette. "But you're better than your brother."

She starts to laugh, but it quickly turns into a thick cough. Deacon watches her with concern, despite her words. His compassion is the greatest part of him. He deserved better than this.

When she finishes coughing, Deacon's mom takes a swig of her beer to clear her throat. I touch Deacon's arm to remind him that we have to go meet Marie. He nods.

"Good-bye, Mom," Deacon tells her, and moves in to kiss

her cheek. She tilts her head, letting him, but she looks more interested in fishing out another cigarette from her pack.

"Bye, now," she says. She doesn't tell him that she loves him. I wonder if that's why he had such a hard time telling me. I wonder who he would be if his life had started differently—if he'd been born with a different family. And then I wonder if I might have started in a place like this too.

Deacon sniffles, keeping his back turned to me so I can't see his emotions. He puts his hand on his mother's shoulder and then he walks out of the kitchen. I follow behind him, giving the living room one last glance before going outside into the gray and cloudy morning.

Deacon is quiet on the ride back to Roseburg. My thoughts keep drifting to my father, and I worry about him. Seeing Deacon's home life has made me appreciate what I had. Sure, most of it was a lie—but I was well fed and looked after. And in my heart I think my father loved me. In my mind I know I loved him.

I hope he's okay.

We're meeting Marie in an hour, and although I was terrified when I called her at first, now I feel more myself. I'm not exactly sure who that is, but with Deacon, I'm always myself.

I text Aaron while we drive, completely disregarding Marie's direction to keep him out of it. He's my partner, even if neither of us is a closer anymore. What affects me and Deacon affects him. I won't leave him hanging on his own, unaware of all the shit that's happening with the department. Turns out, he didn't plan to get left out anyway. He's already on his way to Rose-burg, so I text him the address to the diner in Myrtle Creek.

When we pull up in front of the Hash House at 10:05, we take a moment to scope it out. There is no one lurking out front, and I wonder how long it will be before the grief depart-ment tracks us down. Roger found me pretty quickly. Then again, maybe they already know where I am, and they're just waiting for the right moment to strike.

Deacon puts the car in park and we exchange an *Are you sure about this?* look before he finally cuts the ignition. The wind has picked up, and it sends a chill over my skin. My nerves aren't helping my composure either.

I lead the way to the heavy wood door of the diner, and it creaks loudly when I pull it open. My heart is in my throat as I turn to survey the room. It's dimly lit, with paneling on the walls and the smell of grease and potatoes in the air. I find Marie sitting at a half-circle booth in the back of the restaurant with two other people. There's a coffee cup in front of her, as if this is an assignment. She lifts her eyes to meet mine, and my stomach knots in part nostalgia, part anger.

Deacon puts his hand on my arm, steadying me as if he can sense my hesitancy. I'm not surprised when I see Reed Castle sitting with Marie, chowing down on a plate of morning nachos. His timing at the school was certainly suspicious, but he's here now, so Marie must trust him. He's always been one of her favorites.

Next to him is Shep Donavon, a closer from Albany. He's

short with painful-looking acne; he wears his baseball cap backward, thick tufts of black hair poking out.

The door squeaks open behind us, and when I turn, I see a tiny redheaded girl, no older than fourteen. I guess that she's Tabitha. She notices Deacon immediately and flashes him a smile when she walks past us. When she gets to the table, Marie stands to give her a hug, smiling affectionately and twisting me with a bit of jealousy.

Deacon watches me, his eyebrows hitched up, telling me we still have a chance to leave this all behind. But like I told him last night, closers have each other's backs. "They deserve to know what's happening within the grief department," I say.

When Deacon agrees, I turn and lead us toward the table.

Reed looks up, and smiles when he sees me. Whether he notices Deacon or not, he pretends he doesn't. Reed scoots in closer to Marie to make space for me. "I knew I'd be seeing you again," he whispers.

"Hi, Reed," I respond, politely taking the seat he offers. Deacon grabs a chair from across the aisle and flips it around to sit at the end of the table near me. Reed glances up at him.

"Deacon?" he says as if surprised. "Good to see you again. Marie didn't tell me you'd be joining us."

"He's here with Quinlan," Marie says, watching Deacon with a hint of a smile.

Reed's expression registers the information, and he lets his charm slip away. "Fantastic," he mumbles, and starts picking at his nachos again.

"It's really great to see you, too!" Deacon says, sounding overearnest. Marie gives a quick shake of her head as if telling him to control his attitude.

Shep is playing a game on his phone, ignoring all of us, and Tabitha watches curiously. She leans in to the table, getting my attention.

"Hi," she says. "You're Tom's daughter?"

The question is a shot to the gut, but I nod, avoiding eye contact with Marie.

"That must have been fun," Tabitha says with a little laugh. She darts a look at Deacon. "Heard you quit," she tells him. "And that you disappeared. Hell, I thought you were dead until you called."

"Still alive," Deacon says. "But believe me, I wish I had disappeared."

Tabitha smiles at him, as if she can relate, and turns to Marie. "All right, Marie," she says. "Why did you drag us all down here?"

"There's a suicide cluster," Shep answers for her in a bored voice, his eyes not leaving his phone. "People are dying left and right." His thumbs stop moving, and he looks up. "I heard about it on the news," he adds. "They said it's contagious."

I should have figured that most of the closers would have been listening—we deal in death. Unless they were on the run, like I've been, news like this would have been unescapable.

"A behavioral contagion," Reed corrects. "Copycat behavior."

"Ahh . . . ," Tabitha says. "Mass hysteria. Well"—she leans

forward to take a chip off Reed's plate—"I'm just glad it's not zombies." She smiles and bites the chip.

Reed curls his lip, clearly annoyed, and turns to Marie as if disappointed in her choice of closers. "So . . . ," he says. "What does this have to do with us? Why this covert meeting? I'm already prepping for an assignment."

Across the diner, the sound of the door opening draws my attention. Both Deacon and I turn toward it, and the moment I do, my heart leaps. It's Aaron.

"Oh my God," I say, jumping out of the booth and rattling the glasses on the table. I meet him halfway, let him sweep me up into a hug. I didn't fully know how much I missed him until just now.

I pull back, still holding on to his forearms like he might disappear, and see how his dark eyes are glassy with the same emotion that I'm feeling. He looks good, not sick the way he did when he was on his last assignment. He adjusts the straps of his backpack on his shoulders.

"I'm so glad you shaved that beard," I say, making him laugh. He runs his palm over his cheeks.

"Naw," he says. "I miss it. But now I'm all *GQ* up in here." He smiles and reaches behind me as Deacon walks up. They slap hands and hug.

For a moment my heart is full. Me, Aaron, and Deacon back together again. They're my family, and not because they were brainwashed to be. Deacon and Aaron laugh about something, and then Marie waves us over, checking around the diner and looking uncomfortable with the attention we're garnering. The closers in the booth move in tighter, allowing Aaron to slide in next to Tabitha. She smiles at him, probably impressed because Aaron Rios is very cute. He's also very attached, so he politely nods and sets his bag between them. He turns to stare intently at Marie.

"You forget about me?" he asks her. "Because I'm seeing a closer convention in here that I wasn't invited to."

Marie's expression is decidedly chilly. "You shouldn't have come," she says. "I gave you an out."

I'm taken aback by her demeanor. I know how she cares for him; she's always had a soft spot for Aaron. Sure, he made a choice to leave, but that was before we knew the scale of this problem. I guess Marie just wanted to keep him out of danger.

So what does that mean for the rest of us?

Reed and I exchange a glance, and I see the same doubt in his eyes. Like we're being played. We both turn to Marie.

"You said you had to talk to us," Reed says to her. "Off the record. But you're not our advisor anymore."

"I couldn't contact your reps," Marie says, folding her hands in front of her. "I couldn't take the chance of them informing the grief department. But before I continue, I need you all to be completely honest with me. Are any of you compromised?"

I furrow my brow, wondering if she expects them to straight-out tell her if they are.

"I'm asking this as a friend," Marie continues, her voice thick with loyalty . . . and emotional manipulation. "If you're working as a handler, walk away now, no questions asked. Give us a chance to make it through this—for old times' sake."

The table quiets, and I look around at the faces, none of them giving anything away. Deacon's eyes are lowered, and Aaron is watching Marie in silence. But when Shep leans forward to talk, my body tenses.

"What the hell's a handler?" he asks. I sigh out my relief, and both Reed and Tabitha jump in to question the term. Marie nods to me, comforted by their ignorance. I have to admit that I'm eased by it too. We've found closers to trust.

Deacon and I stay quiet while Marie tells the others about the grief department and their plan to transition all closers. I watch as their faces reveal shock, horror, terror. Marie tells them that the alternative is memory manipulation, and thankfully, she doesn't mention that they've already tested it on me. It's not my fault, of course, but it still humiliates me—as if it makes me different.

And after she's scared the shit out of them, she gives them another option: running.

Aaron sits quietly, his arms crossed over his chest, looking lost in thought. When Marie is done talking, Reed is the first to speak up.

"So we can still run from this?" he asks. "What about our money? I've worked years to fulfill this contract. I'm only a few weeks away."

"Gross, Reed," Tabitha says. "Who cares about the money?"

"Says the person who's already retired," he snaps at her. Marie holds up her hand to stop their argument.

"I can gather some of the funds," Marie says. "Enough to help you all get out of town and set up. It won't be as much as your contract, Reed." She presses her lips together apologetically. "But if you choose to run, it's the best I can do."

"Where are you getting the money?" Reed asks. "If it's not coming from the grief department."

"Her name is Dr. Evelyn Valentine," Marie says. "She's a friend of mine, and she's concerned about the outbreak. She's offering to pay. . . ." Marie hesitates. "But—"

"There's a catch," Deacon says, narrowing his eyes as he watches her. Marie glances over at him.

"Isn't there always, Deacon?" she asks. "Always a side deal to be made." Deacon flinches, and I think we both wonder if Marie knows about him and Arthur.

"So yes," Marie continues, looking back to Reed, "Evelyn wants something in return. She believes in closers; she sees the merit in what you do."

"What does she want?" I ask, unsure of where Marie is going with this.

"She wants you all to close one last time. Undercover and off the record. She wants you to try to stop this epidemic. She thinks you can. She wants you to be the alternative to Arthur's memory manipulation."

"You lied to us," Deacon says. "You told us this meeting was to warn the closers about the grief department, but instead you're recruiting them."

Marie turns to him, her eyes flashing. "I'd be careful of who you're calling a liar, Deacon. Throwing stones and all . . ."

They watch each other for a long moment, and it's clear that Marie does know about his past, which in itself is troubling. How long has she known? She turns away from him.

"Now," she tells the rest of us. "Whatever your decision, I ask for your complete secrecy. You'll risk our lives otherwise. Can you give me that?" Slowly, everyone nods or murmurs yes.

"But what about my current assignment?" Reed asks.

"It's void," Marie tells him, wrapping her hands around her coffee cup, even though she doesn't take a sip. Reed scrunches up his face to argue. "Finish if you want," she says. "But they're not going to pay. They never planned to. They're going to offer you a new contract as a handler." She pauses and looks around at all of us. "So you have a choice," she says. "Stay and be transitioned, leave with almost nothing for your past work, or close this out and help people."

"But without the grief department," Tabitha begins, "how do we know our assignment? Who will we be role-playing?"

"You will be yourselves," Marie answers. "Your names. Your identities. No role-playing. You know how to do this; you don't need to hide behind another identity."

I can't help but feel a little slighted by her choice of words.

"Do you agree?" she asks, and stills as if waiting patiently. One by one they all say yes. She doesn't ask me or Deacon. She doesn't even make eye contact with Aaron.

"Now," Marie continues, her voice taking on a parental tone, "Tabitha and Shep, you'll go to the high school. Talk to the students and see who's in need of advice. You're trained counselors; use that to help them."

Tabitha smiles, seemingly excited at the prospect of regular school, but Shep rolls his eyes like it's the last thing he wants to do.

"And watch out for others," she says. "Those who seem too friendly, those who seem like closers. I have no doubt the grief department has dispatched some people to the area. They're looking for Quinlan and Deacon," she adds, side-eyeing me. "But if they know you're involved, they'll take you, too. Stay under the radar and buy yourselves some time."

Tabitha's smile fades, but this threat seems to bring a bit of life to Shep's expression. Like he finally just woke up to what's going on around us.

"Deacon," Marie says, turning to him. "Are you in or not?"

Deacon looks at me, waiting for a cue either way. She's changed the plan and he doesn't like it, but ultimately, if this other doctor is right and we can stop the epidemic by being closers . . . it's worth a shot. And while I'm at it, I'll find a way to get Virginia's memories back to her and find out my real identity. No pressure. I nod to Deacon, and he inhales deeply.

"Yes, Marie," he says with little enthusiasm. "I'm in."

"Good," she responds, not missing a beat. "I need more information on Arthur Pritchard. His ties with the department have been mostly cut with the exception of this new treatment he's planning. I want to know what he's doing to his patients. I'm sure it'll be of interest to you, as well." Her eyes dart momentarily to me, and I know she's really asking what he's doing to Virginia's memories—and mine. She glances back at Deacon, a moment of vulnerability there. "And after that," she adds, "find out his plans for me."

Deacon tells her that he will, but he lowers his head, looking troubled. He's broken his contract too, so what threatens Marie threatens him.

"The rest of you," Marie says, glancing at Reed, me, and Aaron, "I want you to meet with Virginia Pritchard. Track down everyone she's had contact with in the past few weeks and assess their condition."

"Why?" Reed asks. "Do you think she has something to do with the outbreak?"

"I think she may be the one infecting people, Reed," she says. I tense, because I'm one of the people she's had contact with. "Now, I don't fully understand this outbreak," she adds. "But Evelyn is concerned, and Virginia does seem to be at the center of it. We need to figure out why."

Marie checks her watch. "You should go," she tells us. "And limit your contact with each other in public. Certainly with your advisors. And again, don't breathe a word of this to anyone at the department."

We all agree, and stand up from the table, a little paranoid as we look around the diner. I say good-bye to the others, and Deacon and I are the first ones outside.

The minute we're out the door, he wraps me in a hug, his lips close to my ear. "I hate leaving you right now," he whispers, and then pulls back to look down at me. "She's just like your father. Always trying to separate us."

I laugh softly and untangle myself from his arms as I gaze up at him. "Don't let Arthur find you," I tell him, voicing my worry. "I don't want you getting screwed over by the fine print of your contract." I try not to sound terrified, but I make a poor show of it.

"I'll see you later tonight," he says casually. I know he's scared too. He just doesn't want me to be. "Oh, and hey," he adds. "Don't fall in love with Reed Castle while I'm gone."

"Reed already loves himself," I say. "There's no room in their relationship for me."

Deacon snorts, and then he turns, tucking his hands into his pockets as he heads toward the car.

But there's a shadow of doubt crawling through my veins, a panic in my chest. I suddenly worry that Marie has set in motion a series of dangerous events, the kind we might not survive. The kind that might be the end of us. One way or another.

PART III
THE EPIDEMIC

CHAPTER ONE

I'M STILL STANDING IN THE MIDDLE OF THE SIDE-walk when Aaron and Reed walk out. Reed checks the streets, like he's wary of being watched, but Aaron sees me and his concerned expression slips away. Or is covered up. He stoops down in front of me, offering his hands to slap.

I do, but then laugh and tell him to stop embarrassing himself.

"Aw, come on, now," he says. "I took the bus to get here. Give us at least a few minutes to be normal. You know it's already getting weird. It always does."

"How far did you and Myra get?" I ask.

"Idaho," he answers with a laugh.

"And where is the love of your life now?" I ask. "She didn't want to join you on this misadventure of bad ideas?"

"Didn't really ask her to." Aaron's easy expression tightens.

"Myra doesn't need to get mixed up in this shit. I told her I was coming to bail you and Deacon out of a closer mess and that I'd catch up with her in a few days. I gave her the car, but let's just say she's not exactly happy with me right now."

"I bet," I say.

"Luckily I'm damn sexy," he adds, pushing my shoulder to make me laugh.

"You should let Reed know how funny you are," I say. "In case he can't tell."

Reed smirks, looking over. "Oh, I'm already laughing on the inside." He motions toward his red sports car and clicks off the alarm.

"Shotgun," Aaron calls, and gives me a look like *of course he drives that*, and we follow Reed toward his vehicle.

"I'm really great at reading people," Reed tells me, opening the door and resting his elbow on the frame as I climb past him into the backseat. "And I've got you all figured out."

I lift one eyebrow, asking him to elaborate, but he just smiles and walks around the car. When I get inside, I'm immediately surrounded by the scent of coconut air freshener. Aaron tosses in his bag and drops into the front passenger seat. He looks back at me.

"I like this guy," he says. "He's the perfect blend of arrogance and immaturity. Can't believe you didn't pick him over Deacon."

"He was never really in the running," I tell him. "Now are we going to talk about this tension with you and Marie? She wasn't happy to see you."

Reed opens the door and Aaron turns away.

"Later," he murmurs. I don't want to discuss this in front of Reed either; we don't know him well enough. We don't totally trust him. Still, I don't like how Marie treated Aaron. There has to be more to the story.

Reed glances at me in the rearview mirror, and I decide to focus on the mission at hand. "It's barely eleven," I tell him. "If we plan to meet with Virginia, school doesn't get out for a while, so—"

Reed holds up his phone, his screen showing the school's website. "Don't you guys do any research?" he asks. "Early release Tuesday. Virginia's on the roster for the volleyball tournament. The game starts at noon."

"Research?" Aaron says, incredulous. "We just got our assignment five minutes ago, you overachieving bastard."

Reed hitches up the side of his mouth in a smile. "What can I say? I'm good."

I shake my head, amused, while Reed brings the car engine to life. I'm impressed that he checked into Virginia so quickly; then again, it sounds like he wants to run from this. But he wants to get paid first. I don't blame him. There was a time when the money was important to me, too—although maybe not as much as it is to Reed. He must have plans for his life after. Most closers do.

"All right, let's go, then," Aaron says, taking a moment to recline the seat to the perfect angle. "I'm curious about Virginia Pritchard. I like that she's an athlete: Healthy competition is good for the soul." He beams at me, reciting a phrase from one of our training classes. "While we're there," he continues, "we'll get a chance to survey the crowd."

Reed turns to me for agreement, and I nod my chin. Truth is, I want to help people. My favorite part of being a closer was the difference I made. This is our chance to change things, and it's literally life or death.

Since Myrtle Creek is only twenty minutes from the high school, Aaron asks if we can swing by the motel so he can check in and drop his bag. I discover that Reed's a fast driver—the kind that swerves in and out of traffic, irritating all of the other drivers only to end up at the same red light.

When we get to the motel—in record time—Reed and I wait in the idling car as Aaron goes inside the lobby. Reed laughs quietly, and I look up to find him watching me in the rearview mirror.

"What?" I ask.

"So you and Hatcher, huh?" he asks, his blue eyes sparking with amusement. "Thought you broke up."

"Classic us, right?" I say with a sarcastic eye roll, making Reed chuckle. "But yes," I tell him, "we're back together. It's a long story."

"I bet," he responds. "And I bet your father's thrilled too. I don't know if I told you, but he tried like hell to get me to ask you out. Even offered me a better contract."

I flinch, but Reed completely misreads it. "Sorry," he says, "but you're just not my type."

"Too bad," I say, playing along, although the revelation about my father is sickening. There was no end to his grab for control over me.

"Yeah," Reed says, taking his eyes off me to stare at the lobby door, where Aaron has just exited, folding a receipt. "I don't date girls who are in love with someone else," Reed adds.

I feel a splash of warm affection, and Reed glances in the rearview again and smiles at me. The passenger door opens and Aaron gets in, exhaling heavily before tucking the receipt between the dashboard and the windshield. Reed stares at the paper, probably annoyed at its placement, but then, in an obvious attempt to look casual, he turns on the radio and starts driving us back toward the school.

By the time the volleyball game starts, the gymnasium is loud with shouts from the crowd and the grunts of the players on the court. We overhear that this is a major tournament, one people have been excited about because both teams are good.

As we enter, we check the crowd for Arthur Pritchard, relieved to find him nowhere in sight. That would have certainly complicated our mission. Reed opts to split off when he sees the girl he was here to research. In the car, Reed mentioned that the girl's boyfriend had recently died. He was going to take on that role to help her, but after what Marie told us, he doesn't want to take on the assignment. Instead, he said he'd talk to the girl and see if he can get some information about the student population.

Aaron and I sit in the middle, and when I look back, I see that Reed has joined the girl and her friend high up on the bleachers. They look like they're talking freely, giving away secrets.

Next to me, Aaron watches the game as I scan the players,

surprised to find Virginia sitting on the bench, especially since I thought she was one of the stars. Aaron bumps my shoulder with his.

"Is that her?" he asks, nodding toward the sideline.

"Yeah," I tell him, furrowing my brow. "How'd you know?"

"Because she doesn't look good."

He's right. Although Virginia is wearing the same uniform as everyone else, she seems smaller now. Like she's folded in on herself. Her shoulders are slumped forward, and her head is lowered as she follows the game with just her eyes. She looks nothing like the girl in the parking lot yesterday, before she took me to the lighthouse. Before she helped me break into her home. I lied to her when I told her I had a lead on her memories—I hope this isn't my fault.

"Come on, Deidra," Virginia calls out, clumsily clapping her hands together. Her friend misses the save, and Virginia jumps to her feet.

I can't be certain, but there are what appear to be scratches on her arms and on her thighs just under her uniform shorts. I turn to Aaron and he meets my gaze, looking equally concerned. I open my mouth to ask what he thinks, when a whistle blow startles me. Virginia runs out onto the court and helps her friend off the floor. Then she lines up, joining in the game. I can see from her coach's expression that Virginia's demeanor is worrying her, too.

And suddenly I start to think that everything is off. I turn slowly and scan the faces of the crowd. Sure, there are people cheering. But mixed in are those sitting quietly with dark circles under their eyes—like they haven't slept. Those with long sleeves, wringing their hands in their laps as they watch the game, looking uneasy. I check back with Reed and see that a deep crease has formed across his forehead. The two girls he's talking to are absorbed in their words; whatever they're telling him disturbs him, though. I watch as his throat bobs, and then he turns to look down at me from the upper rows, his eyes wide with fear.

Some of these people look *unwell*. They remind me of Roderick at the party, his expression as he walked himself off the balcony. The referee blows the whistle again, and I visibly jump. Aaron puts his hand on my leg to steady me.

"You all right?" he asks, his eyes trained on the court.

"I don't know."

The game continues, and Aaron leans forward, his elbows on his knees as he studies Virginia's behavior. Virginia is diving for volleys she has no chance of reaching. She's tossing her body around as if she can't feel it when she hits the floor, her skin squeaking against the polished wood. A patch of blood appears on her knee, another on her elbow. The ref notices and calls time.

The coach comes onto the court with a white cloth and some bandages. She motions for Virginia to go to the bench, but Virginia shakes her head no. The coach puts her hand on her shoulder, but Virginia shrugs it off and then slaps her coach's hand away when she reaches for her again.

"I said I'm fine!" Virginia shouts, her voice echoing throughout the gymnasium. The gym goes quiet, and my stomach knots up with a deep sense of dread. The referee comes to stand next to the coach, and the two women take a step toward Virginia, their hands held up in a nonthreatening manner.

"We want to treat your cuts," the coach says, her voice audible in the silence. "I just need you to come to the bench for a minute." But even I can tell she's lying. Virginia won't be going back into the game.

Virginia laughs wildly, shaking her head, backing away from the approaching women. "There's nothing wrong with me," Virginia snaps bitterly. "But you don't really care about that, do you? Just like you didn't care about Diana or Roderick or Micah."

The coach takes a wounded gasp, lowering her hands. "Of course I care," she says. "I cared about all of them. Care," she corrects.

"You want us all well behaved," she tells her, and looks back at the crowd. Several of the students straighten up, as if she called on them specifically. They're hanging on her every word, entranced by her. She's a burning building you can't look away from.

Virginia turns back to her coach. "I know you're working with him," she says flatly.

This makes the coach stop in her approach. She fumbles for a response. "You need help, Virginia," the coach says, not addressing the comment. "Now come off the court. We'll call your father and have him pick you up."

Virginia laughs and walks toward her coach, making the woman puff herself up in case there's going to be an altercation. Virginia stops just in front of her. The referee watches from a few feet away, ready to break up a fight. The players stand in shock, staring at them.

Virginia leans in, blinking slowly, erratically, and says, "I remember *everything*."

The coach drops her supplies and grabs Virginia to spin her around. She locks her in a hold to restrain her, as if Virginia was about to attack. Which wasn't what I saw. Aaron is the first to stand, reading the situation same as me. Half the crowd stands up with us, some covering their mouths. All looking horrified.

Virginia starts to thrash, telling her coach to let her go. She snarls, wild. Unhinged. In the struggle she splits her lip, and blood sputters out as she shouts and kicks. The referee comes over to help the coach pull her from the court.

My heart is in my throat. I don't know what to think, but I'm watching in horror as Virginia Pritchard seems to disintegrate in front of our eyes.

"You won't erase me again!" she screams, kicking at the air as she tries to free herself. "I'll die first. We'll all die first!"

I see at least one person nod.

"Call Dr. Pritchard and tell him to get down here!" the coach yells to the player that Virginia helped on the court. Without a second thought the girl runs toward the bench and grabs her cell phone out of her bag, biting her nail as she watches Virginia get dragged toward the locker room.

"No!" Virginia yells to her friend. "Don't call him!" She seems to choke on some of the blood and spits it out on the floor. Tears stream from her eyes. "No, Deidra," she tells her friend again, her voice shaking. "Please don't call him."

Her friend pauses, but the coach waves for her to continue.

Conflicted, the girl turns away from Virginia and begins talking to who I assume is Arthur Pritchard.

Virginia cries the rest of the way, no longer fighting. Resolved to the unspeakable outcome she's resigned herself to. I grip Aaron's arm hard enough to turn my knuckles white. Aaron's eyes have welled up as he watched. When he turns to me, a tear drips onto his cheek.

"We have to get out of here," he whispers. "And we have to leave now."

I look across the gymnasium just in time to see the locker door close behind Virginia and the coach. They're gone.

"We need to help her," I tell Aaron. "She's scared."

"*I'm* scared," Aaron responds, prying my fingers from his arm. He tilts his head like he can't understand why I would say such a thing. "We can't help her now," he adds. "If what she says is true, if her coach is in on it . . . this is already beyond us. We can't stay here. We need to call Marie."

"No," I tell him fiercely. "That's bullshit, Aaron, and you know it. Virginia said she remembered everything, and if that's the case, we need to find out what that includes. And how exactly she remembered." But I'm being selfish, because part of me thinks that if Virginia can remember, maybe she can show me how to do the same.

Around us groups of students flee the gymnasium, while the ref cleans up the blood from the court with a mop; the opposing team is standing around, staring in shock. I see one of the players scratch nervously at her forearm, scratch until a thin red line appears in her skin.

Reed stops at the end of our row and waves us forward, his eyes already on the exit. Aaron and I make our way toward him, and I hope that at least he is thinking rationally. We can't just leave Virginia behind.

When we get into the school hallway, I hear a whistle in the gym signaling the continuation of the game. I don't imagine the team will do well after Virginia's outburst. I know I'm not doing well.

Reed runs his hand roughly through his dark hair. "I feel like I'm in a fucking asylum," he says, an obvious change in his demeanor since we arrived. "Do you know what those girls said? The ones I was talking to?" he asks. "They wanted to know if I was interested in something called 'quick death.' Poison, apparently," he clarifies. "But they acted like they were selling me weed or something." He shakes his head, horror in his expression. "I'm glad to back out of my assignment. They need more than closers here," he says. "We are way out of our depth."

"Marie asked us to check on Virginia," I say, my voice echoing down the corridor. "And now you want to abandon her? Did you see how they were treating her?"

"Have we considered that maybe Arthur Pritchard has a real strategy to deal with this?" Reed asks. "At least he's a doctor."

"Yeah?" I say. "And did his daughter seem interested in that plan? You saw how she reacted." I look at Reed and then at Aaron. "Would you call that a normal response to therapy?"

"Oh, I wouldn't call any of this normal," Reed says darkly. "But I know I feel like shit after seeing that, after being here."

He shivers as if a thought haunts him. "We *can't* help these people," he adds. "Any of them—including Virginia."

"He's right, Quinlan," Aaron says, surprising me with his firm tone. "We need an actual plan."

I shoot him a betrayed look, and he lowers his chin as if I didn't let him finish.

"A plan to talk to Virginia," he continues in a softer voice. "She's the key to this. Once we know what they're doing to her, maybe we can relate it back to a trigger. That's what Marie and Evelyn really need—a problem to treat. So let's figure out what Virginia knows, make a list of people she's been in contact with, and hand it over. Then we get the hell out of here."

"Okay, look," Reed says, stepping closer. "I'll drop the two of you back at your motel to regroup. I'll find where they're taking Virginia and contact you. Until then, stay put."

I'm about to tell him he can't give me orders when I feel Aaron take my elbow. "Come on," he says. "It'll give us a chance to loop Deacon in."

Deacon is off looking into Arthur's intentions, but after Virginia's complete meltdown, I'm even more worried about what can happen to him.

"Call Deacon and tell him to meet us," I tell Aaron. "He'll know what to do."

Which is, of course, a lie. None of us know what to do.

And with one last glance behind us, Aaron, Reed, and I rush for the exit and out into the uncomfortably bright afternoon.

SUZANNE YOUNG

CHAPTER TWO

I SIT IN THE BACKSEAT OF REED'S CAR IN COMPLETE silence, listening as Aaron calls Deacon and tells him to stop what he's doing and come to the motel. Once he hangs up, he dials Marie and relays the events of the past hour. He mostly listens as Marie gives instructions. At one point he stiffens and says, "Yeah, she's with me."

When he hangs up, he turns. "Marie said she's delaying Tabby and Shep's placement," he tells me, "and that we should wait for information on Virginia's condition before moving forward. You okay with that?"

"I think I'm outvoted," I say. "And how are we supposed to talk to Virginia if we're sitting around in a motel being useless? Telepathy?" Aaron scoffs and gets out of the car.

"Dial it back, Quinn," Reed tells me, glancing in the

rearview mirror. His skin has paled, and his blue eyes are serious. "I'll find where they're taking Virginia," he says. "But this is obviously a bigger conspiracy than we initially thought. If you're losing your grip on this, we should—"

"I'm not losing my fucking *grip*," I snap, and then immediately regret my attitude. Shouting isn't the best way to prove control. "I'm just . . ." I continue in a softer voice: "I'm worried about her."

"Then I will do absolutely everything I can to help her," Reed says kindly. "I promise you, Quinlan." This particular tone combined with Reed's good looks is useful for manipulation, I'm sure. The fact that he's trying to use his closer skills on me should be irritating, but instead it actually offers me a small measure of comfort. And for that I'm grateful.

"Thank you," I say. "That means a lot."

"Anytime, Quinlan," Reed murmurs. He tears his gaze away from me, seeming lost, and adds, "Every time."

Reed swears he'll be in touch the minute he tracks Virginia's location, and he leaves. Aaron stands in the parking lot with his fingers locked behind his neck and stares up at the motel. When Reed's car is gone, Aaron turns a suspicious eye on me.

"What's really going on?" he asks. "Because I love you, girl—but I'm not going to blindly follow you into the abyss."

"But I'm supposed to trust *you* with no questions asked?" I shoot back. "Tell me what's going on with you and Marie."

Aaron exhales and turns his back, but he doesn't walk away.

"I don't trust her anymore," he says. "We've been with her for years, but look what she kept from you—how she lied to you. As soon as you called, saying she disappeared, things started to click into place."

"How so?"

"She had me watching you for a while," he says, looking back guiltily. "Hell, when you were Catalina, I staked out the house on her command. She had me worried, said you were losing it. And maybe you were.

"But then I got sent on an assignment, same situation as you. It wasn't right—timing too coincidental. Both assignments came directly from Arthur, both of us Marie's closers. I don't know what it means, but I just got a feeling. I don't think Marie is fighting against Arthur—I think she's working *with* him."

I shake my head, seeing the logic in his argument, but not buying it completely. "That's a pretty big accusation," I say. "I . . . I don't believe that. Marie's scared of Arthur—I can see it, hear it in her voice. She thinks he's going to erase her memory for breaking her contract. Besides," I add, "she let you leave and she gave me my closer file. Do you really think she'd double-cross us now?"

"Did she let me leave or was she trying to get rid of me? Because there's a difference," he says.

"I'm not defending her," I say, holding up my hands apologetically. "But she did want us to run. She was *protecting* us."

Aaron puts his hands on his hips like he can't believe I just said that. "So if she's protecting us, she can lie to us?" he says. "I know you don't buy that." He pauses. "Does that apply to your father, too?"

And, of course, now that he says it . . . I think maybe it does. I asked Deacon how he could love the woman who'd mistreated him so badly, and the only answer was because she was his mother. I get it now.

"He's still my father," I tell Aaron, my voice starting to shake. I've been keeping the fear at bay, but the fact is, I have no idea about my father's condition. I have no idea if he's okay.

"Aw, shit," Aaron says, and steps over to hug me. "I didn't mean to bring him up. I'm sorry, Quinn."

"Will you find him for me?" I ask, my cheek pressed to his chest. "Will you just check if he's okay?"

"Yeah," Aaron says. "I have a few contacts in Corvallis. I'll get in touch with them." He pulls back and stares down at me. "I'm sorry about what I said," he adds. "I know Marie loves us. I just want to be careful. And now that I've said my piece, why don't you tell me what's going on with you and Virginia Pritchard."

I sniffle and a take a step back. Aaron knows I'm a good person, but not that good.

"I need to find out how she remembered her past," I tell him. "That means she knows everything that her father's done. She knows the methods and reasons. And she might know how to trigger my memory. If she can, then I won't need Arthur Pritchard to find out my identity. I'll get it my damn self."

"So you want her help?" he asks.

"Yes. And I want to help her, too. If she already has her memories back, the only thing I can offer is freedom from her father. So if Marie can't get him shut down, I think we should help Virginia run away."

Aaron's lips form a perfect O, and he forces a laugh. "That's enough conspiracy talk for today, Quinlan," he says, reaching to take my arm. "Let's save this conversation for when your boyfriend gets back."

We walk up the outdoor steps of the motel toward my room. "He'll agree with me," I say, looking sideways. I smile when Aaron meets my eyes.

"Oh, I don't doubt it," Aaron says. "He's a crazy fucker too."

We both laugh, but when we get to the motel room door, we exchange a look that brings the lightness of the moment crashing down around us. We'll have to try harder, do everything we can when all around us darkness is pushing in. So we force bigger smiles and go inside the motel room.

Deacon jumps up from where he was sitting on the bed, surprising us. I didn't know he was already back.

"What took you so long?" he asks, obviously worried. The news of Virginia getting dragged off the volleyball court must have been disconcerting, even though he wasn't there. Aaron and I are immediately grounded again in the horror of our situation.

"Sorry, man," Aaron tells Deacon in a low voice. He goes

to sit in the hard chair next to the window. "Where were you when I called?"

Deacon shifts his eyes to mine, checking to make sure I'm okay since I'm not the one who answered. "I was at Arthur's medical office," he says to Aaron, although he's still watching me. "His car wasn't in the lot, though. I'm thinking about breaking in."

"Of course you are," Aaron says with a heavy sigh.

Deacon ignores him and crosses the room to pause in front of me. "Are you really okay?" he asks quietly.

I lean in to him. All at once I feel vulnerable again. "You should have seen her," I tell him, the image of Virginia fighting and bleeding and helpless burned into my memory. "It was awful."

He tightens his arms around me, whispering how sorry he is that he wasn't there. For a second I let myself pretend that if he had been, he would have run onto the court, grabbed Virginia's hand, and taken off with her. He would have saved her. That wouldn't have happened. But I need to think it could have. The chance that we're not all completely helpless in this comforts me.

There's a buzz, and Aaron takes his phone from his pocket to check the caller ID. "It's Myra," he says. "I gotta take it." He points the phone toward the door. "I'll be in my room. Let me know when Reed gets in touch."

I nod, and after Aaron leaves, Deacon checks me over, seeming uncertain. "You look miserable," he says. "What can I do?"

"You can stop treating me like I'm made of glass," I say. "I won't smash into a million pieces."

"Yeah, well, I don't even want you to get a hairline crack, so let's take a minute to think."

He's right. If we let ourselves dwell on the terrible, it can become us. We know that from being closers. Right now we just have to fake it as long as we can.

"You hungry?" he asks. "I picked up lunch."

"Sure," I say. "I am kind of—"

Deacon motions to the bed across the room, and I see a mountain of vending-machine snacks. I laugh, and when I look back at him, he grins.

"What?" he asks. "I'm a stress eater."

Deacon has fully stocked us with salt-and-vinegar chips, Red Vines, Dr Pepper, and Hostess cakes. We're adulting pretty hard as he spreads it out like a picnic on the extra bed. I sit cross-legged in front of him, our phones set out where we can see them, and I tear open the Red Vines.

"Appetizer?" I ask, holding out the package. Deacon shakes his head and reaches for the Ho Hos.

"Going straight to the main course," he says.

The sounds of crumpling cellophane can barely cover the sadness that's hanging around, and soon enough our attempts at levity become pointless. I adjust the pillows behind me and lie back.

"What do you think they're doing to her?" I ask Deacon, sick at the possibilities.

Deacon lowers his eyes to his food, but he no longer looks hungry. "Well," he says, "I didn't get far, but while I was waiting in the parking lot, I managed to make a few calls, find out the names of a few employees."

This isn't unusual; as closers we've done this sort of research for assignments. We don't always leave it all up to Marie. "And?" I ask.

"I tracked down a receptionist—Magdalena. She had her profile on private, but she accepted my fake friend request. Anyway, she was complaining about work. She said the doctor was making her move boxes and her back was killing her. She suggested he was moving out. So I think that whatever Arthur's doing, it's happening somewhere else. Different facility, possibly."

"You have to break in and find out for sure," I tell him.

"Exactly. And I feel stupid, you know? Even though I never trusted Arthur, part of me believed he really was trying to protect you. That was the one part of him that seemed true. That all changed when he assigned you to Catalina's case. He changed after that."

"Because he thinks I discovered his daughter's connection to the suicides," I say. "And now I'm a liability. Which is why we need to get to Virginia before he erases her. I need to know what she remembered."

"I think . . ." Deacon scrunches up his face like he doesn't like where his thoughts are leading him. "I think part of what's happening to her is my fault, because the memory manipulation with you seems to have started before Virginia's," he says.

"You're Arthur's patient zero, and since I always told him you were fine and well-adjusted, because I lied to him, he went ahead and started testing it on his daughter." Guilt crosses his expression. "So I'm basically the worst person alive." He reaches for a can of Dr Pepper, staring down at it.

"Deacon," I say softly, sitting up, "you were trying to protect me. You didn't know what Arthur was planning. Hell, we still don't. But what matters is that we're here together now. We'll beat this. We'll beat him."

Deacon looks up, his finger on the tab of the soda. "I'm crazy about you," he says, setting the drink aside. "Do anything for you." He crawls up the bed, crushing some of the food under his knees.

I pull him to me and kiss him, threading my fingers through his soft hair. And when his tongue lightly touches my lower lip, I moan against him. We lie back on the bed, brushing the snacks onto the floor. The mood here isn't quite right, but if we waited for that, it never would be.

So I slowly strip away our clothes, and we pay attention to each other, to every need and whisper. We don't speak a word about the epidemic, about Virginia, or about how the chances of us getting out of here alive grow smaller every day. For now we just live.

CHAPTER THREE

THERE'S RADIO SILENCE FOR NEARLY TWO DAYS.
Although we can leave the motel room to eat or run errands,
Marie bars us from contacting anyone other than the closers
involved. She also forbids Deacon from breaking into Arthur's
office or going to his home. As the only adult in our lives, one
that we've all counted on in the past, I guess she still has power
over us.

Reed suspects that Virginia is being treated at home. He
saw an older woman at the house, but he wasn't sure who she
was. Marie guessed it was Dr. Evelyn Valentine and said she'd
follow up. We haven't heard from her since.

There is nothing about Virginia on the news. Despite the fact
that her meltdown took place in front of two teams and half the
school, her name is completely absent from the broadcasts. Absent

from the websites. Like it never happened. Even when I check social media, I find only a few vague references to the event. And then I find a whole slew of accounts that have been locked.

"Do you think the grief department could do this?" I ask Deacon, looking over to where he's sitting at the table, going through a list of former closers, now presumed missing. He's researching them, but he hasn't found anything unusual yet.

"No," he says. "I think the threat of the grief department is causing people to police themselves. Intimidation at its finest." He glances out the window, brow furrowed. "Where the hell's Aaron?" he asks.

Deacon's phone vibrates loudly on the table, and he snatches it up. When he sees who it is, he slips his phone in his pocket and puts on his jacket.

"What are you doing?" I ask. "Who was that?"

Deacon bites down on his lip. I scoff, letting him know that *not telling me* isn't even an option. "I was hoping Aaron would be here by now to take the heat off of me," he says.

"Uh . . . that's an encouraging start," I tell him. "Now, who just texted you?"

"Marie," he says. "She's staying in a short-term apartment across town, and I demanded a meeting. I can't wait around here anymore. I need to know what's going on."

I tilt my head, slightly confused. "Don't we all?" I ask. I'm not sure why going to see Marie would be a secret. I climb off the bed and walk to the chair to grab my jacket. "Fine," I say. "Let's go."

He winces. "She said just me."

Deacon and Marie have had a strained relationship since he left the grief department. His work with Arthur would make them more colleagues than the typical advisor and closer. And when Aaron told him his theory on Marie working for Arthur, Deacon didn't disagree.

"I don't trust Marie, and I think she's hiding something," Deacon says. "She said she wanted the closers to warn them, but instead she recruited them to work for Dr. Valentine. Not far off from transitioning into handlers, wouldn't you say?"

I swallow hard, not wanting to believe that Marie would betray us. Lie to us, sure—she's done it before. But work for Arthur Pritchard and actively put us in danger? No.

"I need to know whose side Marie is really on," Deacon continues. "And if it's not ours, we leave."

"Say it's all true," I tell him. "Say she's working for Arthur and is royally screwing us over. Why would Marie tell you any of it? She isn't exactly an open book."

"Because I plan to drug her with her own truth tea," Deacon says innocently.

I stare a moment and then laugh. "What?"

"Tabitha was able to track some down," he says. "We're not the only ones who don't trust Marie anymore. We just want to know the truth."

"This is absolutely not going to work," I say. "You know that, right?"

Deacon smiles and comes to a pause in front of me. "Oh, baby, with that sort of confidence, I can do anything."

"Be quiet," I say, putting my palm on his cheek. Worried. Terrified. You don't drug a person and go on like nothing happened. I mean, not unless you're their advisor.

Deacon leans in and kisses my lips softly—an obvious, but not unpleasant, distraction. "I love you," he whispers.

"Just be sure to come back," I say, knots tightening in my stomach.

There's a knock on the motel room door, and Deacon goes to open it.

"What's up?" Aaron says with a big smile, but he immediately senses that something's wrong and sucks in a tentative breath. "Aw, shit. What now?"

Deacon slaps his shoulder and starts past him, stopping in the doorway. "I'll be back," he tells Aaron.

"Where you going?" Aaron asks.

Deacon looks past him toward me. "I'm going to get answers," he says, and turns back to Aaron. "I'm sure Quinn will fill you in on my idiotic plan. Now, both of you stay safe. Back as soon as I can."

Before Aaron can ask any more questions, Deacon is out the door. And I'm left in a motel room with a huge weight on my chest.

Reed arrives an hour later, saying he's happy we got in touch. Aaron and I had grown bored, and since we're not allowed to contact nonclosers, Reed was the only choice, since we actually like him.

Reed moved to a place across town with Shep. He'd been staying at a Best Western downtown, but Marie wanted him to keep an eye on Shep since he's only fourteen. But Reed says his roommate barely looks up from his phone, and when he does, it's to be sarcastic.

"It's like living with a younger version of me," Reed says, yanking off his black jacket before tossing it on the chair. "Except terrible and not at all awesome. Please fucking save me," he adds, and sits at a table near the window.

Aaron laughs, lounging back on one of the beds while I sit cross-legged on the other. "Sorry, man," Aaron says. "I only got a double bed, and you look like a snuggler."

Reed smiles. "Oh, I am." He begins to sort our latest pile of vending-machine food on the table, picking through until he finds a pink Sno Ball. He tears open the plastic wrapper and takes a bite, flakes of flavored coconut dusting the chest of his blue Nike T-shirt. "I feel disgusting eating this," he says with a full mouth. "I'll have to find a gym later."

"Wrong crowd," I say. "In fact I don't think Aaron has ever seen the inside of a gym."

Aaron tsks, looking over at me like I'm crazy. "Please," he says. "You think I get this good-looking naturally?"

"No," I say, wide-eyed as if he's wrong about the good-looking part.

Aaron cracks up and then asks Reed to throw him a bag of Doritos. As the two of them happily snack, I lie on my side, facing them. This is nice. I take a moment to enjoy it. I've lived many lives, even if just short-term. I've met many people. On my last assignment I got a chance to hang out with regular people, and I liked it.

But here, now, I am myself. I'm a closer around other closers. I don't think people can understand the freedom in that. These guys understand what my life is like, what my experiences are like. These are my people. These are my friends.

"What's that about?" Reed asks, nodding at me. "You look like you're a million miles away."

"No," I say, smiling softly, "I'm right here. And don't think I'm being weird, but . . . I'm glad we're all together. I'm glad we're all closers."

Aaron and Reed exchange a glance, ready to play off my comment, but they don't say a word. I think they realize it too. This is who we are, and together we don't have to fake anything, pretend anything. Our souls can be stripped bare in the best kind of way.

Reed crumples up the empty cellophane packaging and tosses it into the trash. "You're a nice person, Quinlan," he says, licking the marshmallow off his fingers. "I'd like to say Hatcher doesn't deserve you, but he probably does."

"Naw, he don't," Aaron adds, and turns to give me a quick wink.

"Since we're sharing," I say, digging into a wound he opened earlier, "can I ask you something, Reed? You mentioned the other day that my dad tried to bribe you?"

Reed scrunches his nose, looking embarrassed. "Sorry,"

he says. "I shouldn't have told you that. It wasn't a huge deal, mostly just a passing mention. But on the bright side, it's good to know I didn't take him up on the offer, right? You would have certainly fallen in love with me."

"Did he say why?" I ask, ignoring his joke because my heart aches at the depth of my father's manipulation. "Why he thought I needed you?"

"Not really," Reed says with a shrug. "He just said you were lonely and that he was worried. And honestly, that's normal. What we do? That's *not* normal. Not at all."

"But why you?" I ask.

"Ouch," Reed says, putting his hand over his heart. "Maybe he knows I'm a catch, Quinn. Jesus."

I laugh, admitting the slightly insulting tone of my question. I realize that Reed probably doesn't know my father's true motives, much like I don't. Like I never will. And of course it makes me think of Marie, and how Deacon's right: She's probably hiding something. Knowing my track record, I wouldn't have seen it until it was too late.

"Let's change the subject," Aaron calls out. "The last person I want to talk about is your father." He looks sideways at me to let me know he doesn't mean that cruelly.

"Agreed," I say. I take a moment to sigh out a topic-cleansing breath. "Okay, Reed," I start. "What do you do for fun when you're not on assignment? And please don't say work out."

"I work out." He grins and leans back in the chair. He

stretches his legs so that his sneakers rest on the side of the bed where Aaron's lying, the soles of his shoes not actually touching the sheets. "But, yeah. I do other things too."

"Like?" I ask.

"How detailed you want me to get, Quinn?" he asks, as if daring me.

"Well, we're trapped in this motel for a little longer, so I guess you could tell me all of it."

Aaron sits forward, hitching up the side of his mouth like he's waiting to hear something juicy. Life stories—we just can't get enough of them.

As I figured, Reed comes alive at our interest, not exactly unattractive in his need for attention. It's weirdly endearing.

"Okay, yes—there was a girl," he says, as if that's my real question. It isn't, but no need to burst his ego bubble. "A few girls," he corrects, "but only one that mattered."

"Uh, they all matter, Reed," I say, making sure he's not about to go locker room on me.

He laughs. "Sorry, not what I meant," he says, holding up his hands. "There's only one girl that I *loved*." His expression softens. "One I won't forget."

"Aw . . . ," Aaron says, tilting his head when he looks at me. "My insides feel all tingly."

Reed snatches a package of peanut butter crackers and throws them at Aaron's head, purposely missing him. He's smiling, though, knowing that Aaron has a girlfriend with whom he readily admits he is stupidly in love.

"I had a girl once," Aaron says, pretending to sound forlorn. "But then I left her in Idaho, and I'm pretty sure that by the time I get back to her, she'll hate my guts." He looks at me. "Thanks, Quinn," he sings out.

"Hey!" I say, feeling incredibly guilty. "She'll forgive you. She always does."

"Better be right," he responds. "Enough about my relationship, though. I think Reed was about to get deep with us."

"Whatever," Reed says as Aaron chuckles. "Nothing left to tell. It's over now. Instead, here I am stuck with you guys. Such is life."

"That was incredibly vague," I tell him. "I thought I was getting details."

Reed's expression falters as the closer part of him falls away. His pain shines through. "I'm not sure it's the right story for the mood we want now," he says, holding my gaze. There's a touch of fear in his eyes, like after the volleyball game. Maybe it's been there since.

Sometimes you can know a conversation is disingenuous, but you'll buy into it anyway—like polite small talk. Like the way people will tiptoe around a subject they want to avoid. I once worked with a family who would change the topic of death to one of birth nearly every time. It was a tic, one I came to understand. They replaced the bad memory with a positive one. They adjusted.

Reed, Aaron, and I are here in a motel room, trying to forget, even though we obviously can't. We're trying anyway, stubbornly. Reed's story is going to be sad; it will pull us out of our illusion. But all at once I decide I want to hear about his pain. I want to *feel* it. I want to stop pretending.

"Tell me," I say simply. Across from me Aaron's expression grows somber, and the veil around us drops completely. Our motel room is dim and poorly lit, and these closers are sad and scared. We have nothing left but our past, and only a small bit of that actually belongs to us.

Reed swallows hard, nodding his chin like he agrees to go on. "She was my assignment's sister," he says. "And before you say anything—I know. Unethical doesn't even begin to cover it."

I'm not judging him. He has no idea that I thought I was in love with my assignment's boyfriend. "Okay," I say, not willing to delve into my own failings as a closer. Aaron doesn't out me either.

"It didn't start as anything," Reed says, watching the toes of his sneakers. "In fact she was completely uninterested in the process. For the first two days she wouldn't even sleep under the same roof. It was Sunday night, and I was leaving in the morning, when there was a knock on my bedroom door. When I opened it, she was standing there like her world had just collapsed. She asked if she could come in, and it was the first time I actually looked at her. I tried not to," he says, "since I was supposed to act like her brother, but I thought she was beautiful.

"The minute I opened my mouth to talk," he continues, "she asked me to stop. Asked me to be myself or she would leave. And . . . I didn't want her to. It was right at the end of the assignment—that feeling, you know?" He taps his chest and looks from me to Aaron. "That feeling like it's all ending, you're ending. It's too fucked up to explain."

"I get it," I tell Reed, watching as he starts to unravel the carefully crafted exterior he's shown us until now. "I've been there. Truly."

He presses his lips in a grateful smile. "Katy and I ended up talking all night," he continues. "I told her my real name, and she asked all sorts of questions about closers. I don't think we mentioned her brother once. The next morning, before I left, I stopped at her door to say good-bye, but she was gone. She never wanted to be part of the closure; she'd already made her peace before I got there."

Reed exhales. "I'd been home two weeks when she showed up at my apartment," he says. "She'd tracked me down because I'd given her my name."

"Dude," Aaron says, shaking his head. "Closer 101."

"Yeah, I know. It was stupid. I can't believe Marie didn't find out, to be honest. She must have been having an off week."

"What happened after that?" I ask. "How did you . . . make it work? It's a pretty bizarre set of circumstances."

"The way all terrible ideas work," Reed says. "We snuck around. At first we tried to be friends. But a few nights in the backseat of my car . . ."

"Ew," I say, making him laugh. "I sat back there."

"I've had it detailed since," he jokes. "But for real, we had a good thing. Katy wasn't a closer, but it was like she understood. It's strange, but . . . I've been noticing that. Lately I meet people who are good at disguising themselves—regular people. Although some seem to be getting weaker, a few others are getting stronger. Guess it all depends on how a person reacts to tragedy."

"I've seen the same," Aaron says. "It's like there's a divide between those who can hack it and those who can't." He looks over at me. "It's like closers are predisposed to handle the disappointments of life. They're trying to be like us."

"This isn't life," I tell him, nodding toward the window. "What's happening out there is a mass hysteria being fed by a delusional doctor."

"Yeah, maybe," Aaron says. "Or maybe our way of life is how they can avoid it. Never get attached—right, Quinn?" He says it like a mantra, one that we sucked at following. It's our biggest failing and, at the same time, our greatest quality.

I turn back to Reed. "What happened to her?" I ask.

"Katy?" he says, seeming lost in his thoughts. "Oh, well . . . she died. She, uh . . . yeah. She died in a boating accident a few months later. Of course . . . she was on the boat alone. She . . ." He swallows hard and lowers his eyes. "She killed herself."

My lips part in surprise, and I think about her poor family. They lost two children—how does one recover from that? Is that what will happen if the epidemic gets worse?

"I couldn't go to the funeral for fear her parents would see me," Reed says. "It would have compromised their healing, and I couldn't make it worse for them." His cheeks pale, and tears dull his blue eyes. "I loved her, you know," he says quietly. "God, I *still* love her. We were going to leave town when I finished my contract, use the money to go to college. She was going to be a teacher. The money was always for her."

"I'm sorry," I say, although I know it's not enough, and I know it doesn't matter if I say it. It doesn't change a damn thing.

"I think the worst part was keeping her a secret," he adds. "Even more so after she was dead. I was pulled from my next assignment, stuck in therapy by Marie for three weeks because they said I was acting erratically. Do you have any idea how hard it is to lie to them? To find a way to evade the chemicals in their truth tea? I did it, though," he says. "Not because I had to—Katy was already dead. I lied because she was mine, and I didn't want them to have her. She was my secret."

The air in the room has grown heavy, and Reed drops his feet to the floor and leans forward, his elbows on his knees as he rests his head in his hands, his fingers shielding his tears. I realize then that he's never told that story before; he had no idea how much it would hurt.

I get up and go over to where Reed is sitting and bend down to wrap my arms around his shoulders. He doesn't hug me back, but he does turn his face against my side. We stay like that a moment; when he pulls back, his eyes are red and watery.

"We should have been friends sooner, McKee," he says, looking up at me.

"We are now," I say. "And at least now is real."

Reed smiles sadly. "Sometimes."

And the three of us fall quiet after that, alone in this little motel room. Lonely in the life that we've made for ourselves.

CHAPTER FOUR

REED GOES INTO THE BATHROOM AND SPLASHES
water on his face while Aaron and I sit quietly in the room.
I'm worried that Deacon hasn't texted yet. I told Aaron about
Deacon's plan when he first arrived and it caused a permanent
crease between his brows. But when I look over now, Aaron
seems to read my thoughts and tells me to wait a little while
longer before getting really worried. Luckily, I have my own
plan on how to get information.

When the water turns off, I look over at Aaron and find
him watching me. He waits a beat and then laughs to himself.

"You're thinking," he says.

"You're right," I tell him. Reed walks out of the bathroom,
wiping a towel over his face, and notices our demeanor.

He stops abruptly and groans. "What are you about to

make me do?" he asks, and tosses the white towel back over his shoulder onto the bathroom floor.

There's a car parked in Arthur Pritchard's driveway, one none of us recognize, but a check in the garage window proves that Arthur's car is gone. He's probably at his office, but it's nearly five o'clock, so I worry he'll be home soon.

"Try her again," Aaron whispers.

I dial Virginia's number, but it goes immediately to an automated voice mail. Reed is standing off to the side, staring up at the house, his brow furrowed. When I told him we were going to find Virginia and rescue her, he wasn't exactly keen on the idea. Especially since Marie told us not to come here. Reed eventually relented, because, honestly, none of us are great at following rules. But also because we want what's best. And we know that keeping a girl locked away in her house is cruel and unusual, and we want to find out why. Why is Virginia being punished? What does she remember?

"Do you know which room is hers?" Reed asks. I think back to when Deacon and I broke in, but I didn't get a chance to fully explore the house. I remember the layout, though, so I guide us around the side of the house and point to the gate.

Reed jumps and catches his hand on the top, pulling himself over, the huge muscles on his biceps flexed. I turn to look back at Aaron, and he rolls his eyes.

I chuckle and walk up to the fence. Aaron bends his knee next to me, and I step on it for a boost. I find Reed on the other side, a hand stretched out to help me over. Once we're all in the backyard, we cling to the wall and slowly make our way around the house.

There are several windows, but they're high up from where we stand in the sloped yard. Based on the layout of the home we saw, I use process of elimination to guess which one is Virginia's.

We pause under the window, debating the best way to get the attention of the person inside. We want to be able to hide if it's not her.

"This is going to sound completely implausible," Reed says, crouching down to pick up a handful of small pebbles from a garden pathway. Aaron looks at him like he's crazy, but I'm not sure we have a better option. The three of us go to hide behind a small shed near the corner of the house.

"How's your aim?" I ask Reed. He laughs and looks sideways at me.

"Perfect, obviously." He pokes out his head from behind the shed and tosses a pebble at the window, making a hollow click. We wait, hidden enough that we can slide out of sight if someone we don't know appears. A minute passes, and Reed gets ready to throw another, when the curtains slip open. I hold my breath.

"It's her," I say, pushing Reed's shoulder. Virginia opens her window, looking confused as she darts her gaze around the yard. I step out from behind the shed, and she gasps like I startled her.

"Hey," I say awkwardly . . . since I'm hiding in her back-yard. "Can, uh . . . can you talk for a minute?"

Virginia looks behind her and then turns back to me. "Who are you?" she asks.

My heart sinks to the ground. She's been erased again—we're too late. "My name's Quinn," I say, no longer bothering with my other identity. "I'm your friend."

Virginia's hands slide over the windowsill, gripping it like she's steadying herself. Does it shock her? Or has she come to expect the fault in her memory at this point? After a moment she holds up her index finger.

"I'll meet you out front," she says. "Do you have a car?"

I tell her that we do, and without a word she lowers the window before turning away and disappearing inside. I look at Aaron and Reed, and both seem concerned.

"She really doesn't remember," Reed says, sounding horri-fied. "She had no idea who you were."

"Just like last time," I tell them. "They did it again." I curse and run my fingers through my hair, frustrated. Scared. "We shouldn't have let them take her," I say, struggling with my own guilt.

But beyond the horror of Virginia's memories being wiped out, I'm also disappointed. I'd hoped she would help me recover my own. Arthur didn't just steal her memories; he stole the pos-sibility of me getting mine.

We need to trigger her memory again.

"There's a place," I tell Aaron and Reed. "A lighthouse on the coast. We have to get her there."

"Uh . . ." Aaron looks alarmed. "And why would we do that?"

"Because her memories are there."

Aaron, Reed, and I all get to the front and wait near the car, just down the road from the house. As the minutes tick by, we start to fidget, worried that Virginia couldn't get out or that her father's been alerted. But then, suddenly, she appears in the bushes on the side of the house and picks her way through until she stumbles onto the sidewalk. She has a backpack, like she's set to run away.

"Shit," Reed murmurs under his breath. "I thought we were just going to talk to her."

"Looks like it's going to be a little more involved than that," I say to him, and hold up my hand in a wave for Virginia. She smiles, and I realize that I may have given her the wrong idea when I said "friend"—she won't like it when she finds out we're all closers.

"Hey," she says, blushing when she notices Reed and his alarmingly good looks. "We'd better get out of here," she adds. "My father will be on his way home."

We rush to the car, and Virginia and I hop in the backseat while Reed starts the engine. Virginia stashes her backpack behind Reed's seat, hope shining in her eyes as we pull away from her house. When we get around the corner, she turns to me without even a flicker of recognition.

"Who are you people?" she asks, perhaps not as naïve as I'd

thought. Reed glances at her in the rearview mirror, and Aaron doesn't react at all.

"We're closers," I say.

Virginia's jaw tightens. "So my father sent you," she accuses. "Why bother? He's already—"

"We don't work for your father anymore," I tell her. "I swear it. We're here to help you. I . . . I was there the other day at the game. You were upset, enraged. You said you remembered everything."

She tilts her head, trying to figure me out. "What game?"

In the passenger seat Aaron turns to look out the window.

"You were at a volleyball game," I say, hating that I have to fill in the blanks of her life. "You told your coach that you remembered everything. She called your father." Virginia tenses at the mention, but I press on. "You begged them not to erase you again," I say. "But they dragged you away."

Virginia bites the inside of her lip and lowers her eyes to the floor. I can tell that she's searching for the memory, but after a moment she takes in a shaky breath like she might cry, and I know that she can't find it. I put my hand on her shoulder to comfort her.

"This has happened before," I tell her. "And last time you took me to the lighthouse. Maybe if we go there—"

"Lighthouse?" she repeats.

"The lighthouse you said you and your friends called the End of the World."

She stares back at me as if she's never heard of it, and I have a new spike of worry. She's forgotten it. And if that's true, than this erasure goes deeper than the others. I swallow past the dryness in my throat. Maybe she can't be fixed this time. But then again, maybe this is how they meant to fix her.

"I know where the lighthouse is," I say calmly, even though my insides are in knots. I lean forward and give Reed the directions, the mood in the car shifting to melancholy. Reed nods, taking the turns as directed. Aaron checks his phone.

"Anything?" I ask him.

He shakes his head. "Not yet," he says. Aaron looks back and tries to smile encouragingly, but I know he's starting to worry now too. "I'm sure he's fine," he adds. "Deacon's always fine."

Although it should have taken us nearly an hour, Reed gets us to the lighthouse in about forty minutes. His race-car driving skills seemed to impress Virginia, who gazed at him in the rearview the entire time while Reed tried to dodge her attention.

Reed pulls up to the walkway in front of the lighthouse. I've tried Deacon's phone a dozen times, but he's not answering. I bury my panic as best I can because there's nothing I can do to help him right now.

The scenery of the lighthouse is just like it was the last time I was here: peaceful, beautiful, and lonely. I look sideways at Virginia and wait for some sign of recognition, but when she turns to me, she just smiles.

"It's pretty," she says.

"We should go inside," I say, turning back to the lighthouse.

We all climb out of the car and come to a pause at the walk-way. Aaron sighs heavily, reluctant to walk into an abandoned building. The wind is strong here, and his jacket billows in the breeze as he hangs back a step. I start forward with Virginia, strands of her windblown hair sticking to her lip gloss.

I'm about to ask for her key when the door comes into to view. My heart stops. The padlock is gone, a dead bolt now in its place. I shoot an alarmed look back at Aaron, who comes over and tries the handle. It doesn't open.

"That wasn't here last time," I tell him. "Someone's been inside."

Aaron takes a step back and then rams his shoulder into the door. There's a crack of wood, but it doesn't open. Reed sniffs and comes to stand next to Aaron, looking more than ready to show off.

"On three?" Reed asks.

"Yeah," Aaron says, rubbing his shoulder. I assume that hurt him more than it hurt the door.

They count down, and on three Reed bursts forward, slam-ming his shoulder into the door and popping the lock open. The wooden door cracks at the frame and slams into the wall behind it. Reed pulls his face into an exaggerated expression.

"Ow!" he says, and looks at Aaron, who is still standing at the starting point.

"Sorry," Aaron says. "I figured you were strong enough to get it on your own."

"Asshole," Reed mumbles, rubbing his shoulder. Virginia watches him, taken by Reed's baited heroics. Despite his disinterest, Reed is a good closer: He turns and flashes Virginia a winning smile.

"After you," he tells her, holding out his arm like a gentleman.

Virginia walks inside, fading into the shadows before Reed, looking uneasy, heads in behind her.

Aaron pauses next to me and murmurs, "Here we go." We both walk in and are immediately struck by the toxic smell of fresh paint. Standing in the center of the circular room, Virginia puts her hand over her nose to block the scent.

But my breath is caught in my chest as I spin to look around the room. The walls have been completely painted over with sterile white paint. I run to the stairs and start up them, shoes echoing on the metal and all around the cylinder. I search for Catalina's note. But it's gone—every single word covered up.

"No," I say, finding the spot where I think it used to be. I begin to scratch at the paint, but a chip lodges painfully under my nail. I cry out and tear my hand away. I feel desperate to find the words, to find Catalina. I start to cry.

Aaron appears next to me and pulls me away from the wall. "Calm down," he whispers, putting his arms around me. "You're okay."

"It was all here," I tell him. "All of Virginia's memories. Catalina had been here. Other people. But they're all dead now, and this was what was left of them."

"I believe you," Aaron says. "But obviously someone else got here first. Which means we have to leave. Now."

I look down the stairs at Virginia. "Do you remember any of this?" I ask her. "Does it look familiar?"

I see that she wants to tell me it does, but I read the lie before she speaks it. I cover my face, trying to regain my composure but failing. I thought this could work. Those memories were here, triggers for her. But someone found out, and they didn't want her to remember.

It can't end like this. I go downstairs and stop in front of Virginia, an irrational wave of betrayal in my chest, even though it was her life on these walls. "Who else did you tell?" I ask. "Who else knows about this place?"

"I don't know," she says. "I don't even remember it myself. I have no idea why we're here, Quinn. What does any of this mean?"

I stare up sadly to the top of the tower, the place that was supposed to be filled with hope. But now it's just another dead end. There's no point in telling her about the notes, even if I could remember them all. There will just be another roadblock, and another. And I wonder how many I'll need to hit before I give up entirely.

CHAPTER FIVE

THAT LIGHTHOUSE WAS THE ONLY SAFETY NET VIRGINIA had. I'm devastated for her, and as she stares out the window of the car, she doesn't even know what she's lost. I do, though. And it feels like I've lost too.

Aaron wanted us to bring Virginia back to our motel until we heard from Deacon. He didn't think her house was safe. I told him our motel probably wasn't safe either, but he reminded me that our options were limited. Fact remained, someone had learned of Virginia's lifeline and decided to erase it. The leading suspect is her father.

We still haven't heard from Deacon, and I can only hope he's okay. And curse myself for letting him go in the first place.

When we get to the motel, Virginia looks around the

meager complex. Aaron leads the way up the stairs, but before I get to the landing, Reed reaches out to take my hand.

"Quinn," he says quietly, "be careful. I don't know what's going on with you right now, but your behavior at the light-house . . ." He narrows his eyes to study me. "I think you're too attached to this. It's compromising all of us."

He has no idea; he has no idea what I went through with Catalina Barnes's family, with her boyfriend, and how I know what it's really like to be compromised on assignment. I don't know how to *not* get attached.

I squeeze his hand. "Thank you," I say. "I'll be careful; I promise." I don't provide an explanation, even though I can see that he wants one. I'm sad that Catalina's words are gone; part of me was still connected to her. Now I've lost her last mark on my world.

There were ways to get the information on the lighthouse; I doubt Virginia gave it away. If only she knew what they've stolen.

Aaron and Virginia are at the room door, and I step ahead to swipe my key card. I push the door open, motioning for Virginia to go on in. She studies me as she passes, like she's concerned about my behavior too. Reed follows her in, but Aaron and I hang back to talk.

I let the door close, and we go to the railing, facing the parking lot. "You okay?" he asks quietly.

"Not really," I tell him. We both check our surroundings, the threat of being followed real now that we've seen how far Arthur will go to keep Virginia from her memories. Because of course it's Arthur who's done this. Who else would be so cruel?

"What does he want?" I ask, looking sideways at Aaron. "What does Arthur want for his daughter? I don't understand why he's wiping her memory. Why did he do it to me?"

Aaron stares at me a long moment and then blinks rapidly. "Wait," he says. "What are you talking about?"

I realize that he doesn't know. I told him about my father not being my father, but Deacon and I never told him about my memory or about Deacon working for Arthur. We didn't mean to shut him out. At least, I don't think we consciously meant to. My skin prickles when I swallow hard and say, "Arthur's erased my memory several times."

Aaron swings around, his back against the railing, and furrows his brow. "That son of a bitch," he growls.

"There's more," I start, wishing Deacon were here to explain this next part himself. But he's not, and I can't keep our friend in the dark anymore. "You remember back when Deacon quit and we broke up?" I ask. "Right before that, Deacon was brought in to meet with Arthur." Aaron shifts uncomfortably. "Arthur told Deacon that I was an experiment of sorts, his patient zero. He said I'd undergone memory manipulation and that he needed me monitored for any changes. He . . . he, uh, hired Deacon to do that. He made Deacon a handler."

Aaron's expression is immediately stricken. "Please tell me you're fucking with me right now," he says.

I shake my head no. "But Deacon didn't tell him anything," I explain quickly. "He only took the job so that Arthur wouldn't hire someone else in his place. He's been looking out for me. He had no idea that Arthur had continued to manipulate my memories. He—"

"So you're telling me that your boyfriend is a liar?" Aaron says, his tone ticking up in volume. "You're saying that the thing Marie is supposedly trying to help us get away from is exactly what Deacon willingly signed up for?"

This is not going well. "Yes," I say. "But—"

Aaron widens his eyes, taking a step back from me. "Stop," he says. "I . . . I left Myra to help you guys. You've fucked up my life and it didn't occur to you to tell me what Deacon's gotten into?" He shakes his head, his face pulled into a sneer. "I've got to go," he murmurs suddenly, and starts to walk away.

"Aaron?" I call, surprised he didn't give me a chance to explain. "Wait!" He doesn't look back and continues down the corridor.

The door opens, startling me, and Reed pokes his head out. He notices Aaron walking away and then sees me with my hand still on the railing, staring stupidly back at him.

"Everything all right?" Reed asks.

"No. Not quite," I respond. *Aaron needs time to cool off,* I assure myself. *He'll be back.* I should have waited for Deacon to explain, even if that meant lying to Aaron a little longer.

"Let's get inside," I tell Reed, not wanting to have this same discussion with him. Reed steps aside in the doorway so I can walk in. Virginia sits on the bed, and I take the spot nearest the window so I can fold back the curtain and watch the parking lot for Deacon's car.

I feel Reed watching me. The room has grown uncomfortably warm, a burning scent in the air from the heater running on high. I glance over at Reed. "What?" I ask.

He shakes his head. "Nothing," he says. "I'm going to grab a Coke. Want anything?" I tell him I'm not thirsty, and he asks Virginia if she's interested in a chilled beverage.

"Sure," she says. "Thanks."

Reed leaves for the vending machines downstairs, and once he's gone, Virginia comes to sit on the bed closest to me. I keep my eyes on the parking lot.

"Deacon?" Virginia asks after a moment. I let the curtain fall closed. "You mentioned him earlier," she continues. "Is he your boyfriend?"

"Deacon's my everything," I tell her. Not in a lovesick way—we're way past that. It's my truth. Deacon is my boyfriend, my best friend, my family. And right now I don't know where he is, and the fear in that is starting to suffocate me.

The corner of Virginia's mouth turns up like she thinks the words are meant to be romantic. "I thought maybe you and Reed . . ."

"No," I say. "Reed and I are just friends. Like I told you, we're all closers."

She nods and eases herself down on the edge of the bed. "Closers," she says as if reminding herself. "My father once told me that closers don't feel the same way the rest of us do. He said he handpicked all of you for exactly that reason."

This revelation twists in my stomach. "What else did he

say?" I ask. I want to tell her that her father took custody of me at one point when I was a child, but I'm not sure what that would accomplish. She can't remember. She seems even emptier than before.

"He never mentioned any of you by name," Virginia tells me. "But he said closers can mimic people really well because they don't want to be themselves. He says all of you are abandoned." She pauses and looks at me. "Does my father know you're here?"

"No," I say. "At least I don't think so. He's lying, by the way. Closers do want to be themselves—they want their lives. Your father and the grief department kept us from them, though. They used us. Anything he says to the contrary is a lie."

"Do you have a family?" she asks gently. I flinch at the question.

"Not anymore," I say. "And we made an agreement earlier, you and me. I was going to help you find your memories, and in return you were going to get me access to your father's files. I got into his computer, but I didn't find anything. When I saw you had recovered your memories . . . I thought you'd be able to help me." My eyes start to well up. "Your dad has hidden my identity—he erased my memories too. And now he's taken my best chance to get them back."

"So it's not just me," she says, but the thought of this seems to horrify her, to displace her. Virginia studies her hands in her lap. "I'll look into it for you," she offers quietly. She lifts her eyes to mine. "But I'll have to go home first."

There's a click, and I turn to see Reed standing in the doorway, holding two sodas. "She's right," he says. "She has to go home." He puts the drinks on the table and steadies a hard gaze on me. "Can I talk to you for a second?" he asks in a lowered tone.

"Uh . . . yeah. Sure," I say.

I tell Virginia we'll be right back, and I walk outside with Reed, noting the chill that has crept into the air. Reed goes to the wood railing, grips it, and turns to me.

"Arthur knows we're with Virginia," he says.

The world seems to drop out from under me. "What?" I ask. "How do you know that?" I look around, afraid I'll find Arthur rushing up the stairs to grab me. But it's just me and Reed out here.

"Marie called while I was downstairs," Reed says. "She told me Arthur contacted her and said that if his daughter isn't home within the hour, he'll put out an Amber Alert. He's saying we kidnapped her."

"She came willingly," I snap, as if he's arguing. "We didn't throw her in a sack and drag her away. And what about Deacon?" I ask. "What does he say?"

"Marie didn't mention him," Reed responds. "I barely got five words out before Marie told me that Tabitha is missing. She wants us to meet right now at her apartment for a debriefing. Deacon's probably waiting there. Marie said she's sending us home."

"Home?" Aaron says, and I turn to see him walking down

the hall toward us. "Which of us has a home?" Reed furrows his brow, confused at Aaron's bitter tone.

But my entire body has tensed with fear—why wouldn't Marie mention Deacon? Why wouldn't he have just gotten on the phone? He went there to drug her with truth tea—obviously that didn't happen. "Aaron," I say, sounding desperate. "Have you heard from Deacon?"

"Nope. Maybe he's with his boy Arthur."

"I'm not fucking kidding," I say.

Aaron's face grows serious. "Neither am I, Quinlan." We stare each other down, but more than anything I'm hurt that he's not more worried. Although I shouldn't judge him so harshly. When I thought Deacon had betrayed me, I left him in a bus station.

"I'm sure Deacon's okay," Reed tells me, reaching to put his cool hand over mine. It startles me, and when I look at him, I note the dark circles under his eyes.

"This isn't like him," I tell him. "He wouldn't leave me here to worry."

"Deacon doesn't always do what we expect, now, does he?" Aaron interjects. I nearly start to cry at his harshness, and Aaron's eyes soften slightly. "I'll see you at Marie's," he murmurs. He passes by and goes down the stairs.

"Do I want to know what that's about?" Reed asks me.

"Not really." I take out my phone to dial Deacon's number again. With each ring my concern grows. *Where is he?* When the line goes to voice mail, I hang up and dial Marie. Again no answer. I turn to Reed.

"I have to get to Marie's," I say. "Can you take Virginia home for me?"

He flinches. "I'd really rather not," he says. "If I'm being honest, she scares the hell out of me." He looks at my closed door. "I mean, it's not *her*, exactly. But if everyone around her is dying, Quinn, I'd like to keep our interaction to a minimum. I'm not in a good headspace right now."

"I have to check on Deacon," I say, my voice softer. "Please help me with this."

Reed watches me a moment, and then he nods. "Of course," he says.

"Thank you," I say, and hug him. "You're a really good closer, Reed."

After a moment he pulls back and looks down at me, my hands still on his forearms. "I think I'd rather be a good person," he whispers.

The door of the motel room opens, and Virginia walks out, her backpack over her shoulders. She looks between me and Reed and then presses her lips into a smile. "Well, let's go," she says.

Reed straightens, seemingly taken aback by her eagerness to go home. He tightens his jacket around himself.

Virginia shrugs. "My father's already erased my memory," she tells us. "What more can he do?"

Without missing a beat, Reed goes over to her. "Let's not think about that. Here"—he offers to take her bag—"I'll give you a ride home." And even I'm charmed by his boyish tone and chivalry.

Virginia hands over her backpack, and as Reed heads for the stairs, she looks at me. "I'm going to help you," Virginia tells me. "I'll find out who you are."

"I promise I'll help you, too," I say, hoping that I can. Instead of looking relieved by my words, a bit of sadness colors her expression.

"It's too late for that," she responds quietly.

And before I can ask what she means, she rushes after Reed. I call for a taxi, hoping that Deacon will indeed be waiting for me at Marie's. He has to be.

Like Aaron said earlier: Deacon is always okay.

CHAPTER SIX

MARIE IS STAYING IN A STUDIO APARTMENT JUST outside downtown Roseburg. When I get dropped off out front, I practically sprint up the two flights of stairs and bang on her door. I'm surprised when Shep opens it, but I rush past him, bumping his shoulder.

"Hey," he calls after me. "Nice to see you too."

Once inside, I quickly dart my gaze around. The room is hardly furnished, with only a twin bed and a folding chair—not what I'd expect from Marie. Then again, she's only been here a few days.

Shep plops himself down on the floor, and I find Aaron hanging near the sink in the efficiency kitchen. His eyes are downcast and his palm is flat over his mouth.

Marie sits in the folding chair, legs crossed and her hands

on her knee. She's normally a vision, but today I see someone different. She is stripped down with no lipstick and her braids gathered up in a messy bun. Her clothes are wrinkled, and her feet are bare. I've never seen Marie as anything other than what she wants to portray—perfection.

But my chest is burning and my fingers begin to tremble. "Where is he?" I demand, glaring at her. "Where's Deacon?"

"Tabitha disappeared last night," she says calmly. "And now it seems . . . so has Deacon."

"I don't understand," I say, starting to shake. "He was here with you. He came to see you, Marie. Where did he—"

"No." She shakes her head, her expression solemn. "He never arrived. I only found out he wasn't with you because Aaron just told me."

I turn to Aaron, so lit up with fear that my voice cracks. "You said he'd be okay," I tell him, hoping he'll still claim that it's true. But Aaron winces and lifts his eyes to the ceiling.

"Keep your head," Marie says to me. I look at her, tears spilling onto my cheeks as my emotions spin out of control. "You have to keep your head, Quinlan," she repeats, "if we hope to get him back."

"Back from whom?" I ask, putting my hand over my heart to stop the pain there.

"I'm not sure," Marie says sympathetically. "Not yet. That's why you're all here." She reaches down to pick up a file from the floor under her seat.

I do what she asks—I temper my emotions, trying to lock

them away so I can think rationally. *Deacon's fine.* I won't believe anything else. But it's an impossible task. I want to scream and run and do everything in my power to find Deacon. That won't work, though. I need a plan.

"This is Tabitha's file," Marie continues. "She didn't return to her apartment last night, and her phone has been disconnected. Since no body has turned up, there's no reason to think she's deceased." Marie opens the folder on her lap. I know what she's done. She's compiled Tabitha's history, breaking her entire life down into a file-size report. I'm relieved that she doesn't have one for Deacon.

There's a quick knock, and Reed opens the door. Marie waves him in impatiently, and I nod as Reed passes me on his way to the kitchen, pausing at the counter next to Aaron. I notice immediately how his expression has darkened. Aaron leans in and whispers to him about Deacon, and Reed flashes me a concerned look. I press my lips together and let him know I'm okay. Or, at least, I'm trying to be.

"I've been unable to get in touch with Dr. McKee," Marie continues. She doesn't even glance at me when she mentions my father's name, and fresh fear of his condition burns my skin. But it's just one of my many problems. "It is entirely possible that Tabitha has run away to Portland," Marie says. "And that is her right. So now I'm giving you the same option. It's too late for closers here. There is no cure for this epidemic."

Reed shifts on his feet. Aaron walks out from behind the

counter and crosses his arms over his chest. Marie sees them both, still avoiding my eyes, and closes the folder on her lap.

"And what about Deacon?" I ask, panicked at the lack of immediate answers. "What happened to him?"

Marie sits quietly, letting dread and fear surround us in the room. "I know he wouldn't leave without you," she says in a measured tone. "So the fact that he's not here means that he's in danger."

No, I think. *No, please.* "Then we're going to save him," I say simply. "And you're going to help us."

Marie gives me a stoic look of admiration, agreement. She glances past me to Shep. "There's money in an envelope on the counter to help you get out of town," she tells him. "Let me be very clear—go far. Any interference will only cause more complications for us. We have bigger things to consider now." She stands, her rigid posture shutting down further conversation on the topic. "Thank you for your time, Shepard. Please go."

Shep gets to his feet, slapping hands with Reed before grabbing the envelope and heading to the door. Attachment is clearly not one of his difficulties. The minute the door closes behind him, Aaron scoffs.

"What was that about?" he asks Marie. "We need him to find Deacon."

"No we don't," she says. "He's a handler for Arthur. I only found out about Shep yesterday morning—Tabitha told me. And then she disappeared."

"That's not possible," Reed says, sounding stunned. "Shep..."

He runs his fingers roughly through his hair. "I was staying with him. He's a kid."

"You're all kids," Marie responds, standing up. "And yet we've used you anyway."

The words are harsh, and Aaron flinches against them. Marie notices his reaction and takes a step toward him before stopping herself. "I wish you'd stayed away," she tells him quietly. "You and Myra had a real chance. But now . . . now we need your help."

Aaron's jaw is clenched. Although he cares about us, he misses Myra. I took that from him when I asked for his help. I'm to blame for this. He tilts his chin up defiantly. "Yeah, no shit," he says. "I'm not leaving without Deacon."

I press my lips together, holding back a cry. My gratitude. Aaron shifts his dark eyes to mine, and they glass over. No matter what, we don't abandon each other. We're family.

"I hoped you'd say that," Marie tells him. "Now, I need you to trail him, track him, I don't care how," she says. "You need to find Deacon and bring him home."

Aaron looks at me when he answers. "We'll get him back. I promise."

Marie turns to Reed, a slight crease between her eyebrows. "We could use you too, Reed," she says. "You in?"

"Yeah," he says, and forces a small smile. "I didn't have much to go back to anyway."

I walk over and put my hand on his arm, grateful for his help. But he lowers his eyes at my touch, his thoughts seemingly clouded. Marie notices too.

"And, Reed," she adds, "stay away from Virginia Pritchard. She . . . she's not well, and I'm concerned. So please, under no circumstances should you contact her. Do you understand?"

"Not a problem," he says.

Marie studies him for another second before saying thank you. Reed's demeanor alarms me, and I do the same, noting the strange mood that seems to plague him. As if he got some really bad news. As if he's really sad . . . deeply sad.

"Now," Marie says, drawing my attention again, "I suspect Shep will tell Arthur everything we've said. So be careful. Get new places to stay. I know you'll want to go searching now, but we need to be smart about this. Start by tracing his car and phone; see if you can get a location on them. Do *not* go charging over to Arthur Pritchard's house. He's a dangerous man."

She pauses. "In fact," she says, "leave Arthur to me. Perhaps there are still deals to be made. Get set up and I'll contact you the minute I know more."

"You'll contact us?" Aaron repeats, taking a step toward her. "You want us to trust you . . . after everything?" The mention of Marie making a deal with Arthur has clearly gotten under his skin. In his career he never once doubted Marie. But in the last week he's learned what she did to me, how she lied. I'm not sure he'll ever truly trust her again.

"You have no choice, Aaron," she says simply. "We have to work together on this."

"And who do you really work for, Marie?" he asks. I look

from him to Marie, scared of the answer. "Who are you running from?" Aaron adds. "We deserve to know before we get in any deeper with you."

Marie's expression grows calm. "I work for myself, Aaron," she tells him. "And part of that is making sure you're all safe. The rest is really none of your business. Now get started. I'll be in touch." She turns away and grabs her laptop from the bed. "We don't have much time."

We wait a minute to see if she'll admit what's really going on, but she doesn't say a word more about it. It might be our training or our past with her, but we allow her silence.

And so we walk out her door without the answer.

Aaron and I exit the building with Reed trailing behind us. He's been quiet since he returned from dropping off Virginia, and I plan to discuss it with him, but I'm a fucking mess. So instead I walk over to Aaron and hug him—my friend seeming to need it just as much, because he buries his face in my hair and squeezes me tight.

We don't lie. We don't promise. We give ourselves one second to fall completely apart. And then, like good closers, we bury our feelings and straighten up. Aaron turns away, wiping his cheeks. I don't bother.

Outside, it's dark, and cold droplets of drizzle paint the windshields of the cars parked at the curb. I bury my hands in the pockets of my coat, and Reed pauses near us.

"I just wanted a normal life," Aaron says into the wind

before turning around. "I just wanted to get my girl and live my life."

His words hit me in the chest. "I'm so sorry," I say. "I shouldn't have called you."

Aaron curls his lip. "Are you crazy?" he says. "This is *not* your fault, Quinn. None of us are to blame. The system, the people we trusted—they've wronged us."

"We're trapped," Reed adds from behind us. "Don't you see we've always been trapped?"

The words are heavy, and I look at the wet sidewalk, thinking about something my father told me before I left town. He told me that if I stayed, the grief department would find a way to get me back under contract. *By any means necessary,* he said. Whether it be money, or blackmail, or threats. I turn toward Marie's building. Whether it be our advisor.

"She's the one who brought us together," I say, mostly to myself at first. But then I furrow my brow as the thought comes together in my head. I look at Aaron. "Marie gathered all of her scattered closers. Sure, I tracked her down—but was it really that hard?" I ask. "Her number was practically waiting for me. She said she was warning us, but instead . . . Deacon was right," I say, my voice ticking up in volume. "She's trying to make us into handlers. And now two of us are missing."

Aaron curses, and glares up at her building. "Then we have to find Deacon on our own," he says darkly. "We're done trusting people."

"Agreed," I say, courage building in my chest. "And I think

I know where to start looking." I turn to Reed. "You want to drive or do you want to jump in with us?" I ask, motioning to Aaron's car.

"I have something to do first," Reed says, taking a step back. "It's stupid and dangerous and I don't want you involved."

"You should know by now that stupid and dangerous are exactly the kinds of things that Quinn does best," Aaron says.

Reed hesitates, but I reach out my hand to him. Both as support and a plea for help. I need him right now. And after another second of thought he takes it and lets me pull him along to Aaron's car. The rain has started to pick up, so I flip up my hood while we wait for Aaron to unlock the door. He opens the passenger side before rounding the front to get in.

I push the seat forward, and Reed climbs into the back, his confidence and humor now missing. I get in and close the door. As Aaron starts the engine, I look back at Reed, concerned.

"You sure you're okay?" I ask him. I want to ask what else he had to do, but as closers, we don't demand people's secrets. It may end up hurting us in the end, but privacy in our world is something we covet.

Reed smiles, and I can't decide if he's faking it or feeling genuinely glad he's riding along. "I'm good," he says. "Thanks for asking."

I nod and turn toward the front. Next to me Aaron glances in the rearview mirror at him. "You know what?" he says, maybe picking up on the same melancholy that I am. "When this is all over, I'm going to miss you, you handsome bastard."

Reed sniffs a laugh. "We've had quite the summer-camp romance, Aaron," he responds.

The misery of our moment is temporarily replaced with care and compassion. This has been the most twisted, heartbreaking week of my life, but Reed has become one of my best friends. And for that I can be grateful.

"So where do we start?" Aaron asks, looking sideways at me. When he sees my expression, he laughs. "You're just like him," he says, shaking his head and shifting the car into gear. "You and Deacon have always had that in common—dumbass plans."

And at the mention of his name, all the air is sucked out of the car. We can't hide our pain and worry. A small whimper escapes from between my lips, but I pinch them closed with my fingers. *Keep your head. Be a goddamn closer.*

I pull myself together. I harden myself against my fear and turn to stare out the windshield. And I tell Aaron to head straight to Arthur Pritchard's house.

CHAPTER SEVEN

I HAVEN'T SPOKEN TO MY FATHER SINCE I CALLED him at the taco shop. Marie said she hasn't been able to get in touch with him—although at this point I have no idea if she's telling the truth. Still, as we drive my thoughts turn to my father, replacing one fear with another. If something's happened to him, if he's really gone—I'll be an orphan. Unless my real parents are alive.

But even if they are, I don't know them. They didn't raise me. I've set in motion a series of events that have taken everything from me. It wasn't worth it. I had a father—and yeah, he was messed up, but he loved me. And I had Deacon. We could have run. We could have saved ourselves.

I was stupid to think that finding my identity would change me. Now I might have lost who I really am. But once

I get Deacon back—and we *will* get Deacon back—I'll set it right. We'll be on the run for the rest of our lives, but at least we'll be free from the control of Arthur Pritchard and the grief department.

I try to call Virginia, but there's no answer. Despite Marie's warning, we can't stay away from her.

"So what exactly are we thinking?" Aaron asks from the driver's seat. "Virginia is in some sort of negative loop, right? She'll be fine for a while, but then she starts spiraling down. And whoever's around . . . they sort of catch it. A behavioral contagion."

"Pretty much," I say. "It's like Arthur's studies—there are certain behaviors that inspire copycats. This is one of them. It's been true for years: clusters and outbreaks with only death as the trigger. Somehow the emotional state of others affects us, affects our behavior. But this is slightly different from the usual suicide cluster. Here you have a person who tells you there's no way out. Virginia feeds that misery, and by doing so, maybe she feeds her own. She digs into it. That's why her father resets her after each death—she gets too deep into the pain. She can't get out. But her hopelessness . . . In one way or another, Virginia is encouraging hopelessness. She's causing this outbreak to spread." It's a crazy theory, but I believe it wholeheartedly. It makes sense . . . enough sense, at least.

And now this is our world. People are killing themselves for no apparent reason other than the loss of hope. Or maybe there is another reason. Maybe we'll never know the actual truth.

SUZANNE YOUNG

I turn to Reed in the backseat. "How did Virginia seem when you dropped her off?" I ask him.

His jaw tightens. "I ended up parking around the block. She was worried her dad would see me. We talked for a bit."

I narrow my eyes slightly. "What'd you talk about?" I ask.

He seems taken aback by the question. "Uh . . ." He hesitates before answering. "We talked about her father. I asked her what his plan was to stop the epidemic. I wanted to know if it would work."

My heart skips. "Did she know?" I ask.

"No," he says simply. "She didn't."

But something about the way he says it . . . I kind of think he's lying. I look at Aaron to see if he heard the same thing, and he swallows hard and stares at the road. Although I want to give Reed his privacy, his state of mind has me worried. I turn to ask him to elaborate, but just as I do, bright blue and red lights flash across his face. He squints against them, and I spin around.

Police cars line Virginia's street, sending the light into the shadows. I sit forward, and Aaron tenses next to me. There are four police cars, a fire truck, and an ambulance parked diagonally in the driveway of the Pritchard residence. One of the lights flashes in my eyes as we get closer, and I hold up my palm to block it.

Every interior light in the house is blazing, including from the attic window—a bright circle cut into the siding. There are half a dozen people crowded on the small front porch; a small, older woman cries as an officer consoles her.

The ambulance. Arthur knew Virginia wasn't really kidnapped; we got her home in time. That's not why they're here. A chill starts up my arms, and I feel the blood drain from my face.

"Stop the car," I murmur, watching out the window. Aaron slows, easing to the side of the road, but I open the door before he fully stops and nearly trip. I stumble but catch myself on the curb. I start to run toward Virginia's house, disregarding any worry of being caught by Arthur.

I make it all the way to the door before an officer stops me, grabbing me hard by the arm. But I'm not scared of him—not now.

"You can't go in there," he says in a clipped tone. I pull away from him and glance around at the people on the porch, noting how pale and miserable they look. I've watched people grieve my whole life—I know what it looks like.

"Is she okay?" I ask the officer desperately. "Is Virginia okay?"

"I'm sorry, but I can't give out that sort of information," he says. He motions for me to leave, but just then a woman is led from the house, clinging to the uniform of another officer.

"Why would she do it?" the woman murmurs. "I don't understand."

I glance up at the policeman in front of me, and he winces like he didn't want me to overhear that. I stagger back a step, and he tilts his head, studying me.

"And who are you exactly?" he asks.

He's looking for symptoms, I think. "I'm her friend," I say, painfully aware of the tense when I see a flash of sympathy cross his face. I *was* her friend.

Because Virginia Pritchard is dead.

I walk off the porch into the rain before the officer can ask me any more questions. I'm struck down by my grief, my guilt. Before I can list all the ways I could have stopped this, I find Reed standing in the driveway next to the ambulance, staring up at the attic as rain soaks him through. He looks completely lost, alone. I've never seen someone look so alone. It terrifies me, but our only choice is to be brave right now. Strong.

I walk over and stand next to Reed, looking at the side of his face. "We have to go," I say quietly.

Reed continues to watch the house, rain still falling and running over his lips. "We didn't save her," he says. "We didn't close her loop of grief. It's our fault."

I blink back my tears, picturing Virginia, the girl who was nice to me that first day, who bought me a slice of pie. Who met a boy she liked at a party. Who was a star athlete. She promised to help me, even though she must have been suffering from her own loss. She knew that she was being erased and that she had no control over it. And I did nothing.

"We shouldn't have let her go home," I say. "So you're right. It is our fault. But now it's too late." I look around us, feeling vulnerable out in the open now that I know what happened. "We have to go," I tell Reed. I pause, putting voice to my other fear. "We can't fail Deacon, too."

Reed turns to me, seeming devastated at the thought. He reaches for my hand, and then together we hurry back to Aaron's car. We find him waiting, still in the driver's seat while he stares blankly at the road.

"She dead?" he asks wearily when we get in.

"Yeah," I murmur, hearing Reed shift in the backseat. "She is."

"Can you take me back to my car?" Reed asks, the emotion drained from his voice. "I have to grab some things from my place. Where are you guys staying tonight?"

I hadn't even thought of it. I won't sleep—not until I find Deacon. Aaron must have sensed that, but he answers immediately.

"I called and got us two rooms at a hotel on Curry and Fisher," he says. "I'll stay with Quinn. You take room three eighteen. It's already paid for."

"Thanks," Reed whispers, and rests his head back on the seat and closes his eyes. We don't talk, not even about our plan for Deacon. It's up to me and Aaron now. Reed needs some time to recover.

We drop Reed off at his car, and then Aaron and I drive to Arthur's office, even though it's long past business hours. We don't have to break in. There's a FOR LEASE sign in the window, and a quick peek through the glass doors shows only a few moving boxes and empty desks. The place is deserted. There's no sign of where Arthur's gone. There's no sign of Deacon.

A wave of hopelessness rolls over me, and I stumble back a

step. My heart is heavy, pained. "What are we going to do?" I murmur, putting my hands over my face.

"We're going to keep it together," Aaron says, emotion strangling his voice. "We'll find him, Quinn. You know we'll find him."

I look over at him, trying to find proof of his statement in his expression. And I do. I see fierce loyalty. I see love.

And so I nod, and together, we go back to the car.

Aaron and I drive to an all-night diner so we can regroup. We're the only people in the small, out-of-the-way restaurant. Aaron sits across from me in the booth, and we search business databases on our phones, but don't come up with a new address for Arthur's office.

"So where's Deacon?" I ask him, my hands wrapped around my coffee cup. "Because if he's with Arthur . . . it's bad. Arthur could be—"

"Don't go down that path," Aaron interrupts. "Focus on finding him, not on what could be happening to him."

"And what about Reed?" I ask. "What if he's not at the hotel when we get there?"

Aaron sets his phone aside and exhales heavily. "What do you suggest we do about Reed?" he asks, looking tired—overwhelmed. We're barely surviving this.

"I think Virginia said something to him." I lean forward. "When he dropped her off, he said they talked. Whatever it was . . . she killed herself after. Now Reed is nearly catatonic. What did she do to him?"

"He might just be upset," Aaron asks. "We're all in a shitty situation, but Reed's a good closer. Maybe you need to trust him."

"And maybe he needs our help," I point out. "Don't forget, we came here because Virginia's last two friends killed themselves. It's one thing for us to willingly put ourselves in harm's way. It's another to let our friends walk blindly into it. Aren't you a little concerned?"

"When you put it like that," he says, "yeah. I guess so." He reaches over to grab a container of sugar, dumps a spoonful into his coffee. He sets the sugar down with a clank next to his cup. "I'll tell you one thing," he adds, staring down. "I sure as hell wish your boyfriend were here right now. He'd have a plan. But he's the one that's fucking missing." Aaron's face scrunches up, and he turns away from me, staring out the window toward the street.

His small breakdown brings on my own tears. Deacon never used to cry. Even in the really dark assignments, the heartbreaking ones, he was always level-headed. Only once did he ever crack while on assignment.

He was playing the role of Ethan Gallagher, a freshman football player in Albany. Ethan's family had been broken by the death—a heart attack after a practice. Ethan's seven-year-old sister held Deacon's hand whenever he walked in the room—as if she refused to see the difference between him and her brother.

I went in to extract Deacon from the case and to bring him to Marie, but he asked me to take him home first so he could shower.

I found him crying on the bathroom tile, saying that he should have been the one dead instead of Ethan—as if they were tradable. Deacon needed therapy after that assignment. He didn't break down again.

So what would he think if he saw me crying in a diner instead of out looking for him? How disappointed would he be? Guilt begins to eat away at my conscience.

For now we have no real way to track Deacon. Our best shot will be following Arthur Pritchard when he goes into work tomorrow. But would he really go to work the day after his daughter's death? I won't underestimate his callousness.

"What should we do about Reed?" Aaron asks, drawing my attention.

"You need to tell Marie," I say, earning a disgusted look. I hold up my hand, asking him to let me finish. "I don't care who she's working for," I tell him. "She wouldn't let any of us die. I know you believe that too. Ask her what to do about Reed."

And although he hates the idea, Aaron nods and picks up his coffee, taking a loud sip.

"Fine," he says. He stands, and we pay at the counter and head to the new hotel. Aaron said we should wait for morning to get our things, especially since we really don't need anything beyond a change of clothes. Right now I just want to check on Reed.

And then I'm going to cry myself to sleep.

CHAPTER EIGHT

I DRIVE AARON'S CAR WHILE HE CALLS MARIE. SHE hasn't heard about Virginia, so Aaron relays what we know and then asks for her advice. When he hangs up, he rubs roughly at his face. "She wants to meet," he says.

I'm about to flick on the turn signal to turn around, but Aaron shakes his head no. "You go to the hotel and check on Reed. Stay with him. I'll go see Marie myself."

"Are you kidding?" I say, and look at him. Deacon did something similar and now he's missing. Aaron must realize the circumstances too, because he shrugs one shoulder helplessly.

"Our options are limited," he says. "But man—I wish Deacon had gotten his hands on some truth tea. It would be nice to know exactly where Marie stands."

"And I wish we didn't need to," I say. But obviously, Marie's motives are shady at best. Still, I won't even entertain the thought that she had something to do with Deacon's disappearance. It wouldn't make sense.

I pull up to the hotel and get out, leaving the engine running. Aaron walks around the car, stopping to give me a hug in the glow of the headlights, and tells me to call him after I talk to Reed.

"I will," I promise. But just before he gets in, I call his name. Aaron meets my eyes over the roof of the car, almost like he knows what I'm going to ask.

"You still think Deacon's okay, don't you?" I need to hear it. I need him to say it.

"Yeah," Aaron says. "I really do."

I close my eyes, relief flooding my chest. I thank him and turn away, knowing that I'm just like one of my clients: I'll cling to any thought right now. Any hope—even if it's a lie.

Aaron pulls out of the parking lot, and I check in at the lobby and get a key. I take the elevator and hit the third floor; when the door slides closed, I dial Deacon's number again, just like I've done at least a dozen times tonight. The sound of his voice on his voice mail gives me one millisecond of hopefulness each time. It also tears me apart.

I just want him back. I don't care about the rest of it anymore.

When I get off the elevator, I decide to stop at my room first, wanting to wash the dried tears off my face and compose myself before going to Reed. I feel broken—empty. Useless. I swipe my key card through the lock and push open my door.

I gasp when I find Reed sitting on my bed. His head is

down as he writes in a small journal on his lap. When he hears me, he puts down his pen and closes the book.

"I was just coming to find you," I say. I shut the door behind me and walk in. But I don't get more than two steps before Reed lifts his head, startling me with his appearance. His clothes are still wet from the rain, and there's a slight pink on his cheeks, almost like windburn. He sits rigidly, uncomfortable in his own skin.

"Hope you don't mind that I let myself in," he says quietly. "I wanted to talk to you." Reed's eyes are so bloodshot they're almost entirely red. His lips are dry and cracked, with a small sliver of blood where they split. I think he's been crying for a while.

"You should have called me," I say. "I would have come back sooner." I sit across from him on the other bed, but my heart is thudding hard against my ribs. He's gotten worse since we dropped him off. I've seen this lost look before, the one he wears like a mask. I've seen it in grief counseling, and I saw it on Roderick when he killed himself at his party.

Reed sets the journal on the nightstand and folds his hands in his lap, looking me over. "I always thought you were different, Quinn. Different from the other closers."

He smiles, but there's no humor behind it. "Do you know that your father once asked me to take you out?"

"Yeah," I say. "You already told me."

"Did I?" he asks, sounding surprised. "Well, Tom told me you were mixed up in something; he hoped maybe I could bring you back. I thought he meant an assignment. But I guess he meant your whole life, huh? You aren't Quinlan McKee."

My skin chills. "How did you . . . ?" I stop, knowing who told him. "Virginia," I say. He nods.

"She found your file," he tells me. "After we talked in my car, Virginia checked the house while I waited. When she came back out, she had the papers. It was in her father's office. She said he must have brought it home earlier in the day. We were going to give them to you. But . . ."

"But what?"

Reed rubs his face roughly, as if he's got a headache. And the change is there. Virginia Pritchard made him sick. Whatever secrets she told him before she died, she made him ill. Panic, bright and red, blooms inside my chest. "Reed, what did Virginia say?"

"That it's too late now. None of us are getting out of here. Not fully intact, at least."

"What are you talking about?" I demand. "Jesus, Reed—what did she tell you?"

Reed looks down at his lap, lost in thought. "Arthur has already started. You, Virginia." Reed pauses and looks up. "His new program has been passed. This is step one. We'll all be rounded up in the morning. Remaining closers have been flagged as a danger to ourselves."

"When did this happen?" I ask.

"Earlier this afternoon. Marie already knew."

"She *what*?" She betrayed us. She knew Arthur's plan but didn't warn us—didn't send us away. "Why would Marie do that?" I ask.

Reed shrugs as if it doesn't matter—as if nothing matters to him anymore.

I cross the room and sit across from him on the other bed. I lean forward and touch his knee. "Reed?" I whisper, panicked.

I think Tabitha found out and ran. We'll never get that chance, though."

"Please—"

"Do you know that for an instant," he says, as if I'm not talking, "I considered it? I considered letting Arthur take her away from me. I didn't think I could live with the pain anymore."

"Take Katy?" I ask. I knew he was grieving for his dead girlfriend, but I didn't consider how much it's been eating him up.

"In the end," he says, "I wanted to keep her, but I can't live with it. Virginia showed me that. She knew her father would erase her again, and she was so scared of him, Quinn. You can't imagine. He left her completely powerless in her own life. Now he's doing the same to us."

Reed stands, and my hand falls away from his knee. He bites down on his lower lip, and measures his words. When he drags his eyes to meet mine again, a tear drips onto his cheek. "I shouldn't even be here," he says. "But I wanted you to know that I think you're special. I always have. You've got something we don't: a soul. The rest of us closers have lost ours somewhere along the way, but you—you still care. Maybe that will be enough."

"Enough for what?"

Reed doesn't finish the statement. He starts for the door, but I jump up and block his exit. I'm not about to let him leave when he's obviously having some sort of psychotic episode. I move in front of him, my hands on his chest to stop him.

"Reed," I beg. "Please, just wait here." The terrifying fact is that Reed was not like this earlier in the week. But ever since the day he met Virginia Pritchard, he's steadily gotten worse. I just didn't realize it. I'm the one who asked him to take her home. I've done this to him. This behavioral contagion is fast—too fast to stop. What the hell are we going to do?

Reed looks down at me and reaches to trail his fingers down my cheek. His touch is cold, and it sends an icy shiver down my back.

"Virginia's right," he whispers. "There is no hope. If Arthur catches you, he'll change you. He'll take away everyone you love. It's just like being dead." Reed's fingers stop at my collarbone. "Don't try to save them," he says. "Any of them—even Deacon. Just save yourself." He leans in and presses his dry lips to mine.

I jump back fast as if he shocked me with static electricity. I slap him across the face, hoping to knock some sense into him. He stares at me for a moment, his tongue licking at the blood that's begun to trickle again from his lip. It's as if he doesn't recognize me. Then he blinks quickly.

"I shouldn't have done that," he mutters, wiping his hand over his mouth and looking down at the spot of blood. He turns and starts for the bathroom to wash it off.

"Reed, wait," I call after him. "I didn't mean—"

He pauses at the door and turns to glance over his shoulder at me. My stomach sinks. His expression is empty, lost. "I'm going to kill myself, Quinlan," he says in a quiet voice. "I just wanted to say good-bye first."

I take a startled breath at his words and rush forward. But before I reach him, Reed moves into the bathroom, slams the door, and locks it.

Panic explodes through my body, and I pound on the door with my fists and try the handle over and over. There's a loud smash and the shatter of glass from inside.

"Reed!" I scream. "Reed!"

This isn't happening. This can't be real. But as I kick, bang, and throw myself against the door, trying to break the lock, I know exactly what's happening. And I'm reminded of Catalina and her sister's story about the day she killed herself.

There is a heavy thud behind the door, followed by silence. I take a step back, staring at the handle. "Open it," I sob out. "Please, Reed." I put my sore fingers over my lips, terror raging through me. "Reed," I say weakly. But there is no answer.

The quiet goes on for another moment, and I numbly reach into my pocket and slip out my phone, keeping an eye on the door. I'm shaking nearly too much to dial, but I manage 911 and give them my address. I call Aaron, and when he answers, I can only whisper, "Come back."

"Quinn," he says. "What's wrong? What happened?"

I don't respond immediately because the beige carpet at the edge of the bathroom tile starts to darken. And I watch in horror as blood seeps under the door, staining the carpet red.

Reed Castle broke the mirror in the bathroom with the soap dish and then used a shard to stab himself in the neck, severing his anterior jugular vein. The paramedics told me he bled out in less than two minutes. By the time they arrived, the bloodstain on the carpet had grown to nearly three feet wide.

Aaron arrived shortly after, never having made it to Marie's. I gave the paramedics as much information as I could without compromising myself. I used Elizabeth Major's name and abandoned my friend's body—I didn't even see him. I left Reed there with strangers because I had no choice. I left him all alone.

And I hate it. I fucking hate it so much, because he belongs with us. We're his family.

Reed was my friend and I ruined him by getting him involved with Virginia. I've ruined everything.

Tomorrow, when I turn on the TV, they'll be talking about Reed, his privacy stripped away as they dwell on the horror of it all. Sparing no detail. Because the concern has led to calls for transparency. And really, the news wants ratings. Clickbait. People find coroners' reports and post them online. Their morbid obsession is fueling this crisis, and yet . . . they can't see it.

Grief ravages through my chest, and I turn to Aaron, crying against his shoulder as we stand in the rain, letting it soak us through. Aaron gathered Reed's things before we came outside. Reed hadn't checked into his room, so he'd left his stuff in ours. Aaron haphazardly shoved the items into a bag and put them in the backseat of his car.

Aaron helps me into the passenger seat and walks around the car and gets in. He parks around the corner, away from the police, so we can catch our breath. In the dark car, we sit and listen to the rain against the windshield. "Make it okay," I murmur. "Please just bring him back."

Aaron sniffles hard and turns his eyes toward the roof of the car.

"I wish I could," he says miserably.

I try to build myself back up, sliding each piece into place until I'm almost a whole person. A broken plate superglued back together, all cracks and chipped corners. "Where will we go?" I ask in a scratchy voice, my thoughts a jumbled mess. I've lost Reed. I've lost my father, my advisor, my identity. And I've lost Deacon. "I have nowhere to go," I say.

I've never really had a home. I had a place where I lived with a man pretending to be my father. I had houses where I stayed with families who had recently lost a child. Nothing of my own.

I had Deacon, and together we made a home. He knows my lonely soul better than anyone. Arthur Pritchard is trying to take that away from me: my last bit of home. And if Reed was right, Arthur plans to take even more than that.

"He took Reed," I say. "Arthur Pritchard murdered him. And I led him straight to him." I choke on my cry.

Aaron closes his eyes, his hands on the steering wheel. I know he wants to console me about our lost friend, but he doesn't get the chance. His face contorts in anguish, his shoulders hunching over as he sobs, hard and filled with pain.

I lean in and rest my head on his shoulder while we both cry. We go on for nearly twenty minutes, and when we're done, Aaron sits up, wiping his tearstained face with the sleeve of his sweatshirt. And he starts the car, his breath still hitching on his tears.

CHAPTER NINE

AARON DRIVES AIMLESSLY AROUND TOWN WHILE I call Marie. I tell her that Reed is dead without crying, trying to detach myself from the story. A defense mechanism. A disturbing one at that.

Marie seems devastated by the news. I leave out the part where Reed said Marie knew of Arthur's plan for the closers. One tragedy at a time. I can't even stand the sound of her voice right now.

The night is a blur. We stop for gas, and then stop again later so Aaron can call Myra. He tells her everything. He promises he'll be back with her soon, but even I can hear the doubt in his voice. Reed's death is a heavy weight dragging us down. Like it's killing us too.

We just keep driving, because if we stop for the night, we might not be able to start again. I don't know where the time goes. I only know it's morning when the sun rises at five thirty, making a rare appearance. It cuts through the gray clouds and illuminates one side of the road. I close my eyes and lean my head against the car window, letting the warmth onto my cheeks.

Reed, I think. *He's sending this to me to give me hope. To tell me not to give up.*

It's a sweet sentiment—one I hold on to as I fight off the darkness creeping up my throat. I drift off, and when I open my eyes again I see that along the road the trees are thick and green, the branches curling toward the sun as if yearning for life. Asking for help to thrive.

A thought occurs to me, and I reach into the backseat and grab the bag with Reed's things. I remember seeing a journal on the side table. I start to rummage through the bag, feeling around for it.

"What are you looking for?" Aaron turns to me, his voice rough, and I realize we haven't spoken out loud in hours.

"Did you grab Reed's journal?" I ask, my heart beats ticking faster.

"Uh . . ." Aaron furrows his brow. "I'm not sure. I grabbed whatever I saw. Was it in the room?"

"Yes," I snap, although not at him. "He was writing in it when I got there. He set it aside." I grow frantic. "I can't find it!"

I tear open the zipper on the front pocket. Whatever Reed was writing could be a clue to what happened—how he spiraled so quickly. How this epidemic works.

My hand closes around a small leather-bound book, and I pull it out. The sight of it makes pain well up in my chest, a reminder that its author is dead. I turn around in the seat and immediately open it.

The journal starts nearly a year ago. All closers keep one, although most of us opt to do it electronically. To be honest, my own journal was mild observation, plain. I imagine Reed's will be the same. I quickly pass through the pages, skipping ahead, even over the mentions of me somewhere in the middle.

"Oh my God," I say, my fingers stopping on a page.

"What?" Aaron takes his eyes off the road to look over at the journal. He immediately flashes his gaze at me and then turns back to the road. "When did it start?" he asks.

I stare down at the black spiral drawn on the page, the words underneath blocked out. I check the page before and see it was from the day we met with Marie at the diner. So the spirals started shortly after he saw Virginia Pritchard on the volleyball court. After talking to the girls at the game.

I skip ahead, finding nothing but dark spirals page after page, the outward expression of how lost he felt. Of the darkness that was taking over his soul. A tear falls from my eyes and dots the page. It waters down the ink, and a gray river runs off the paper.

My hands are shaking, but I turn to the last page—what he was writing just before I arrived at the room. I'm surprised when I don't see a spiral.

Quinlan,

My breath catches at my name.

I know you're going to be angry with me. I know you'll be sad and I'm sorry for that. Believe me when I say I would never willingly hurt you. You are one of the truest friends I've ever had.

I was with Virginia tonight—she found your file. She also told me what it was like to be erased, showed me what was left of her. She said it was like being an empty shell. She said her father took her soul.

She also told me that he'd done the same to you. And that he's planning to use this procedure on all of us. Arthur has a new facility on Old Garden Road, and I think that's where he's taking the closers.

This memory erasure is his cure—not just for suicide, but for misbehavior. Noncompliance. It will pinpoint memories and erase them. Loved ones are typically the first to go, she says.

But I couldn't lose Katy. Her memory is all I have left.

Don't trust Marie. Don't trust anyone. You should run. Hide. I want you to know that I care about you. To me, it doesn't matter who you used to be, because I know who you are now. You're you. And that's enough. That's

The words end and the absence of them rips through my heart. I must have walked in when he wrote the last bit and he closed his book. I would give anything to talk to him again. To take back everything—keep him safe. But it's too late for everything except regret. I read it aloud to Aaron.

When I close the journal, Aaron looks over, his jaw set hard. "Am I a bad person for hating Virginia?" he asks quietly.

"No," I say honestly. "But she was a victim too. Imagine living with a monster. Imagine waking up with no hope every day. I can't hate her; I understand if you do. But right now we have to be focused. We can't absorb this pain. We can't take this all in. Reed tried, and it killed him."

"He killed himself," Aaron says flatly.

"No," I say, glancing over. "Arthur's plans did. And that's the problem. This behavior is a contagion. I can only hope that Virginia's death hasn't triggered something worse. Reed felt like he had nowhere to turn—it had all gone black for him. One deep, dark spiral. And fear is a force all its own. Arthur Pritchard and Virginia are spreading fear. And for that . . . there is no cure."

"And if they got to Deacon?" he asks, turning to me. "If they erased him? Then what?"

"Then we'll burn it all to the fucking ground," I say, and stare out the windshield. "I won't let him take Deacon too."

I take out my phone and look up directions to Old Garden Road. Aaron looks over and asks what I'm doing.

"Something," I say. "I've got to do something, and if the choice is run or show up on Arthur's front fucking doorstep, I choose to face that bastard head on. I will *take* Deacon back, even if it means handing myself over.

"Stupid plan," Aaron mutters, and with a glance at the map on my phone, he makes a U-turn. And drives us directly to Arthur Pritchard.

Aaron's dark skin has taken on a greenish tint. We're heartsick. But our courage grows as we drive down the nearly abandoned stretch of road. We pass old factories with their crumbling brick façades. I start to worry that Reed misled me—he wasn't exactly thinking clearly. But Aaron was right: Reed was a good closer. His observations would have reflected that.

"There it is," I say, pointing ahead. It's unmarked. It's unremarkable. But I know it's the right place. A two-story building with whitewashed bricks, a wheelchair ramp out front. Aaron pulls into the lot and drives around to the back. When I see Arthur Pritchard's car, I take in a shaky breath. This really is it.

Aaron parks under a curved tree, and little droplets from last night's rain fall from the leaves. Neither of us moves. Our grief has made us careless. Reckless. Brave. We watch the building, and when no one comes or goes, we look at each other.

"Should you keep the getaway car running?" I ask. An attempt at levity in an otherwise heavy situation. Aaron smiles.

"Although I'll be the first to admit you're probably stronger than me," he jokes, "I'll come with. I think you need the backup. Strength in numbers and all."

"I can't protect us," I say seriously.

Aaron nods. "I know. But no matter what, we've got each other's backs. So if this is a giant-ass mistake, at least we're in it together."

I check the time on my phone and see it's just after eight a.m. I could call the police, but ultimately, Deacon wasn't kidnapped, not if he's going through "mandatory therapy." And I'm a ward of the state. I pause at the thought. No, I'm a ward of Arthur Pritchard. I bet even my father didn't know that. And Arthur will have the police on his side.

There's still a chance I could find out who my real parents are, ask them to fight for custody—but it would be too late. Besides, they're strangers. And although the idea sounds impossible, they could be worse that Arthur.

It *is* too late. Too late to fight for a past I never had. I won't lose anything else.

I grab the door handle and tell Aaron to stay close.

We get out in the cool morning air and round the building to a side door, hoping it's not locked. It's a drop-off for lab pickup, with a red delivery box attached to the wall. I take a deep breath, grip the handle of the door, and turn. It opens.

I look back to Aaron, stunned because I didn't think we'd get this far. He seems to understand, because he gulps and then takes the edge of the door to open it wider so I can walk in. Tentatively, I enter the building, glad I'm not going in alone. Hoping I'm not about to lead another friend to his death.

The walls and floor are bright white, fluorescents above us shining on every corner and chasing out the shadows. It reminds me of Arthur Pritchard's kitchen: sterile and lifeless. And of course that leads to thinking about Virginia, and my pain threatens to derail my mission.

There's an empty nurses' station at the end of the hall, and I plan to look through the files until I find Deacon's name. It's an asinine and improbable plan, but I can't think of anything better at the moment. Now that I'm inside, the idea of storming into Arthur's office and demanding answers doesn't seem very appealing. We're almost to the station when the sound of approaching voices startles us.

"The patient in room one fourteen is ready to be moved," a woman says. Aaron and I dart around the corner, our backs pressed to the wall. The woman continues talking, and from her authoritative tone I guess that she's one of the nurses. A man answers her, using a hospital code I haven't heard in the grief department. We wait, and once their voices fade, Aaron and I move back into the hallway.

"That was close," I say, and start toward the nurses' station. "We should—"

"Stop right there," a man calls, freezing me in place as his voice echoes around us. I exchange a look with Aaron, one that debates if we should run—but that would mean leaving Deacon behind. And that's not going to happen.

I spin and find a man in medical scrubs. He's big and bulky, and I wouldn't have a chance against him. Neither would Aaron, but he looks like he's considering it anyway. I decide to defuse the potential of the situation. I can't let Aaron get hurt. It's time to face my demons.

"I want to see Arthur Pritchard," I demand. "And I want to see him now."

CHAPTER TEN

I'M TERRIFIED. BUT AS A CLOSER I'M TRAINED TO hide my emotions, even when I can't control them. Like the panic currently raging in my chest and strangling me. But my face is a portrait of calm as I wait on a hard chair in the middle of Arthur Pritchard's office.

Aaron was taken to a different room for questioning. When he refused to be separated from me, the male nurse spoke a code into his walkie-talkie along with Aaron's name. Static returned, but then a cool female voice said, "Bring Aaron to room one twelve. Marie would like a word with him."

So yeah—everything sucks. Everything is terrible. Marie has been working for Arthur, and the confirmation of that would break me down if I processed it. She double-crossed us, but I can't yet. So I'm left sitting here, helpless, hoping I can talk the world's biggest asshole into letting us walk out of here with Deacon.

But as Virginia would tell me if she weren't dead: *There's no hope*. I feel that now. Then again, maybe she's why I feel it.

I hear the door open behind me. I don't turn, refusing to give in in any way, not even to curiosity. Footsteps tap on the linoleum floor, and then he appears: the well-dressed bogeyman of my nightmares.

Arthur Pritchard smiles, but it doesn't reach his eyes. He sits on the edge of his desk facing me. He wears a striped button-down shirt with a patterned sweater-vest over it. His salt-and-pepper hair is neatly combed to the side, while his beard is perfectly trimmed. And yet his pale blue eyes are haunted by dark circles like he hasn't slept in days.

"It's good to see you again, Quinlan," he says. His voice holds the warmth of a closer. The strength of an advisor.

I don't respond, and he puts the edge of his index finger along his lips as he studies me. Eventually he nods, and he gets up to round his desk and sit in the leather chair behind it. I continue my silence as he opens a drawer and takes out a file, setting it in front of him and folding his hands on top of it.

"We have so much to discuss," he says. "After all, I doubt you would turn yourself in if you didn't have a compelling reason. Where should we begin?" His expression doesn't change, like it's only a mask of normalcy. Then again, this man just lost his only child.

"Where's Deacon?" I demand.

"Ah, yes," he says. "Deacon Hatcher—your handler."

He catches me off guard and I flinch. Arthur notices, of course, and smiles before continuing. "Deacon is fine, Quinlan," he says. "In fact, by the end of the day he'll be better than fine. He'll be immune."

"Immune to what?"

"The epidemic," he responds. "We've erased the triggers. There are only a few left to go, and then his risk factors drop dramatically. You should be grateful."

There's a sick twist in my stomach, and I take in a sharp breath. I'm too late. "You erased his memory?" I ask, any ability to cloak my emotions falling away. My eyes well up and tears spill over. "What did you take?"

"Would you rather he died?" Arthur asks, furrowing his brow. "Are you that content with letting your friends kill themselves? Like Reed Castle. Like *my daughter*." His teeth gnash together, but he's quick to rein in his bitterness.

But I lean away from the accusation, a wound reopening at Reed's name. Arthur straightens the collar of his shirt and runs his tongue along his back teeth, watching me.

"Are you angry with yourself?" he asks. "Don't you feel guilty? Your existence here has led to two deaths. You are directly responsible."

Whether he's trying to mindfuck me or not, it works. The guilt crashes down around me, but I force myself to look stronger.

"No," I say. "I'm angry with you. I think you're a deranged lunatic, and I'm pissed about it. I'm getting Deacon and Aaron and we're leaving."

Arthur lifts one shoulder. "I'm sorry," he says, "but I can't let you do that."

Subtle threats are his specialty. But this is the start of more. Dread crawls over my skin.

"I'll call the police," I say, reaching in my pocket to take out my phone. "Better yet, I'll call someone in the media, tell them what you did to your daughter's memory. Tell them you're a monster."

"Stop," he says, pointing to the phone. "If you do that, you'll never get answers."

"I already know them," I say. "Your daughter was a trigger for the epidemic, so you erased her memory. You drove her mad. And last night you meant to do it again, only you didn't get to her in time."

Arthur's nostrils flare, and I know I've struck a nerve. I can read him, too. I see a grief-stricken father who blames me because he's not brave enough to blame himself.

"You want to pin this on somebody else," I continue. "But it's not just my fault. I didn't know what was happening until it was too late."

Arthur sits forward in his seat, his eyes wild with anger. I keep my phone in my hand, not willing to completely give up the idea of calling the police. "Not your fault?" Arthur asks. "That's where you're wrong. You and Deacon Hatcher were not honest with me. You hid the truth. There are side effects to memory manipulation, and if I had known—"

"Then you wouldn't have experimented on your own daughter?" I ask, feeling little sympathy for him. Not now.

Not when he's here to threaten and intimidate me.

I watch as Arthur's anger fades; possibly he's telling himself that I'm the sick one. But the danger is real, and I don't want to spend another minute with him. I'll have to take my chances with the police. I open up the keypad on my phone and start to dial 911.

Arthur stands, smoothing down the thighs of his khaki pants. "Really, now, Quinlan," he says, looking at me impatiently. "Hang up so we can have a discussion."

"You're a psychopath," I tell him, my thumb hovering over the send button. "I don't think there's going to be much of a discussion."

"Well, how about we start with this," he says calmly. "This isn't the first time we've had this conversation."

I tighten my jaw. "I already know," I tell him. "I suppose you're going to tell me next that Marie still works for you? I know that, too. So you're not so fucking smart after all."

Arthur narrows his eyes. "I must say you're taking this well. Better than the last time." He succeeds in unsettling me. The idea that he's seen me desperate and crying, that he's treated me, and that I can't remember a single moment of it is horrifying. It makes me feel vulnerable.

I lower my phone in my lap and glare at him. "Then tell me," I challenge. "Tell me all the secrets you've been keeping. Tell me why we're here. What more could you possibly want from me?"

Arthur goes back to his chair, looking smug. He sits and rests his elbows on the desktop. "When I found you as a child," he begins, "you were wandering the halls of the hospital."

This revelation shocks me. He's going to tell me the truth. Although I'm no longer searching for it, I feel my stomach upend with anticipation. "What hospital?" I ask.

"St. Joseph's in Portland," he says. "You were wandering the halls, filthy. Your mother had died days before, but no one noticed you at first. Your father was gone—no idea who he was; he wasn't on your birth certificate. So really, you never had a father."

The comment stings me, but I swallow hard, willing him to continue.

"You barely spoke to anyone," he says. "A very withdrawn child. But I noticed you. I knelt and talked to you in front of your mother's old room. You'd go back there again and again, hoping she'd show up. But of course she couldn't, because she was dead."

There's a sharp pain in my heart, and I know that his words are true. I miss her. I miss my mom even though I only have one fragmented memory of her. Of the dark-haired woman in a hospital bed.

"And after speaking with you for a bit," he says, "I noticed certain quirks in your personality. The way you could mimic the nurses who would talk to you. How you could bend your personality to suit the situation, even as a child. I knew right away that you would make an excellent closer."

He presses his lips together like the memory is nostalgic. Maybe for him it is. To me it sounds more like kidnapping.

"You were consumed by your grief," he continues. "You wanted your mother so much, would cry for her. It worried me, because I saw how it would limit your potential."

"You bastard," I say at his coldness, tears dripping onto my cheeks.

"Yes, well," he adds, unfazed. "At the time I'd been deep in development at the grief department. I wanted something more effective, so I tried something new. It's not very complicated," he says. "I used my influence to take custody of you so that I could have access to your medical care. I brought you home. My wife had died, you see, and my daughter needed a friend. You worked brilliantly for that."

"You're sick," I murmur, horrified. He brought me to his house, to Virginia's life. It explains how I felt when I met her, as if I'd known her before. He stole that from both of us. It's possible that Arthur's been unwell since his wife died. It's also possible that he's always been deranged.

"Needless to say, while you were in my care," he continues, "I began to unravel your mind. Trial and error until I erased your identity completely. Marie Devoroux came to me shortly after that, and I knew I had the perfect case study. The reason you were such a suitable closer for Quinlan McKee was because you didn't remember who you really were."

"I was a *child*."

"Oh, we had setbacks," he allows. "Especially that first year. Memory crashbacks. Bits and pieces of your past would haunt you, wake you at night. Some mornings I'd find you asleep in Virginia's room—the two of you clinging together, joined in your grief for your mothers. It was imperative that I separate you—get a true study free of influence. Tom McKee took you home, but the memory crashbacks continued. Your father . . ." He pauses. "Your new father would call us, and he'd bring you in, kicking and screaming. But you always left a well-behaved child. You always adjusted.

"It could have gone on forever," he said, "but Marie and your father stopped cooperating. And with Virginia's problems getting worse, I knew of only one solution to help her, one that seemed to help you—memory manipulation. Only I didn't have a way to know the long-term effects. I assigned a handler to you to monitor your emotional state and warn me of any problems."

I already know the part where Deacon comes in, so I stare at Arthur, searching for any memory of him that might still be hidden in my head somewhere. He continues talking, and I study the way his mouth moves, his gestures. It's how I remember people. And soon a hazy memory starts to surface. Moments in his white-walled office. Sixteen years old. Eleven. Nine . . .

My heart seizes at the realization that each time, he made me over. The real me, the fake me—there was no distinction. I'm an imposter in my own skin. It's not just my identity that he fabricated. They continue to erase and rebuild me like some twisted version of role-play therapy. They've taken my truth and filled me with lies.

"And you plan to do it again?" I ask, fear strangling the words. "Even though Virginia's dead?"

"I'm afraid so, yes," Arthur says. "We need a cure—we need to learn the breaking point of this therapy. Virginia was pushed too far." He lowers his eyes. "I see that now. But she also fought it. I only wanted to help her." He stops abruptly, his body going so still he's like a statue. After a moment his eyes flick to mine. "She was all I had left," he adds. "And now, without her, there is only The Program." He rises. "Perhaps if you came willingly, we could strike a deal."

That's not going to happen. I grab the phone from my lap and throw it as hard as I can in his direction. There's a pop as the phone ricochets off his forehead, and Pritchard cries out in pain. I jump to my feet to escape, but at that exact moment the door opens and two men come rushing in.

I shoot a panicked look at Arthur and find him bent forward, watching me with his cold eyes as if he's seeing right through me. Blood trickles from a gash on the corner of his forehead, a bruise darkening just above it. I wonder then if he hates me as much as I hate him. I'm the child who survived—not Virginia. There's pain in that. We were both his experiments.

One of the men grabs me around the waist, while another stabs me in the arm with a syringe. There's no way I'm getting out of this. It's too late. The room starts to fade, and my eyelids grow heavy and start to slide shut.

I should have made a deal for Deacon's and Aaron's safety. But I already know what my father tried to tell me before: Arthur Pritchard isn't the kind of man you can make deals with.

I hear Arthur tell the men to take me to the treatment room and prep me. He says to erase everything.

Erase.

I'm not sure if there's a more terrible word.

CHAPTER ELEVEN

THE FIRST THING I NOTICE IS BRIGHT WHITE WALLS
that are so stark that I feel an immediate sense of unease. How
can anything be so void of life? I try to move and realize my
wrists are strapped to the arms of the wooden chair I'm sitting
in, thick leather bands lashing me in place.

I'm panic-filled, my eyes flicking throughout the room as I
analyze any means of escape. I see none, but it's possible that the
way out hasn't presented itself yet. I'm about to be erased—the
last thing I can afford is to be irrational. I have to keep my head
clear, my emotions detached. It's the only way to survive this.

The door opens, and Marie Devoroux strides in. A painful
cry catches in my throat as I look her over. Her hair is neatly
tied back, and she wears a long white doctor's coat. But it's still
her. It's still Marie.

"Please," I say, pulling against my wrist straps. "Please help us, Marie. Arthur's crazy. You have to help us get out."

She watches me with a careful gaze and sits down on a rolling stool across from me, a clipboard in her hands. "And where's *out*, Quinlan?" she asks calmly. "Where would we go?"

My lips part, and I try to assess the situation. "We can go—" I wince. A headache has formed behind my eyes, a fracture through my consciousness. Warmth rises in my chest, weakens my muscles. I blink against the pain and shoot a betrayed glace at Marie.

"It's their brand of truth tea," she says. "Stronger than what I use. They're still adjusting the formula."

"And you're still letting them experiment on me?"

She clenches her teeth but doesn't deny it. I wonder if it hurts her, seeing me like this. I wonder how many times she's seen me like this before.

"Now," Marie says after a moment. "Where is home, Quinlan?"

"It's with Deacon," I say. "And you've taken that from me."

"It's not with your father back in Corvallis?" she presses.

"He's not my father."

"But you love him anyway?" she says.

I tilt my head, surprised by the question. Especially since Marie seemed to think he was in danger earlier. "Yes," I tell her. "I do."

She nods and makes a note on her clipboard. I'm not even sure what she's after, how they plan to erase me. But I have to believe that the woman who helped raise me will be on my side now.

"Don't let them do this to me," I whisper, hoping to appeal to the part of her that might still care about me. "You don't have to go along with this."

"Would it matter if I told you that I didn't have a choice?" she asks.

"No," I say honestly.

She presses her lips together as if admiring my answer. She takes in a deep breath, her dark brown eyes studying me. "The truth is," she says, her voice hushed, soothing, "I had a choice and I made it. I gave you the Quinlan McKee file. I sent Aaron away. Deacon was clear, or so I thought.

"Yes, I knew what was coming," she continues. "I'd been watching Arthur Pritchard dissect his daughter for months. She was never going to get better, not with him. He was losing his grip on reality, becoming more zealous. I knew you were next. So I made the choice to get you out of the department, much to Tom's dismay. I'm sure he'll never forgive me for the danger I put you in."

"Why didn't you just tell us what was going to happen?" I ask, thinking that her methods led us to this place.

"I thought knowing we were liars would be enough to keep you away. I underestimated your attachments. Your bravery. When you contacted me and asked for my help, I knew it was too late anyway. I doubt you found my number by chance. Arthur probably left it for you. It ensured he'd trap both of us."

In a matter of an hour I'd found Marie's whereabouts. I feel stupid for thinking it would be that easy.

"You could have run again," I say.

She shakes her head slowly like I'm not understanding. "No, I couldn't," she says, "and Arthur knew that. It was a message to me that he'd found you. He had you already, even if you didn't know. And then I had my second choice: an exchange." She closes her eyes and swallows hard before continuing.

"I offered up my best closers in your place: Tabitha, Shep . . . Reed. In return I asked that Arthur leave you alone. You, Aaron, and Deacon. Initially, he agreed."

My eyes well up, and my bottom lip quivers. "You got him killed," I say. "You brought Reed in, and it got him killed. You fucking murdered him, Marie. I thought it was Arthur. Thought it was *me*. But Reed's dead because of you."

She turns her face away and brushes the tears as they fall on her cheeks. I let mine fall because there will be more for Reed. So many more. Unless they erase my memory and take him away forever.

"He was only supposed to become a handler," Marie says, her voice rough. "He was supposed to be fine. I didn't protect him the way I should have; you're right." She looks at me. "I will bear that for the rest of my life. That is mine. But it's only one of many weights." Her expression grows wary, and I know there's more.

"What else did you do?" I ask.

"Your father was serious when he told you not to make a

deal with Arthur. He changes the rules. After Tabitha disappeared, Arthur wanted to amend the deal. He'd already converted Shep. He decided Aaron would be next. And then he gave me one last choice to make." She takes in a shaky breath. "You or Deacon."

"You didn't," I say, leaning forward, eyes wide. "Please tell me you didn't just hand him over."

"I chose to keep you safe, Quinn. Deacon would have come willingly given the option; you know that. When he arrived, the handlers were waiting for him. They told me nothing else. I had second thoughts—that's when I asked for your help to find him.

"Eventually, I discovered that Arthur brought Deacon here. He's been slowly picking through his memories, trying to find the right ones to erase. Deacon won't know you when it's done."

"Then stop it," I growl.

"There's still one more deal to be made," she says with a small smile. I'm utterly confused when she gets up and goes to the desk with her clipboard. She moves a metal skull paperweight to the side and presses the intercom on her phone. "The patient in one fifteen is prepped," she says.

"No," I tell her, thrashing against my restraints. "Don't let them erase me, Marie! Please don't do this!" I start to scream.

The door behind me opens, and I'm a sobbing mess, trying to cling to every memory desperately. My mind spins through big and small moments as if they all have the same importance. They do—because they all filled my heart.

Deacon kissing me for the first time. Aaron and Myra fighting over a video game. My father holding the seat of my bike as he taught me to ride. Marie bringing me to pick out my first bra. Reed telling me he wanted to be a good person.

"Please don't take them," I whisper, squeezing my eyes shut as I feel the handler's fingers close around my arm. I realize that all these memories combined are me. They'll erase *me*.

There is a wet thud, and I feel a spray of warm liquid splash across the side of my face. It startles me, and when I turn, I see the man next to me contort his face. In the next second his eyes roll back and he falls to the floor. Blood begins to seep from under him.

I gasp and dart my gaze wildly around. I find Marie standing at the doorway, a bloody paperweight still raised in her hand. A long drip of red runs off it and streams down her wrist and into the sleeve of her white coat. Staining it red like a moving inkblot test.

"Oh my God," I say, trying to catch my breath. Marie lowers her arm and lets the metal skull fall to the ground. It leaves a crack in the linoleum and rolls next to the unconscious man. "What are you doing?" I ask her.

"My choice is you," she says. She walks over and undoes the leather straps. I watch her face, smell her perfume—a bit of home here in hell.

"Aaron is—" I start.

"Aaron is waiting outside in the car," she says. "Arthur can do as he wishes with me, but I'm not letting him take my kids." She undoes the other strap, and when I'm free, I jump up.

Marie pauses, looking me over. Her expression is a mixture of sorrow and regret—but mostly love.

She grabs the clipboard from her desk and rips off the top page to hand it to me. Confused, I look down and see a building map. Room 134 is circled with a key code scrawled next to it.

"Deacon?" I ask, my adrenaline spiking.

She nods. "Now hurry," she whispers.

I'm about to dash out, but I stop and look down at the body at our feet. Marie might have killed that guy—surely she'll have to face up to that. What will they do to her? "You have to run, Marie," I tell her. "If you—"

"I can't go with you," she says her eyes softening. "Evelyn Valentine and I . . . we're trying to find an alternative to all of this." She motions around. "We're trying to stop what The Program wants to do. Arthur isn't thinking clearly—hasn't been for a while. With Virginia gone, I can only imagine how bad it will get." She takes a step back from me, and I can feel her tearing her heart away from me.

"Go," she says. "Deacon's in the lab, probably in the final stages of his therapy. Get him and go." She closes her eyes and presses her lips together. "And please tell him I'm sorry."

Final stages. I move to the door and pause only a second to look back at Marie. But it's long enough to memorize every feature—because memories, I realize now, are what build us.

"I love you, Marie," I tell her. She puts her hand over her heart as if my words hit her straight there, and then I turn and bolt for the laboratory.

CHAPTER TWELVE

I'M STILL SLIGHTLY DISORIENTED FROM THE MEDI-
cation, but I do my best to follow the map toward the lab. I get
confused, turned around. I have to stop once or twice to push
the heel of my palm into my temple, willing myself to pull it
together. At least this one last time.

I manage to dodge a nurse who's exiting a room, and eventually I find the lab in room 134. I enter the code from the paper
and then shove it into my pocket when I hear the click of the
lock opening. I quietly slip inside the room.

The room is larger than the other two I've been in. It's set
up like triage, a long rectangular room with several curtained-off
areas. There is the murmur of conversation in the corner, and I
see the silhouette of two people standing behind the white fabric.

I duck down near a set of cabinets and work my way around

until I see who it is. My breath catches when I find that it's Arthur himself. There's a small, older woman in a doctor's coat next to him; she has dark hair and glasses. I assume she's Evelyn Valentine.

I see them standing over a kid—someone I don't recognize. He's asleep, and Arthur and Evelyn are looking him over and discussing his condition. With them distracted, I make my way to the closest curtained area and peek inside.

My luck holds out when I discover it's Deacon. He's strapped down to a bed, and his eyes widen when he sees me. He darts a terrified look around to make sure it's safe and then purses his lips as if saying *Shh . . .*

I don't have to ask if he remembers me—I can read it on his face. I can see it when his soft brown eyes well up with tears. But his condition is terrible. There are scratches on his cheek that look like fingernails, a bruise under his left eye. He didn't come here of his own will. I can't imagine what it's been like for him. I don't know what they've taken from his memories. But it's him. My heart is full because I've found him. My love. My home.

I go to him and work the strap from around his chest. He doesn't speak, afraid to draw their attention, but he watches me, inches from my face. When I get him free, he pulls me fiercely into a hug. I have to choke down my cry of relief.

I move back and level our gazes. Now we have to get out of here.

I help Deacon off the bed, when I realize he's unsteady.

He has to hold on to my arm. He's wearing hospital scrubs, this terrible yellow color, and his feet are bare. I poke my head around the curtain and see the route to the door is clear. Our best option is to run for it.

I slide my fingers between Deacon's, and then I yank him forward as we make a mad dash for the door. But just before we get there, a handler in the hallway appears in the glass cutout of the door, blocking our exit.

"Come now, Quinlan," Arthur calls. I spin around and see the doctor walk out from behind the curtain. "You think we don't monitor our rooms? I must say, I admire your tenacity. You could have just saved yourself."

"You can't keep us here," I say with a quick look at the other doctor as she walks out into the open. "We won't willingly stay. We will continue to defy you. So what are you going to do about it, Arthur?" I ask. "Kill us?"

"That's the last thing I want," he says, as if I'm ridiculous. "I'm trying to avoid death. Don't you see—I want you to live, both of you. You were right. I was angry. I did . . . *do* blame you for Virginia. But you've proven to me that memory manipulation can be effective. Look at you! Look how you still love! You've proven how viable the option is. You're the cure for the epidemic."

"I don't want to be your cure," I tell him. "You have no idea what you've done. The lives you've destroyed. The ones you will continue to destroy if you keep doing this."

He shakes his head. "Would you be able to watch the people

SUZANNE YOUNG

you love die?" he asks. "If you could stop it, wouldn't you do anything? Anything at all?"

Deacon turns away, not even slightly moved by the doctor's speech. But I am. Looking back, I would have saved Reed. I would have done *anything*, as Arthur says. But it's too late for Reed.

I'm throwing my cards in with Marie. She and Evelyn want to make an alternative. It's the best chance. So, no. I won't help Arthur ruin people's lives. Even if he means to save them.

"I'm done, Arthur," I tell him. "I won't manipulate people anymore."

"The truly strong have to fight for the greater good," he says. "Even at the loss of the weak. It's not a popular position— I know that. But my daughter is *dead*. I would trade every single one of you to have her back. So if we have to erase a few memories to save other kids, believe me when I say it'll be a lot less painful than watching them die."

Deacon reaches to take my hand, strengthening my resolve. "Let's go," he says, sounding shaky but determined. Arthur has no choice but to let us leave. Aaron's already out. The police could even be on their way. It will take time to explain what he's done, but we'll be long gone. I turn my back on Arthur and his laboratory.

"You're a coward," Arthur calls after me, his voice cracking.

I look back. "You're wrong," I say. "I'm not a coward for walking away. I'm choosing to walk away and live. Live a life you tried to steal. I won't help you. I won't champion your cause. Believe me when I say this: Your grief is blinding you. Maybe it's been building since your wife died; I don't know. But it's driving you mad. Stop before you make this all so much worse."

"She's right, Arthur," Evelyn Valentine says. She comes to stand next to him and places her hand on his arm. "She's gone," she whispers to him. "Virginia's gone now. We can't help her anymore."

Arthur visibly sways, his body seeming to crumple at the words. For the first time I find a small sliver of compassion for him. For his grief. Together Arthur Pritchard and Evelyn Valentine remind me of what my father and Marie must have been like after Quinlan died. This is their loss—their shared grief.

And for that I can pity the doctor who ruined my life.

Virginia died just yesterday, and although he must have tried to compartmentalize the grief, it floods Arthur now.

"Let them go," Evelyn whispers. "We don't need them anymore. It's time we start fresh. It's time we stop hurting them. We're not that cruel, Arthur."

Devastation works over Arthur's posture. I watch as he starts to feel again. Like a closer, he's been able to shut out his pain. But not anymore. It contorts his features, steals his face, and breaks him down. And as he starts to cry, he looks up at Evelyn and grabs the bottom of her jacket.

"But we can't let anyone else die," he tells her. "We'll move forward with The Program. The grief department can't know what it did to Virginia—delete her records. Don't let them know that my daughter had any part in the spread of the epidemic."

Evelyn stares down at him with compassion, obviously

seeing a different man from the one I've known. "For Virginia, I will keep that secret," she says. Arthur buries his face in her jacket, melting away. I watch him be reduced to the pile of grief I've seen my whole life. I'm no longer afraid of him.

Evelyn puts her hand on the back of his hair, soothing him, and looks up at me. And there's something there: something conspiring and crafty. She will fix this—I know it. There will never be a Program.

The doctor motions to the desk on my right. Confused, I walk over to it and find a single folder sitting on top. I look back at her.

"It's yours," she says. "It belongs to you now."

The entire world stills. I recognize the folder; it's the same kind we have for assignments. The same one they had for Quinlan McKee. It's *my* folder.

"You could have saved lives," Arthur says, wiping tears off his cheeks. He turns to us. "You could have helped so many."

"I'm starting with us," I say. "And I feel pretty damn good about that."

"Now go," Evelyn says to me, putting her hand on Arthur's arm.

I look at Arthur Pritchard one last time. His eyes judge me, blame me, curse me—but he'll get over it. He needs to examine his daughter's death. He's the one who needs help.

I thank Evelyn, and then Deacon and I open the door and leave. The handler outside puffs himself up, but Evelyn calls for him to let us pass. He seems reluctant to do so, but he steps aside, and we rush toward the exit.

Deacon and I make it out the side door into the blinding sunlight, both of us shielding our eyes. "It's not raining anymore," Deacon says absently. We look at each other, overwhelmed by the moment. So much to say.

"It's about time," Aaron calls. I turn and see him standing on the driver's side of the getaway car. He smiles and waves us forward.

Deacon and I make our way to him, and both of us get in back, still catching our breath. Aaron doesn't say a word, but he drives fast enough to make Reed proud. Deacon's shoulder is pressed against mine in the seat as I stare down at the folder in my lap.

I look sideways at Deacon. "This is all of me," I tell him, holding up the papers like they're the messed-up consolation prize from the worst game show.

He presses his lips together. "No," he says. "That's just your name."

In this moment my thoughts don't drift to my father or to my past. Not to my real family, which is no longer imaginary. I don't try to put the pieces together. Instead . . . I think of Reed. I think of how he said he knew me. And I realize he was right. He did. He was kind and he was brave. The world is worse without him. I'm worse. But I have his memory. He knew me. And now I know myself, too.

Because in the end it doesn't matter what my name is. Or where I came from. After all the lives I've lived, all the people I've become, I've finally found my real identity. I've found me.

I'm more than a name on a piece of paper. I'm more than what Arthur or my father or even Marie wanted me to become.

And so I set the folder aside in the seat, not even glancing at the name. Maybe later. Maybe not. Because it doesn't matter.

I'm the real me.

Deacon looks on curiously, but he must see in my expression that this isn't the time to discuss it. He takes my hand and kisses my fingers. We'll have to talk about Reed's death—Virginia's, too. We'll have to figure what pieces Arthur removed from Deacon's memory with his Program. And Deacon will have to explain to Aaron about being a handler—that is, if he can remember it. But for now we'll ride into the brightly lit day. Out into a world that's losing hope.

"We can't help them, can we?" I ask both Aaron and Deacon. "The ones who are getting sick?"

Aaron meets my eyes in the rearview mirror but doesn't respond. I turn to Deacon, and he seems to think it over before answering.

"Maybe it's time we live our own lives for once," he says. "Like you said, you're saving us first."

My heart hurts at the truth of his statement: We're all drowning without life preservers. So for now we can only run and save ourselves. But we'll keep hoping that things will get better.

After all, they can't get any worse.

CHAPTER THIRTEEN—ONE YEAR LATER

DEACON AND I SIT ACROSS FROM EACH OTHER IN A diner just outside Weed, California. It's a small place near the border of Oregon, and although we could have met my father halfway, we've vowed not to return to our home state until The Program is stopped. But it's not looking so good for us. Marie and Evelyn failed.

It turns out that the bulk of the memories Arthur erased from Deacon were those of his family. Deacon doesn't remember his mother or brother, or the years he spent suffering and then protecting them. I debated whether or not to fill in the blanks, but ultimately he deserved to know his past if he wanted it.

I took him to his childhood home so we could stop in and meet them. It went as well as expected. After we left, Deacon turned to me on the sidewalk and laughed. "I must have been a really nice fucking guy to put up with them," he said. I assured him he was.

Of course, there were other things missing—Reed and Virginia never existed to him. I've filled in those, too. Aaron and I painted a pretty glorious picture of Reed for him—complete with jokes in history. It hurts less to talk about him now—like I can imagine he's still alive, just off on an assignment. Sometimes I imagine he's with Katy.

Together, Aaron, Deacon, and I made up. It may help that Deacon can't remember working for Arthur and yet still feels absolutely miserable about it. You can't stay angry about something like that.

The one upside is that Arthur didn't take Deacon's memories of me or Aaron. I got to him just in time.

"What are you thinking about over there?" Deacon asks, sipping from his Coke. He never used to ask me questions like that; he gave me my privacy. But I don't mind—I like telling him everything. I like when he does the same.

"I'm hoping he's okay," I respond. I wring my hands in front of me, my blue nail polish chipped off at the edges. We've been living in California, although we're thinking of moving because the cost of living here is too high. We don't want our money to run out. It's not like we can go back to being closers—they don't even exist anymore. Now they're known as handlers. And they're not the remedy for grief; they are instruments of fear and intimidation. It hurts to see how something meant for good has been used in such a dastardly way.

"Aaron thought he looked well," Deacon says conversationally. But I know he's worried too. With all that we've heard about The Program, what they do to people, there's no way to assess my father's condition.

"Yeah, but Aaron saw him over a month ago," I say. "Things change."

Deacon lifts up one corner of his mouth. "Your father doesn't change. I'm sure he still hates me. Bet on it?"

I pause a minute, knowing I shouldn't place bets on my father's emotional state, but I nod my agreement and reach to take a shaky sip of my Dr Pepper.

Aaron was in Corvallis recently, passing through with Myra. They had a rough patch, Myra feeling abandoned and all. I don't blame her. But they loved each other too much to break up. Now they live up in Washington together. North Dakota was too cold for Aaron, the spiders in the cabin too many for Myra. They have a cute bungalow and assumed names. We don't get to see them often, but one day. Deacon and I count on *one day* being our future.

There's movement by the glass door of the diner, and I immediately straighten up, my heart leaping into my throat. Across the table Deacon reaches to put his hand over mine, his eyes steady, and gives my fingers a squeeze before turning to the man who just walked in.

My father looks the same. Sure, he's slightly thinner, and his clothes are unexpectedly casual—a green polo shirt and a pair of jeans with tan loafers. He looks older, too, something that pinches my conscience. But I know him.

I smile in his direction. When his eyes pass right over me, I wilt. My dad pauses in the middle of the diner and puts his hands on his hips as he scans the room. Deacon shoots me a concerned gaze, and then he stands.

"Tom," he calls kindly. My father looks at him and smiles politely. Deacon waves him to the table.

Deacon sits down, his face registering momentary shock before he slides over in the booth to make room for my father.

"Hello," my dad says in a formal tone. "Sorry about that." He sits down and looks between us. "Wasn't sure who I'd be looking for."

"Hi," I say, quickly moving my nervous hands under the table. I don't want to give anything away. I don't want to be creepy, either, so I don't stare too long. "Glad you could make it," I tell him, and lower my eyes.

"I have to say I was intrigued," my father tells me with a little laugh. "You said we all worked together." He looks at Deacon. "I'll have to apologize in advance—my memory's not the greatest."

Deacon nods like he understands, but I think we both feel sick. We suspected this, figured it out based on information Aaron collected, and one very confusing phone call with my dad.

My father, Thomas McKee, was erased a year ago. The last time we spoke, when he was at the taco shop and I was in Eugene, a group of handlers recovered him. The grief department decided he was in breach of contract, and one of the penalties was complete erasure. However, since he was a long-time employee, they spared some of his past. They let him keep his name, his life with his dead wife and daughter, and his early history in the department. I was erased entirely, like I never existed. Sometimes I wonder if that means that maybe I didn't.

After he was reset, they gave him a severance package and sent him to a doctor who told him that his memory loss was a side effect of his job, and that it was a good thing he was retired.

The grief department no longer exists. Now it's known as The Program. My father isn't part of what happens there. Instead he's in the home I grew up in, gardening and putting little ships inside bottles. It makes me think he would have been an excellent grandpa. But I'll never know.

"Yeah, Tom," Deacon says when I don't—*can't*—speak. "We worked together at the grief department, before your uh . . ."

"Breakdown," my father says for him. "It's okay, son. I'm not embarrassed. It happens to the best of us, right?"

"Yes," I say, earning his gaze. "We just . . . we wanted to make sure you were okay. We heard about it, and . . ." My words continue to fail me. I want to say, *Do you remember, Dad? Please tell me you remember. Please tell me you still love me. Please tell me I'm real.* But when my eyes begin to well up, Deacon clears his throat loudly and signals for the server.

My father grabs a menu from between the condiment bottles and starts to peruse the selections. "What'd you say your name was again?" he asks, looking over the top of his glasses at me.

"Nicole," I tell him. "Nicole Alessandro." It's still weird to use my real name. But in the end it doesn't matter what it is. I haven't called myself Quinlan McKee in a long while. She's finally at rest.

The corner of my father's mouth lifts slightly, and then he goes back to the menu, giving his order to the server when she arrives at our table. Together the three of us share a meal, letting my dad do most of the talking. It's all good-natured and upbeat, but I don't say much. I'm afraid of exposing us. I'm afraid of hurting my father. The latest word on The Program is that patients shouldn't be messed with; it could lead to a meltdown. And after what happened to Virginia Pritchard, we know all too well how dangerous the consequences can be.

I finish picking at my fries, barely touching the burger on my plate. My father and Deacon are laughing about an old football rivalry when Deacon's phone buzzes on the table. He picks it up and checks the message.

"Nic, we should go," he says, putting his phone away. It's Aaron, I'm sure. He told us not to spend too much time with my dad, just in case people were watching him. He was checking on us.

I shoot Deacon a pained look, not ready to say good-bye to my father. But my dad wipes his hand on his napkin and lifts one side of his hip to work his wallet out of his back pocket.

"I should probably head out too," he says. "I have a date tonight." He laughs, his cheeks growing red from the admission. In all the time I knew him, my father was never in a relationship—other than his highly dysfunctional friendship with Marie. It bothers me that I'm missing this new woman. What if he marries her? Would she be my mom?

"It was nice seeing you, Tom," Deacon says as my father gets out of the booth and tosses two twenties on the lunch ticket. Deacon tells him he doesn't have to do that, but my dad waves off the sentiment.

I get to my feet, watching him; my lips are unwilling to say the words. Just then my father turns to me and smiles warmly. It makes my heart swell in my chest, and I have to take a steadying breath.

"I'm glad you called," he tells me.

"Thank you for lunch," I return, because it seems like a normal thing to say in this very abnormal moment. I hold out my hand awkwardly, and he reaches to take it.

"Can I . . . ?" He stops, dropping his arm and laughing like he's embarrassed. "Never mind."

"What?" I ask. "What were you going to say?"

He scrunches up his nose. "I was going to ask if I could give you a hug," he says. "I don't know . . . you just look like you really need one."

Without hesitation I step in and hug him, my cheek against the soft cotton of his polo shirt. I squeeze my eyes shut; his clothing smells like my childhood. It doesn't make me think of lies or grief. It smells like home.

I straighten out of his arms and step back, quickly wiping the tears from my cheeks. I smile self-consciously. "You take care of yourself," I tell him.

"You too, Nicole," he says simply. And for a moment I'm sure I see a flicker of recognition in his eyes. But then it's gone. He touches my arm in good-bye and walks out of the diner.

The second the door closes behind him, I turn and grab my jacket off the seat, biting back the rest of my tears. Deacon watches me carefully as he grabs his coat, and then together we walk outside.

My father is gone.

The icy wind blows against my jacket, and I pinch the zipper closed with my fingers, standing and facing the snowcapped mountains with Deacon beside me.

"I'll never see him again," I say quietly. I sniffle, tears fighting to get out once again.

"The Program can't last forever," Deacon tells me.

"I hope you're right," I say. "But either way, the department took my father from me. They erased me. I'm forgotten."

Deacon turns, and his eyes are wounded at my sadness. "I'll never forget you," he says. "I love you like crazy. I love you to eternity."

I still enjoy it every time he tells me. I gaze at him for a long moment, thankful for what I do have. Thankful of what we can still be. It's nice to have possibilities.

"I'm ready," I tell him. "I'm ready to start living." Seeing my father one last time was the final piece. And now my old life is over.

I reach for Deacon's hand, slide my fingers between his. He smiles and pulls me closer. He leans in and kisses me, whispering again how much he loves me.

After that I lead him to the car. We're free to go where we want, but we don't have to find a place right away. Home is with the person you love, the person who loves you back stupidly and completely. Home is the space of peace in your heart.

And I'm finally home.

EPILOGUE

THOMAS MCKEE WIPES THE TEARS FROM HIS CHEEKS as he drives through the mountains toward the Oregon border. The radio plays loudly in an attempt to drown out his thoughts. His regrets.

"Nicole," he repeats aloud, as if he enjoys the sound of it. She looked well, and for that he was relieved. His daughter is finally safe. Deacon was annoying as ever, but of course in a way Tom could understand.

The music cuts out as a call comes through on his cell, and Tom sighs when he looks at the caller ID. He presses the hands-free option and answers.

"Hello, Marie," he says dryly. "I would have called when I got closer to home."

"How is she?" Marie asks instantly. "How does she look?"

Tom smiles, knowing that his affection for Quinn—Nicole—is matched by Marie's. "She's going by Nicole now," he says. "It really suits her. She was nervous." His lips start to shake, and he presses them together. "But I got to hug her." His voice breaks, and the tears flow anyway.

The road grows blurry, so Tom pulls to the side and parks his sedan. He hears Marie sniffle on the other end of the line. Together they cry for the girl they raised as Quinlan. They cry that they'll never know her as Nicole.

After a moment Marie clears her throat. Her voice is a stern echo in the empty car. "You know it was for the best," Marie says. "If she knew you remembered her, she'd come back here. She'd never leave. And you see what Arthur has been doing to those who reject therapy. There's no telling what he'd do to keep her quiet. We can't let that happen to her."

"I know," he says miserably. "I know."

"We'll protect our girl, Tom. We'll always protect her."

Tom puts his hand over his eyes, trying to pull himself together. His daughter can never know how much he misses her. She's too kind—she'll come for him. This really was the only way.

A year ago the grief department gave him a choice—they give everyone a terrible choice. But he asked to be erased, refusing to tell them anything about Quinlan. Marie arranged for Evelyn Valentine to do his procedure. And instead Tom began working with her and Marie. He's had to fake memory loss since, and it grows tiring at times.

"There is something else," Marie says, a new urgency in her

voice. "I just got off the phone with Evelyn. She's testing her theory. She thinks she has the right boy."

Tom straightens, slipping back into work mode. "And?" he asks, checking his mirrors before swerving back out into the road.

"She's given him The Treatment. Now she's waiting to see how it takes. She thinks it's the only way to counteract The Program."

"Good," he says with a small measure of hope. "Now what's the bad news?" Because of course he can hear that in her voice too.

"She thinks Arthur and the board are onto her. She's going to run."

"Damn it," Tom curses. After a few measured breaths he adds, "Then she should. The last thing we need is for her memories to compromise us."

"I agree," Marie says.

Tom continues driving toward home, thinking that every step they've taken toward ending The Program has been thwarted in some way. "Well then, let's hope this boy is the cure for The Program."

Marie laughs softly, almost desperately. "Yes, let's," she responds. "I'll see you when you get home."

Tom says good-bye and hangs up, watching the road that winds higher and higher. He thinks about Nicole again, hating how sad she looked, but happy that she was okay. But of course she would be okay—she's strong. She's brave and wonderful.

And he dares to let himself hope that one day, when this is all over, he'll get a chance to see her again. So that they can be a family.

SUZANNE YOUNG

TURN THE PAGE FOR A PEEK AT BOOK 5 IN THE PROGRAM SERIES:

THE ADJUSTMENT

I CAN'T REMEMBER THE LAST TIME I CRIED.

It's an odd thought to have in the middle of English class, but for years the threat of being taken, against our will, to a facility for memory manipulation had terrified all of us. Any moment of weakness, one show of emotion, and we could have been flagged as unstable. Once flagged, we would have been handed over to The Program, where the doctors would steal our memories, our experiences, and our lives—all in the name of their false cure. I barely escaped that fate.

But it turns out that although The Program no longer exists, its effect is long lasting.

I stare ahead in class at the whiteboard, the words there blurring together. Around me, pencils scratch against notebook pages and the movement of other bodies mimics learning. I sit still and apart from all of them.

I'd gotten used to small classes, some with as few as twelve students. But now we're pushing thirty in here. Former patients of The Program have been flooding in—wide eyed and confused. I mostly feel bad for them. They've been erased, some only partially.

Months ago, when The Program was shut down, there was no follow-up therapy offered to its patients. Many were sent uncompleted, un*cured*, to Sumpter High, a private school just for those who were treated: a school filled with broken people. Returners were left to their own devices, and some didn't make it. Some didn't want to.

But as the criminal trials carried on in the media, The Program decimated and supporting politicians questioned and shamed, Sumpter was shut down. One senator filed an injunction to ban returners from our district, citing the possibility of another suicide outbreak. As a result, students were left for weeks with nowhere to go—abandoned by their government. But that asshole politician got voted out of office, so returners have come back to the lives they had before The Program. Now that their lives have been thoroughly ruined by The Program.

Even now, former patients still occasionally freak out. Break down. Crack up. To them, The Program is forever.

I glance around at the other students in my class, some dressed in black, dark and dramatic. Others even wear Program yellow ironically. Some say their emotions are heightened now that we're suddenly allowed to "feel" again—built-up angst and anger getting release. Lust and love intertwining so that no one knows the difference anymore. Everything is about now. Everything is about living.

But not me. It's like I've forgotten how to feel—always set to numb. I wonder how many others are just mimicking what they think is sadness. What they think is joy. What if The Program took away our ability to feel by making us hide it for so long? What if none of us is real?

I shouldn't sit here feeling sorry for myself, though. Not when there are those worse off. I look sideways at Alecia Partridge, watch as she flinches—a post-Program twitch she hasn't lost. She occasionally murmurs to herself during class, but the rest of us pretend not to notice. Alecia talks to the ghosts of her past—a friend who died during the epidemic. A friend who was only partially erased from her memory and is, therefore, familiar enough to still be in her present.

Alecia laughs under her breath, brushing her knotted brown hair behind her ear. "Yes," she whispers to no one. "Yes, I know." She looks back down at her notebook and continues to work. She does this at least once a week. This is her normal—and by extension, ours.

I swallow hard and turn away, reminded that returners are still considered unstable, even if the purpose of sending them to The Program in the first place was to make them stable.

"I'd ask to copy your notes," Nathan says in his scratchy

voice from the desk behind me, "but you're obviously going to fail this test."

I turn my face toward him, keeping my eyes on the floor so as not to draw attention from our teacher. "Bet my F will be higher than your F," I say.

Nathan laughs, low in his throat. "No fucking way," he says. "I'll take that bet."

"Done," I say, and look toward the front. I'm almost ready to write down a line or two from Shakespeare's Sonnet 30. I get as far as picking up my pencil before the classroom door opens.

There's a flash of white fabric, and I immediately imagine crisp white jackets and blank expressions. I imagine silence and dripping fear. Although handlers have been out of our lives for months, I still have nightmares about them. And so I hold my breath until my eyes can adjust.

A guy steps into class wearing the same stupid clothing most of the returners do: a stiff button-down shirt, khaki pants, belt—like he's on his way to become our new math teacher. Most returners have had their clothing replaced, and it takes a while for them to figure out their style again.

And maybe it's because of that, or maybe I don't recognize his newly buzzed hair, but Nathan reacts to his presence before I do.

"He's back," Nathan murmurs, putting his hand on my shoulder. But I feel a million miles outside of my body, and his touch is just a breeze past my soul. My pencil falls from between my fingers and drops on the floor, before rolling under my desk.

I stare at the guy in the front of the classroom, my mouth agape, my heart racing. Guilt smacks me, scolding me for not recognizing him immediately. Several students look in my direction, anticipating a reaction. They're curious, maybe. Horrified?

"Wonderful," the teacher says, barely hiding her annoyance. "I see they still aren't worried about class size." She pauses. "Welcome back, Weston," she adds, softening her voice. "There's one last seat." Miss Soto motions toward an empty desk near the front.

Wes watches her for a moment like he's trying to figure out if he knows her, but then he turns and starts down the aisle. He sits two rows away from me. After a moment of silence, Miss Soto goes back to teaching, and the other students go back to pretending to learn.

Nathan's hand is still on my shoulder, attempting comfort, but I lean forward and out of his reach. I stare at the back of Wes's head, willing him to see me. Begging him to turn around.

As if he can sense me, Weston puts his chin on his shoulder and covertly turns. When he finds me, when his dark eyes lock on mine, tears I didn't know had welled up spill onto my cheeks.

And I smile.

Weston Ambrose is the love of my life, and I don't mean "the like," I don't mean "the obsession." We were together for two years, until the day men in white coats showed up at his kitchen door. Although handlers would occasionally take people from school, it was more common for them to come straight to the house. Most patients were turned in by someone they knew. Turned in by their parents.

Of course, parents didn't know the truth of what was happening in The Program—the lasting effect it would have. The paranoia that became the curse rather than the cure to an epidemic.

Wes's parents turned him in. The handlers arrived and pulled Wes from his home as I fought, holding on to his shirt until it tore at the collar. Until a handler physically removed me from the house.

And when Wes was gone, stolen away, his mother came and sat next to me on the curb. It was the first time I cried in public. The only time until now. Mrs. Ambrose held me tightly and let me sob into the shoulder of her blouse, and when I was done, she kissed the top of my head and told me never to come back. Fair or not, she blamed me for her son's condition.

She called them. She called The Program on her son. I'll never forgive her for that.

I blamed myself, too. I replayed the last few months of us over and over, trying to figure out what I could have done differently. Trying to take responsibility for his actions. Most of that time was a blur, really. But eventually, with therapy, I accepted that it wasn't my fault.

My love for Wes is pure, forever. And so I waited for this moment. I waited for him to come back.

But Wes doesn't return my smile, and instead he turns around and opens his notebook. He jots down what I assume are notes from the board.

My skin is on fire, waiting for him to look back. When the bell rings, Weston gets up and walks out without even a backward glimpse.

I sit still and watch after him. There is a sympathetic glance or two in my direction from other students; even Alecia nods at me like she understands how I feel. Truth is, people have wondered about my stability for a while, and I'm sure that if The Program didn't end when it did, the handlers would have come for me next.

"Tatum?" Nathan calls, his voice always set to a quiet hush that gives every word an extra layer of depth, like he's confiding in you.

I don't turn immediately, and I hear his chair scrape against the linoleum floor before he crouches down next to my seat. I turn to him, feeling my bottom lip jut out.

Nathan's eyebrows pull together as he looks me over, like I'm the most pathetic creature on all of Earth. He leans in and puts his forehead against my arm and whispers, "I'm sorry."

HE SHOULDN'T BE SORRY. MY NEIGHBOR NATHAN
Harmon has been my constant companion since Wes was taken
away—unwaveringly by my side. I've known him since we were
kids, and although he and Wes were never friends, Nathan was
devastated when he was taken. If for no other reason than
because of how it affected me.

When we heard that Weston had been released from The
Program, I begged Nathan to help me find him. He reluctantly agreed, and we went to Wes's house. But Wes's mother
told us he'd moved to California to live with his uncle, a devastating fact I hadn't expected. Mrs. Ambrose wouldn't give
us a forwarding number or way to contact him. She told me
he needed space.

I didn't give up, though. When the district ban was lifted,

and students started returning, I'd hoped he'd show. Fantasized about it. But, of course, I was imagining *my* Weston walking in—wearing his worn, tan leather coat. His dark wavy hair to his shoulders. His busted-up motorcycle parked illegally in the teachers' lot.

He'd walk in, wink at the teacher, and then say to me, "Come on, Tate. Let's get the fuck out of here." And then we'd be free.

I'd confided that fantasy to Nathan once, to which he replied, "Sure, that sounds just like Wes. If he were a character from *Sons of Anarchy.*"

But no matter how I pictured it, I always imagined Wes would look at me and know me instantly. Know me always. And now all I can hope is that he does, but decided not to show it.

The rest of the morning passes quickly; I don't share any more classes with Wes. Nathan is in advanced courses, so I don't see him, either.

At lunch, Nathan and our friend Foster are waiting at the usual spot on the half wall near the flowers in the courtyard. There were murmurs at the beginning of the year that students would be able to leave campus for lunch this year, but it hasn't happened yet. Some terrified parent always speaks up, worried about a car accident. Most of the time, I think the parents in this district will only be happy when we're all put in individual bubbles, completely protected (and isolated) from the outside world.

Nathan must be telling Foster what happened this morning, because they both look miserable, conspiring quietly without me. Nathan is first to lift his head as I approach, his hazel eyes squinted against the sun. Foster casually sips from his soda and turns away. Neither of them speaks as I sit on the wall next to them.

I set my chips aside and try to pull back the cardboard top on my juice carton to open it, but it keeps shredding. My fingers shake. Nathan watches me, and then he takes a bite of his sandwich before putting it on top of his lunch bag.

"Gimme," he says through a mouthful of food. I hand him the carton without argument, and he refolds the triangle top and opens it easily. When he passes it to me, I murmur a thank-you.

"So . . . ," Foster starts carefully, "I heard Weston came back. That's good news, right?" He presses his freckled lips into a hopeful smile, the kind you give someone as they're loaded into the back of an ambulance.

"Seriously, Foster?" Nathan says with a heavy sigh. "I said don't bring it up."

Foster scoffs. "Yeah, I figured you knew I would anyway. Of course I'm going to bring it up—her boyfriend just came back from the dead!"

"He wasn't dead," I say quietly.

"I know," Foster whispers, reaching to pat my leg. "I was just trying to make Nathan feel shitty."

Foster Linn is cute with bright red hair, freckles, and the

sort of personality that makes guys and girls swoon alike. I've known him since seventh grade, when he and Nathan were on swim team together. For most of middle school, the three of us were inseparable: video games, pizza, and cliff diving—Foster being the reckless diver. Fearless, always.

But two years ago, his older brother Sebastian was taken into The Program. None of us realized he'd been suicidal, something that I know haunted Foster afterward. The entire situation was obviously traumatic. When Sebastian finally came home, he was like the other returners: quiet, reserved . . . empty. We stopped talking about him. Ever since, Foster spends his free time with his family, with his two older brothers. They work weekends in their dad's shop together.

Foster's friendship with me and Nathan is mostly lunch oriented now—which is also just the evolution of high school, I guess. We still love each other. I know he understands what I'm going through right now—better than most. And to prove it, he grabs my hand and squeezes it.

"Wes doesn't remember," I tell him, pain welling up in my chest. Foster lowers his eyes, feeling the heaviness of the moment. We all fall silent.

I'd been waiting for Wes. I'd built the future around the idea of him coming home.

"What does that mean for you?" Nathan asks, leaning forward. He may not show it the same way, but Nathan knows my devastation too. He tries to carry it for me.

I take a sip of my juice, the sour taste stinging my tongue. I swallow it down. "I don't know," I say. "I don't know who that was this morning."

The real Wes would have asked someone to move so he could sit next to me. He would have made a show of it—completely fine with his affection. A Wes who doesn't smile at me is something different entirely. And we know what it means: He's forgotten me.

Around us, the courtyard is buzzing, other people going about their lunch period, their day seemingly unaltered by the aftermath of The Program. Tears tickle my cheeks, and I wipe them away quickly.

"Tatum," Nathan says, "I know this is hard, but you have to pull yourself together. I just . . . I don't want you to get caught up in it. You were getting better," he adds, then looks at Foster. "Wasn't she getting better?"

Foster opens his mouth to answer, but I'm quick to cut him off. "No, I wasn't," I say. "And you both know it."

They exchange a look, and Foster widens his eyes and picks up his Tupperware and fork, stabbing his pasta salad.

"Okay," Nathan concedes. "Then you were good at pretending. And as the counselors say, that's part of it. Believing it can get better. I think you started to believe it."

"Then you're an idiot," I say.

"And you're being an asshole," Nathan replies just as quickly. I'm not offended—I know I'm projecting my frustration, my hurt, onto him.